AMONG THE LOST

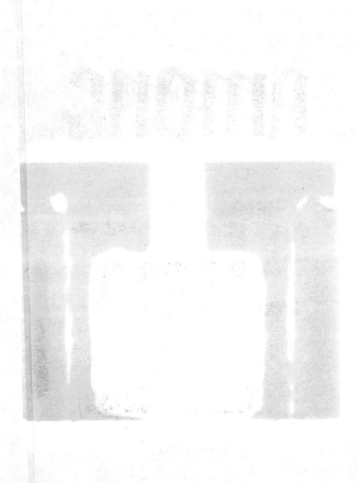

AMONG
the
LOST

Emiliano Monge

translated from the Spanish by
FRANK WYNNE

SCRIBE
Melbourne • London

Scribe Publications
18–20 Edward St, Brunswick, Victoria 3056, Australia
2 John St, Clerkenwell, London, WC1N 2ES, United Kingdom
3754 Pleasant Ave, Suite 100, Minneapolis, Minnesota 55409 USA

First published in Spanish as *Las tierras arrasadas* by Literatura Random House in 2015
Published by agreement with Casanovas & Lynch Agencia Literaria S.L.
Published by Scribe in the UK 2018
Published by Scribe in Australian and North America 2019

Supported using public funding by
ARTS COUNCIL
ENGLAND

This book has been selected to receive financial assistance from English PEN's Writers
in Translation programme supported by Bloomberg. English PEN exists to promote
literature and its understanding, uphold writers' freedoms around the world, campaign
against the persecution and imprisonment of writers for stating their views, and
promote the friendly co-operation of writers and free exchange of ideas.
www.english.pen.org

Typeset in 11/17pt Adobe Caslon Pro by the publishers
Printed and bound in the UK by CPI Group (UK) Ltd, Croydon CR0 4YY

Scribe Publications is committed to the sustainable use of natural resources
and the use of paper products made responsibly from those resources.

9781947534797 (US edition)
9781925322804 (Australian edition)
9781911344643 (UK edition)
9781925548655 (e-book)

CiP records for this title are available from the British Library
and the National Library of Australia.

scribepublications.com
scribepublications.com.au
scribepublications.co.uk

Author's Note

All passages set in italics in this novel are taken from Dante's *Divine Comedy*, or are quoted verbatim from the testimonies of Central American migrants making their way through Mexico, hoping to reach the United States. The author would like to express his gratitude for the work done and the information provided by the Comisión Nacional de los Derechos Humanos, Amnesty International, Hermanos en el Camino, Las Patronas, La Casa del Migrante, Sin Fronteras, and La Casa del Menor Migrante.

Translator's Note

One of the challenges in any translation is preserving a sense of place, affording the reader a glimpse of otherness, of another life, another culture.

Emiliano Monge's novel *Among the Lost* recognisably takes place in the desolate mesas of Mexico and Central America. It is a story — a threnody — of migration, of the desperate and the lost. But the novel also takes place in a mythic landscape, directly inspired by Dante's *Divine Comedy*, and often reminiscent of the worlds of Hieronymus Bosch. In Emiliano's writing, the particular is universal, the allegorical all too brutally real. In trying to recreate the cadences and inflections of the novel, I have drawn on translations of Dante, but also found inspiration in Milton, and the King James translation of the Bible.

One of the most difficult decisions to make was how to approach names. Almost all of the characters in the novel bear names that reek of death: some are clear to an English language reader — *Epitafio* (epitaph), *Cementeria* (cemetery) — others are less so: *Estela* (gravestone), *Sepelio* (burial), *Hypogeo* (a burial chamber). Many of the characters are also referred to by nicknames — often in the form of strings of unspaced words. In the end, I elected not to translate those names by which characters address one another, feeling more would be lost than gained, but to translate the sobriquets which appear in the narrative but not the dialogue. Place names in the novel are at once real and allegorical. The arid plateaus, the impenetrable jungle and the rocky sierra are palpable, but the names given to locations and natural formations sometimes come directly from Dante, others — like *La Caída* (The Fall) — sound biblical, still others, allegorical — *El Ojo de Hierba* (The Eye of Grass). For these, I have chosen to preserve the Spanish names, while glossing the first time they are mentioned.

Throughout the novel, are brief passages set in italics. Some are quotes or rewordings of lines from the *Divine Comedy*, the others are taken from interviews with migrants who have made, or attempted, the long, brutal, dangerous trek to an imagined paradise.

The terrains through which Epitafio and Estela traffic migrants are enduring landscapes that have forever existed in visions, dreams and waking nightmares, but they are also the harrowing no-man's-land many of us glimpse only in news footage, where desperate migrants risk their lives 'seeking liberty, which is so dear, as he knows who gives his life for it'.

> *'If the present world go astray, the cause is in you,*
> *in you it is to be sought.'*
> DANTE, *PUGATORIO*

For Alejandro, Iván, and Jose

'Through me the way to the suffering city; Through me the
everlasting pain; Through me the way that runs among the Lost'
DANTE, *INFERNO*

'You who believe the gods are indifferent to human affairs, what
say you to those paintings that show the great number whose
prayers saved them from storm and returned them safe to harbor?'

'That may be,' rejoined Diagoras, 'but there are no paintings
of those who drowned, and they are a multitude.'
CICERO, *ON THE NATURE OF THE GODS*

The Book of Epitafio

|

It also happens by day, but now it is night. On the expanse of wasteland that neighboring villagers call El Ojo de Hierba — The Eye of
Grass — a clearing ringed by gnarled trees, primeval liana and roots
that snake out of the earth like arteries — there comes an unexpected
whistle, the clatter of a diesel engine revving up, and the darkness is
suddenly ripped by four huge spotlights.

Fearful, those who have come from afar stop, cower and try to
look at each other: but are blinded by the powerful spotlights. Then,
drawing nearer, mothers to children, children to men, those who have
been walking now for many days begin to sing their fears.

> *Someone whistles and spotlights*
> *suddenly blaze ... We cannot see ...*
> *We huddle against each other ...*
> *sheer fearful bodies.*

The words of these creatures whose bodies strive to merge into
a single being cross the space, the man who whistled does so again
and advances two paces. Confronted by his body, the thrumming of
the jungle, like the shadows a moment earlier, falls away and for a
few seconds all that can be heard are the whisperings of the men and
women crossing the borders.

Some say we are already fucked
that we are not worth shit ... Others
talk but say nothing ... as though
praying or swallowing their words.

Listening to these whisperings, paying them no heed, the man in command removes his cap, wipes a hand across his brow, turns his body and reveals his face. As yet, it is impossible to discern anything particular about this man who now raises both arms and, whistling once more, sets in motion the boys operating the powerful spotlights.

Having advanced several meters, the four pushing the powerful spotlights hear another whistle from their boss and halt their advance across the grassy clearing. Yawning contentedly, the man in command turns his head, looks up toward an old truck and smiles at the woman dozing there.

For their part, when the cage of light in which they find themselves ceases to close in, the men and women who left their lands some days, some weeks ago, feel something drain from the entrails and huddle ever closer to each other, their tremblings merging into one, their hollow voices fusing into a single voice. The shock is passing and the terror is charged with questions.

We did not know what had happened ... or knew what had but
not what would ... They began:
Who sees something ... those who are
on the other side ... who?

4

The glare of the spotlights that fashions the intangible bars makes it impossible for those who have come from afar to see anything; not the mountains they crossed some time since, nor the jungle where they were so recently, nor the thick wall of vegetation they breached in order to enter this wasteland and stumble on their waiting captors, whose boss is still looking at the woman sleeping in the truck.

Removing and replacing his cap, revealing his large nose, the man tears his eyes from the woman he first met in El Paraíso, turns his head and reflexively makes another inventory of his things and his people: all his men are here, his huge trucks, his large trailer, two ramshackle vans, three motorcycles, the blazing spotlights and the diesel generator that has just begun to sputter.

The sudden belching of the machine signals that it is about to stall, and the commander, the man with the big nose and bushy eyebrows whose name is Epitafio, says: 'I told you that thing was on its last legs!' Shaking his head, the man with the nose and the eyebrows, who also has two disproportionate lips, takes off his cap again and waves away the smoke enveloping him as he approaches the generator, lights a lamp, hunkers on the ground and begins to tinker with various levers. Seconds later the machine's hiccupping stops and Epitafio gets to his feet and extinguishes the lamp, and listens doubtfully to the clanking gears as a doctor might listen to a patient's chest.

It won't hold out much longer ... We don't have much time today, thinks Epitafio and, turning on his heel, he walks towards the old truck: his ears, intent on nothing, take in the sounds that emanate from the dark jungle: the screeching of the howler monkeys, the singing of the frogs on the riverbed, the shriek of bats in the air, the drone of cicadas in the grass.

An hour at most ... There'll be no time to do the selection today, thinks Epitafio, as he reaches the old truck and scowls to see his reflection in the window. Then he turns away and stares at the cage of light and sees the creatures that now form one single being whose voice chants *the fears that suddenly teem inside its multiple heads.*

I knew it back in Medias
Aguas ... we aren't worth shit ... I saved
myself by sheer luck ... They will beat us ... They
will drag us away and beat us again.

Bad enough, there've never been so many before, thinks Epitafio still staring at the floodlit mass in the center of the night, then, taking off his cap, a red cap emblazoned with an albino lion pouncing, he walks away from the old truck: Still, at least I get that big guy there.

In the center of the cage, between the bodies of a stooped old man and a big-headed girl he can make out a young giant.

Imagining all the things this giant can do for him and for his boys, Epitafio is excited and is about to whistle when from somewhere in the jungle there comes the roar of the panther of these latitudes. When the jaguar is silent again, Epitafio finally whistles and the four men operating the powerful spotlights begin to move once more.

When each has counted to fifteen, the four men stop, turn toward their boss and for the first time whistle in return. This startling chorus causes two children to collapse and heightens the terrors of the men and women whose bodies are illuminated by the approaching spotlights.

> *Be careful not to fall … They shoot at*
> *anything on the ground … That is how*
> *it was in Medias Aguas … Then they wrapped*
> *them in nylon … Do not buckle!*

This is it … We will not have much time today … We have to beat this lot and quickly! thinks Epitafio, watching as those who have come from other lands drop their bundles and fall on the ground. Turning away and putting on his cap, the man whose men secretly call him Thunderhead walks back to the ramshackle truck and the still sleeping figure of the woman who is in command here when he is at rest.

Perhaps he should wake her, thinks Epitafio staring at the window, and he is about to tap on the glass when the panther of these forests once again roars in the distance. But it is not this roar that numbs the arm of Epitafio: gazing at the woman he loves so much has brought to mind what she said a little while back: 'Remind me that I have something to tell you … When you wake me, say to me: "You said you had something to tell me."'

If I wake her now she will not want to tell me, thinks Epitafio, and turning away he focusses all his energy on his cage: with that one there, we have nine … and those three make eleven … plus the six there, eighteen … There have never been so many … and with those five there … and those ones on the other side … I don't even know how many there are … there must be about forty … more, maybe fifty.

Removing and replacing his cap again, Epitafio shakes his head, contents himself with knowing that these creatures he is looking at are fucked, and putting his fingers between his lips and, for the first time, he whistles a sequence.

These whistles, short and knotted, alert two boys camouflaged within the crowd. Clearing a path with elbows and shoulders, these boys, who were born in the jungle and will drag the men and women here into its depths, surge from the crowd, screaming: 'Here we are!'

They tricked us ... those two
little shits who are hardly more than children ...
and they ran off laughing ... I heard them
they were laughing ... I never saw them again.

Without turning their faces, the two sons of the jungle break through the border where the light meets the shadows: we are breaking out! Then, once outside the luminous enclosure, both boys stop, allow their eyes to adjust to the darkness, seek out the silhouette of Epitafio and, having found it, they go to join him.

But before they can reach the man who commands here, a colossal shadow rises up before the boys who fall on to the ground. Protected from the laughter of Epitafio, by the ear-splitting flapping of wings of the flock of birds that had been sleeping in the grass and is now taking wing, the two boys leap to their feet, set their legs to working, hiding the shame of having been trounced by their kingdom.

'Don't be scared!' roars Epitafio, his laugh dying away.

'Scared, us?'

'We didn't see them.'

'You kept your part of the bargain.'

'I told you,' says the older of these two sons of the jungle.

'You told me.'

'So when do we do it again?'

'First you have to keep your side of the deal.'

'If you pay us what you promised, whenever you like,' says the younger of the sons of the jungle.

After a brief silence, Epitafio brings his left hand to his pocket and, as he takes out a wad of money to give to the boys, he feels a pressure in his bladder. I'm pissing myself, he thinks, handing over the money, then, unbuckling his belt, he adds: how about we say same place, next Thursday? Fine, we'll be here, promises the older of the two boys, who, dragging the younger boy by the hand, heads back into the jungle.

As his body empties, Epitafio watches how the two boys hop over a root and how they pull back the curtain of liana. But he does not see the two disappear beyond the wall that separates the clearing from the jungle, because at that moment the diesel generator belches again and he looks anxiously at the old truck: *Puta madre* ... I'll have to wake her up.

||

'How many times have I told you?' says the woman who woke up a moment ago, and then adds, 'I haven't had a wink of sleep for nights.'

'I didn't want to wake you ...' Epitafio says again, and before the woman can demand a reckoning, '... but the spotlights are about to go out ... the generator is seriously fucked.'

'I can't get to sleep, and when I finally manage to fall asleep you wake me up,' the woman grumbles again, turning her head. 'You know how much I need my sleep and you don't care!'

'Why do you say? ... Fuck ... You started it,' Epitafio gets confused and, turning his face to hers, he tries to explain, 'You know very well that I care ... but we don't have time.'

'Why do you think she did it?'

'What difference does it make why she did it?'

'That way ... why that fucking way?'

'That way she didn't feel anything,' says Epitafio, 'or that's what she must have thought, that she wouldn't feel anything.'

'You think she thought about it ... that she planned it?'

'What I think is that we have to get to work,' says Epitafio, 'go make the selection while the lights ... the generator is going to give up the ghost any minute now.'

Looking away from the woman who is now yawning, Epitafio turns around in the seat of his old truck, takes out a coin, holds it between his fingers, flicks it into the air, watches the arc it traces, catches it and slaps it on the dashboard. Heads or tails?

Turning up the volume of the aid in her ear, the woman with the incongruous features — it is hard to believe this tiny nose perches above that crude mouth, beneath those deep, amber eyes — looks at Epitafio's hand and says: 'Why are you asking me, when you already know what I'll chose?'

As Epitafio lifts his hand, the woman in whose face one can see three different but equally attractive portraits — her beauty is a riddle — cheers. 'Next time, I get to choose first. You always get to choose first … I never win a single toss!' complains Epitafio, as he tosses the coin into the ashtray, sending two cigarette butts flying and spitting ash. Then he pleads, although, even as he does so, he knows he shouldn't: 'Just don't pick the giant.'

'What giant?' asks the woman who loves Epitafio, folding down the sun visor and, seeing her reflection in the mirror, opening and closing her mouth several times. Then she brings both hands behind her head and, dividing her hair into three strands, begins to braid them, exposing her shoulders, the nape of her neck and her slender throat, from which her name hangs in letters of gold: Estela.

Meanwhile, Epitafio puts on his cap again and, repeating the words he should not have said, gives form to a warning: 'Down there, there's a huge guy … Seriously, you don't want to choose him … I saw him a while ago.' 'If you hadn't said anything,' says Estela with a flicker of a smile, 'but now that you have, of course I want him!' Epitafio suddenly laughs, too, and asks: 'Whose fault did you say it was that you're not sleeping?' '*Hijo de puta!*' Estela roars in surprise and, losing her smile, growls: 'Seriously, don't make jokes!'

In the silence that descends after Estela's last words, Epitafio opens the door of the old truck and, saying, 'Don't be long,' heads back to the clearing known as the Eye of Grass to be engulfed by the stifling heat and by every interwoven fiber of the thrumming forest: the howls of the monkeys, the chant of the frogs, the chirrup of the cicadas and the shriek of the bats.

For her part, Estela is thinking: Fucking Cementeria … Why the hell did you have to do what you did? … You've even robbed me of my sleep. Her eyes follow Epitafio as he walks to the center of the vast expanse of waste ground, where he stops, takes off his cap again, mops his temples, tosses back a few stray wisps of hair and whistles once more.

This last whistle brings from the shadows some creatures who had not allowed themselves to be seen and who emerge from the tall grasses brandishing the threat of their weapons. As he divides these boys into groups, Estela relaxes and she finally comes down into the clearing. The first thing she sees, this woman with her slim body that looks as though it is armoured with pieces of other bodies, are the mountains like walls that encircle *the great sorrowful terrain in which they find themselves.*

Then, having seen the highest treetops framed against the night sky, Estela, as the man she loves did before, silently makes an inventory of her possessions: the three motorbikes, the little vans, the diesel generator, the two ramshackle trucks and the trailer against which a number of dark forms are silhouetted.

Who are those morons? she is about to ask, when suddenly, in spite of the fact she is still half-asleep, she receives a jolt from her memory and clenches her jaw, trapping the words inside. They are putting together my surprise, Estela thinks and, as she does so she looks away from the trailer, its white lettering flaked by time now spells 'king minos', where it should read 'trucking caminos'.

Having stretched, seen the tiny lights of an airplane against the darkening sky, and yawned twice more, Estela scans the clearing for Epitafio and, having spotted him, begins to walk across the damp, misty jungle floor.

Two meters from the spot where Epitafio is standing, her shoes clagged with mud, Estela sees the men and women who have come from afar and excitedly thinks … He's right, there's more than we've ever had before. Taking Lacarote by the shoulder, Estela is about to express her delight, but the man she adores whistles yet again and everything whirrs into motion.

The twenty men who emerged from the shadows grip the barrels of their guns, those pushing small carts step forward, while from those who have come from other lands comes *the gnashing of a thousand fearful teeth*.

When all those present have taken up their new positions, Estela whistles for the first time and this is how she communicates new orders to her boys. The first burst of gunfire rings out and those who have spent many days walking fall to the ground, vomiting *a few words that spew raw from the mouths*.

> *This was where they first used their weapons … those who were still standing crumpled … pushing, scrabbling and jostling … desperate to be at the bottom of the heap … No one wanted to be left on top.*

'Why do they always think it belongs to them?' asks Estela when the metal falls silent, and silently thinks to herself: It's incredible how well I hear with these things. It was only a few days ago that the woman stroking her ears bought new hearing aids.

When the thrum of the jungle has recovered its rhythm and Estela is enjoying certain sounds she has never heard before, Epitafio moves away from her and declares: 'Get up! … sons of bitches … What are you all doing on the ground?

'Shift your fucking asses or we really will shoot you,' says Epitafio, stepping closer to the luminous cage, taking his cap off again and mopping the sweat streaming down his temples. 'How can it be so fucking hot in the middle of the night?' he says, turning around, but rather than answer him, Estela spits. 'Which is the one you don't want me to choose?'

'That big bastard on the left there,' says Thunderhead, turning towards the enclosure again and pointing.

'The one next to the old man and the little girl?'

'Exactly.'

'You take him, I don't care,' says Estela, moving closer to Epitafio. 'Why fight over him when there are … how many exactly?'

'I was going to count them, but I came to wake you up,' says Epitafio, then, pointing to a spotlight that is blinking, says, 'We won't have much time today … I told you that generator is about to croak.'

'I suppose I'll have to count them again.'

'Sixty-four, total,' Estela announces after a moment and, moving even closer to the enclosure, is surprised to be able to hear *the timid words, the muffled howls, the accents of fear, the sighs and the pleas* of the men and women who fled their lands. These new hearing aids are very good, excitedly thinks the woman who adores Thunderhead and once more brings her hands up to her ears.

But in a second Estela's excitement is transformed and, turning around, she looks at Epitafio and asks, the color draining from her face, 'What are we going to do with all of them?' 'That's your business,' says Epitafio, scornfully waving her away. 'You're the one who wanted them … the one who was bitching about how we didn't have enough … and anyway, in La Carpa you can never have too many.'

The words Thunderhead is speaking crumble as the jungle is desecrated by a noise that quickly becomes a rumble: a helicopter is crossing the night, dragging its clatter of metal. While the men and women who crossed the borders raise their heads, Estela covers her new prostheses, and Epitafio draws his flare gun.

Moments later, as the helicopter hovers over the clearing known as the Eye of Grass, and ignites *the powerful spotlight that illuminates the vault of darkness*, Epitafio aims at the sky, Estela stares at the ground, and those lying in the pool of light cease trembling for a moment.

Suddenly other vehicles appeared …
… someone screamed: 'It's the Border Patrol!'
and it was true … but they don't care … They
saw what was happening and went on their way.

'Haven't seen those fuckers in a while,' Epitafio mutters, and with a weary shrug he fires into the night. The silver-blue flare shrieks through the darkness and the helicopter switches off its huge spot-lights, ceases its hovering, recrosses the waste ground and vanishes into the distance.

When the drone of the aircraft can no longer be heard, Epitafio stows the flare gun and says: 'Poor deluded fuckers ... They think they're ...' But before he can finish, Estela interrupts: 'Isn't this what they wanted? For everything to be different ... Now they'll know what's really good for them!'

'Turn them on!' snarls Epitafio. It is the first order he has not whistled. 'The rest of them ... turn on all the rest.' At his command, the men pushing the little handcarts turn on the spotlights illuminat-ing the outside of the cage of light, and those who have come from far-off lands can finally see their captors.

'I thought you came to find another country?' Epitafio roars, his voice hoarse, and feeling the eyes of these creatures who *curse his ancestors and his seed* upon him he looks to the men still clutching their carts and orders: 'Let them feel the heat of our country.' Obediently, the men who emerged from the shadows march towards the throng, shouldering their rifles.

Trembling even more than they did when the first spotlights ripped through the darkness, the men and women who have fled their lands, countries that had long since become wastelands, *feel-ing the imminent terror and the pain*, open their bowels, and as they watch the approaching men who hearken to the orders of Estela and Epitafio, they hear the ultimate threat of this woman, screaming: 'They will know what the Fatherland is ... They will know who the Fatherland is!

'Who is the Fatherland?' Estela roars, turning around.

'I am the Fatherland!' Epitafio responds, dramatically flinging his arms wide.

'And what does the Fatherland require?'

'The Fatherland wants them to kneel.'

'You heard him, on your knees, all of you, right now!'

'The Fatherland says: Lay flat on the ground,' Epitafio adds, shouting and waving his arms in feigned politeness.

'Everyone, face down!' roars Estela, 'And don't move ... I don't even want to see you tremble!'

When all the men and women from the ravaged lands are no more than prostrate creatures, Epitafio slowly approaches Estela, embraces her and whispers into the hearing aid in her left ear: 'The Fatherland wants them searched.' 'Search them!' Estela barks. Those still in shackles shuffle forward, bend over the creatures who have lost all hope, frisking and manhandling each of them.

There are some who still long to resist, to say something, anything, but the words of these creatures who all too soon will lose their very names perish before they can be thought.

'The Fatherland does not want the giant searched,' Epitafio whispers into Estela's ear and, pointing to her left, she shouts, 'No one is to touch the giant.'

Thinking that no one is coming for him, one boy crawls away, jumps to his feet and runs towards the jungle. Out of the corner of his eye Epitafio sees *he who cannot flee for having tried too often*, moves away from Estela and shouts: 'Grab that one, he's trying to escape!' Two men quicken their stride and chase the boy, they beat him with their rifle butts and drag him back to the heaving mass.

Just as Epitafio is about to tell his men to finish the boy off, Estela grabs the flare gun from his belt and, raising her arm, opens fire: the silver-blue flare hurtles through the air and busts the eye of the fugitive, who falls writhing in the mud, while the gunpowder still spews its fiery rage.

Gradually the flare gutters and, with a last shower of sparks, falls silent, prompting Estela to say: 'Perhaps this is not what the Fatherland wished.' But before Epitafio can answer, two of the huge spotlights flicker and in the distance the generator belches: 'I told you we had to move quickly ... We have to divide them up before the lights go out.'

'But I get first pick ... What do you think, should I take the giant ...?' Estela taunts Epitafio with a wink.

'I already said: you can have him,' says Epitafio, not seeming particularly surprised. 'What do you want in return?'

'There are a lot of them ... I'll let you have him if you help me with the others.'

'All right, then,' Epitafio sighs, 'but no children.'

'...'

'And don't give me that look — what difference does it make if we leave them here?'

'That makes things difficult ... I'm not planning on going back to El Paraíso,' Estela says, tensing her jaw. 'I was going to tell you later.'

'On my mother's life, you'll go to El Paraíso!' Epitafio thunders, suddenly furious. 'You'll go, and you'll spend the night there.'

'You take half of them and I promise I'll go.'

'Half of them, my ass!' Epitafio screams at the woman he so loves, 'and don't even think about arguing … We have to get a move on!'

When the spoils have been divided and the followers of Estela and Epitafio have taken the creatures who crossed the border away in the trailer and the battered trucks, Estela allows her eyes to stray to the clearing for a moment and takes Epitafio in her arms: 'Does the Fatherland have nothing to say to me?' 'What do you want me to say?' Epitafio replies, bring his forefinger up to her ear and running his fingertip gently over the antenna of the tiny hearing aid. *Hijo de puta!* says the woman who loves Epitafio, but before he can get angry, she wraps her arms around him.

'I want the Fatherland to tell me that he loves me … to hear that you are tired and that all you want is to be with me,' blurts the woman whose men called her IhearonlywhatIwant, and, pressing her body against Epitafio, she adds, 'I wanted to hear you say you have the courage … that you are really going to give it all up. That we're not going to start all over again,' pleads Estela as another explosion rumbles in the distance.

The generator finally dies and the spotlights surrounding Estela and Epitafio flicker and are sightless. Darkness invades the clearing, which the men and women of the neighboring village have recently come to call El Tiradero — the Shooting Range — and plunges the world into blindness. 'Best we go,' says Epitafio, as Estela slips from his arms and says, 'I don't want to stay here in the dark.'

Urged on by the screams of the howler monkeys, by the shrill chir-rup of the cicadas hiding in the grass, by the screech of the bats that will soon be heading home, by the croak of the frogs and toads resting on the banks of the creek that flows on the far side of the curtain of liana, past leprous tree trunks and tangled roots like ruins, Epitafio and Estela cross the vast wasteland.

Not looking back, nor even looking at each other, Ihearonly-whatIwant and Thunderhead give the final orders to the men and go their separate ways without returning to the subject that torments Epitafio: when will he have the courage to give it all up? In the dis-tance, farther off than before, the beast of these latitudes roars again and, for an instant, the jungle falls silent.

While the men busy themselves with their final tasks in the clearing, Epitafio goes to the battered old truck, jumps in, tosses his cap on to the empty passenger seat and, picturing the woman he so loves sleeping there, wonders: What was the thing you wanted to say to me earlier? ... You said, 'When I wake up, remind me to tell you something.' Estela climbs into her Ford Lobo, rolls down the window and, seeing the headlights of Epitafio's Cheyenne blaze into life, wonders: Why didn't I say anything? Why did I chicken out again?

The growl of the engines drowns out the single thought that unwittingly unites Epitafio and Estela: It's high time we talked ... told each other what's happening. As one, they accelerate, this man and this woman who have loved each other so much for so long, each taking the lead of a convoy to leave the vast wasteland by different roads.

When the clouds of dust from Epitafio and Estela's trucks have settled, the two sons of the jungle who had only pretended to run away, emerge from the liana and the aerial roots of the ceiba trees. Behind them, on the distant mountaintops, daybreak lights up the horizon, and in their lairs and dens and burrows, the jungle animals shake themselves awake in dapple-gray dawn.

|||

Neither uttering a word, the two sons of the jungle cross El Tiradero, indifferent to the abrupt metamorphosis of the jungle: the shrill sobs of the bats has been replaced by the song of waking birds, the screeching of the howler monkeys gives way to the hoarse wheezing of wild boar, the cicadas are lulled to sleep by the drone of crickets, and the mosquitoes depart, leaving the space to the bees.

When they reach the center of the waste ground once more, the elder of the two boys switches off his flashlight and orders the younger to do likewise. Like the sounds, the very space is mutating: this is the hour when dusk shrinks.

Having stowed the flashlight in his pocket, the elder boy scans the horizon and, pointing to the mountains, says: 'How did it get to be so early?' And yet before the elder boy looks towards the hills, there comes a scream from above and both boys look up: up in the sky, which is also transforming at a dizzying pace, an eagle announces its presence.

'Soon it will be daylight,' says the elder and turns his eyes back to the earth. Then, unfolding the hessian sacks he carries in his belt, he adds: 'Stuff everything you can find into these.' Obediently, the younger boy begins to search the bundles and the bags strewn across the waste ground, only to immediately stop.

'*Puta madre!*' says the younger, taking two steps back.

'Fucking one-eyed freak! Don't frighten him!' says the elder, look-ing down at the corpse, then, turning to the younger boy he says, 'How can the flare still be burning?'

'...'

'...'

'You think it's gone out?' the younger boy says after a few seconds, advancing the two paces he just retreated. 'It looks like it's just smoke.'

'It looks like it's coming out of the guy's head,' says the elder. 'We should get going.'

Turning from the smoldering, one-eyed corpse, the two boys go back to stuffing the sacks with clothes, shoes, bracelets, identity papers, hairbrushes, pictures, photographs, chains, nail-clippers, soap, earrings and votive cards lost by those who abandoned here their hopes and their names.

It is not until the day has almost completely devoured the shadows and workmen can be heard in the distance — an axe is striking a tree-trunk, a tractor plowing furrows in the soil — that the eldest throws his shoulders back and announces: 'Now the dawn is truly breaking … We have to hurry.' But his words are interrupted by the younger shrieking excitedly: 'A medal!'

'A medal?' the elder says, but before he can reach the younger's side, an unfamiliar sound makes him turn towards the trees: 'On the ground! Down on the ground, NOW!' the elder growls, watching as the clearing known as El Tiradero is invaded by *the swarm of fleas or flies or gadflies come to prey on things and on men.*

'Get down or I'll get up and knock you down!' the elder boy roars for the third time, looking up and pounding the earth with his fists.

'What the fuck are they doing here? It's not their time,' says the younger, finally sliding to the ground.

'Just shut up and don't move!' says the elder and these words are the last they hear for some time.

When at last the swarm moves on, the two boys get to their feet, examine each other and pluck from their skin the barbs and stings they have been unable to avoid. When they have finished delousing each other, they laugh nervously and, grabbing their hessian sacks, return to the moment before the plague descended and contemplate the medal the younger boy has discovered hidden in a bundle.

But all too soon, they are itching from the bites and stings: scratching his neck, the elder, soon to turn sixteen, emerges from a daze: 'Take whatever's left!' he orders in a voice that does not sound like that of a lone man, then he says: 'I want to get out of here before that fucking swarm comes back.'

In the minutes that follow, the younger boy, who turned fourteen two months ago, and whose lips and eyes do not move even when an expression distorts his face, finished filling his two sacks, and the elder, on his knees, scours the grass: there is always an earring, a necklace or a ring that the jungle tries to keep.

Rays from the sun, still hidden beyond the horizon, have now reached the treetops and new sounds join the thrum of the jungle: ravens caw, migratory *chepes* sing, turkey buzzards croak, mountains of oil rumble, dawn breaks to the screech of metal and scattered gunshots in the distance.

Urged on by one of these, the elder boy, whose face looks as though it is permanently cast in shadow, gets to his feet, and in a voice like a chorus, announces: 'They are close, the poachers … We need to get away.' It is then that the two sling their sacks over their shoulders and walk away from the packs and bundles they have looted.

A few meters from the liana curtain that separates the wasteland from the jungle, the two boys are once again startled by a cry that convulses the sky and, looking up, see the eagle as it plummets towards the earth. But twenty meters before it reaches El Tiradero, the bird realizes its prey has made it safely back to its burrow and, deploying its great black wings, it pauses in mid air.

After hovering for a moment, the eagle beats its wings and once more takes flight: the two boys pay it no more heed, they shoulder their sacks, leave El Ojo de Hierba and vanish into the thick jungle just as the eagle vanishes into the distance.

Soaring into the air as the two boys head back to the house where they live with their children and their women, the eagle scans the horizon and, after a moment, once again espies an animal on the ground. Swooping from the vastness of the sky once more, the bird crosses the space where daylight now reigns and, in seconds, lands, disappointed, in a dusty furrow.

Contemplating the dead animal that caught its eye, the eagle scans for a mouthful amid the half-eaten remains left by nocturnal creatures. When, finally, it sees a gobbet it might pluck with its beak, it senses an approaching vehicle and, unfurling its great black wings, takes to the air.

The sight of the eagle he has almost hit rouses Epitafio from his daydream: he had been walking with Estela in far-off El Paraíso; now he turns his attention to the dirt track blazing in the sunlight: the sun finally appears between the mountaintops.

Inside Epitafio's Cheyenne, a shaft of light ricochets off the rear-view mirror, and again off a stray coin in the ashtray, and strikes the left pupil of the man who so loves Estela. It is unbelievable that I still let you decide things on the toss of a coin, thinks Thunderhead and, reaching out, plants four fingers in the ashtray. Taking the coin, he sets it on the dashboard and, thinking about Estela, he says aloud: 'Never beat you, not even once.'

The smell of ash brought unwittingly onto his fingertips triggers a furious urge to smoke and he reaches out again, grabs his cigarettes and, remembering Estela's smile, looks in the rear-view mirror at the bars on the truck following behind, knowing that, inside, bound and helpless, are those who have come from other lands. What he does not know is that inside the huge Minos trailer truck, there are also five packages put there on the orders of the woman flickering through his thoughts.

Clutching the pack of cigarettes, Epitafio stamps on the brake, turns the steering wheel several degrees and heads east, staring into the rising sun and, addressing it directly — as he always does when speaking to inanimate objects — says: 'I'll probably reach El Teronaque before you reach your zenith.'

Lighting the cigarette twitching impatiently between his lips, Epitafio coughs several times — the first lungful always chokes him — shifts gear and accelerates, forcing the three outriders to do likewise, and the hulking Minos, whose shoddy suspension judders and jolts those who have been walking for so many days.

As the others pitch and roll, one of these creatures who, *without death, are going through the kingdom of the dead*, is trapped between the boxes Estela has despatched, and though he tries to wriggle away, to scream, having heard the noises coming from inside the cargo and feeling something move inside, he cannot free himself.

> *They bound us and they tossed us in here …*
> *feet tied with shoelaces …*
> *hands with mobile charging cables …*
> *mouths gagged with our own socks.*

The last puff of smoke Epitafio exhales dances before his face only to be quickly whipped away by the void: Thunderhead rolls down the window. The Cheyenne is invaded by the sound of the wind and, reaching out again, Epitafio turns on the battered old stereo, which is only half-fitted to the dashboard.

Discovering that Estela left her disc behind, Epitafio once again calls to mind her face and immediately begins to address her absent presence: 'I'll bet you listened to it before you fell asleep … while I was down there working … I thought you said you were tired … that you just wanted to sleep … I'm busting my balls and you're listening to this shit … This always happens to me because … because … Jesus fuck … that's fucking disgusting!'

The Cheyenne is also invaded by the fetid stench produced by the fertilizer factory hidden on the border between the jungle and the patch of woodland Epitafio can make out up ahead. 'It's amazing that they haven't closed it … It's not as if they don't know this shithole is here,' grumbles Epitafio, though he knows how ridiculous the protest sounds coming from his lips.

Just as it invaded the Cheyenne a moment since, the stench from the manure factory leaches into the Minos, chafing the lungs of the men who obey Epitafio, but not those of the men and women who have come from other lands *plagued by the doubt that takes root in each of them as a voice that is never silent,* those who have crossed frontiers heed nothing but the desperate wail that comes from the packages.

> *We were lying in the trailer truck when one of us began to shudder and howl …
> howls of such pain they were not human sounds … and we felt terror take hold once more.*

Rolling up the window against the stench of manure, Epitafio ejects the disc Estela left behind and scans for the only radio station whose signal reaches this place where the jungle gives way to scrubland and thickets. But even as Thunderhead spins the dial of the radio, he changes his mind and slides the CD back into the slot: 'You always have your way with me … even when you're not here with me I can't listen to what I like.'

Humming Estela's favorite song, Epitafio accelerates again and the three outriders and the trailer truck behind do likewise. Those who breached the borders, those who have not ceased *to listen to this disturbing voice, to the wails of this creature in torment*, are thrown across the floor of the container, crushing the one who is lying trapped between the packages, causing one of them to split.

> *The wails grew worse and worse ... the*
> *poor man writhed and screamed as though*
> *something had been ripped from him ... I could*
> *feel him shudder ... It went on for a long time.*

The howls of the man lying beneath the sack that has split trail off only when the bile surging from his stomach through his throat finally fills his mouth. And even more than the wails the sudden silence that swells inside the vast container of the Minos terrifies those who have come from other lands.

> *Suddenly he stopped making a sound ... but*
> *what was worse he stopped shuddering ... I*
> *tried to think of something else but I heard*
> *someone crying ... and I started sobbing.*

Meanwhile, in the Cheyenne, Epitafio has turned off the stereo and, as he does so, he notices the three black dots forming a triangle on his wrist: like the other tattoos that disfigure his skin, it is a sign to the world and to his memory, that he, too, grew up in El Paraíso.

Seeing how the jungle and the frost merge, Epitafio thinks of the first time that his skin was marked, and the memory of the smell of burning flesh makes him shake his head with rage. Why am I thinking about this? Thunderhead wonders and, as though he might outrun his past, he urges the pickup truck faster: but he cannot shake the memory of Father Nicho's needle and his heart pounds faster in his chest.

Controlling his breathing in the way Estela taught him, Epitafio gradually calms himself and manages to drive out the disturbing memory, as the image of the woman he so loves resurfaces in his mind and he is struck by another memory: You said you had something you wanted to tell me.

'Remind me I've got something important to tell you,' that's what you said, Epitafio thinks, accelerating again, this time without realizing. Later, after you wake up, 'I need to talk to you,' you said that, too, thinks Thunderhead, opening up the Cheyenne and heading towards the ditch, to the surprise of the drivers following, who are trying to catch up.

Feeling his heart race again, Epitafio decides to dispel the doubts once and for all and is about to take his cell phone from his pocket and call the woman he so loves when suddenly, in the middle of the dirt road, a man appears, waving his arms. Behind him, in the distance, the sun climbs, unperturbed, its rays giving form to the heat that will soon be unbearable.

What's he doing here, the little shit? Epitafio wonders and the Cheyenne slows, as do the motorcycles and the Minos, where the boy Estela ordered to hide in the container assumes that his moment has come. Taking advantage of the fact that the convoy has stopped, the boy struggles to his feet, turns on a flashlight, jumps over the bound bodies, pushes aside a young man who has choked on his own bile, and, taking a knife, slits open the other boxes.

Meanwhile, Epitafio stares hard at the boy standing in the ditch, observes him for a long moment in silence, then, forgetting what he was thinking about earlier, he stretches himself and, releasing the lock on the passenger side, throws open the door and calls: 'What are you doing standing there?'

'Nothing ... no lights, no sound, no.'

'Why aren't you where I told you to be?' Epitafio interrupts the boy.

'There weren't no people there even,' says the boy, climbing into the passenger seat and slamming the door behind him, 'that's why I came straight back.'

'Why do you never listen to me?' says Epitafio, slapping the dashboard of the old pickup truck. 'Why the fuck do you never fucking listen?'

'I got a surprise for you.'

'What the hell are you talking about?'

'You'll see how easy they are to unload,' says the boy from the ditch with a smile. 'I watched them and I thought ... He's gonna love this.'

'I don't want to hear about it ... Shut up, I don't want to know,' bellows Epitafio, interrupting the boy again.

'Why not?'

'I said shut your mouth,' says Epitafio as he sets off once more, leading the convoy.

Having skirted the copses and thickets where the forest peters out and driving for a long while, each immured in silence, Epitafio raises his arm and points to the house in the distance and, in a gruff voice, announces: 'El Teronaque!' 'I know where we are,' mutters the boy from the jungle, then adds, 'How could I not know, when you keep me locked up there all the time?'

Still staring at this building that was once a slaughterhouse, Epitafio turns toward the boy from the ditch and says: 'I'm not even going to ask whether you've got everything ready … Everything better be fucking ready, Sepelio, for your sake … and my breakfast better be on the table … I'm half-dead from starvation …'

When silence falls again in the Cheyenne, Epitafio accelerates for the last time, as do the three outriders and the hulking Minos trailer truck, in which the men and women who came from far-off lands are suffering the attacks of the creatures that emerged from the sacks, creatures recently freed by the stowaway planted by Estela; Estela, the woman who is only now crossing the Tierra Negra, having had to stop to fix one of the broken-down trucks.

We shouldn't still be in the sierra … We should be in hiding by now, Estela thinks, gazing at the plains that stretch out all around and spill over the horizon. 'Better not to be outside at this time of day,' she says and the driver next to her thinks that he should say something, but cannot bring himself to open his mouth.

Cursing the time they have wasted, IhearonlywhatIwant rolls down the window and the dust entombing the plains rushes into the cab. Tiny particles embed themselves in the eyes of both driver and passenger and, furiously rubbing her eyelids, Estela hastily closes the window and growls again: 'Fucking shitty, busted trucks … We should be miles from here by now!'

Then, when her eyes have wept out all the dust of the plains, IhearonlywhatIwant removes the hearing aids and decides to doze for a little while. But a second later, the sun blazes on a strange mass in the distance and her fingers immediately replace the little devices in her ears: 'What the hell are they doing over there … When the fuck were they sent here?'

IV

Moments before the Ford Lobo stopped and the soldiers manning the roadblock noticed, Estela fixed her eyes on one of them and muttered: 'When the fuck were they redeployed?

'"When the fuck were they redeployed?" I asked,' Estela repeated, jabbing a finger at the soldier she is talking to. 'You're new — I ain't seen you before.'

'I ... I ... can't,' the soldier stammers, instinctively clutching his rifle.

'When did you join them?' IhearonlywhatIwant asks, only to instantly modify her question. 'Where's your commander?'

'Capitán!' yells the soldier, without turning around, his fingers gripping his weapon tighter still.

'I said you were new — he doesn't like it when people shout.'

'Capitán!' the soldier calls again, not daring even to turn his face.

'So is the lazy fucker coming out or what?'

'He'll be here in a minute.'

'Which minute?'

Exasperated, Estela opens the door of the truck and jumps down. But before she can set off walking, a roar comes from the hut behind the banks of sandbags and a door slowly opens.

For two seconds that could be two minutes, the whole world is reduced to the rasp of three hinges, the wind whipping across the plateau, the idling engines of the Ford Lobo and the two battered trucks, and the tense, wary breathing of the soldiers and the men loyal to IhearonlywhatIwant.

Then the voice from the hut is heard again, and words: 'We were redeployed at short notice!' This reassures everyone, everyone except Estela, who mutters, *'Hijo de puta!'*, pushes aside the soldier she has never seen before and walks towards the shack, where the captain buttons his uniform shirt and comes towards the door, tugging at his shoelaces.

'This door is broken,' the captain says under his breath, then, noticing Estela — he has always been fond of this woman who stands before him — adds, 'They redeployed us during the night … They ordered us to come here with no advance warning.' 'With no advance warning?' IhearonlywhatIwant fumes, and as she grabs the captain's elbow and drags him back inside the hut, she hears her phone vibrate.

'ALREADY IN TERONAQUE. WHERE U???' reads the message Epitafio sent a moment earlier, to which Estela hurriedly replies: 'PROBS W/ PICKUP JUST ARRIVED CHECKPOINT … IT'S MOVED!!!'

Slipping the phone back into the pocket of the tight leather pants that hug her figure the way a punching bag hugs its contents, Estela looks at the captain, steps towards him, cornering him next to the window and, as though she has not heard a word he has said before now, asks: 'Why the fuck aren't you up where you're supposed to be?

'And don't tell me, they didn't give us any warning … Don't tell me you don't know, because I'm not going to believe that shit,' splutters

IhearonlywhatIwant, taking two paces towards the window and forcing the captain up so close to the glass that he nervously turns and opens it.

Seeing the two beat-up trucks and thinking he might still be able to negotiate, the captain grasps at straws, saying: 'How many you got in there today?'

'I'm not going to give you any unless you tell me what I want to know ... You don't want to see me ... Don't take me for a cretin,' Estela growls, poking her head out the window, then, playing to the captain's greatest weakness, she adds: 'Today I might even let you take your pick.'

'And let me tell you I've got a little girl in there who can't close her mouth,' Estela stokes the captain's unease: IhearonlywhatIwant does not remember that the little girl in question is in the Minos, that the girl with the big head is not in her trailers, where *prostrate, the wretched gnash their teeth and pour out their sufferings.*

What happened to me does not matter, but what they did to all those women, that really hurts. There were seventeen. Seventeen women who each night came back battered and bruised. I will never forget what I saw done to them.

After a brief silence that infuriates Estela still further and sets the blood in the captain's groin tingling, IhearonlywhatIwant turns her body and presses herself to the man, who can no longer tear his eyes or his urges from the two battered pickup trucks and, angrily grabbing his rigid prick, she threatens: 'If you want them, you'll tell me … What the fuck are you doing posted here? … What the hell happened?'

'The orders came yesterday afternoon … I swear,' the captain says in a voice quavering with lust. '"Get your shit together, you're moving down to the plateau."'

'Then who the fuck is up there?' Estela asks, her fingers squeezing harder. 'Unless there's no one manning the checkpoint in La Cañada?'

'Why would you think there's no one … stationed up there?' the captain says, the words almost disintegrating in his mouth. 'They must have dispatched men … from somewhere else.'

'You're telling me that you don't know who's stationed at La Cañada?' IhearonlywhatIwant says, releasing the captain's penis and then kneeing him in the balls. 'In that case I'll just have to take you with me!'

'…'

'You're coming with me and you're going to make sure that whoever's up there doesn't give me any shit!'

'You know … you know I can't do that.' The captain gasps for breath and re-opens the eyes that snapped shut when her knee made contact. 'I can't …'

'Who said it was a request?'

When the door of the shack finally opens again, Estela drags the captain out and shouts to her boys: 'Back in the trucks! We're out of here!' Meanwhile, the captain, whose voice has recovered its gravitas, says to his soldiers: 'Get that barrier up now … I'm going uphill with them, I'll be right back ... No fucking around while I'm gone.'

With an obvious limp — one leg is six centimeters shorter than the other — the captain follows Estela, who calls to her driver: 'You get in the back, I'll be driving from here!' Without a word, the boy turns and walks to the battered trailer trucks in which the women who have come from other lands lie gnawing on their pain.

> *Two of the women they raped daily. They were like rag dolls, these women, the ones they raped. And the girls, those who were raped over and over, day and night, they reminded me of my daughter.*

As Estela and the captain climb into the Ford Lobo, the boy passes the blue trailer and hears: 'If you hurry, you might land yourself a fresh one!' while the driver of the red pickup, seeing the boy scuttle past, adds: 'Get your ass in gear and you're well in.'

With a leap as deft as it is agile, the boy who drove here bounds into the trailer carrying the women who have come from other lands and, listening to the *cries of despair ... the tormented spirits as they lament in chorus,* clambers inside just as the convoy following Estela moves off again.

Revving the engine of the Ford Lobo, IhearonlywhatIwant forces the trailer trucks behind to accelerate and leaves the checkpoint, where she has wasted too much time. 'Just look at the time ... It's your fault we're running so late,' Estela complains to the captain next to her, a creature so scrawny his skin seems to stick to his bones.

'What the fuck do I care that you're late?' says the captain, looking out the window. 'I'm going to be in deep shit if anyone finds out I left my post!' 'You wouldn't be in the shit if you'd warned us,' bawls Estela. 'If you'd phoned Epitafio. He trusted you, and this is the thanks he gets.' As she rants, she feels the fury coursing through her body and she grips the steering wheel, trying to resist the overpowering urge telling her: Beat the shit out of the bastard!

Bowing his head, seeing Estela raise her fist, the captain opens his mouth and is about to apologize when the fist becomes an open palm, stopping him in his tracks as a policeman stops traffic: 'Because of you, we'll be running a serious risk up there … Fucking hell.

'We could have taken the other route,' Estela says, gesturing to vast plateaux as the sun continues to scale the ramparts and a phalanx of birds skirls in the sky, searching for the corpse that will set them plummeting like a cyclone, just as in the blood-red trailer truck the boy who arrived driving the Ford Lobo is searching for the female cyclone writhing beneath him.

That one raped me. Laid me face down and raped me while the others chatted. Another one said I was pretty and wanted to stick it to me, too. Two raped me at the same time. One kicked me in the face. One beat me with the flat of a machete until I bled.

After driving in silence for a while, Estela realizes the captain has been glancing at her painted green fingernails and, not quite knowing why, breaks the silence, murmuring: 'They're not the color he likes them.

'What the hell has it got to do with you, anyway? What the fuck are you looking at?' snarls IhearonlywhatIwant a moment later and, hiding her nails behind the steering wheel, angry that she is justifying herself to this man, who ventures a smile. Without changing his rictus grin, the captain allows his gaze to shift to the horizon, where, a moment later, he sees the vultures in the distance whirl and swoop.

Then, when the carrion birds have vanished from the sky, the captain looks down at the ground and is surprised to note that the dirt track they are following has already left behind the vast plateau and begun to wind its way up toward the sierra.

As the track becomes ever steeper, Estela and the captain, who have both rolled down their windows, listen as the hushed drone of the plains gives way to sounds of the mountains and watch as the black soil of the massif becomes streaked with bone white. Only now does the soldier dare speak again: 'A zebra. The ground around here is like a zebra.'

'A zebra?' Estela says mockingly as she slows the truck, the convoy is hemmed in by monolithic escarpments. 'What the fuck are you babbling about? What makes you think you can just blurt out whatever shit pops into your head? … Didn't you hear me when I said shut up?'

Gravel crunches beneath the tires of the Ford Lobo as the track grows steeper, raising a cloud of dust that envelops the trailer trucks where the men loyal to IhearonlywhatIwant cover their faces and the women *whose bodies have been penetrated by the miasma of other beings* long for the dust that would clot into earth and bury them by the shovelful.

Some kilometers later, at a point where the road levels out for a stretch, Estela gazes down at the plateau in the distance, turns back to the captain and, with a calm brought on by this vision of the void and the time they have spent in silence, asks: 'What do we do if you can't come to a deal with whoever is stationed up here? ... If there's trouble at La Cañada?' 'Why wouldn't they deal with me,' says the captain also calmer now and staring down at the plains. 'They might have been redeployed from elsewhere, but they're all the same!'

'It's true ... Why wouldn't they want to make something out of it?' Estela mutters in a low voice, then, staring down into the void and the plateau below and dropping her voice even lower: 'I'm tired.' The calmness spreading through her body suddenly becomes deeper, heavier, and, almost without realizing, IhearonlywhatIwant yawns and whispers, 'I feel sleepy.'

But this phrase, I feel sleepy, is enough to rekindle Estela's unease: I'm tired because I haven't had a wink of sleep ... and I haven't slept because of fucking Cementaria ... I was just about to nod off when you came and woke me up ... and you didn't even bloody remember ... I said, when you come to wake me, remind me I've got something to tell you.

No sleep. 'You didn't say anything and I didn't say anything either!' Estela suddenly roars, startling the captain, as her inner calm evaporates. 'Why didn't I say something? Why? I'd already said I've got something to tell you that changes everything!'

The Ford Lobo accelerates with the worries whirling in her mind. Estela is beside herself as she hurtles towards the narrowest stretch of the road. 'Jesus fuck!' yells the captain, staring at the sheer drop to his right. 'There's no need to drive so fast!'

Jolted back to the reality of the mountain pass by the sound of the captain's voice Estela gives a loud laugh and, steering towards the edge of the cliff, threatens: 'You scared? Want to see how close I can get?' 'What's wrong with you? What the fuck are you doing?' screams the captain, squeezing his eyes shut and cowering in his seat.

'Who'd have thought you'd be such a chickenshit? You should be ashamed!' Estela taunts between howls of laughter. 'And these are the men sworn to defend our Fatherland!' At this word, *Fatherland*, Estela's thoughts once more fragment, and Epitafio is with her here in the high sierra.

Slamming on the brakes and snapping, 'Don't get out and don't move a fucking muscle,' Estela opens the door, jumps down and climbs the steep road, then leaves the path and heads to an outcrop of rocks jutting from the ground like ribs from a corpse, while the drivers of the battered trailer trucks brake suddenly and wonder: What the fuck is going on?

When she reaches the promontory, a bevy of larks pecking for food in the scree takes wing, and the drivers, still wondering what is happening, watch the frantic flutter as the birds are drawn back to the ground by hunger, and their boss scales the tallest of the rocks.

Having reached the top, IhearonlywhatIwant takes out her phone and is disappointed to find she can get no signal: Why was I so fucking stupid when I woke up ... letting you think you were waking me up? ... Why did I pretend to be asleep when you were talking to the boys? ... Why didn't I say, 'Come here, I'm already awake? ... Come here, I want to tell you something?'

Climbing down again and rejoining the road, Estela continues to reproach herself. Why didn't I talk to you after they'd gone ... when

I saw you there on your own? … Why didn't I get out of the truck? As she reaches her truck and realizes that she cannot talk to Epitafio from here, IhearonlywhatIwant climbs in and tries to dismiss the man she so loves from her mind: I'll call you when we get back down … at least this fucking phone might get a signal there.

Flooring the accelerator of the Ford Lobo again, now completely focussed on the road, Estela manages to forget Epitafio for a while, but not the boys of the jungle: I should have got out when I saw them leaving. The same two boys still lugging the sacks they filled in El Tiradero.

'I can smell eggs!' says the elder, and, almost without realizing, quickens his pace: 'First back gets second helpings!' 'But you started before me!' whines the younger boy, dropping his sack and, pointing to a fallen tree, says: 'When we get to the log, we run!'

When the door of the house opens and the two boys pile in, panting for breath, their wives get up and lay their babies in the hammock that divides the space. Each still claiming victory, the boys allow their women to hug them, and then immediately demand: 'Who won, who won?'

Her face hardening, the elder of the women says: 'We didn't see you come in,' and the other quickly adds, 'You're too old for games … Why are you so late today?' The elder of the two boys says: 'It took us ages at the clearing … There was a whole shitload of stuff today … We couldn't cram it all into the sacks.'

'We've left them outside … you go and fetch them, but first give us something to eat,' says the younger boy, sniffing the air and slipping an arm around his wife. 'We're starving.'

As the women move toward the fire, a litter of puppies appears from the shadows and they scamper, yapping, to the table where the two boys are tucking in to the *huevos con camarón seco* and tortillas set in front of them.

The whimpers of the puppies wake the babies sleeping in the hammock and the boy who acts as leader raises a hand and, his mouth full, splutters: 'Shut those kids up and then go bring in the sacks.'

When they have finished eating, the two boys get up, go over to the hammock, lie down and announce: 'We need to sleep.' But before either of them can close their eyes, a voice makes them turn back to the door: 'You planning to take everything away today?'

'Only the clothes and the shoes,' says the elder boy, lifting his head from the hammock.

'So you'll be going out again today?' says the younger of the girls.

'I already told you,' says the younger boy, jumping to his feet.

'They told me,' says the elder girl.

'I've told you a million times, we can't just work for one client,' says the younger, hurrying to the door.

'You never said anything about that,' says the younger woman, turning on her heel and disappearing into the forest.

'Let her go ... I'll calm her down,' says the older woman, looking at the younger boy.

'You heard her, she'll calm her down,' says the older boy, then, glancing at his partner, he says, 'Wash the clothes and clean the shoes. Everything needs to look new.'

No one says anything else. The two women go out into the forest. The two boys go their separate ways: the house is divided in two by the table and the fire; the left-hand side is occupied by the elder boy and his family; the right-hand side by his subordinate and his brood.

But before the two boys can get to sleep, the mother of the puppies appears in the doorway and, yelping, they scurry from under the table. They will not shut up now until the bitch lies down and they are latched on to her dried-up teats.

And the cats prowling under the big table far away in El Teronaque will not be quiet until one of Epitafio's men gives them a scrap from their breakfast.

V

'Give them whatever's left on your plates,' says Epitafio, looking from his men to the cats mewling under the table. 'I don't care if you're still hungry … We have to go unload the container.'

Resigned, the boys loyal to Epitafio tip their food on to the floor, get to their feet, grumbling angrily, and head for the door, where each takes a rifle. 'Maybe the sun will have finished them off … They've been in there for ages,' says Thunderhead as he leaves the house overlooking El Teronaque and walks quickly to the patch of ground where the Minos is parked.

> *We could hear nothing now. We even thought they might leave us here forever. Lying face down on the white-hot steel. There we were gasping for air. Waiting for whatever to happen.*

But halfway there, realizing that not all of his boys are following, Epitafio stops in his tracks. He removes and replaces his cap, scans his men to see who is missing and, feeling a fire in his belly, he roars: 'Where the fuck is Sepelio?'

'Where is the little shit?' He throws his hands up and, surveying the yard of the former slaughterhouse and the fringes of the forest enclosing everything, he growls, 'Why the fuck does he always do whatever comes into his head?'

Hearing him, the men loyal to Epitafio race across the red volcanic rock called *tezontle* and take up their accustomed positions for unloading, grateful that they are not Sepelio. 'Fucking moron … I suppose I have to do everything, as usual!' gripes Thunderhead, walking on and thinking: I wanted to have a little talk with that giant, then he gestures to the first men he sees and barks: 'You! Go fetch the ladder!'

Then, quickening his pace again and silently muttering to Sepelio, '*Hijo de puta* … You'd do well not to show your face,' Epitafio arrives at the spot where the trailer is parked. Talking a run-up, he leaps and grabs the door handle: 'Jesus Christ, it's burning hot!'

The sound that comes from Epitafio's body as it hits the steel goes unnoticed in the courtyard of El Teronaque, where the air is pervaded by the voices from the forest, but inside the trailer it sounds like an explosion, a violent sneeze that startles the boy who stowed away on the orders of Estela, and the tiny mammals that have escaped from the hessian sacks, and the men and women who have crossed borders and who suddenly *feel the dread cling to their skin and fresh grief to their soul.*

Before he can raise the bolt that operates the lock-rods, a sound unlike any he has ever heard captures his attention like a dog tugged by a leash: at the sight of Sepelio, leading a group of men who are dragging a huge ramp, Epitafio feels his black rage swell and he jumps down from the container.

'I told you I had a surprise for you!' Sepelio shouts when he sees Thunderhead looking at him. 'I saw it and I thought, It's better than the ladder.'

'What are you doing?' says Epitafio, walking towards him. 'Where the hell did you get that thing?'

'I spotted it over in Hortaleza when they were using it,' says Sepelio. 'I saw it and I thought, This is better than the ladder.'

'You saw it and you thought … How many times do I have to tell you … we have nothing to do with those people?' roars Epitafio, stepping aside so as not to be knocked down by the ramp.

'Don't worry. I explained things to them. They don't want it back,' says Sepelio as he reaches the container truck. 'You'll see. We'll have them out of there in seconds.'

'You explained things to them? Fucking hell … Why do I even bother? … Why do I put up with you?'

'See? I knew it … Fits perfectly!'

Jumping over the ramp, Epitafio grabs Sepelio by the throat and, this time to himself, he mutters: 'I don't have to put up with you forever … It's been years now. When you're done here, you take it straight back and you tell them it was just a joke.' Then, squeezing Sepelio's throat, which still bears the mark of the branding iron at El Paraíso, Epitafio mutters ominously, 'And they'd better fucking believe it was a joke!

'But right now, get your ass in gear,' says Epitafio. Releasing Sepelio and turning to his men, he bellows: 'Everyone get ready!' Then he takes several steps away from the container, takes off his cap, cursing the bright sunshine, wipes his face with the back of his hand and says: 'What are you waiting for? … Open her up!'

The five men who dragged the huge ramp here hoist themselves on to the Minos, slide back the lock-rods sealing the doors, loop ropes round the bolts and jump down on to the volcanic rock. The piercing sounds of their bodies against the steel echo inside the container, and those who left their lands many days since *begin to sob, to speak one by one: they know that the words they hear are seeds with fruit of infamy.*

> *Every time we relaxed the noise would start up again ... and we knew by now that noise was not good ... the silence lasted thirty minutes at most ... maybe forty ... never an hour ... I thought it would be better if we could not hear ...*
> *if we were deaf.*

Using the weight of their bodies, the men who help drag the ramp here pull on the ropes, but in vain: still welded shut by warm solder, the hinges of the doors refuse to budge. 'Come on! Don't just stand there staring!' Epitafio yells at the men still clutching their guns ... 'Quick, before they run out of air in there!'

One after another, the men loyal to Epitafio put down their weapons, approach the container and lend a hand, but though many are pulling on the ropes, they cannot open the Minos. What the fuck is going on? Thunderhead wonders as he watches the men heave, and thinks, If they run out of air in there, my giant will die. Then he booms: 'Put your backs into it, like real men!'

When finally the hinges of the container begin to creak — Estela ordered her stowaway to weld them shut — Epitafio peers into the Minos, but before he can make out anything, he and his men are thrown backward by a dark, dense living cloud that billows out with a deafening clamor.

Humiliated by what they can see, Thunderhead and his men shamefacedly pick themselves up; meanwhile, the cats that followed them from the house give a frantic yowl and dart toward the container. The cloud of frantic, beating wings wheeling aimlessly in the sky serves only to fuel Epitafio's rage: 'What the fuck is going on?'

In the silence that follows, Epitafio watches the cats prowl, maddened by hunger and the sudden appearance of the flock, until the silence is broken by a booming laughter that echoes inside the hulking Minos.

Tearing his eyes from the jaws of the cats fighting over the three or four animals they managed to catch, Epitafio watches as the figure of a laughing boy emerges from the shadows: 'She told me … "It'll scare the shit out of him," she said!' 'How did you get into my container? … When did you sneak in?' says Thunderhead, taking two paces forward, shooing a cat with a bat in its jaws that scurries off and hides in the undergrowth.

'What the hell are you laughing at …? How did you get them in there?' Epitafio says angrily and the boy, who has now stopped laughing, comes down the ramp and explains what happened. Suddenly Sepelio appears from nowhere and slaps the boy. 'What are you doing?' Epitafio barks and slaps Sepelio. 'Go stand over there, let the boy talk.'

'That's another thing she said … "Sepelio is bound to interrupt," she said … Tell him I send my love to him, too … Tell him: "Maybe we'll see each other next time" … It's been a while since Epitafio brought you along,' says the boy, glancing at Sepelio. Then, looking into the eyes of the man in command, he says, 'Did you shit your pants or just piss yourself?

'That's what she told me to say: Did you shit your pants or just piss yourself?' says the boy who stowed away in the Minos. 'And she also said to say: Maybe this will teach you a lesson ... You're not the only one who can pull cruel pranks!'

Unable to contain himself, Epitafio bursts out laughing and the men clutching their guns, who until now have been standing to attention, relax and go back to their appointed posts, while Sepelio and his boys climb the ramp and go into the container.

Hearing the sound of footsteps circling their bodies, those who came on foot to the clearing called El Ojo de Hierba, those who will shortly be dragged from the metal box and tortured in the courtyard of El Teronaque, *curse God, their ancestors, their race, their seed and that of their descendants.*

> *When everything started again, I have to admit I cried ... I have two children, I made this journey because I have no money ... no future ... This is why I was making the journey ... and this was what God had done to me ... I hated Him, I hated my parents and my homeland.*

Still laughing, Epitafio takes his phone from his pocket and sends a message 'LMFAO!!!' then, slipping it back into his pocket, he conjures the face of Estela and is about to speak to her absence, when the voice of Sepelio interrupts: 'They nearly fucking suffocated!

'They're pretty much cooked!' Sepelio laughs, and it is his laugh rather than his words that brings Epitafio back to earth and he feels a rush of concern. I don't want the giant to suffocate ... I want my giant to be all right! he thinks as he stares at Sepelio and shouts, 'Stop wasting time and get them down here! … Get them out here right now!'

'You heard him!' Sepelio calls, assigning tasks to his men, who set about doing what they should already have done; the men who put the ramp in place go inside the container while those clutching their rifles form a guard of honor in the courtyard of El Teronaque.

But just before Sepelio and his men begin to carry out those who have come from far-off lands, there is another cry from Epitafio: 'Look around, there's a big guy in there … Bring him out before the rest of them. Bring him here to me … Sepelio … Bring the giant to me here and then you can bring out the others.' Then, turning to the boy sent by Estela, he says, 'Don't move from this spot.'

Clearing his throat and aping Epitafio's words, Sepelio, whose face seems to have shrunk in his head, goes back inside the container, cursing those lying on the floor as he steps over them. As he scans the container for the giant, Sepelio starts to hum the song he sings every time they unload: 'Eeny, meeny, miny, moe.'

Just as when the fog lifts and the eyes refashion the form of what was merely insinuated by the mists, those who hail from other lands but not from other tongues recognize the song being sung above their heads, and so they realize they *must abandon all hope.*

'*Eeny, meeny, miny, moe, catch the giant by the toe,*' sings Sepelio, stumbling around inside the container, where the temperature is several degrees hotter and the air as dense as it was in the jungle. '*Eeny, meeny, miny, moe, catch a giant by the toe. Eeny, meeny, miny, moe, catch a giant by the toe,*' Sepelio counts off until he finds the one he is looking for and points.

'Catch the giant by the toe … Catch the giant by the toe …'
Sepelio sings as he and his men surround the giant, grabbing his arms
and legs: 'Has to be this guy, there's no one bigger in here.' Taking the
blindfold from the giant's eyes and the gag from his mouth, Sepelio
brings his constricted face close to that of the young man now suddenly begging: 'Please don't hurt me!'

'He wants you out before the others,' Sepelio whispers, cutting the
ropes that bind the giant's hands, then, ordering him on to his knees,
adds: 'Who knows, maybe this is your lucky day?' Unable to understand what has been said, the giant again fires off the words burning
his tongue: 'Please, don't hurt me … I never did nothing to no one!'

Turning on his heel, Sepelio reaches the entrance to the container,
waits until the giant is by his side, and shouts: 'Get a fucking move on!
The boss is waiting and you don't want to make him angry!' But one
step before he reaches the edge of the ramp, the giant's terror betrays
him and he stumbles and falls on his face.

Laughing at his fall, the men loyal to Sepelio lift the big guy from
the floor and deliver him to their boss, grabbing him by the elbows
and dragging him down the ramp: 'You were right … He's a giant
… but his legs don't work … or his head … He's afraid something is
going to happen to him … that you're going to do something to him!'

Hearing the *tezontle* crunch beneath the weight of the giant,
whose pleas trailed off as terror numbed his throat, Epitafio says:
'Leave him with me and go unload the others … You need to work
quickly … We'll need some rest. It's going to be a long night … If we
don't get some sleep now we'll never get it done … We won't have the
strength, you and me.'

'So I'm going with you ... You're taking me with you tonight?' Sepelio asks, feigning surprise, and his shriveled face expands once more as he listens to the words of Epitafio, who feigns surprise that Sepelio is surprised: 'I've told you a bunch of times ... tonight you come with me.' As they stare at each other, the two men are planning to put an end to each other before the day is done.

A second before Sepelio and the giant reach him, the phone in Epitafio's pocket beeps and he fishes it out with two fingers: YOUR MESSAGE CANNOT BE DELIVERED, read the twenty-eight characters that, in the mind of the man who so loves Estela mean: So you're up in the sierra now ... Let's see whether you heed me this time. Let's see whether you show up at El Paraíso.

Taking advantage of Epitafio's inattention, Sepelio looks over his shoulders and calls to his men: 'Untie the rest of them quickly ... I'll be there in a minute. In the meantime, make a start ... We haven't got all day ... We have to lock them in the rooms ... We have to get some sleep ... I want to feel strong for tonight.

'Here's your giant,' Sepelio says when Thunderhead finally looks up from his phone and they both listen in surprise to the disjointed, half-finished words of the giant: 'Where are ... They think that ... came with m ... don't want hu ...'

Eagerly examining the giant that has been delivered to him, Epitafio responds and at the same time issues a new order to Sepelio and the first of many orders to the boy who stowed away in the Minos: 'Don't pretend to know what you want and what you don't want ... You might have been misinformed ... You, go back to the container ... and you, go and help him ... No one stands around idle here.'

When Sepelio and the boy who welded shut the hinges of the container have disappeared inside the truck, Thunderhead looks into the eyes of the giant, and, seeing them scan for Sepelio, he says: 'Don't be afraid of the halfwit … My dogs don't bite unless I tell them to … Anyway, he's not going to be around for much longer.'

Epitafio wraps his arm around one of the giant's arms and, turning him around, they walk to the place where the *tezontle* is interspersed with tufts of the yellowed grass that extends all the way into the shadows of the trees and shrubs of the forest, where every creature has fallen silent, beaten down by the sun still rising in the sky.

'You're with me now … Nothing bad is going to happen to you … No one is going to hurt you if I say so,' Epitafio whispers into the ear of the giant, and then adds: 'This is your lucky day … Thanks to me, this is your lucky day. You can relax now … I mean it, stop that quivering,' says Epitafio, causing them both to halt and, turning both bodies once more, points back to the trailer.

'I want you to see what they do to them now,' says Thunderhead, sitting down on the anemic grass. 'What I am not going to let them do to you.'

'…'

'See the guard of honor the men have formed? Watch the terrified creatures come out.' Epitafio gestures, then, pretending he had forgotten he hastily asks, 'How rude of me … I haven't even asked what you're called.'

'What I'm call—?' ventures the giant only to be immediately interrupted.

'No … Don't say anything … Better I give you a name,' says Epitafio, increasingly excited. 'But don't look down … Watch what our men are doing over there … What is not happening to you.'

'…'

'That's right … Watch and learn,' says Thunderhead, then, turning back to the giant, 'What was I saying? Oh yes, I was going to give you a new name … So, tell me what you used to do.'

'Boxed and gave lessons,' sputters the big guy, barely registering that he has spoken and eager to tear his eyes from what is happening in the courtyard. 'I even won an Olympics once.'

'Are you serious?'

'I had a medal … It got lost … out there in the jungle,' babbles the giant not knowing what part of him is still speaking. 'After I gave lessons … not long … the gym closed.'

'What was the name of it … of the gym?' asks Thunderhead, his eagerness mounting.

'El Mausoleo.'

'The Mausoleum? That's your new name … Mausoleo … It fits you perfectly.'

Throwing a few punches at the empty air, Epitafio repeats: 'The Mausoleum!' Then he turns back to the giant, who closes his eyes, picturing his medal: the medal that now lies beneath the body of the elder of the two sons of the jungle: the two boys who are back in the home, sleeping like the dead, despite the fact that the puppies have begun to whimper again. Then, growing angry again, Epitafio growls: 'How many times do I have to tell you? — Don't look away.

'Open your eyes ... You need to see what the men are doing ... What'll they say about Mausoleo if he can't even bring himself to watch? ... What do you care that they're bawling like babies? ... If even one of them could hold it in ... stifle their screams ... maybe he would be lucky like you ... But no, not even one ... They don't even have the balls to choke back tears!'

First they lashed out with fists and feet ... then they beat us with boards ... we sank to the ground, legs splayed and they started to hit us ... every day I dream they're killing me ... that the boards are bursting my heart ... by now we were not ashamed to sob, we were howling dogs, animals.

When Mausoleo finally looks up toward the courtyard of El Teronaque, Epitafio throws another couple of punches, remembering the boxing matches he had with Estela and, smiling at the memory of this woman he has always loved, he takes out his phone and types: TOLD YOU HED B VALUABAL. EX–BOXER, OLYMPIC TEAM, MY GIANT. EVEN 1 A MEDELL!!!

Hearing her phone beep, Estela reaches an arm across the steering wheel and suddenly resurfaces from the abyss — her thoughts have strayed again to Cementaria and her suicide — grabs the device she left on the dashboard and reads the message that, this time, has been delivered. Her mind whirls, three thoughts intertwine: the memory of the friend she loved, the message from Epitafio, and the excitement at finally being able to get a signal.

But before the excitement she feels can be transformed into

joy, the signal disappears and IhearonlywhatIwant screams: 'Fuck!'
Meanwhile, silently thinking to herself: I need to get a move on …
I need to get to the summit soon. Then she tosses the phone on to
the dashboard, shifts up a gear, floors the pedal of the Ford Lobo and,
spotting a rocky outcrop in the distance, thinks: I can call him from
there.

VI

Incredulous, the drivers who, only seconds before, had seen their boss make a second unscheduled stop, watch as Estela clambers out and runs up the path. They are even more surprised as they see Ihearonly-whatIwant climb the escarpment and walk to the cliff edge.

Staring down into the vertiginous abyss that gives birth to the wind that whistles through the mountains, Estela holds up her telephone and complains: 'Shit ... I had a decent signal a minute ago!' and at the same time silently grumbles: Why didn't I say something ... or at least send you a message? ... What the fuck am I saying? How could I explain all this in a message?

Two meters from IhearonlywhatIwant, in a nest built into the rock face, two hatchlings cheep and the sound attracts the attention of this woman, who, on seeing the nest, shifts her thoughts to another person, thinks for a moment about Cementeria: back in El Paraíso, they were responsible for feeding the chickens.

Turning back from the sheer drop, Estela stares at the fledglings and once again wonders what happened to Cementeria, where she was all that time she was missing, and why the hell she took her own life. But her mind quickly accepts that now is not the time to think about such things, and her friend's suicide is once again replaced by thoughts of Epitafio: *Carajo* ... I didn't even respond to your message!

I bet you're pissed off ... You probably won't want to hear me out

… Even if I could get through now you probably wouldn't talk to me … One missed message and you go crazy! Estela thinks, transforming her worry into nervousness. So why bother calling you? IhearonlywhatIwant adds silently, but before she can extricate herself from this new spiral of doubts and fears, she hears a cry in the distance, looks up and sees a falcon returning to the nest.

Suspending its flight less than half a meter from the rock face, the falcon folds its wings, contracts its body and, as though walking on air, enters the nest. Disgusted by the sight of the hatchlings eating what the falcon vomits over them, Estela looks away, her gaze plunging into the void as she thinks: I'm not going to let you get angry … I'm not going to give you an excuse … Your whole life, you've been like this. Even when we were kids you'd get mad if you couldn't get an answer.

Looking away from the abyss and hopping from one rock to another, Estela smiles, remembering the first time she ever saw Epitafio angry, and writes: *WTF DO I CARE THAT HE 1 A MEDELL!!!* Then, praying that her phone will get a signal if only for a second, IhearonlywhatIwant waves her arm in the air, spins around and looks at the Tierra Negra massif in the distance.

Seeing the sandworms of dust raised by the vehicles crossing the mesa, which she herself crossed only a short time ago, Estela thinks: I'd get a signal down there … Shit … I was dumb not to call you from down there. Looking away from the mesa, just as she is about to launch into another rant, IhearonlywhatIwant hears her phone beep: it has managed to send the message to Epitafio.

Taking a deep breath, Estela hops to another rock and begins to calm down: at least this time I responded. Then, as she retraces her steps to the huge truck, she feels another surge of calm: Anyway, what would I have said if I'd called you from down there? I can't tell you what's going on with us like that … It needs to be face to face … That's another thing that pissed you off … when I'd leave little notes in your room … when I didn't tackle things head on.

Just as she is walking away from the chasm, she is hit by a gust of wind, but it is a different blow that almost knocks her off her feet: Worse than leaving you little notes was when I made a joke … That really got your back up … Why the fuck did I write *WTF DO I CARE THAT HE 1 A MEDELL!!!?* Each time IhearonlywhatIwant cuts a head off the Hydra of her fears, two more grow in its place and shriek at her: You're going to think I don't care … that I'm taunting you … that I don't want you to call or write or tell me anything … that you're just a pain in the ass!

Increasing her pace even as the Hydra's heads of fear in her mind increase, Estela takes out her phone again: *IT WAS A JOKE. U KNOW I CARE ABOUT U. YOUR ALWYS RIGHT ABOUT THIS STUFF!!!* Then she puts away the phone and heads back to the convoy, where her men are frantic and the willpower of the men and women who have come from other lands is waning.

I should never have tried … never have left … to think I thought I could succeed … like an idiot … I should have known it was impossible … that every man is broken eventually … that this place breaks him … these people break him … turn him into a dog … no better than an animal.

As she runs faster, Estela prays that her last message has been sent. Then, shaking her head, she realizes: What difference does it make whether it was delivered or not? … The problem is not the text messages … The problem is that we need to fucking talk … I need to tell you we can't carry on like this … to call you … I have to say it, even if it's not face to face.

Puta mierda … I'll have to go to El Paraíso … I have to go, though I don't want to … At least I can call you from there, Estela thinks as she braves a whirling gust of wind: I'll have to go to El Paraíso, even though I told you I'm not going … even though I told you something strange is going on there … Something you and I don't understand …

That's another reason why you're probably angry … Why the fuck did I say: I don't want to go to El Paraíso, there's something weird going on there, but I didn't tell you what is going on with us? How could I imply that the people there are plotting against us and not say, there's that, and there's also what is going on between you and me? Estela thinks as she reaches the door of the truck and, looking up, sees the falcon, which has left its nest, at the moment it swoops on a flock of birds, scattering them and picking off the weakest.

The quail captured in mid-flight still fluttering in its claws, the falcon flies off and disappears into the ravine just as Estela climbs into the Ford Lobo and slumps into the driver's seat, tosses her phone on to the dashboard and glances at the captain and asks: 'What the fuck is up with you?' Her voice, he cannot help but notice, is like a bugle call, and she continues: 'You should have phoned us yesterday … or at least called Epitafio!'

'Still whining about that … I'm with you now, so what does it matter that I didn't call!' says the captain, surprised to hear himself

THE BOOK OF EPITAFIO

raising his voice and casually saying what he just said. In an instant, the tension in the truck swells like a balloon. The captain looks away from Estela, points to the keys that fell on the floor earlier and says: 'There's your damned keys.'

Turning the ignition of the Ford Lobo and flooring the accelerator, IhearonlywhatIwant realizes that she needs to calm down, but though this is what she wants, she snarls: 'He always stands up for you with the boss … No one defends you the way he does at El Paraíso … I can't believe you just left him hanging … that you didn't say anything.' Then Estela takes a slow, deep breath, convinced that now she will be calm, only to erupt again: 'He always says, "I like him better than the last guy … I trust El Chorrito more than any other soldier."'

For a moment she is mute, then the woman who loves Epitafio once again breaks her silence: 'Do you know what Epitafio calls you?' The captain's face hardens and he says: 'How could I not know? I was there when he shouted: "Just look at this guy, the way he walks, it's like he's got the shits" … And Sepelio got to his feet, laughing and cheering and imitating my limp … "I was walking down the lane … And I felt a funny pain … diarrhoea, diarrhoea …"'

'And you still didn't call him … He gives you a cool nickname and you go and betray him!' Estela taunts El Chorrito, who flies into a rage: 'He gave me a cool nickname? … Gave me … Don't fucking make me laugh, and anyway, I didn't betray anyone! Stop trying to piss me off … How do you expect me …?' The captain trails off, recognizing that it is dangerous for him to broach this subject. I always say more than I should, thinks the captain and, in an attempt to divert attention, says the first thing that comes into his head: 'You'd be better off telling me how many women we're carrying ... I need to know before we get to La Cañada!'

'I don't know exactly how many there are,' Estela says. 'There were about sixty of them back in the clearing ... He took about twenty of them ... We should have about fifty.' 'Fifty?' says the captain, while IhearonlywhatIwant shifts up a gear and takes a bend that runs perilously close to the cliff. 'That's what I said ... Approximately fifty ... Minus the ones my men have already finished off. Their dicks always get the better of them.'

> *They said it would go easier if we cooperated ... that was lies ...*
> *they never stopped ... until one of the women couldn't take any*
> *more ... she's fucking hot they said and they took her from both*
> *ends ... she was on her period but they didn't care ... they all*
> *raped her ... afterward she couldn't stand ... the bitch is dead,*
> *one of them said and they left.*

'I'm serious, I need to know ... I can't tell them: "We've got fifty, more or less,"' El Chorrito says, looking at Estela, who continues to accelerate. 'If you need to know so badly, you can count them ... when we get to El Paraíso ... but right now, just shut the fuck up.' 'I thought we were going straight to La Cañada,' the captain says. 'Now you're telling me I'm going to waste a whole day.' He is about to continue when Estela interrupts: 'We go where I say we go! And we're going to El Paraíso whether you like it or not!

'That's where we're headed, and when we get there we're going to make like everything is wonderful ... like we've been dying to get back there,' says Estela, speaking not so much to the captain as to herself. When finally she trails off again, the silence that falls in the huge truck seems barbed and filled with echoes.

And like all silences that bristle with what has just been said, the silence in the Ford Lobo is pregnant with what is about to be said: with no choice but to listen to each other, Estela and the captain open their mouths, activate their tongues and talk over each other: 'I can't be away from we'll eat and I'll call Epita my checkpoint all day and all nightsome shut-eye even for a few hours don't even know I've gone while we can they find out they can court martand it's not so dangerous to be out!'

'Shut up, I'm trying to talk,' screams Estela, slapping the steering wheel of the huge truck. 'Besides, you do what I fucking tell you … What do I care if they court martial you and lock you up? … What the fuck do I care if they kill you? … You should have called him … You shouldn't have double-crossed us … How could you betray Epitafio?' 'I already told you, I didn't betray anyone,' the captain tries to say, but Estela interrupts: 'I said shut the fuck up … I don't want to hear you!'

Silence falls again, gouging out the time in the Ford Lobo while IhearonlywhatIwant shifts the truck and her mind into neutral: the convoy she is leading begins its descent just as, in her mind, she begins another descent; Estela slips into the memories of the years she spent living in El Paraíso, while her Fordo Lobo and the two battered pickup trucks coast down the slopes towards the hanging valley and El Paraíso.

Estela cannot help it, the memories of the days long since gone resurface, clearer than the things she can see before her: two eddies of dust whipped up by the wind, a distant coyote loping across the horizon, the acacia bushes that line both sides of the ravine are superimposed by the wooden door that kept her locked in her room, by the bed where she spent years tossing and turning, unable to sleep, by the window she spent hours peering through so she could escape her present.

What is it about El Paraíso that makes me so suspicious? ... Why have they turned their backs on us? Estela wonders, as memories of this place where she first saw the man she now adores come flooding back, and as she snakes down the mountain road, the rocks lining this stretch of road are superimposed by the rocks where she and Epitafio used to hide, while the towering cacti dotting the landscape are overlaid with the memory of the cactus where they once left messages for each other.

Meanwhile, as the trucks hurtle down the sierra, led by a woman who will remain lost in her memories for some time yet — rather than the track the Ford Lobo is following, Estela sees the sandy patch of ground where once she played with Epitafio, Osaria, Ausencia, Hipogeo, Sepelio and Cementaria — the bodies of *the nameless whose souls were betrayed by the deaf God they called upon when they realized they were doomed* are tossed about.

I pleaded with God for help ... begged Him not to allow this to happen to us ... I prayed and they laughed ... then they dragged me outside and tossed me in the mud ... keep praying, they said, see what happens ... and I lay there ... in the darkness and the smell of putrefaction ... now I dream of that stench ... now I no longer pray.

When finally the jolting stops, the oldest of all those who have come from afar finds himself lying face up, staring at a tiny hole in the canvas that is his tarpaulin shroud. For the first time this morning, the oldest of the men and women who have come from other lands might see a patch of sky, if he chose to. But rather than look at this, the old man thinks of the little girl he was tasked with looking after and weeps bitterly that she is no longer by his side.

Meanwhile, the little girl no longer with the old man, the girl with the oversized head and the mouth that does not close, is being dragged, insulted and beaten in the courtyard of El Teronaque by those loyal to Epitafio. Hurrying across the *tezontle* and urging his giant faster, the chatter of a magpie transports Epitafio — as always when surprised by a magpie — to the courtyard of the house in which he was born, a house that seemed happy for many years, those years when he and his brothers did nothing but play beneath the boundless sky.

Then, one day like any other, the years of confinement began: Epitafio and his brothers were allowed out only for a brief period every day. Later still, for only a brief period every three or four days, and only accompanied by their father or their mother.

In the end, the boys were never allowed out of the house, something was lurking, though Epitafio never understood what it might be. Epitafio, this man who right now wants nothing more than to go and rest in this building that was once a slaughterhouse and this is why he is urging Mausoleo across the blood-red rocks.

VII

'I don't want you trembling when we get inside ... is that clear? ... You have to walk in there like you own the place,' Epitafio orders the giant and, as he does so, thinks about the days he himself spent imprisoned: when he and his brothers could no longer leave the house, when his mother spent her life in bed, when, day and night, his father could not tear himself away from the windows: 'They'll come today, I know it.'

Shaking his head, Epitafio tries to drive away this memory and once more says to Mausoleo: 'You have to walk in like you own the place ... In there, you have to look strong. You have to act like they —' interrupted by the bleep of his phone Epitafio breaks off: *WTF DO I CARE THAT HE 1 A MEDELL!!!* reads the message that sets Epitafio roaring with laughter.

A startled magpie answers Epitafio with a loud cackle and he is once again transported to the courtyard where he spent his childhood: it had been filled with magpies just like this one on the morning when the men his father had so often warned about finally arrived. The morning when Thunderhead and his brothers pressed their terror to the windows, while their mother sobbed in her bed, and their father screamed and argued in the courtyard.

Shaking his head again, Epitafio once more dispels the memory of the day when his family ceased to be a family. He quickens his pace, pockets his telephone, and comes back to the present time and place. And to what he was saying: 'If they see you trembling I won't lift a finger to save you … I can't fail them … Stop that trembling or I'll stop … I'll take away your luck!

'That's it … make sure your body doesn't quiver … I don't want to go in there and have you break down … What we did out here was just the start!' Thunderhead says as they reach the building in which they have just locked *the shadows and the mute whose very souls have been ripped from them*. Then, blocking his thoughts from drifting back to the months of his own imprisonment, Epitafio strokes his pocket and fills the void in his mind: What did I do to you today to make you so angry? … Why the fuck are you sending me these messages?

A few meters from the rickety edifice that overlooks El Teronaque, Epitafio stops his giant, turns to Sepelio, who has been waiting for them, and gives the same order he gave earlier: 'Get moving, take that ramp back where it belongs!' Thunderhead squeezes Mausoleo's arm and reiterates: 'I don't want you missing a single detail … You'll be expected to do the same thing often enough.'

In the doorway, where the eyes and the ears of the giant leave his body open to a hundred stab wounds, Epitafio once again wonders what he could have done to annoy Estela, and can calm himself by deluding himself: It must be something to do with Cementeria … You're upset because of what the stupid *chica* did and, as usual, I get the brunt of it. Meanwhile, inside the slaughterhouse, the men obedient to Thunderhead continue to terrorize the men and women who have come from other lands.

You're upset and you're taking it out on me … *Puta* Cementeria … Why the fuck did you have to do that … and why did you throw yourself into the road? Epitafio silently accuses, not realizing that the giant next to him has begun to totter: the daggers planted in his body a moment ago and ripping through his entrails. Why again? thinks Mausoleo, tensing his jaw, half-closing his eyes and longing to clap his hands over his ears.

> *They put us in a building that reeked of something dead … They beat us again, they burned us … 'Kill the first one that moves' … They asked for our phone numbers, our families' phone numbers … They demanded ten thousand dollars … They laughed at them, at us … It was just talk … They knew they would get nothing.*

As the creatures who crossed the border howl, Epitafio's men smile and chat about a soccer match that took place some time ago to block what they are doing from entering their minds. 'Hey, what d'you think, *jefe*?' comes a voice, and talk of the match banishes Estela from the mind of Epitafio, who snaps irritably: '*Hijos de puta* … We were robbed … No way that was a penalty.'

But just before he loses himself in the match his men are reminiscing about, Epitafio feels a sharp tug and turns his face to Mausoleo: the daggers that entered his body through his eyes, now tightly closed, and the ears over which he has finally clamped his hands, force the giant to take two steps back.

'What the hell? Where do you think you are? Don't block your ears … Open your eyes this minute!' Epitafio roars angrily, but the big guy is not listening: the pain of the creatures who came from other lands shakes him, turns every muscle in his body to jelly. '*Puta madre!*'

Epitafio screams, but Mausoleo retreats another two steps, staggers, falls to his knees and, without opening his eyes or taking his hands from his ears, vomits.

Hearing the gale of laughter from his men, Epitafio steps towards the giant, grabs him by the hair, shakes him violently, kicks him in the ribs: 'Stop that now, I'm not fucking kidding … I warned you about this shit!' It is fear rather than the pain of the blows that forces Mausoleo to open his eyes, uncover his ears and once again turn his attention to Epitafio, who bellows: 'Stop that, and clean up that mess!' Then, turning to his men, he says in a hoarse voice, 'And you lot can shut your traps … Who said you could laugh?

'Get a move on, do what I told you … clean up your mess!' Epitafio says again, still shaking the giant, who wants to do just that, but cannot tear his eyes from the vomit in front of his face: he can feel them, the stares of the men clutching their weapons and the eyes of those creatures who, like him, have been walking for many days, they are heavy as lead weights on the back of his neck.

Just then, in the sepulchral silence that has gathered around him, Mausoleo feels the barrel of a gun press against his collar bone and hears the man taking aim at his existence ask Epitafio: 'So, should we toss him in with the rest of them?' 'You watch, he'll get up!' says Thunderhead, pushing the gun away from the giant: 'Get to your feet, I don't want to see you shot … I don't want to take your luck from you … Get up and prove to them you can stand on your own two feet!'

Laying both hands flat on the floor, struggling to make sure he does not slip on his own drool and vomit, Mausoleo gasps for breath like a man who has almost drowned, tenses his jaw even harder than before and, with a brutal headbutt, pushes aside the gun barrel threatening his existence. Then he looks around him, listens as the *wails of those who no longer expect anything of fate* take over the space, and gradually gets to his feet.

Shaking off the last crumbs of his fear, Mausoleo recovers from his collapse, feels as though his legs belong to him again and, balling his hands into fists, takes two steps forward. 'I ate something that didn't agree with me,' he mumbles to Epitafio, who smiles and orders: 'Clean up that shit ... Clean it up or get one of them to do it!'

The giant does not think twice, but strides through the house overlooking El Teronaque and, as his eyes survey the creatures suffering the torments of this Fatherland that has swallowed their hopes and entombed their memories, he hears an unfamiliar voice from deep within his belly: 'Who do you want to clean up your shit?' Exhilarated, Epitafio watches Mausoleo and, fumbling in his pocket for his cigarettes, says to his men: 'See? I told you so.'

I left them in the truck, Thunderhead remembers a moment later and is about to turn back towards the door: if he does not do so it is simply because he feels as though the energy radiating from the giant is his, the almost electrical force that gives voice to the new language that Mausoleo is muttering to himself, a language that startles the men clutching their weapons and terrifies those who were captured in the clearing known as El Ojo de Hierba.

Feeling his bravura heal the wounds opened up by his fears, *the blind newcomer in the kingdom of the blind* reaches the mass of tortured and humiliated men and women, and, for the first time today, his face relaxes. He grabs an old man by the throat, drags him several meters, throws him to the ground and, pointing at the consequences of his nausea, orders: 'Clean up that shit right now!'

'You heard him … clean up that mess!' Epitafio excitedly echoes and, slumping into a chair, he replaces and removes his cap: 'Leave him to it and come and sit next to me … The dumb *pendejo* knows what he has to do.' Obediently, Mausoleo lets go of the old man and walks over to Epitafio: 'I told you today was your lucky day!'

'I am the lord of luck and I am offering it to you,' says Epitafio. 'I'm doing you the biggest fucking favor anyone has ever done you.'

'…'

'I am Fortune and I am the Fatherland,' says Thunderhead as Mausoleo draws alongside, then, nodding to a chair, he adds, 'Sit down and watch what happens next … This is something else you will have to do.'

'What are they going to do?'

'You mean, what are we going to do to them!' Epitafio corrects the giant. 'We have to shut them up once and for all … lambast their head … turn them into nobody.'

> *They were constantly screaming at us, beating us, pissing on us …*
> *They did not let us speak to each other, look at each other … Anyone*
> *who spoke was whipped with a wet rag … Anyone who looked*
> *around was burned with matches … then they'd say … 'You're*
> *dead now' … We stayed there until they assigned us to the rooms.*

'We have to make sure they don't remember … that they don't know who they are, who anyone is,' Thunderhead explains after a long silence. 'Then we have to divide them up … the ones that are ours … the ones that will be taken away.'

'The ones that will be taken away?'

'That bastard, Señor Hoyo, will come and collect some of them …' Epitafio explains. 'He'll come and take away his own.'

'…'

'The rest are ours,' says Thunderhead, 'we'll move them out tonight.'

'Tonight?'

'That's why we need to get some sleep … to get some rest, once we put them in their rooms.'

'Where?'

'You'll go in there,' Epitafio interrupts Mausoleo, pointing to one of the rooms in which his men are imprisoning those who have come from other lands. 'You'll watch over them … make sure they don't make any noise … I don't want to hear a peep out of them.'

Once Mausoleo is in the room crammed with half of those from the far side of the border, Epitafio orders his men back out into the court-yard to burn the clothes worn by *those who no longer expect anything of heaven now their God has forsaken them*, torch the body of the one who did not survive the journey, decide on a rotation of sentries for the coming hours so that the others can sleep a while.

Then, when all the men loyal to him have left the building, Epitafio remembers his cigarettes, gets up from his chair, yawns once or twice, and, addressing the absence of the woman he so loves, says: 'Better to smoke and not think about your tantrums,' he goes out into the yard and silently adds: I could sleep in the truck today.

Gazing at the mountains that are a mirror image of the sierra that Estela and her men are still descending, Epitafio reaches his battered truck, clambers in and searches for his cigarettes, still talking to IhearonlywhatIwant: 'I'll phone you as soon as I wake up ... Right now, I have to get some shut-eye, even if only for a while ... Tonight promises to be long and tedious.'

Coughing and spluttering from the cigarette he is holding between his fingers, Epitafio lays a cushion between his seat and the passenger seat to make up a bed, and thinks: The night will be long, but I'm going to be rid of that idiot ... I won't have to look after Sepelio any more. Then, he tosses aside Estela's CDs, takes off his cap, finishes his cigarette and lies down: You could have tidied away the CDs ... You didn't have to leave them lying around.

You're always leaving things lying around: still thinking about Estela, Epitafio feels sleep invading his body and, reaching out, manages to heed one last order dictated by his caution: he grabs the door handle and tugs it hard. The sound made by the door slamming is indistinguishable from that produced, moments earlier up in the sierra, by the car door slammed by Estela, who has reached El Paraíso.

VIII

Without explaining anything to the captain traveling with her, Estela slams the door of the Ford Lobo and walks towards the huge dilapidated stone building in the distance: El Paraíso rises and is camouflaged in the only hanging valley in the sierra, a mirror image of the sierra in whose foothills Epitafio is now sleeping.

Looking at the fountain, the stone benches, the sentry plants and the nopal cacti as one might look at a relative one would prefer not to see again, Estela quickens her pace, but is stopped by the sound of footsteps. Looking over her shoulder, IhearonlywhatIwant glares at her men: 'Get back in the trucks … Don't move until I get back!'

Swallowing their anger, the men loyal to Estela climb into the trucks. Hearing their executioners return, those who lost their faith in God call on Him again, all except the women who no longer have the strength to rip even a single word from their silence.

> *They got back in the trucks … I thought it will all start up again … I didn't even beg … Why bother? … Sooner or later they would climb on top of me again … I thought … I no longer had the strength or the will to live … Why bother? I thought … They had already left their mark … deep inside … those marks that go on hurting forever … hadn't they?*

The only man who remained silent, like the women whose voices are broken, is the oldest *of all the creatures who have come so far*: a little while ago he suceeded in freeing his hands and, staring at the patch of sky through the hole in the tarpaulin, has managed to dismiss the thoughts of the little girl with the oversized head he could not keep with him.

Reading the lines that mark his palms, the oldest of *all the creatures to whom God has turned a deaf ear* now smiles and accepts that this is the first of the last moments left to him: Perhaps they will come and let us out now. Why don't they just fucking come and kill us?! he silently rails, convinced that he has screamed the words: but no one hears him, not the creatures trussed up beside him, nor the men clutching their weapons, nor the woman in the distance hurrying towards El Paraíso.

Circling the fake well and gazing at the pepper trees shading the façade of the ancient workhouse, built as a monastery almost two centuries ago by an order that has since disappeared, Estela forces her legs to walk faster and, as her eyes adjust to the shadows cast by the pepper trees, she exclaims with feigned irritation: 'What kind of welcome is this ... is no one here happy to see me?'

A few meters from the flowerbeds teeming with jasmine, Estela unthinkingly slows her pace and says in a low voice: 'I shouldn't have come ... I should have followed my instinct ... There's something strange going on here ... I said to Epitafio that they're plotting something,' IhearonlywhatIwant mutters to herself as her heart beats faster in her chest: so many things, so many memories, and, suddenly, so many fears.

Slowing until she all but comes to a halt, Estela silently complains to the absent Epitafio: I told you something was going on, something you and I don't know about, while at the same time calling out: 'Is no one going to come out ... does no one come out to welcome a daughter of El Paraíso when she comes home?' But the only response is the cackle of a few hens and a solitary bark that might not have been a bark.

Fretfully circling the wishing well, at the bottom of which the tiles spell out 'Welcome to El Paraíso', IhearonlywhatIwant admires the main entrance to the monastery built with stones quarried in these mountains, tightens her stomach and steels herself: *Stop being afraid ... Why would anyone here want to hurt you?* The solitary bark turns out to be a bark; it is followed by the baying of a pack of hounds reacting to the call of their master.

The chorus of howls drowns out the cackle of the chickens and swallows the whistle of the wind eroding the sierra. More irritated than anxious, Estela is about to turn toward the dogs when Father Nicho finally appears, dragging his ancient body through the gates of El Paraíso: he is pocketing a cordless phone he has just finished speaking into.

Picking up her pace again, Estela regrets her misgivings. *How could he harm me? ... I'm not the little girl I once was ... and besides, why would he, when he has always been fond of me ... when he and Epitafio are so close ... so reliant on each other?* IhearonlywhatIwant adds silently, even as she loudly apologises for her lateness: 'One of the trucks broke down in the forest ... and they've moved the checkpoints ... but here we are, at last.'

'A truck, a checkpoint ... always some excuse, huh?' says Father Nicho, taking several steps towards her, then he turns back to his hounds and whistles for the pack to be silent. 'What are you thinking of, being out at this hour? What would Epitafio say if he knew you were breaking his rules?' grumbles the priest, throwing his arms up to indicate that he is not interested in the excuses of this woman who has just arrived: 'I didn't want to be out and about ... they really have moved the checkpoints.'

'What do you mean they've moved the checkpoints?' Father Nicho asks, pretending to be surprised by what he is hearing, as he takes another step forward and surrenders to Estela's embrace and the sun's rays as they filter through the leaves of the two ancient pepper trees. 'We don't know what happened ... Why the hell they moved them ... but I forced El Chorrito to come with me,' IhearonlywhatIwant gestures to the Ford Lobo as she releases the old man.

'El Chorrito? What were you thinking bringing that jerk here?' Father Nicho says, genuinely surprised this time. 'You had no business bringing that bonehead here ...,' he growls, peering at the huge truck and thinking to himself: I'll have to go and tell him ... I'll have to remind that idiot not to open his mouth! 'I had no choice ... I need him to do the talking at La Cañada,' Estela apologises, and is about to continue but the priest cuts her off: 'He can stay where he is ... I'm not having him in my orphanage.'

'If it was up to me, he'd wait in the well,' says Estela, following Father Nicho as he hurries back into the shade cast by the building: 'The stupid bastard didn't even phone Epitafio ... Epitafio, that's it ... I have to call Epitafio.'

'There's no hurry ... He knows you're here,' says Father Nicho, now two steps from the main door of El Paraíso. 'I was speaking to him a minute ago … when you were getting out of the truck … I saw you from the window.'

'So Epitafio called you … just now?' IhearonlywhatIwant splutters in surprise.

'Well, not just now … A little while ago … but we had a long chat, the two of us,' Father Nicho explains as he pushes open the heavy door. 'Then I saw you coming and I said to him … Here she is now.'

'And he didn't ask to talk to me?' says Estela, closing the huge door behind her.

'Tell her I need to get some sleep … that I'll talk to her this afternoon … That's what he told me to say,' explains the priest. 'Tell her I'm too tired … I know I've got another long night ahead of me.'

'The bastard … so *now* he wants to sleep … he'd rather sleep than talk to me!'

'That's what he told me … but don't think of it like that,' says the priest, crossing the space that was once the monastery tithe-barn. 'Better to think that you're tired too … that you'll talk to him in a little while … You should go upstairs and rest awhile.'

'You're right … no point getting upset,' says IhearonlywhatIwant, and not realizing she is muttering aloud, thinks, '*Hijo de* fucking *puta* … stupid of me to even worry.'

'Sorry?'

'I'm worried about my men.'

'Well, don't fret. I'll send someone to fetch them right now,' says Father Nico and then, crossing what was once the refectory, asks, 'Why do you have two trailers today?'

'There were more than usual.'

'So you're not going to go without leaving a few here with me.'

'There are five or six that you could use,' Estela says, and then, betraying her worries once again, adds, 'Maybe I should call him.'

'Leave six of them with me and leave him to get some rest … You should be asleep yourself … Aren't you tired?'

'All I feel right now is hungry,' says Estela to avoid saying that she is angry, that her anxiety is making her furious.

'Well, you go up to your room and I'll bring up some breakfast … though at this hour, it might be more accurate to say lunch,' says Father Nicho, nodding towards the corridor that leads to the stairs.

'Is it empty?'

'They came for her a few days ago … They wanted a boy, but as soon as they set eyes on her, their decision was made,' says the priest, 'so your room is empty … Now go up there and I'll be up in a minute.'

As the priest walks away, Estela turns, crosses the main hallway of El Paraíso and climbs the stairs, trying to calm herself: Maybe it's because I was angry … Maybe that's why you called here and said: Tell her it's better if we talk later.

The ancient wooden stairs creak beneath the weight of Estela's body, which is heavier than she admits and heavier than it appears, while in her gut hunger begins to rumble: I'll get something to eat soon, thinks IhearonlywhatIwant, but her mind continues to rail: You didn't want to talk to me because of my outbursts.

On the second floor of the orphanage, as the woman who so loves Epitafio negotiates the labyrinth of corridors she knows by heart, as hunger begins to cramp her belly, her mind insists: You decided to get some sleep because you're angry with me.

IhearonlywhatIwant is so self-absorbed she does not even hear the sounds leaching from beneath the doors she passes: the mutterings and whisperings of children who finished the day's work an hour since, cursing their lives.

Only when she comes to the end of the corridor, to another staircase she is about to climb, does Estela notice the drone of voices and, clicking her tongue, she says, 'You'll see, you'll get used to it … It will make you stronger.' Hearing her own words, she remembers Cementeria, Hipogeo, Ausencia, Osamenta, Osaria and Sepelio: but of all of them, the only one that will stay in her mind is the one who was already there.

IhearonlywhatIwant no longer cares about the suicide of Cementeria, the murder of Hipogeo, the sale of Osamenta, the life of Sepelio: she cares only about the fact that Epitafio did not want to talk to her: I always end up doing something that pisses you off.

Turning into a new corridor, Estela moves away from the whispered voices, passes several rooms, one of which was once Epitafio's, and arrives at the wooden door that once kept her prisoner.

With an empty gesture. IhearonlywhatIwant reaches out, grabs the rusted doorknob, thinking: Still as cold as ever here, then, turning the handle, she decides: I'm not going to think about you any more, pushes the door open and says: It doesn't matter … I'll make you happy later.

The squeal of the hinges, the whispered voices she can no longer hear, but which still echo inside her head, and a sudden, precarious sense of calm transport Estela back to her past and, as she steps into the room, she steps into a different era: one when she was first brought to this orphanage, clutching the hand of her mother's partners. Her mother, a woman whose twin legacies were the constant refrain, I made you with no help from anyone, and jokes about her father's identity.

'What a bitch you were … *Mamá*,' Estela says, caressing the walls, approaching the window and reading the names scratched into the bare stone years ago: Mario, Sixto, Valentín, Abelardo, Juan, Esteban and Ramiro.

'You always were a bitch … Just look at all the names you gave me … telling me over and over: that one there … that was the name of your *papá*.'

Shaking her head, Estela drives from her mind the names she read a second earlier and allows her gaze to leave the orphanage: through the window, beneath the pitiless sun that reached its zenith some time ago, IhearonlywhatIwant watches the comings and goings of her men and utterly forgets her past, brooding on something that Epitafio once said: 'The past is closer in memory than it is in time.'

As she watches the six nuns marshalling her men, Estela feels that she is finally safe and, trusting her eyes, allows her guard to slip: immediately, the glassy distance is transformed by the sunlight into reverie and she witnesses something long past: her mother's friends walk away from El Paraíso after leaving her here, cursing her for what she did at the funeral of the woman who gave birth to her.

The pain is all in her mind, not in her body, Estela thinks, paraphrasing Epitafio, and, without realizing, rubs those parts of her body bruised by her mother's two partners that day. The same parts where

IhearonlywhatIwant now bears the mark of Father Nicho's branding iron: the tiny squares tattooed onto every girl as soon as she is brought here.

The nuns who burned her flesh and those now marshalling her men in the courtyard of El Paraíso meld into a single image, Estela returns to the present day and takes two steps back. Then she crosses the room and slumps onto the bed, recognizing the creak of the springs that were already worn out when she was a little girl, and says aloud: 'I'll get some sleep and then I'll call you.'

But the words that Estela has uttered are shattered by four sharp raps at the door. Without waiting for her to answer, Father Nicho pushes it open and his eyes lock on to those of IhearonlywhatIwant: 'I see that they've already been unloaded … I imagine you've taken the children … are you going to mark them now, or later? I'd like to help with the branding when I wake up.'

Father Nicho approaches the bed where Estela is sitting and, setting down a tray with water and food, says: 'I have told you often enough … those who leave cannot take part in the branding.' 'But are you going to mark them now or later?' IhearonlywhatIwant asks again, not turning to look at the water or the food, then she asks: 'How many do you have here, including the six I just brought?'

'Including the six you brought, nineteen,' the priest says, pushing the tray towards Estela. 'But not all of them serve me … There are some whose hands have grown too big … Maybe you could take them away with you?'

'I didn't come to take anything away.'

'Well, give them a weapon … Go on, you know that they know the ways of the world.'

'Bastard.'

'Your hands grew, too … You too were forced to leave,' says Father Nicho, 'and you cannot say that you left here unprepared.'

'I don't want to argue about it any more … Besides, the trucks are already full,' says IhearonlywhatIwant. 'I'm tired … yes, I'm really starting to feel tired.'

'That's what I thought.'

'I haven't slept since she … that *hija de puta*, Cementeria.'

'Do not mention her name … As though she lacked for anything here … I am serious, do not mention her name.'

'Why the hell did she do it … and why do it the way she did?'

'Because she was ungrateful … She always wanted more than she had,' says the priest. 'But don't think about her … better to get some rest … sleep a while.'

Before Estela can lie back on the rickety mattress, Father Nicho has left the room and is hurrying along the corridors and down the stairs: he does not want the branding of the children in the cellar to begin unless he is there to do it, unless he is holding the iron, and so he quickens his pace.

Meanwhile, Estela lies back on the bed, staring up at the six beams that she has seen so often, and that have so often seen her slip off her restless wakefulness. Closing her eyes, almost without realizing, the woman who so loves Epitafio slips into unconsciousness, leaving the world just as Thunderhead has done in El Teronaque, and just as, much earlier, the two sons of the jungle did in their house.

Three floors below, Father Nicho takes out his telephone: he will call Sepelio and the men he has hired on the Madre Buena plateau: the men, who, with the help of Ausencia, first tortured and then drove poor Cementeria mad, forcing her to wonder and to question what happened to Osamenta, why she committed suicide … and why she did it the way she did.

So Crumbled the Horizon

|

On the walls of the room in which Mausoleo and the men and women who have come from other lands are confined, the monotony of brickwork is broken only by the door slammed shut by Epitafio, a few stains on the concrete, and the window that allows the sun to pour in like a penance.

Leaning against the door, his eyes bloodshot, his nose congested and his face flushed from the tiredness he cannot allow to overcome him, Mausoleo watches over the men and women now sleeping, huddled together and pressed against the walls.

'If I hear a sound, you're responsible,' Epitafio threatens Mausoleo moments before pushing him into the place that reeks of captive creatures: though there is no glass in the window, those who are sleeping *because only in sleep can they mock their suffering* suppurate with sweat and fear.

'I don't want to hear a sound from them ... I don't want them moving around,' Mausoleo remembers Epitafio's order as he witnesses a woman shaking and letting out a wail that might be heard in the main room, or even outside where the sentries are patrolling and where the sun has passed its zenith three hours since.

Leaping to his feet, Mausoleo strides across the room, but before he can reach the corner where she lies, the woman who woke a moment ago has curled up and fallen asleep again.

Peering out into the courtyard of El Teronaque, Mausoleo watches the guards move away and listens as their voices and their laughter also fade.

When all is silent once again, the giant gazes out at the horizon and what he sees transports him back to the place where he was born: not that what he can see looks anything like the places that he remembers, but Mausoleo wishes that it did.

Rubbing his eyes because he knows they are trying to deceive him, Mausoleo see a solitary cloud, then a pair of giant birds, and then, for a brief moment, he stares at the sun, blazing so fiercely that the giant can feel his retinas burning.

In the distance, beyond the wall of trees masking the dense forest, he hears again the murmur of the sentries' voices and the twisted echoes of their laughter.

But beneath the closed eyelids of the giant, these voices, this laughter are the voices and the laughter he used to hear on the wharf, just as the stench all around is the stench of piles of fish. Mausoleo is back on the *barra* — the spit of land where he was born — staring at his house, at the village beyond, and farther off the boxing gym where he trained.

I should never have left! the giant thinks as he opens his eyes, retreating a few steps, then turning and, with a heavy heart, going back to the door. More than all the things he left behind on that spit of land, Mausoleo is thinking about the one thing he brought with him and, as he leans back against the door, he brings his hand up to his throat and feels the space left by his medal.

Sinking to the floor, Mausoleo throws two, three, four punches at the empty air and, forcing a smile, he talks to the medal: 'It's not as though you brought me much luck. It's not as though you brought me much of anything,' says the giant and in saying this, comes back to himself, to the one who watches over everyone. Rubbing his eyes, where the sand of sleep has formed a crystalline crust, the giant surveys the men and women left in his charge.

But a new sound forces him to his feet again: though still asleep, the little girl with the outsized head mutters something unintelligible, a growl that sounds like a clap of thunder and sets Mausoleo's heart beating faster: 'You'll watch over them … Make sure they don't make any noise … I don't want to hear a peep out of them.'

Hurrying across the room, the giant comes to the place just as the little girl growls again and is about to hunker down when some strange new impulse stops him. Then he kicks the girl a couple of times and the fear that he sees as her eyes snap open excites him: Maybe this really is my lucky day?

This excitement, as new to him as the impulse that caused him to lash out at the little girl, and the voice he heard speak to him earlier, are transformed into conviction when, leaning back on the door again, Mausoleo feels his fears transformed into pride: he is the one chosen to keep watch over the men and women who, in addition to the fact that they *no longer expect anything of heaven*, should not expect much here on earth.

II

Staring wearily at a pipe from the mouth of which two timid wires protrude, Mausoleo continues to shadow box, silently hoping that one of the men will wake and make some noise, although aloud he says: 'Just let any of them dare make a sound … *Hijos de puta!*

'Let them dare open their mouths!' says the giant staring up at the ceiling, at a piece of cardboard the builders forgot to remove when it was plastered. When the building was a slaughterhouse, this room did not exist. People are always leaving shit like that behind, Mausoleo thinks, rubbing his glassy eyes and remembering similar pieces of cardboard back at home and, surprised at his thought, he wonders: Why the hell did I ever leave?

Alarmed by the sudden void that has opened up inside him, the giant closes his glassy eyes and, pressing his finger against his eyelids, tries to drive out the past. But the sounds that inhabit his memory drag him back to the spit of land and the giant listens to a crackle of flames, the whispering of a radio, the barking of dogs, the beating wings of a hundred seagulls, the slapping of gloves and a strange rattling.

But this strange rattling is not a sound he ever heard on the *barra*, and so Mausoleo opens his eyes again and recognizes the commotion that has brought him back to earth: on the other side of the door, several of the men clutching their rifles have burst out laughing.

At the sound of this commotion among those loyal to Epitafio, the giant gets to his feet, startling two boys who have come from afar; they glance at each other, hug each other hard and exchange a few prayers. As though on springs, Mausoleo bounds over to the boys: Don't let them make any noise … Don't let these two ruin your lucky day.

Before the boys who have crossed so many borders realize what is happening, Mausoleo jumps on them and, ordering them to be silent, turns his glassy stare on these boys *who can no longer expect anything of a man.*

When the eyes of the boys he is subduing are finally subdued, the giant gets up and returns to his post by the door. Here, thinking of the words that Epitafio said to him earlier: 'I'm doing you the biggest fucking favor anyone has ever done you,' he watches as those who came from other lands drift off to sleep once more.

But shortly afterwards, while he is throwing a few punches, the giant's fists fall to the ground like wounded birds: his glassy eyes have met those of a man who is also awake and who is staring at him with an inexcusable air of dignity and pure hatred.

For a second that could easily be an hour, Mausoleo and the young man defying him weigh up their silences, their angers and their fears. Then, *he who cannot bear to suffer the scorn of justice and mercy*, smiles at the giant, sits up, throws his arms wide and takes a deep, dramatic breath.

Convinced that he knows what the boy still staring at him is about to do, Mausoleo gets to his feet and, in a trice, crosses this cell that he embodies, and growls: 'Don't even think about it … *cabrón* … Don't you dare fucking scream!'

Half a meter from the young man about to scream, Mausoleo leaps and the two bodies roll across the floor, waking those still sleeping, who watch in terror as Mausoleo's arms and legs close around the young man who dared defy him.

As he squeezes the body he is subduing tighter, Mausoleo covers the boy's face with his hands and whispers: 'Stupid *hijo de puta* ... You didn't have to do that! No one gets to do that to me!' The giant's voice begins to rise as, out of the corner of his eye, he looks at those who have crossed so many borders and are now huddled even closer to the walls.

When he has finally subdued his rival, Mausoleo feels all tension drain from the body and, listening to the voices that have begun to whisper all around, he pinches the nose of the man fast losing his foolhardy strength.

One after another, as the defeated boy's lungs grow weaker and the giant's anger is transformed into pure hatred, those who have come from afar fall silent, turn their faces away, cover their ears with their hands, and *turn their howls into hushed sighs.*

Feeling the panic of the chest that can no longer breathe in his own chest, Mausoleo realizes what he is doing and, without quite knowing why, releases his fingers: the choked lungs greedily gulp in the stale air of the cell and, for a brief instant, the boy the giant is subduing begins to struggle again.

But before the lungs of the young man being reborn can expand completely, Mausoleo pinches the nose again, feels panic take hold of the creature he is crushing and, smiling, releases his forefinger and thumb: he repeats the exercise two, three, four times.

When the young man he is asphyxiating finally succumbs, Mausoleo's arms and legs feel the life draining from the body that they will not, that they cannot let go.

Without relaxing his grip, Mausoleo turns his attention to the window and stares at the deep blue sky: there is no sign now of the solitary cloud. But the birds that crossed the space earlier now fly back in the other direction. The last breath of life leaves the body of the young man and in that moment Mausoleo is looking at the horizon, which seems to quiver.

Thinking about the seagulls on his spit of land, Mausoleo returns his gaze to the inside of the cell and hugs the body of the boy ever harder: he will not let him go until his own body begs him to stop, until his legs, his arms plead with him to give up, for the love of God.

When it is all over, Mausoleo lays the body of the boy on the floor and feels a shudder run through him: he cannot understand while he still feels as though he were clasping something. Why he feels as though something is clasping him.

Shrinking back, the giant looks at what he has done; then, he looks out the window as the horizon comes crashing down, seems to collapse, and then he tries to look at his hands: in that moment his glassy eyes explode as though someone, the someone who is clasping him, were pummeling them from inside.

The liquid trapped inside his head streams out in torrents, transforming the face of he who has been re-baptised, while this man, Mausoleo, repeats the words that Epitafio said to him: 'Take that look off your face, stick out your chest ... I've freed you from having to be one of them!'

Getting up off the floor, Mausoleo jumps across the corpse and paces his cell, while the creatures who crossed the borders continue to stare at the walls and cover their ears.

Leaning against the door, the giant closes his eyes and runs his fingertips over his face. But he cannot manage to work out whether these are his cheeks, his cheekbones, whether these are his features.

The Book of Estela

|

'Like the dead,' Epitafio says again, breaking the sudden silence that has come between him and the woman he so loves.

'You were very tired,' says Estela, pushing away the plate of food she has hardly touched, simply toying with the food while they talked.

'But I slept longer than I should have ... Now I'm running late.'

'I tried to wake you ... I called twice, maybe three times.'

'I didn't even hear the phone,' says Epitafio, sitting up and looking out at the courtyard of El Teronaque. 'I wish I had, that way I'd have had more time.'

'I wanted to tell you about the checkpoints and to ask how things are going with that giant of yours.'

'They'll show up here and we won't be ready ... I bet they're all still asleep inside.'

'No ... you don't know that,' Estela says, finally deciding to take the plunge and, half-closing her eyes she adds, 'Aside from what I said about El Chorrito, there's something important I wanted to tell you.'

'Now ... you want to tell me now?'

'What?' Estela yelps in surprise, clenching her jaw.

'Do you ... do you really have to tell me right now?' Epitafio says, prepared to accept the consequences of these words.

'No, fine ... whenever you like.' Estela mutters through gritted teeth, 'It's not going to change anything anyway.'

'I'm looking out at the courtyard and they haven't brought any of them out yet,' Epitafio says, by way of apology. 'So it's not fair, you saying that.'

'It's not fair ...? Not fair? ... *vete mucho a la chingada*!' Estela explodes. 'Fuck you! You always get to decide.'

'Calm down a second ... Please ... Don't start now,' Epitafio pleads, clambering out of the Cheyenne and racing towards the building that overlooks El Teronaque. 'I swear, I'll call you as soon as I've got things sorted.'

'When you've got things sorted ... Bastard!' Estela screams, jumping to her feet. 'Fuck all the things I need to get done ... I'm such a pushover.'

'Please, I'm begging.'

'A pushover, and a fool for worrying ... for thinking you might actually give a shit.'

'Seriously ... Estela,' Epitafio pleads, coming to a sudden halt as he sees a convoy approaching El Teronaque. 'Fucking hell ... He's arriving right now!'

'Just let me fucking tell you what the fuck is going on with us,' Estela snarls, pacing her room furiously.

'I can't ... Señor Hoyo ... It's a disaster here,' Epitafio splutters, breaking into a run again. 'We'll talk later.'

'Are you going to hang up on me?' Estela asks, looking through the window at the dying day.

'...'

'Did you hang up on me?'

Taking the cordless phone from her ear, the woman who so loves Epitafio takes two paces back, brings her gaze back into the room and shouts: 'Fucking bastard! ... You hung up on me!' she stares up at the roof beams and amuses herself, gazing at the shadows that hang there like water-filled balloons.

A shriek of bats that have just emerged from their refuge, the decommissioned water tank and the cellar that can no longer be used because the air is toxic and unbreathable, rouses Estela, and ShewhoadoresEpitafio tears her eyes from the ceiling, tosses the telephone on to the bed and, smiling at the silence, announces: 'You'll be desperate to know later, and I won't fucking tell you.'

For his part, having stumbled once or twice crossing the courtyard of El Teronaque, Epitafio bursts, shouting, into the rickety building where his men and the nameless who have come from other lands are sleeping. One after another, as the sons of the jungle are doing in their house, the men obedient to HewhosolovesEstela open their eyes, just as *those who will soon be unable to put an end to their weeping* begin to stir.

In the minutes that follow, in the house perched on the summit of El Teronaque, and in the house buried deep within the jungle, everything will happen at breakneck speed: the boys will prepare to set out again; Epitafio's men will enter the room that Mausoleo has not been guarding; the two boys will bid farewell to their wives and their children; Epitafio's men will once again lash out at the soulless creatures born beyond the borders; the two boys will creep into the jungle, while those loyal to Epitafio will dress the godless come from other lands in white waterproofs.

In the orphanage of El Paraíso, meanwhile, everything is happening at a leisurely pace: sitting on her bed, looking around for her stockings, as the calm brought on by sleep drains from her face and her features harden, Estela warns: You'll ask me ... You'll beg me to tell you and I won't tell you a damn thing.

Stretching out her leg and trying to hook her stocking with her left foot, Estela studies her nails for a moment and her face hardens until it is almost stone: she is angrier than ever for giving in to Epitafio's whims, for painting the nails the color he wanted. Swallowing a thick clot of saliva, never imagining that what she is about to say is a prophecy, Estela announces: 'I'll never give in to you again and you'll never know what's going on with us.

'I won't tell you a thing, not even if you beg ... not even if it means leaving you for ever,' Estela continues with this prophecy she does not realize is a prophecy and her features relax. Then, she puts on her stocking, pulls on her boots and, as she ties the laces, thinks about Cementeria: ShewhoadoresEpitafio cannot know that the death of her friend is the crux of her prophecy.

Getting up from the bed again, Estela walks over to the window, opens it and hops up on to the sill: before her eyes the day is dying and memories flood back as they did when she arrived here. Shaking her head ShewhoadoresEpitafio once again reads the names carved so long ago: but this time, she tries to scratch out the words with her fingernails.

When the green of her nails has flaked away and her ten fingertips have spilled her red blood, Estela stops scratching the ancient stones and turns her attention back to the daylight guttering out and in doing so sees, between her room and the mountains that rise like the charred bodies of animals, her men bustling away: this is what she asked of Father Nicho when she went down to the living room for the cordless telephone: 'Tell them they need to be ready ... that we'll be heading off soon.'

Quickly irritated by the commotion among her men and the failing light. Estela spits on the spilled blood, jumps down on to the floor and walks away from the window. In front of the bed, ShewhoadoresEpitafio turns off her telephone, winds the charger cable and reaches over to the pillow to take the bands she uses to tie back her curly hair. Then she surveys the room for a moment and hurries towards the door.

As she negotiates the corridors and the stairwells of the orphan-age, Estela plaits her hair, accidentally squashing the antennae on her right hearing aid, which generates a blast of interference, reminding her of the cordless phone back in her room. But it is not forgetting the telephone that worries ShewhoadoresEpitafio, but Epitafio's voice asking: 'How is Father Nicho?'

'How is Father Nicho?' Estela says aloud and, hears the words, wonders, Why did he ask me that? Then, feeling a new and unfamil-iar warmth in her belly, ShewhoadoresEpitafio hurries on and as she reaches the great hall of El Paraíso she hears the faint, feeble whis-perings of the priest she is thinking about, a few meters away, saying his goodbyes: 'Take care, my dear Sepelio.'

Turning to face Father Nicho, Estela understands that the fire in her belly is a warning and she longs to feel again the terrifying sus-picion she earlier drove out: Something strange is going on here ...

Why the fuck did I dismiss it … when I already sensed it? Stopping in her tracks as Nicho hangs up the telephone and realizes that he is no longer alone, Estela clenches her jaw again and silently says to herself: I shouldn't have come … I didn't need to stop here.

For his part, as he walks with Estela toward the door that frames the ultimate spectacle of every day — in the distance, the sun is dropping behind the mountains — Father Nicho feels his heart pounding in his chest, and, as he wonders whether she overheard what he was saying to Sepelio, he forces a smile, stretches his arms out and presents Estela with his two fists.

'Which one will your surprise be in today?' Father Nicho asks, hurrying to catch up with Estela.

'You seriously want me to play this game?' ShewhoadoresEpitafio says, moving away from the priest. 'Or is this another trick?'

'What the hell are you talking about?' Father Nicho says, catching up with Estela on the threshold of the main door to El Paraíso. 'What have you got into your head this time?'

'As if you didn't know.'

'As if I didn't know what, for God's sake?'

'Best that I leave now … That's all I want you to know,' ShewhoadoresEpitafio says, walking faster and feeling the fire in her belly suddenly blaze white-hot.

'Without even giving me a kiss … You're going to leave without so much as a hug?' The priest takes Estela by the shoulder and, feeling the pounding in his chest grow faster, he forces his smile into a laugh. 'Who knows, it might be your last kiss?'

'What did you say?' ShewhoadoresEpitafio snaps, jerking her shoulder away from his hand. 'What the fuck did you say?'

'What the fuck did I say when?'

'Don't take me for a fool,' Estela shouts, hurrying even faster, then turning her head, she adds: 'Or maybe that's another trap?'

'First you talk about tricks, and now this ... What is this trap you're talking about?' the priest says, still laughing. 'I just wanted one last ...'

'You really want to know?' Estela roars, cutting Father Nicho short and, stopping a few meters from the huge truck, says: 'I'm talking about the fact that I talked to Epitafio.'

'Epitafio ... you talked to him?'

'And he said ... "Give him my regards,"' Estela announces, and as she does so, feels the swelling in the belly ease, '"Maybe I'll get to talk to him one of these days ... I haven't heard from him in ages ..." That's something else he told me to tell you.'

'He was half-asleep,' the priest says, quickly trying to get out of this fix. 'You know as well as I do that he never remembers things when he's half-asleep.'

'He was wide awake when I talked to him,' Estela says as she opens the Ford Lobo, and it is her turn now to force a smile as she says: 'So, now, I pick the left.'

'What?'

'I thought you had a surprise for me?' ShewhoadoresEpitafio revels in Father Nicho's embarrassment, then, keying the ignition of the Ford Lobo, she puts an end to the conversation: 'Just joking ... You've got nothing that interests me!'

As the huge truck pulls out of the esplanade of El Paraíso, followed by the two battered trailer trucks in which those who have come from beyond the borders are once again jolted and jostled, out of the corner of her eye Estela watches the captain, who has turned back to look at Father Nicho. 'What the fuck are you looking at?' ShewhoadoresEpitafio demands as she silently says to herself: Why didn't I ask Epitafio?

But there comes no response, either to the question she posed herself or the one she asked the soldier, and Estela floors the accelerator of the Ford Lobo, eager to get away from the place where she has just left the six children she was carrying in the red trailer truck where the nameless who have come from other countries *have found hope back within their reach*. In the pale blue truck, on the other hand, everything is as it was before they arrived at El Paraíso: *the broken bodies of women strew the floor.*

As Estela rolls down the window, in rushes the dust of the sierra, the shadows falling now like a cloudburst and the screech of bats blotting out the sky. Why didn't I ask you whether you'd called? Estela silently mutters as she flicks on headlights of the hulking truck illuminating the road dappled with the last flashes of dusk: I never ask the questions I need to ask and never say the things I need to say.

How come I can never manage to tell you what I feel sure I am definitely going to tell you this time? ShewhoadoresEpitafio protests, then, shifting gears, she unwittingly accelerates the speed of her thoughts and of the moment in which she finds herself, with her men, with the men and women who have come from other lands, who right now, in the red trailer truck, are clustered around the oldest of the soulless creatures abducted in the clearing known as El Tiradero: he is the unexpected glimmer of hope.

> This line here tells me ... before you die, eleven years will
> pass ... You will have enjoyed a new, rich life ... You will
> have lived through days of light and warmth ... You will
> have left behind this terrible, painful period ... All this
> grief will be little more than a memory ... a turning point
> between one life and the next.

Meanwhile, as he watches the convoy move away, Father Nicho takes out his phone and calls the number that will carry his voice to the heart of the Madre Buena plateau and, when he is sure that the message is being recorded, he says: 'They set off early ... She is heading for La Carpa ... You need to move now ... They won't be able to hold her at La Cañada for long ... I'm not even sure I want them to ... It's better if they don't try to hold her up ... She has more men with her today.'

No sooner has he hung up than Father Nicho begins to have doubts about the telephone that he is holding, and the lines connecting it to the telephone that has just recorded his message: it is something that happens every time technology intervenes in his life. And so, shaking his head, the priest redials and spits out the same message: 'I don't give a shit that we agreed it would happen later ... I want you to be waiting for her as soon as she arrives!'

Despite having recorded his message twice, Father Nicho cannot convince himself that it has reached the men who will soon pile into their fake security van and leave Lago Seco, heading for the mountain range that Estela's Ford Lobo and the two battered trailer trucks are scaling once again. And so Father Nicho taps in the ten digits that connect his unease to the heart of the forest surrounding El Teronaque.

But Sepelio will not answer the ringing telephone, because at that very moment he is in the courtyard of El Teronaque, lining up the nameless creatures that Señor Hoyo is about to buy.

II

We're lucky we made it in time, Epitafio thinks, staring into the distance at Señor Hoyo's approaching vehicles, then, heaving a sigh, he turns and heads back to the spot where his men have just finished lining up the godless and orders: 'Everyone to their posts!

'You too, Sepelio!' Epitafio barks, removing and replacing his cap as the sun dips below the mountains and the sounds that daylight keeps at bay begin to stir. Then, hurrying his legs, grabbing Mausoleo and thinking: Thank God you called, HewhosolovesEstela sees the man he has just shouted at slip something into his pocket and says: 'What the fuck are you doing?'

'What the fuck … am I … doing?' Sepelio mumbles, and says the first thing that comes into his head: 'I couldn't find my pencil!' as he silently complains to Father Nicho. How many times do I have to tell you not to call me when I'm with Epitafio? It's a fucking miracle he didn't hear the phone ring just now! Sepelio says to himself and, taking his hand from the pocket in which he has just slipped his phone, he heads over towards *those who are waiting, newly bewildered, pale as death and paralyzed with fear.*

'You better hope you brought them with you!' says Epitafio, standing where the *tezontle* meets the withered grass, watching as the bats from the forest and those from the jungle come together in the sky above El Teronaque. 'How could you forget your …' growls

HewhosolovesEstela, but before he can finish his threat, he hears Sepelio shout: 'I've got them here! I've got the pencil and the piece of paper!'

'Just the sort of thing I'd expect from that halfwit,' Epitafio mutters to Mausoleo, turning his head and nodding to the vehicles that have just parked up in the distance: 'Señor Hoyo always insists that we give him the numbers.' Then, turning again and thinking: If you hadn't called I'd still be sound asleep, HewhosolovesEstela looks over at Sepelio, who is thinking: I need to call him before he calls me back, as he draws alongside the voiceless who have crossed so many borders.

He won't give up until he's talked to me, Sepelio says to himself as he reaches the trembling figures wrapped in baggy white raincoats of *those whose souls have been ripped from them*. Then, staring at the nameless and with the ghost of a smile, Sepelio clears his throat and bellows: 'What does the Fatherland want right now?'

'The Fatherland wants to hear their names!' Epitafio replies, setting his legs in motion once more, trailing in his wake the giant Mausoleo, who, to avoid witnessing what is happening in the courtyard, turns away and looks at the woodland that surrounds El Teronaque: this is the hour when the day is not yet gone and the night is not yet come.

'You heard the Fatherland!' Sepelio bellows, scanning the faces of the soulless, who have been walking for days, while on a piece of paper he is holding he notes down the names that they utter, which stir not a single echo. The space echoes only with the swift transformation of the hours: the cawing of crows is supplanted by the hooting of owls, the chirrup of cicadas drowns out that of the grasshoppers; meanwhile tapirs, ocelots and peccaries fall silent, giving way to the voices of coyotes, peacocks and foxes.

'You, there! What's your name?' Sepelio barks as he meets a wall of silence. 'You understand what I'm saying or what?' he taunts the man, who, much as he wants to, cannot manage to open his lips: 'Why won't you tell me your name? … *Puta madre* … Why is there always one moron who wants to play the hero?' As though they understand what is happening, the hum of twilight is momentarily hushed, so that everyone can hear the silence of he who will not open his mouth.

Taking a step towards the young man *betrayed by the chorus of tongues that wrong and dishonor themselves*, Sepelio furiously yells: 'Who the fuck do you think you are, refusing to give your name? … The Fatherland itself is talking to you!' When his words serve only to magnify the mutism of the young man who was kidnapped thirteen hours since, Sepelio feels a new hatred kindled in his soul and, gripping his pencil as though it were a knife, forcefully turns the man's face towards Epitafio.

'The Fatherland demands that you say you name right now … Say it now or it's all over!' roars HewhosolovesEstela, resuming his walk and trailing Mausoleo in his wake. In spite of this threat issued by the Fatherland, the young man clenches his jaw, holds to his stubbornness and fixes his eyes on those of Sepelio, whose fingers unintentionally snap his makeshift weapon: fragments of the pencil lie scattered on the ground.

'Say your name right now … Say it or the Fatherland will say: Enough!' roars Epitafio, as Sepelio picks up a thick piece of wood and the young man closes his eyes and resigns himself to being no more than the silence of his passing through the world. 'The Fatherland says: Finish him now!' yells HewhosolovesEstela and the nameless one heard his vertebrae crack: *I shall not say my name nor show them my soul, however much they beat me.*

> *At six o'clock or seven … they dragged us outside again … They asked us whether we had family back there … They demanded their phone numbers … so they could demand a ransom for us … One man refused to speak … They broke him with a stick … but still he would not give them his name … The name given him by his parents.*

Picking up the scattered pieces of the pencil from the *tezontle* and jumping over the body of the man who has just expired there, Sepelio comes face to face with another of the soulless and, more loudly than before, says: 'You know what the Fatherland requires … and you've seen what will happen if you say nothing!' The anguish of the godless who fled their lands rings out again, and with it the twilight hum of the forest.

Suddenly aware of a sound he has not heard here before, a sound that stands out from all the others, Epitafio looks over his shoulder and sees Señor Hoyo approaching moments before he shouts: 'I've come up with a new business arrangement.' Let's see what he'll come out with this time, HewhosolovesEstela thinks and, trailing Mausoleo behind him, he walks toward the figure surrounded by his right-hand men: 'I bet he's going to try and beat me down on price,' Epitafio whispers to his giant, 'but I'm not going to let myself be beaten.

'We've already agreed terms,' Epitafio says, forestalling any greetings.

'How can you be so short-sighted?'

'Three was the price I agreed, and it'll be three or nothing,' Epitafio snaps, removing and replacing his cap.

'You've got far more than you know what to do with,' Señor Hoyo says, stripping off his jacket and handing it to one of the men who are staring anxiously at the giant.

'What do you care how many I've got?'

'Two and a half crates apiece … that's the new deal.'

'Three, and a fence.'

'Two and a half, plus the fence … You'll not get three out of me.'

'In that case, there's no deal,' Epitafio says and turns to Mausoleo. 'Tell them to put them back in the house.'

'Hold up there! Three … and two and a half for the other one.'

'The way you're going, it'll be three and a half.'

'You're a stubborn bastard.' Señor Hoyo reluctantly gives in and, turning to his men, says, 'Tell them to bring the vans over … and tell Macizo to get ready.'

Epitafio turns back to Mausoleo and says, 'Go tell them to board the trucks.'

When Señor Hoyo's trucks have finally been loaded with those *who sense that the next part of their journey will be not less ill-starred, no less cruel, no less long,* and the crates have been unloaded in the courtyard of El Teronaque, where the rain of shadows has become a downpour, Epitafio puts on his cap, gives Señor Hoyo a satisfied smile, and bringing his fingers to his lips, gives the first whistle of the evening.

While his men and those who came with Señor Hoyo bustle in the center of the courtyard and light the torches that Sepelio handed out a moment earlier, HewhosolovesEstela smiles at Señor Hoyo and breaks the awkward silence between them: 'How much do you think you'll lose tonight against my guy?'

Drawn by the glow and the smell of the torches — they blaze with an oil made from fermented oranges — the insects that swarm in the drowning hours of twilight invade the courtyard, their buzzing rising to become a roaring engine. 'I've brought a boy today who's more than a match for Sepelio,' says Señor Hoyo, and before Epitafio can say anything, he walks towards the bellowing circle of men, adding: 'You'll see, he'll whip the ass of that chickenshit *pendejo*!'

Fluttering in feverish circles amid the swarm of mosquitoes, the bats feed while Epitafio and Señor Hoyo continue toward the center of the courtyard and the mounting clamor of the men clutching their rifles and their torches. 'Who said I'm intending to put Sepelio into the ring today?' HewhosolovesEstela says suddenly, and, lifting his arm, points to Mausoleo: 'My giant is going to fight your boy tonight!'

Seeing the supercilious expression on Señor Hoyo's face crumple, Epitafio hurries towards the circle of flames, but the excitement hammering in his chest suddenly crumples too: *Puta madre* … I told her I'd call her as soon as they left. Why the fuck did I ask for a fence? … You're going to be furious that I didn't call you, Epitafio thinks, then he turns and walks over to Mausoleo, while Señor Hoyo is heading over to Macizo.

Next to Mausoleo, who is staring down at the broken-necked corpse and the bloody length of timber, Epitafio imagines Estela's fury, and, grabbing the giant with both hands, he growls: 'You're about to fight a real bastard, and you'd better be quick … You'd better hope you weren't lying … that you really know how to use those fists of yours.' All around, in the mounting excitement, the men clutching their torches and their weapons continue to roar.

'Beat the shit out of him … and make it fast. I've got better things to be doing … Are you listening to me?' Epitafio says, putting a hand under the giant's chin and lifting his face so that he no longer has to look at the broken creature whose face is *split from nose to eyebrow*. 'You're going to fuck this guy up and fast!' HewhosolovesEstela mutters, his eyes boring into Mausoleo, then he turns to Señor Hoyo and the boy next to him in the circle of flames: Why didn't I let you talk while I was running back to the house? All I had to do was pretend to listen.

That way it would all be over now, and I wouldn't have to call you! Epitafio grumbles in the circle formed by his men and those brought by Señor Hoyo. You could have told me what's going on and I could have left them to get on with things! Epitafio thinks to himself as he growls at Mausoleo: 'As soon as Sepelio gets here with the weapons, grab the pipe … I want you to win with a single blow.

'Sepelio … Where the fuck is Sepelio?' roars Epitafio, stepping away from the giant and thinking, If you'd told me what was wrong, we wouldn't need to have a conversation … It's all you ever talk about, and I need to talk to you about La Cañada. 'Is he bringing the weapons or not?' Señor Hoyo interrupts Epitafio's train of thought and, grabbing him by the shoulder, issues a challenge, 'Or do you want them to fight bare-knuckle today?'

Before Epitafio has time to answer Señor Hoyo, Sepelio appears, slipping the phone he has used to call Father Nicho into his pocket, and steps into the circle of light and drops the implements that will give form to rage. The sound made by the implements as they clatter to the ground electrifies the men, calms Señor Hoyo's worries, excites Epitafio's impatience and buries itself in the guts of Macizo and Mausoleo.

The shouting rises to a frenzied roar as Macizo and Mausoleo stand alone in the center of the circle: then, Sepelio takes his torch and, raising it skywards, gives the order to start. 'Lay into him!' shouts Señor Hoyo, while Epitafio yells to Mausoleo: 'The pipe … Grab the pipe!' Macizo rushes towards the pile of weapons on the ground and grabs a machete. Mausoleo does not move a muscle.

'The fucking pipe!' Epitafio bellows, but his words fuse with the chorus of raucous voices and do not reach Mausoleo, whom Macizo is now circling, wary and attentive. Just then, from the sky there comes the cry of a huge bird that cleaves the dark vault of heaven like a shadow and flies off without anyone looking up at the sky: 'Don't just fucking stand there … Grab the pipe!'

Having weighed up his opponent and his hesitation — why the fuck is he just standing there? … Why doesn't he pick up a weapon? — Macizo lunges at Mausoleo, brandishing his machete. But at the last moment, the giant who had been standing, imperturbable, as though his mind is a blank, dodges the blade and with the smallest of movements, trips Macizo and sends him sprawling; Macizo crawls two meters, grabs his machete and jumps to his feet.

'For fuck's sake, grab something … anything!' shouts Epitafio, whose mind is also a blank as he feverishly watches his rival get to his feet and, more nervous than ever, sees that the giant is planted there, like a tree. 'What the hell are you playing at?' Around Mausoleo and Macizo, the circle of men has degenerated into pure noise and sheer slack-jawed fury: one after another, all those present have lost their minds.

Having hesitated for a fleeting moment, Macizo raises his weapon and lunges again at Mausoleo, who, this time, drops to a crouch, grabs his opponent's legs, lifts him a meter and a half into the air and hurls him on to the rough *tezontle*. Before Macizo has time to work out what has happened, Mausoleo lifts the machete, raises it in offering to the darkness, and then brings it down on the neck and shoulder of the young man who came with Señor Hoyo.

A howl erupts from the men, who refuse to relinquish their weapons or their torches as the body of Macizo is split like a log falling to the axe. Señor Hoyo stamps the ground, while Epitafio races over to the giant, raising his hands: 'That's the way … That's what I like to see … But you gave me a scare there at the start … *Hijo de* fucking *puta!*' he says, as he thinks about Estela: I want to call you to talk about the checkpoint and about El Chorrito.

Leaping over the body, *which now seems like two bodies, each with only one arm, only one leg*, Epitafio turns to the giant, who is once more still as a statue and says: 'You gave me a hell of a scare, but you did good!' All the while thinking: I need to talk to that fucking moron and find out why they moved the checkpoints … and if they moved them, why he didn't fucking call to warn me.

Raising the left arm of the giant, who seems to be in a completely different place, Epitafio is about to announce: And the winner is Mausoleo! but the giant anticipates his words and, re-emerging from the place where he seemed to have disappeared, he announces: 'Es ... Este ... Esteban ... That was my name before ... That is who I am ... So the winner ... the winner is Esteban.' As though sucked up by a huge vacuum, the cries of the men and the beasts of night are suddenly silenced.

'Esteban ... That was always my name,' mutters Mausoleo, his eyes boring into those of Epitafio, who bursts out laughing, since he knows no other way to put an end to this moment: 'What the fuck are you talking about? ... That faggot couldn't have handled himself like Mausoleo did ... That's why your name is Mausoleo ... I knew you wouldn't let me down.' Epitafio's words are the only sound to be heard in the courtyard of El Teronaque.

Just then, the vast bird like a shadow that cleaved the heavens a moment earlier flies back across the sky and this time its cry not only captures the attention of those present, but trails in its wake the chorus of sounds that announces the realm of night and stirs those noises that have so far been silent. 'Back to the trucks!' Señor Hoyo barks, just as Sepelio, thinking it is what Epitafio expects of him, says: 'Now on to what comes next!'

'Who do you think you are to decide what happens here?' Epitafio roars, forgetting Mausoleo and turning towards Sepelio as he thinks: Fucking El Chorrito ... You should have phoned me ... That way I wouldn't have to call her and wouldn't need to talk to you now ... I could wait until she calmed down. It is as though he, HewhosolovesEstela, can sense that, high up in the sierra, ShewhoadoresEpitafio has allowed her rage to wax and intensify.

'I am the one who says what happens!' Epitafio mutters and, barely a meter from Sepelio, bellows: 'Is that clear?' 'Crystal clear,' Sepelio says, choking back his anger and, forcing a smile so ambiguous that no one notices it, thinks: It won't be that way for long ... It won't be crystal clear for much longer. Epitafio's face hardens as he thinks: While they're loading the rest of them, I should call Estela.

I hope you answer ... that you're not blinded by rage! Epitafio thinks as Señor Hoyo steps forward to make good on his wager, and as Sepelio thinks to himself: We'll see how long it is crystal clear. We'll see who gets to be in command here very soon. This is the first time that Sepelio dares to think the words in the presence of Epitafio, who, having pocketed his winnings and said goodbye to Señor Hoyo, is giving orders to his men: 'Load the miserable wretches we've got left into the trailer.'

As the last man heads back towards the building, which still serves as a prison for the little girl with the oversized head and one half of the godless who have come from other lands, *their eyes stitched shut by tears and their souls unstitched by fear*, Epitafio mutters: 'I'll call you right now.'

Then this man who has always wanted to marry Estela, but was forced to marry the woman chosen for him by Father Nicho, scans the horizon, studying the cloudburst of shadows, the same shadows that the sons of the jungle are staring at as they prepare to leave, eager to bathe in the pool known only to the two of them, before heading for the village where their path leads them.

Watching as night takes possession of the earth, Hewhoso-lovesEstela takes out his phone and, feeling his chest fill with the dark air of hours spent in contemplation, tries to think of anything that will not prevent him from dialling the number he knows by heart: It must be dark wherever you are, too. Then, as his fingers begin to tap Estela's number, his thoughts betray him and his fingertips slip from the keypad: If it is dark and you haven't reached El Cañada, I'll only slow you down.

Besides, what difference does it make if I talk to El Chorrito now? ... Better to let you get to El Cañada without wasting any more time, Epitafio thinks to himself, and, slipping his phone back into his pocket, whispers: 'And it's not as though we've got time on our hands here ... We have to get moving, too ... We need to load those miserable wretches and get the fuck out of here ... We have to sell them off as soon as possible.'

Three or four meters from the entrance to the ramshackle building that was once a slaughterhouse, Epitafio joins Sepelio and Mausoleo, and, closing the distance between them with a wave, says to the former: 'Go and get the trailer right now ... and get your boys to fetch the ladder.' This would all be much easier if we hadn't given back the ramp, Sepelio thinks as he leaves the two men who are about to step inside the house that overlooks El Teronaque, and he mumbles to himself: 'Stubborn fucking bastard.

'Stubborn son of a bitch ... You've always been that way,' Sepelio mutters again as he takes out his phone, then, glancing around to make sure no one is watching and smiling to himself, he says: 'Things are about to change. You'll see ... Someone else will get to give the orders here.'

Someone else will get to be the Fatherland, Sepelio promises himself and, his smile broadening into a loud laugh, he stares at his phone for a moment and dials a number that he, too, knows by heart. But the line is busy: Father Nicho is talking to the men who left the Madre Buena plateau some time ago.

|||

'We never said you could call,' says the driver of the fake security van that left Lago Seco almost an hour since.

'I'll call whenever I like.'

'We were absolutely clear when we talked to Sepelio ... no calls after we set off.'

'And anyway, this is only the second time I've called,' says Father Nicho, slumping into the armchair in his office. 'I just wanted to know whether you've arrived.'

'How could we have got there?' says the driver of what looks like an armored truck, taking a cigarette from the pack he has fished from his pocket. 'Do you realize how far it is?'

'I'm not assuming you're in the sierra ... I'm just asking whether you're getting close,' the priest says, getting to his feet and growling. 'This isn't some fucking game.'

'Who the fuck said it was?' says the driver, thumping the windscreen. 'Phone us one more time and we'll call the whole thing off.'

'I didn't realize you were in a position to make such decisions,' Father Nicho taunts the driver, striding across the room and grabbing the branding iron he has just used down in the cellar.

'I'm not one of your fucking lackeys ... Call this number again and the whole thing is off,' says the driver of the fake security van.

'At least tell me where you are,' the priest insists and, bringing the awl up to his nose, he adds, 'If you tell me, I won't phone again.'

'Stubborn bastard,' grumbles the exasperated co-driver. 'I'll call when it's done.'

'How about you call me when you're within sight of the mountains?'

'The dumb *hijo de puta* just doesn't fucking get it,' the co-driver mutters, holding the phone at arm's length and glancing at the driver.

'Or when you get to Tres Hermanos,' Father Nicho goads him, and chuckles as he hangs up.

'Jesus ... I've had it with this bullshit!'

Listening to the engaged tone that says that the person on the other end has hung up, the co-driver of the phony armor-plated vehicle turns to the driver, who, like him, is a police officer and says: 'He's going to be calling us every five fucking minutes.' He says nothing for a moment and, thinking: Ignorant bastard hung up on me, he looks out at the ribbon of road that stretches away into the distance, dividing the earth in two.

'I told Sepelio a million times ... we don't want to have to talk to that fucker ... We only want to talk to you ... Don't try playing us off against that old bastard ... just look what happened with Cementeria.' The co-driver's words — as crude as he is, and as rancorous — get no response, and the fake security truck rattles over a pothole and swerves across the road: darkness has fallen in this part of the Fatherland, too, and the driver is severely myopic.

Aside from the driver and the co-driver, the men in the back of the vehicle masquerading as a security truck — who are also police officers from Lago Seco — are tossed and jolted in their seats as they place their bets for the next game: the floor of the truck is strewn with cards, coins, money, cigarettes, shot glasses, bottles, matchboxes, and with the anger and frustrations of these men.

Having hit the tarpaulin and bitten the inside of cheeks that are as plump inside as they are outside, the co-driver of this former garbage truck, this vehicle that for years served to keep Lago Seco tidy, rummages under his seat for the cigarette that fell from his fingers, thumps the driver and, spitting a thin thread of bloody saliva, grunts: '*Hijo de puta* ... Fucking cigarette just burned a hole in my trousers.'

'Shit — and I know how hard it is to find a pair your size,' the driver snaps, resetting the thick glasses the jolt knocked from the bridge of his nose. Before the co-driver can say anything to the driver — though his superior officer back in Lago Seco, in these particular circumstances they are equals — the protests from the men in the back of the truck are punctuated by insults directed at the captain and his lieutenant, who are their superiors, albeit in a different sense.

'They must have taken one hell of a bump!' the co-driver laughs and, picking up the things that fell into the footwell — a couple of CDs, a figurine of Christ dressed as a soldier, several beer bottles, a tiny Christmas tree, an ice bucket, three lighters and a couple of dolls in football strips, he says: 'If you see another pothole —' 'If I see another one, I'm heading straight for it!' the driver snaps, interrupting the lieutenant and, with a chuckle, he adds: 'I bet they're shitting it in the back there.'

When the two men in the cab of the fake security truck realize that their underlings have stopped bitching, the driver rolls down the window, wafts at the air with his hand and, pretending he can smell something, says: 'Are you sure you put out the fire in your trousers?' Picking up a Smurf dressed as Saint Juan Diego, the lieutenant whips round and is about to defend himself when the driver says: 'Seriously, though, where the fuck do you buy your trousers?'

'I'm sick to death of you being all fucking superior ... You're scrawny as an orphanage rat,' the lieutenant mocks the driver, who has lost more than thirty kilos in the past year. 'You're like a fucking mole — you have to snuffle your way around because you can't see shit!' The lieutenant picks up a gold and silver bangle: 'Poor Cementeria ... She left her bracelet here,' he says, and the expression playing on his lips could either be a smile or a nervous tic.

Meanwhile, in the back of the former garbage truck, as they reassemble the board they are using as a table and re-hang the flashlights they are using as lamps from hooks in the tarpaulin, the six soldiers who hear only a remote echo of their bosses' conversation are convinced that they are the subject of this distant discussion: the six men cannot imagine that their bosses are arguing while no one is watching.

'I'd much rather be a fat pig than the way you've turned out ... You're a scrawny fucking beanpole,' the lieutenant cackles and the driver's smile drains from his face. 'Your clothes are too big for you — and just look at the folds of skin you're left with ... You look like you're fucking melting!' the lieutenant mocks, because he wants to carry on laughing and because no one is listening: he would never say this if there were anyone else present.

'You can talk ... You're a beached whale, a fucking elephant's tampon ... Shut your face and stop pissing me off!' The venom with which El Topo spits these last words startles his lieutenant and he bites his tongue, reluctant to carry on the banter — neither of them has ever used this tone before. Inside the cab, the tense minutes tick by, a remorseful silence that hangs in the air, like the vestige of a lover's tiff.

The situation is precisely the reverse in the sierra, in the house that towers over El Teronaque, in the depths of the jungle, and in the orphanage at El Paraíso, where Estela, on one hand, Epitafio on another, the two boys who left their shack an hour since, and lastly Father Nicho are all unleashing a torrent of words: Estela wants to be safe when she reaches El Cañada and this is why she is still talking to El Chorrito; Epitafio wants to be behind the wheel of his truck and this is why he is screaming at the *creatures transformed into shadows who have lost even their bodies such that if anyone should try to hug them they would find no purchase*; the sons of the jungle want nothing more than to reach the cool waters of the forest pool of which they alone know the secret, which is why they are babbling to each other; and Father Nicho wants someone to tell him what is going on, and this is why he is wondering, Should I phone Sepelio now or should I call the other two morons?

The other two morons, weary of the silence to which neither is accustomed, loosen their tongues again and, in doing so, unawares, attempt to erase the conversation they were having only a moment earlier: and so the co-driver goes back to the moment before things swerved off course, the instant when they lost control of their words and their tempers: 'He's going to be calling us every five fucking minutes … He's going to be on our case all day.'

Flicking on the headlights of the fake security van, El Topo turns to El Tampón and nods: 'Yeah, I'm sure he's going to be on our backs all day.' Then, reaching out his left hand, he gestures to the pack of cigarettes wedged between the Smurf dressed up as Juan Diego and the bracelet that once belonged to Cementeria and says: 'Pass me a cigarette,' and as he does so he thinks to himself: Who would have thought it'd be so easy? … That it wouldn't cost us anything to drive Cementeria insane … That she would end up copying Osamenta … That crazy bitch Ausencia was right.

'I don't like it when they call us,' El Tampón grumbles, passing the pack of cigarettes to El Topo.

'Don't answer, then … or turn off your phone. Let the old bastard go fuck himself,' El Topo says, taking the cigarettes and, glancing at the gold bracelet, he thinks: Who would have thought that she loved Osamenta that much … that persevering with the lie would push her over the edge?

'What happens if Sepelio calls?' El Tampón asks, passing El Topo the old lighter lying on the dashboard.

'Then just don't call back,' El Topo says, lighting a cigarette and thinking: It's unbelievable that she acted on the lie I told her … It's as if I said: Go over there and kill yourself.

'Who are you saying I shouldn't call?'

'Sorry?'

'Don't call. That's what you said … What the fuck are you talking about?'

'I meant don't answer,' El Topo says, exhaling a plume of smoke.

'You've got something on your mind … You're not listening to me.'

'I swear, I've got nothing else on my mind.'

'Really?' El Topo says, bringing a cigarette to his own lips. 'That old fucker … I don't like it when he phones.'

'I think it's the old man that you don't like,' El Topo says, handing back the lighter he has just been passed. 'There's only one person you like. Only one man who makes you happy.'

'You're always trying to confuse me … You were thinking about something else … But it doesn't matter … I'm used to it,' El Tampón says and rolls down his window. 'It's fucking freezing.'

'Fuck's sake. It's not as if you're not wearing enough layers,' El Topo grunts, deciding to be aggressive, since he prefers it to the conversations about his constant distractions.

'There you go again,' El Tampón complains and, rolling up his window, adds, 'Why don't you close your window, too … and stop being such a bastard.'

'I don't want to stink of smoke,' El Topo says and, surprised that El Tampón has not exploded, continues to taunt him. 'If you knew it was going to be cold, you should have brought a jacket … or don't they make them in your size?'

'Maybe I'll skin your fat mama and make a jacket out of her …'

'There we go …When you can't think of something to say, you always … Hang on tight, I've just spotted another pothole.'

'…'

'…'

'Another jolt in the back,' El Tampón says as the battered fake security van lands with a judder.

'And that won't be the last,' El Topo roars, and, exploiting the fact that the pothole has calmed El Tampón's anger, he goes back to the subject they already dropped on two separate occasions:

'What does Sepelio have to say about the old man?'

'What do you think he'd say? ... He's known the old man all his life ... ever since he was taken to the orphanage ... when they closed Lago Seco and couldn't find anywhere else.'

'...'

'They sent Sepelio up into the mountains ... That's where he first met the old man ... and Epitafio and Estela,' El Tampón explains, stubbing out his cigarette and hugging himself. 'It's really fucking cold.'

'Poor Estela,' El Topo says, as he, too, stubs out his cigarette, hardly aware of the words that have just passed his lips.

'What do you mean poor Estela? ... She's a miserable old bitch.'

'I don't think she's a bitch ... It's not like she's Cementeria, or even Osamenta.'

'That's ... Don't tell anyone ... It's none of your business,' El Tampón warns, and then says, 'Or maybe you have a thing for that slut, too?'

'Why would you think I fancy her?'

'We're coming to the turn-off,' El Tampón interrupts El Topo, and, forgetting the cold, rolls the window down further and leans out. 'I can't read the sign.'

'What do you mean we're coming to the turn-off?'

'Pull up so I can get out and read the sign,' El Tampón orders, leaning even further out.

'Get back in, you moron ... How many times do I have to tell you not to lean out the window?' El Topo snarls. 'And anyway, we're not there yet.'

'What do you mean we're not there? I can see the silos,' El Tampón says as he slides back into the cab and points to the huge triangular shadows.

'You talk such shit,' El Topo splutters, shaking his head. 'There are silos everywhere.'

Before El Tampón lets go the dashboard his hands grabbed on to a split second before they hit the pothole, the six soldiers in the back of the former garbage truck start to complain, and this time their rage is white-hot: one of them has split his skull and another has cut his chin. Enraged, the one whose chin is bleeding draws his gun, raises it, and without thinking, fires into the steel roof.

The former garbage truck skids several meters before El Topo regains control of the vehicle, and his pounding heart, then he slams on the brakes and it is this, this sudden screech to a halt, that sets off the ensuing chain of events: El Topo and El Tampón jump down from the cab, fuming with rage and rush around to the back of the fake security van, wrench open the doors and roar: 'Which of you fucking morons?' and drag the fucking moron out on to the road.

When they see that the moron's chin is bleeding and hear him explain what happened, El Tampón and El Topo exchange a few words and then burst into a booming laugh: the rest of the men laugh with them, leaning out of the back doors of the truck. Finally, as the moron himself starts to laugh, a symphony of death rattles echoes across the desolate plain and stretches eastward to Lago Seco and those who govern the laws and the ministries.

Drawn by the dark and boundless emptiness, the men who deserted the Madre Buena plateau and deserted their posts stare out into the void, lost in this unfathomable plain. Then, as though they are all pulled by the timeless force and mysterious magnetism of the rocks, the lieutenant, the captain and the six soldiers turn towards the west and silently gaze at the vast, ghostly shadow formed by the sierra, which they will shortly reach.

'Bastard fucking cold!' Tampón says after a moment, his words like a falling curtain, which, when it rises again a moment later, reveals a completely different scene: the six soldiers are in the back of the van and El Topo and El Tampón are sitting in the cab of the former municipal garbage truck.

'What were you saying?' El Tampón asks as the fake security van begins to pick up speed.

'That we're still a long way from Tres Hermanos,' El Topo says, switching the headlights on again and, staring at the twin holes they carve out of the darkness, adds, 'I also said I don't think Estela is a bitch': Estela, the woman who is about to reach the roadblock at El Cañada.

Hesitating about whether or not to stop en route and to tell El Chorrito to continue on foot, Estela looks out at the rocks that mark their progress through the sierra and — since deep down she does not want to stop — wonders whether Epitafio has left El Teronaque. She does not know that the men loyal to the man she so adores are only now loading the crates that Señor Hoyo will be taking from El Teronaque.

'Get those fucking crates loaded!' Epitafio roars, and then, turning towards Sepelio, orders: 'Load them up as well. Make sure their hands are tied!' Surveying his men and signalling to the nameless who have come from other lands, Sepelio shouts: 'You heard … Get this lot loaded up!' Then, when all that remains is the echo of Sepelio's voice, Epitafio and Mausoleo watch the ensuing scene without participating: the giant is thinking that he cannot dare ask what is in the crates, while, without quite knowing why, HewhosolovesEstela is thinking about the sons of the jungle.

Those two boys who, now standing beside the forest pool, toss their sacks on to the ground, the sacks filled to bursting with the objects lost in the clearing known as El Ojo de Hierba by those who have crossed so many borders — they quickly strip off their clothes, scrabble across the ten meters separating them from this place they have been longing to visit and dive into the water.

IV

'Why does it look like there are more lights today?'

'You're right ... There are more lights.'

'Look how close the beams come,' says the younger of the two boys, lifting one arm out of the forest pool.

'And on the far side of the fence, they go farther, too,' says the elder, swimming towards the center of the pond.

'I want to go with you,' says the younger boy, swimming a couple of strokes. 'I want to go to the other side, too.'

'Someone has to wait here,' says the elder, floating on his back, 'to look after all the stuff we've brought.'

'Maybe you could stay behind one day,' says the younger, resting his arms on the older boy's stomach. 'Maybe I could go there on my own.'

'How could you go on your own?' says the older boy, allowing himself to sink again. 'You don't know anyone there ... You don't know even know the way through the fence.'

'You didn't know anyone when you first went.'

'But I know them now,' says the older boy and, cupping his hands like a shovel, sends off a wave of water splashing over the younger boy.

'I'm serious,' says the younger boy, wiping his face. 'If you won't let me go on my own, at least we can go together some day.'

'And what would we do with all the stuff?'

'We'll do it some day when we're done working … when we've sold everything.'

'We can't leave it that late … You know that as well as I do.'

'No, but really, take me with you … I don't care if it's dangerous later,' the younger boy begs, his hands skimming the surface of the water.

'Okay, maybe we could go in a while,' the older boy suggests unexpectedly.

'Are you being serious?'

'We'd have to finish here early,' the older boy nods towards the village twinkling in the distance, then turns and swims back to the bank.

'I swear, we won't have anything left,' says his brother, looking at the village that those on this side of the great wall have named Tonée, though its inhabitants, on the far side of the wall, know it as Oluée. 'I'll sell things really fast.'

'Well then, don't hang around in the pool. We need to hurry.'

'If you'd told me that I could go with you today, I'd be out already,' says the younger boy, swimming towards the bank. 'But you didn't say anything.'

'It only just occurred to me … I know someone this side of the wall who can help us sell this,' the older boy says, climbing out of the pool and unfastening the medal that hangs around his neck. 'He'll know how much it's worth.'

'Are we really going to sell the medal?'

'I thought you wanted to go to the other side?' the older boy says, smiling, as he picks up his shirt, then he adds: 'This way you'll be able to go to the other side, all thanks to your medal ... What else can you do with it?'

When the sons of the jungle have gathered up their belongings and the bundles containing the things lost in the clearing in El Tiradero by those *who no longer know whether their hearts still beat in their chests*, the elder sets off walking and reaches the path that leads to the river: the river that winds through the jungle all the way to the village.

Before he too sets his legs in motion, the younger boy looks up, he sees the treetops of the kapoks and the *chujumes*, hears the calls of the howler monkeys, though he is not really listening: for a couple of seconds he is lost in a dream of this place that he does not really know, this land that extends beyond the great wall. Another cry jolts him from his dream and drags him towards the path where his older brother is impatient: 'Don't just stand there!'

'If we don't get there soon, there won't be anyone to sell anything to ... We'll end up stuck with all this stuff,' the elder of the two boys shouts, looking over his shoulder through the shadows and the liana of the jungle as the young boy finally quickens his pace, thinking: What excuse can I come up with so he can't come with me? Next to him, on the banks of the river, amphibians croak, drowning out the murmur of the forest.

Why put both of us in danger? the older boy thinks silently, then, stopping for a second, he shouts: 'Seriously, get a move on if you want to make it in time!' The younger boy shouts: 'I'm coming!' all the while still imagining this place that he does not know. At this point, the younger of the boys feels his heart pounding in his chest as hard as it did when Epitafio whistled to them back at the clearing known as El Ojo de Hierba and he emerged from the mass of migrants they had been duping all along.

Even those fuck *hijos de puta* know both sides of the wall, thinks the younger boy, and, seeing the one who, of the two of them, serves as leader, he thinks, I'm the only bastard who hasn't visited both sides. His chest throbs with rage, while, without knowing how it is happening, his mind is filled with the faces of the men and women they sold to HewhosolovesEstela: the faces of the nameless right now being caged inside the huge truck back in El Teronaque. El Teronaque, where Epitafio and his men and are still racing to finish their work and the soulless are still singing their fears:

> *We were forced back into the truck ... We were bound again ... tossed on to the floor as they screamed at us, as they beat us ... The fear returned ... but now it was a different fear ... We no longer had the strength to tremble ... We did not have the strength to feel ... There was no reason now to think, to speak, no reason left to weep.*

'Don't just stand there. Go on, get over,' Epitafio says to Mausoleo. 'You're coming with us ... Just make sure that he doesn't do anything when you're not watching,' HewhosolovesEstela adds, gesturing towards Sepelio with one hand and prodding the giant, who has come back to the courtyard, drawn by the dead. Cloaked by the shadows and the darkness, the ten cats who live here wait for Epitafio and Mausoleo to leave, and still they baulk at approaching the corpses.

'Don't leave him alone even for a second … and I need you to keep an eye on everything he does,' Epitafio says, urging the giant to move faster, then, gesturing towards Sepelio, who is standing in the doorway of the rickety building, pleased that they have finished loading the crates brought by Señor Hoyo, and the godless who have been walking now for many days, Epitafio adds: 'Is that clear?' In the distance they hear the mewling of the cats and, farther still, the cries and calls of the forests encircling El Teronaque.

'Is that clear?' Epitafio says again, because he has had no response and because he sees Sepelio turn in the doorway and come towards them. 'It's clear … You don't want me to leave his side … You want me to keep an eye on everything he does,' Mausoleo says. 'You're sick of having him around … You don't want him—' Epitafio cuts him short in case Sepelio might overhear: 'Right, go get in the truck … We'll be setting off any minute now!'

'I was waiting for you,' Sepelio explains, interrupting Epitafio and Mausoleo, and when the giant turns and sees Sepelio standing half a meter away, he immediately understands why HewhosolovesEstela forced him to shut the fuck up. In the distance, the mewling of the cats rises to a shrill screech, punctuated now and then by a menacing growl, while from somewhere high up in the darkness comes the cry of the great bird who has come back to El Teronaque.

As they reach the truck, Epitafio looks up for a moment and, catching a glimpse of the wheeling birds tracing concentric circles in the sky, mutters: 'I've never seen them around here.' Then he tears his eyes from the heavens and looks at Mausoleo and Sepelio, who are staring up at the sky, and snaps: 'What the fuck are you looking at? Why are you still here? … Why aren't you in the truck?' Sepelio and Mausoleo obediently bow their heads, go around the back of the Minos and clamber into the cab of the truck in which are caged *those blinded to all hope, the tongue-tied victims who utter disjointed words.*

*Behind our backs … plastic ropes … huge, ancient, dark …
sharpened pincers … Our eyes are blindfolded … Our limbs
shackled … Cold down our backs … No one screams …
Whimpers, only whimpers … Chains and tubes … The hum of
an engine … lulling us … starting over … neck taut.*

When they are finally ready Epitafio, too, climbs into the cab, hands Mausoleo a bag of food, slams the door, then, surveying his kingdom through the windscreen, opens his door again, pops his head out and shouts: 'I don't want anyone using shortwave!' Then he slams the door a second time, wonders whether he has everything he needs, checks his pockets and realizes he does not have his phone: 'Shit … where the fuck could I have left it?'

If I don't go and find it, how can I call you? HewhosolovesEstela thinks, and, opening the cab door once again — to the surprise of Sepelio and Mausoleo — he jumps down into the courtyard of El Teronaque: I really need to call you now … I need to know whether you've made it past El Cañada … Even if I know you won't pick up. As surprised as Sepelio and Mausoleo, those who lie shackled, chained in the back of the truck, watch Epitafio cross the yard and listen to his words: 'At least I noticed it was missing before we left … I want to talk to you as soon as we're on the road!'

Meanwhile, in the rear-view mirror attached to the passenger door, Sepelio watches the strange wanderings of HewhosolovesEstela, and seeing him get into his Cheyenne thinks: What the fuck is wrong with him? … What the hell is he doing? Then he looks away from the mirror, slowly turns his head, stares into the eyes of the giant and, speaking to Mausoleo for the first time, says: 'Don't put your faith in luck … Don't go thinking that everything is down to luck.'

More puzzled than startled, Mausoleo ignores the words addressed to him and gestures to the rear-view mirror, drawing Sepelio's attention back to the dark reflection: Epitafio has emerged from the Cheyenne and is heading back to the building that was once a slaughterhouse.

Where the fuck can I have left it? HewhosolovesEstela wonders as he passes the place where the cats and the birds he has never seen before are feeding on the corpses of the dead. 'Fucking disgusting,' Epitafio mutters, while silently repeating to himself … I know you won't pick up.

'Where the fuck could I have put it?' HewhosolovesEstela says again, standing before the door of the building that towers over El Teronaque, still thinking to himself: If I don't talk to you, you'll only get angrier, then he breaks off as he spots the telephone: See, I knew I'd find it! As he picks it up, Epitafio has misgivings: 'When did I come over and set it down here?' While in his mind he carries on: Maybe it's this thing you wanted to tell me … 'Maybe that's why you're so angry.'

This time, it is the looming figure of a man, clutching his weapon, carrying a torch and a can of gasoline across the courtyard, that reminds Epitafio that he is speaking out loud and makes him fall silent, makes him forget Estela for a moment and hurry back to the truck from where Sepelio and Mausoleo are still watching him in the rear-view mirror and where the nameless, in the dark, cold, pestilential abyss of metal, are still loosening their tongues.

More waiting ... bound ... The freezing cold ... hand, arms,
strained ... Hanging here ... feet barely ... We hear nothing
... a sob ... a whimper ... skin taut ... muscles cramped ...
Sometimes a trickle ... thick waterproofs ... Someone pissing ...
The smell of shit ... The smell of fear.

As he approaches the container, whose hulking shadow hides him from the prying eyes of the men clutching their weapons and the ghostly presence of the man carrying the gasoline can, a flashlight, and a rifle, Epitafio heads towards the center of the courtyard, where he stops, dials Estela's number and, realizing he has been connected directly to her voicemail, growls: 'Fucking mountains ... Just my fucking luck ... Shit!' Then he hangs up, slips the telephone into his pocket and heads back to the truck.

Opening the door and slamming it behind him, Epitafio climbs into the cab of the Minos without a word to Sepelio or Mausoleo, who are watching him stoically. Epitafio fumbles for his keyring, slides a key into the ignition and, turning it, he stares into the wing mirror at the reflection of El Teronaque: in the distance, the man carrying the gasoline can shoos the ten cats and the birds from their feast, douses the bodies with gasoline and, bringing the flame closer, sets them alight.

While the corpses blaze like firebrands on the *tezontle*, Epitafio shifts into first gear, spins the steering wheel and, easing the accelerator, drives forward in the present even as his memory reverses into the past: this image of two corpses blazing in the shadowy darkness has brought him back to the days when his parents left, when he watched through the window as his father set fire to the men who had arrived at their house earlier.

Leaving behind him the van, the three motorbikes, the building that was once a slaughterhouse and the two lines of men witnessing his departure, Epitafio reaches the road that runs through El Teronaque, and he asks Mausoleo to pass him a sandwich, which he wolfs down, and as he picks up speed, heading towards the jungle, so he plunges deeper and deeper into his past: when the fire eventually guttered out, his father came back into the house, kissed him and his brothers, and left, taking their mother with him.

They shouldn't have left without us, HewhosolovesEstela thinks, shifting gears as the Minos moves further from El Teronaque, while in his mind he is reliving the day following the abandonment, when three men arrived at the house and each took one of the brothers home with them. You should have taken us with you, Epitafio thinks silently, pushing the huge truck to move faster. Sepelio and Mausoleo are still staring into the wing mirror, where the human torches are now no more than tiny embers.

On its own, the hulking Minos glides through the forest to the screech of bats and the singing of cicadas, and from time to time there comes the howl of coyotes, the bark of dogs no one has ever tamed, from time to time peacocks shriek. From this point, no vehicle will follow Epitafio, who prefers to deal singlehandedly with the delivery of the creatures *whose chests and throats are swollen with a pent-up commotion*, and, as he changes gears again, Epitafio feels his memories gnaw at him: You should have come back … You should have taken me from El Paraíso … found my brothers … brought us all together.

I never saw them again … It was their fault we never saw each other again, Epitafio thinks as he approaches the junction where the dirt track meets the tarmacked road, and, as he slows, not realizing he is shouting at the top of his lungs, he says: 'It's your fucking fault that I never saw my brothers again!' Startled, Mausoleo and Sepelio, who have remained silent until now, turn to stare at Epitafio.

'What the hell are you talking about?' Sepelio says as Epitafio turns the Minos on to the tarmac. Only then does HewhosolovesEstela realize that he has spoken aloud and, with a roar, he dismisses the past and this story he does not want the two men sharing the cab to know: 'What do you care? I talk about whatever I feel like …'

'And obviously you do whatever you feel like … otherwise why did you take the turning here?' Sepelio asks, whipping his head around.

'I'll turn wherever the hell I want!' Epitafio snaps, speeding up again as he moves away from the crossroads.

'You promised we weren't going to your house,' Sepelio says, leaning forward. He can guess what is going on.

'If I want to go by my house, we're going by my house and you can shut up!' Epitafio barks, and the void left in his mind by the memory of his brothers is filled by the woman Father Nicho married him to, and the child she gave birth to there in El Paraíso.

'You never keep your promises.'

'I didn't make you any fucking promises,' HewhosolovesEstela bellows as his memories begin to unsettle him: every time he pictures the woman he was wedded to by Father Nicho, a voice from deep down rips him apart: Estela, will our day come some day?

'We're going to be late … If we go by your place, we won't get there on time,' Sepelio says, turning to face Epitafio. 'We agreed we would make the delivery at a specific time.'

'I don't give a shit if we're late … I don't give a shit what we agreed,' Epitafio says, thumping the steering wheel as he hears the voice from within him: Estela … I can't go on waiting … We can't go on like this!

'You know that they're waiting for us … You're going to fuck up the deal,' Sepelio says, punching the dashboard.

'I don't care what they're doing,' HewhosolovesEstela snarls, and then, allowing the voice inside him to merge with his own voice, he says: 'If you're not going to shut up … If you're determined to keep on talking … Call Estela!'

'What?' Sepelio sounds surprised.

'Call Estela right now … Talk to her, ask her where she is … She's pissed off with me … If I call her, I know she won't pick up.'

'You really want me to call?'

'I really want you to call her.'

'What the hell am I supposed to ask her?' Sepelio asks, fumbling for his phone and trying hard not to laugh.

'Ask her if she's pregnant … moron,' Epitafio yells, and as he shifts gears and urges the truck even faster, he thinks: How can I have put up with this knuckle-dragger for so long?

'Whether she's pregnant?' Sepelio says as he pretends to type

Estela's number into his phone.

'What the fuck? … Why would I want you to ask her that?' Epitafio says, shaking his head in exasperation: he'll believe anything, this dumb-ass.

'No answer,' Sepelio says, glancing again at Epitafio and thinking: This idiot really thinks I'm going to call her.

'Hang up and try again!'

'I'm trying again … but no one is picking up,' Sepelio says, turning towards the window where his smile is reflected as a sneer.

'Why the fuck won't she answer?' Epitafio roars. He's losing control as he begins to wonder: What if something happened to you at La Cañada?

'You want me to try again?' Sepelio says, controlling his mounting excitement and, as he turns turning back towards Epitafio, his eyes meet those of Mausoleo: the giant has realized he is only pretending to dial.

'Do I want you to try?' Epitafio splutters, but, rather than respond, he continues to fume silently: Nothing can have happened to you … You're probably passing the checkpoint right now … The reason you can't answer is that you've just reached the checkpoint … What time did you set off from El Paraíso?

'You want me to or not?' Sepelio taunts, his eyes still locked on the giant.

'El Paraíso … Call El Paraíso,' Epitafio orders. 'Ask them what time Estela left.'

'El Paraíso?' Sepelio says, his excitement still mounting, and, tearing his eyes from those of the giant, he turns back to the window.

'Ask them how long it takes to reach El Cañada … That's probably why she's not answering.'

'I'm calling them,' Sepelio interrupts Epitafio and this time, though he is revelling in the moment, he is not lying to anyone.

'Hello … Father? … Father Nicho?'

'Sepelio … is that you?'

'Yes … it's Sepelio.'

'I thought you said this wasn't a good time to call,' Father Nicho says.

'I'm not calling for myself … Epitafio asked me to phone,' Sepelio says, weighing each word.

'Is he there with you?'

'He's asking me to ask you how long it takes to get to El Cañada?'

'How long it takes to get to El Cañada … He wants to … Has he mentioned whether he's talked to Estela … whether she told him that I told her—?'

'From El Paraíso to La Cañada,' Sepelio interrupts Father Nicho. 'That's all he wants to know.'

'Then he hasn't spoken to her … or at least not about whether he and I talked earlier …?'

'He's trying to work out whether she would have arrived yet … whether she would have reached El Cañada.'

'Give her a chance and she'd fuck me over, the bitch.'

'It's just that he's worried,' Sepelio stifles a laugh.

'Worried? … Isn't that sweet … What a decent man.'

'So you don't think she would have got there yet?' Sepelio says, his throat tightening to contain the laughter swelling in his belly.

'That's right … Tell him she won't be there yet … that there's no need to hurry … that she told me she was going to call him as soon as she passed the checkpoint.'

'Is that what she said?' Sepelio signs as Epitafio says, 'What did she say?'

'By the way, I talked to your men,' says Father Nicho.

'So she said she'd phone as soon as she makes it to the far side of El Cañada?' Sepelio's words are not intended for the man on the other end of the line, but for Epitafio.

'I was surprised you've got them on such a tight leash … They don't want to speak to anyone but you,' says the priest. 'Carry on like that and you'll do well … but you should tell them to talk to me if I call … Tell them I'm in charge … that you understand that it's important that they understand it, too … not like that moron Epitafio.'

'You're right … I'll tell them right now … Tell him, I mean … that there's no hurry … that nothing has happened … that she's on her way to El Cañada … that there are problems getting a signal out there.'

'It's something that cretin Epitafio should never have forgotten … He thinks he's really someone … I know you understand … You'll tell your men who really runs the show … in Lago Seco … in La Carpa … every-fucking-where,' Father Nicho says. 'And give Epitafio my regards … Tell him there'll soon be a new boss in town.'

'I'll tell him … you send your regards,' Sepelio says and as he does so Epitafio says he also sends his regards.

'Make sure everything goes to plan.'

'Epitafio sends his regards,' Sepelio says.

'We'll talk later.'

Through the window, beyond the reflection of his eager face, Sepelio watches the mantle of darkness rob space of its perspective and the earth of its contours, and, slipping his phone into his pocket, he thinks to himself: I have to keep very calm now … I can't do anything to raise his suspicion … Nothing out of place … No clue that anything is wrong. Then, turning his face and returning his attention to the inside of the cab, he glances briefly at Epitafio and asks: 'Are you feeling a bit more reassured?'

'I will be when she calls,' HewhosolovesEstela explains, though he does feel a little calmer: his agitation has abated and his mind has returned fully to the present moment. Gazing out at the darkness through the windscreen of the huge Minos, Epitafio is thinking that it is not much farther to his house, and that once there, he will have to move fast or they will arrive too late to sell the nameless. Those soulless creatures caged in the back of the Minos, who, only moments earlier, began to unravel the knots of their lives.

> *I don't know who began but suddenly a man started to talk …*
> *and it was as though talking about the past meant we were no*
> *longer caged here … 'This was my third attempt' … he said and*
> *he suddenly began to speak … 'I come from Kino … from very*
> *far away … I left four children there … I left my parrot and my*
> *dog … My wife went on ahead … two years ago … I have not*
> *heard from her.'*

As he shifts gears and accelerates a little faster, Epitafio reaches out his arm and asks someone to give him the pack of cigarettes on the dashboard, and Mausoleo obediently leans forward and does so. Sepelio takes out a box of matches, strikes one and proffers the tiny flickering flame to HewhosolovesEstela, leaning past the face of the giant, who turns in surprise towards Epitafio, hearing him cough as he exhales a lungful of the smoke that will gradually fill the whole cab.

Lighting a cigarette for himself, Sepelio blows tiny smoke rings and puts the box of matches on the dashboard: as he does so, he sees the car stereo and thinks perhaps music might ease the strained atmosphere between the three men traveling together. 'You mind if I put on some music?' Sepelio ventures, tossing the pack of cigarettes on his lap on to the dashboard.

'Of course you fucking can't,' Epitafio barks, removing and replacing his cap several times with the hand holding his cigarette: 'What happens if she calls and we don't hear it? I don't even want to hear people talking,' HewhosolovesEstela says, exhaling another plume of smoke, and, revving the engine of the truck, he stares at Mausoleo for a second: the giant is playing with the matchbox he picked up from the dashboard.

Striking a match and blowing it out, then another, and another, like an idiot stripping petals from a dead flower, Mausoleo hesitates between the flame and the smoke. And yet each time he blows out the match about to burn his fingers, the giant feels as though he is extinguishing the inferno of doubts blazing in his mind: he overheard the phone call between Sepelio and the man they call Father Nicho.

As smoke continues to fill the cab — the windows of the Minos cannot be wound down, since, like the windscreen, they are bulletproof

— and the three men gradually retreat into their minds, their silence, while the timeless creatures in the back of the truck, their hands bound, their feet shackled to strange weights, continue to pour forth what they carry deep inside and, in doing so, recall their past.

Another said … 'I am from Enseguay … and a migrant … I've traveled this road many times … I've seen a lot of terrible things … but nothing like this … This can't be real … It can't be happening … To have left everything for this … It can't be true … My four brothers … My old woman … My two orange trees … I can't believe it … All my tools … This can't be happening.'

Roused by the lights of a town that has suddenly appeared in the distance, Epitafio stretches out his hand, stubs out his cigarette, picks up the matches Mausoleo put back on the dashboard, grabs the pack of cigarettes, takes out another, lights it and, after coughing once or twice, says: 'We're only going to stop at my place for a minute … I want to drop off a couple of boxes … We'll drop them off, say hello, and set off again … You'll see, we'll be on the road again in no time.'

As HewhosolovesEstela trails off, the silence inside the cab swells and Mausoleo, who opened his eyes when he heard Epitafio's voice, now closes them and nods off as Sepelio laughs to himself: he knows that in talking about his house, Epitafio is thinking about Estela. The woman who has just climbed out of her truck and ordered the captain to get out and come with her.

V

'Hurry up, and don't come back unless you've got good news,' Estela shouts, staring into the distance as the captain turns on the headlights of the truck: El Chorrito has turned on to a road swallowed by the darkness that leads to the checkpoint at La Cañada.

The far-off braying of two donkeys and the bleating of a herd of goats interrupted by the rhythmic tinkling of their tiny bells fills the space with sounds like sparks that puncture the weary drone of the engines of the battered trailer trucks.

'If you're not back in half an hour, we'll go ourselves!' Estela warns, watching as the figure of El Chorrito melts away at the border between the darkness and the light. 'Get back here within half an hour or we'll go apeshit!' ShewhoadoresEpitafio calls after him, and as she does so she hears the little bells tinkle faster, reminding her suddenly of the bells back at the orphanage: Why would Father Nicho have pretended that you called him?

Lying fucking priest, Estela thinks as the bells are hushed then, hearing a distant howl that announces the presence of a coyote somewhere beyond the donkeys and the goats. She turns and tells the drivers to shut off their engines. The stillness of the metal hulks calms the men loyal to Estela, worries the bodiless creatures trapped in the blue pickup truck and startles the nameless in the blood-red truck, who carry on listening to the eldest of all those who have come from other lands.

Your life lines are much clearer ... Your future is obvious
... You will meet the man who even now is waiting for you
... Together you will have many children ... and a good job
awaits you ... The man you have dreamed of for so many
years ... The job you have always wanted ... You will fill
crates with fruit ... Your children will help you.

Hearing the barking of the dogs warning the coyote: Don't come near!, ShewhoadoresEpitafio turns back to the dark road, scans for the figure of El Chorrito in the sea of shadows that drowns the beams from her headlights of her huge truck and, unable to find him, chokes back the warning that has been straining at her gritted teeth: half an hour, no more!

But having already opened her mouth and already loosened her tongue, Estela mutters: 'Fucking Nicho ... What were you doing making that up? ... What do you get out of it?' Then, turning back to stare at the convoy she is leading, ShewhoadoresEpitafio shouts to her men: 'Better be on your guard!

'Everyone needs to be on the alert!' Estela says, and, making her way back to the spot where her men and her battered trucks are parked, she adds: 'Have your weapons at the ready ... You never know, they might appear out of nowhere!' Just as Estela's cry dies away, the coyote howls again, farther off now, but this time no dogs bark: the coyote has announced its departure.

'What the fuck are you still doing in the trucks?' Estela roars a minute later, and to her men the roar is like a brutal shove in the back: they had not realized that their boss wanted them out of the trucks.

'All of you, get behind a rock!' ShewhoadoresEpitafio orders when her men are standing on the rocky sierra: 'They could show up here, all guns blazing!'

This word, *blazing*, violates the soulless creatures still sprawled on the floor of the blue truck and the godless still caged inside the red truck, their legs swinging back and forth, breaking up the circle they had formed around the old man.

Don't pay any heed to what you hear ... Nothing is going to happen to us here ... I don't see any fires up ahead ... I don't see or hear any shots being fired in the air ... Come back over here to me ... You give me your hand ... Nothing is going to happen here ... I swear ... Please, everyone, stay calm!

Fucking bastard Nicho ... I knew you were up to something ... I should never have gone to the orphanage! Estela thinks, curled up behind a rock and, watching her men hunker or crouch down, calls out: 'No one fire, even if they show up firing ... Don't shoot unless you see me shoot first!'

Two minutes pass and then, from the distance, comes the braying of the two donkeys, the bleating of the goats and the howl of the coyote is now so far away that it is difficult to distinguish the howl from the wind, which suddenly whistles across La Cañada, surprising the men clutching their weapons: El Chorrito, who is approaching the checkpoint he commanded until recently, the soldiers who were reassigned here only yesterday, and ShewhoadoresEpitafio, who hugs her knees against the biting cold swept in by the wind. But as she hugs herself, the only thing Estela can do is remember Epitafio's arms around her.

Why do I only want you to listen to me when I decide? ... I should have phoned you already ... I should have told you: told you that something strange is going on! Estela thinks and, hugging herself harder, she adds: But I don't want you listening to me only when you decide ... If I call you, you'll never learn to respect me ... You won't listen to what I need to say. You won't hear what I have to tell you about Father fucking Nicho.

The wind whipping across the sierra grows strong as Estela tightens her grip on her knees, drawing from the rocks the sounds and the voices of the creatures who years ago lived in this place and now are merely dust. This stony, deep and icy song sharpens the senses of El Chorrito, who, moments earlier, reached the checkpoint at La Cañada, of the officers greeting him, of the men clutching their weapons and of ShewhoadoresEpitafio.

I need to tell you what's going on with us and what's going on with Father Nicho ... but first I need you to call me, to realize that I haven't told you, Estela thinks, relaxing her embrace and rubbing her arms in an attempt to bring back the warmth the wind is leaching from her body: I want you to call me ... to call and realize that when it is you who calls, I'm different ... though who knows whether you'll listen when I tell you that that bastard Father Nicho is up to something ... that he's not the man he used to be.

I said as much today and you didn't listen to me ... I don't want to go to El Paraíso ... That's what I said and it was as if I hadn't said a word … You've never listened when it comes to that fucking idiot … 'Why would you listen now that he's changed,' ShewhoadoresEpitafio mutters angrily and, though she cannot know it, her words put a snake on its guard.

The snake slithering between the rocks stops and curls up as it hears the woman threatening: 'You never fucking listen when it comes to Father Nicho … Certainly not that he's changed … as though there's something between the two of you … as if nothing has happened.

'Fucking bastards,' Estela grunts, then suddenly stops herself and addresses herself to someone else: from Epitafio she moves on to Father Nicho, and, in doing so, her voice rises as she spits the words. 'Fucking bastard … I knew you'd grow tired of me … as if I'd never seen you lose interest in others.'

Among the rocks up in the sierra, while Estela continues to mutter to herself, the snake constricts the knot it has become, shakes its rattle and probes the air with its tongue.

'*Hijo de perra* … I knew you'd betray us sooner or later!' ShewhoadoresEpitafio grumbles. 'So what betrayal have you got in store today? … What the fuck have you been plotting?' Then she jumps to her feet, having heard the ominous rattle of the snake. Estela feels a shudder run down her spine as she scans the dark ground for the snake, but carries on talking to herself: Where are you planning to betray us, you evil fucking shit?

It's bound to be at the checkpoint up ahead, Estela concludes and, unable to see the snake, turns as slowly as she can. Evil son of a bitch priest … 'This is what we get after all these years?'

ShewhoadoresEpitafio murmurs as she continues to slowly move away from the sound of the coiled creature on the ground about to lunge at her: 'I said it to Epitafio a thousand times ... but you think that with us everything will be different!'

By the time the rattlesnake falls silent again, Estela has once more changed the person she is addressing: I told you until I was sick of telling you ... in the end, he'll toss us aside, too! But then, realizing that the threat is imminent, she puts even Epitafio from her mind and, quickening her pace, she yells to her men: 'It's a trap ... The checkpoint up ahead, it's an ambush!'

Meanwhile, at that same checkpoint, El Chorrito is explaining to the officers on duty what Father Nicho told him back at the orphanage and what he repeated a moment ago when El Chorrito spoke to him — he has just hung up his phone. He said it would be better not to keep her too long ... keep her waiting, waste her time, but not too much, the captain says, toying with the cable of his phone, coiling it around his fingers just as the words are coiled around his tongue, then he reiterates: no need to make her waste time too much time when they're wasting her time.

'He told me he spoke to his men a little while ago,' El Chorrito adds, untangling the cable as he tries to disentangle the words in his mouth. 'That he's already talked to his men and that they're on time ... That they will be there on time, so you should let her through. Take your time, but let her through. Then, dragging his bum leg up to the barrier where he spent so many years in command, El Chorrito regains his composure and his fluency and says: 'Now go and hide and act like there's no one here ... as if I got here and the place was deserted.

'You have to make sure she gets through after you hold her up,' El Chorrito says again, glancing back at the path that led him to this place, peering into the black darkness, straining to hear the hum of Estela's Ford Lobo or the two pickup trucks towards which ShewhoadoresEpitafio is now running, ranting: 'What the fuck? … Did you hear what I said?

'We're going to head over that way … I'm not going to let myself be fucked over by that bastard,' Estela growls and her voice brings the men springing from their hiding places behind the rocks and dashing across the rocky path: 'We'll show those sons of bitches! We'll ambush the traitors that Father Nicho sent here!' Estela shouts, and this time it is the nameless who hear her words.

Don't be afraid … Nothing is going to happen to us here … Pay no attention to the shouting … Just stay here, side by side … Don't let your hands tremble … What I see in your hands is destiny … You too will live for many more years yet … You too will find a new life over there … on the other side.

Little by little, the voice of the eldest of all those who have come from other lands soothes the soulless huddled in the blood-red pickup: but in the pale-blue pickup, there is not a single word to calm the bodiless still lying on the floor, who now begin to tremble as they hear Estela's voice in the distance: 'Get back into the fucking trucks … He was planning to set a trap for us … Well, we'll show him what we think of his trap!'

Watching her men, who, having darted between the dark shadows are now climbing into the battered trucks, ShewhoadoresEpitafio says: 'I want every man in position with his weapon at the ready ... We'll go in all guns blazing! We'll annihilate them.' Then she walks back to her huge trailer truck, thinking: It was a fucking stupid idea to hang around here ... I should have realized what was going on.

As she climbs into the Ford Lobo, Estela turns her head, surveys the convoy and calls out: 'We're not even going to stop ... When we get there, we shoot anything that moves!' Then she turns the key in the ignition and floors the accelerator, silently repeating to herself: Bastard fucking Nicho ... You don't give a shit about all the work, all the years we gave you.

A roar of engines trails the convoy following Estela and, in its wake, the dust stirred up by the tires slowly settles, like a wave just beginning to swell: with every meter, the Ford Lobo and the two battered pickups accelerate, and from inside comes the clack and clatter of shotgun cartridges.

Alerted by the rumble of the engines, the dogs who were barking at the coyote scrabble to their feet and begin barking into the wind, which is blowing ever stronger. 'That's it ... blow as hard as you like ... cloak the convoy in a dust storm,' ShewhoadoresEpitafio says, just as El Chorrito sees the distant convoy bearing down on him, and those stationed at the checkpoint seconds earlier search for a rock crevice to swallow them up.

What am I going to say to her now? El Chorrito thinks, raising his arms and frantically waving them in the air as the wind sets the dust dancing in the wake of the trucks closing in at breakneck speed that must surely brake soon. 'How the hell am I going to convince her

THE BOOK OF ESTELA

there was no one stationed here?' mutters the man who is only skin
and bone, just as Estela thinks: I forgot about that dumb-ass!

'You have to be mixed up in this plot … You must have cut a deal
with Father Nicho!' Estela mutters, and, as she draws closer to El
Chorrito, wonders whether she should stop or run over the little shit,
who is still silently thinking to himself: How am I going to convince
you? … How can I explain why I hung around for so long if there
wasn't a soul here?

'You're working for the fucker Nicho … How could you do this
to Epitafio?' Estela whispers, still unsure whether to speed up or stop:
a split-second before she crushes the captain, who has closed his eyes
and steeled himself, she makes her decision and slams on the Ford
Lobo's brakes. Then, throwing open the door and jumping down,
Estela says: 'What the fuck is going on?

'What the fuck are you doing?' ShewhoadoresEpitafio repeats,
pacing up and down as the two pickup trucks screech to a halt: the
men clutching their weapons jump down, too, and the voiceless, in
the pale-blue pickup, are thrown across the floor. The timeless in the
blood-red pickup, however, grip each other's hands and manage not
to lose their balance as they listen to the oldest among them.

> My judgment tells me … You will know just vengeance for
> what has happened … Listen to what I have to tell you …
> My words offer you a great verdict … Though the time is
> dark and you can see nothing … the sun will rise for you
> and a sprawling valley of glorious years will open up before
> you.

While her men scatter, and the dust raised by the trucks mingles with the dust whipped up by the wind now lashing the checkpoint and the soldiers who ran off to hide, Estela walks towards El Chorrito: 'What the fuck is going on?'

'It's deserted.'

'What the hell are you on about?'

'There's no one here.'

'How can there be no one here?' Estela asks as she reaches the captain, silently thinking: *Hijo de puta.*

'I've been over every inch of the place, and there's no one here,' El Chorrito insists, while a voice inside him whispers: She doesn't believe a word.

'I don't believe you ... There has to be someone in one of the huts.'

'I couldn't believe it either,' El Chorrito says. 'They must have left this afternoon ... It sometimes happens with new recruits.'

'It sometimes happens?' ShewhoadoresEpitafio takes a step forward, forcing the captain to recoil.

'They get scared in the night ... I've seen it before.'

'You've seen it before?'

'It's not easy, getting through the first night,' says the man all skin and bone, and once again he hears a voice inside him: That's it ... keep going ... She's starting to believe you. 'It gets dark and they want to leave ... They probably didn't have a captain or a lieutenant with them.'

'They wouldn't be hiding around here somewhere?' Estela says, her eyes boring into El Chorrito, and, taking another step forward, she

THE BOOK OF ESTELA

orders her men to shoulder their weapons.

'Maybe they're … in one of those … I don't know … what's going on … Maybe one of them is hiding …,' the captain falters as he sees the guns trained on him and then, in Estela's eyes, sees a flicker of doubt.

'I knew something was going on … It would be very strange for this place to be deserted,' ShewhoadoresEpitafio growls, reaching for the gun holstered in her belt and staring at the shack next to the checkpoint at La Cañada just as a barn owl lands on its roof.

'I've seen that happen, too … Why are you drawing your …? Sometimes when they see people coming they run and hide … Why are you drawing your gun?' El Chorrito hesitates before turning his head too. 'Then they wait for you to get here and *bang* … they swoop.'

'They swoop … You think that's what going to happen here?'

'That's not what I'm saying.'

'Well, what the fuck are you saying?' Estela roars angrily.

'I'm saying they could be anywhere,' El Chorrito mutters, while the voice in his head says: You're falling into her trap.

'Anywhere?' ShewhoadoresEpitafio says through gritted teeth, feeling her chest swell with joy.

'Yeah, anywh … Probably better if you don't draw your … Maybe it's best if we just hit the road,' stammers the captain.

'Best if we just hit the road?' Estela mocks him, looking up just as another owl lands on the roof of the shack.

'We have to get out of here as fast as possible,' El Chorrito says stubbornly, as the voice in his head deserts him: You're in this up to your neck and now you're coming out with this bullshit.

'I thought you wanted to stay here ... Why do you want to come with us?'

'Why do I want?'

'Why do you want us to get out of here?' Estela says again, feeling the exultation in her chest; she has decided that it is all over for the man of skin and bones.

'Why do I want? ... I want ... because ... because why?' El Chorrito stutters, his words cut off by the woman who forces him to take another step back.

'Do you seriously think I'm a fucking idiot?' Estela barks. 'You might betray me ... but how can you dare betray Epitafio?'

'Be ...betra ... please ... put the gun away ... betray Epitafio?'

'You little shit ... Did you really think I wouldn't catch on ... that I wouldn't realize that you're lying?'

'Lying ... What are ... Don't do ... What are you saying?' El Chorrito digs himself deeper, then, clutching at his last hope, he masks his words with brazenness: 'I've never betrayed anyone ... Everything's going to be fine here.'

'You're absolutely right ... Everything's going to be fine, because I'm going to make an example of you,' Estela screams, grabbing the captain by the hair and dragging him to the shack next to the La Cañada checkpoint as the owls on the roof begin to screech.

Startled, the men loyal to Estela watch as their boss throws El Chorrito on the floor of the shack, as she kicks him, as she drags him out again and, pulling him to his feet, leans him against the door. 'I don't know where they're hiding,' ShewhoadoresEpitafio hisses into the ear of the man of skin and bone, 'but I bet they're watching,' then she shouts: 'The first man to try anything will end up like him!'

Though he wants to swear that he has done nothing, the captain cannot utter a word: his tongue has died before the rest of his body, and El Chorrito, who wishes he could beg, can do nothing but listen to the woman ordering him: 'Say his name ... I want to hear it ... Say it, say Epitafio! E-pi-ta-fio! Come on, you piece of shit ... I want to hear you say Epitafio!' Estela's words leave her men shaken, as they do the men hiding in the rocky crevices and the godless who have come from far-off lands.

> I see it clearly ... as clearly as I have ever seen anything ...
> the shadows will eventually recede ... You will see many new
> horizons ... You will be with those you love again ... Those
> who love you will come back ... Life will reward your pain
> and your prayers.

The echo of the gunshot that destroys the teeth, the throat, the hypothalamus and the neck of El Chorrito interrupts the words of the eldest of all those who have come from beyond the borders, puts to flight the owls on the roof of the shack, starts a muttering among the men loyal to Estela and forces those who fled and hid deeper into their rock crevasses: those who are the target of Estela's last threat, as she steps over the body of the captain: 'You'd better not stand in our way!

'If you don't want to end up like this cripple, stay away ... and stop being puppets for Father Nicho!' Estela turns on her heel and, walking back toward her men, she says: 'Right, back in the trucks and let's get the fuck out of here!' Watching ShewhoadoresEpitafio and her men, the soldiers feel their entrails liquefy and, filthy with fear, muddy with shame, they cling to the sides of their stony clefts as Estela climbs into the Lobo.

Even the stench enveloping them cannot force these men to leave their hiding places and return to the checkpoint they are supposed to man: they will not return to their posts for many hours yet, until no trace remains of Estela and her men, by which time Estela and her men will have encountered the men who left the Madre Buena plateau, Epitafio will have finally left his house, and the sons of the jungle will have sold the contents of their sacks in the town where they find themselves.

But it will take some time for all these things to happen: the sons of the forest are only just emptying their sacks of the things lost by those who have spent many days walking in the clearing of El Tiradero; Epitafio is just stepping into his house; the men from Lago Seco have barely reached the foothills of the sierra; and Estela has just keyed the ignition in the Ford. The truck that, a moment later, roars into life as, after a glance in the rear-view mirror to make sure her men are back in their pickups, ShewhoadoresEpitafio pulls away, thinking: I'm sick to death of these mountains.

Actually, I'm sick to death of everything, Estela corrects herself, and, urging the car faster, she loses herself in the mountain roads, where, in a little while, she will stop to call Epitafio at the same time as she becomes lost in the pathways of her mind: How is it possible that all these years are worth so little now … that that bastard priest wants to make us pay dearly for everything we have done for him? And there we were, you and I, always worried … always concerned that he might feel disappointed … letting life trickle through our hands.

Constantly worried that he might think we were abandoning him … Always doing what was best, not for us, but for him … You put up with everything. You even married Osaria! Estela is thinking when her daydream abruptly stops: she knows that if she does not stop to phone Epitafio that she will end up losing her way in these mountains where the wind has finally eased and she can once again hear the howl of the coyote, the bleating of the goats and the braying of donkeys hidden by the darkness.

These same mountains in whose foothills the former municipal garbage truck is wending its way, heading for Estela and her men: it would be for the best if ShewhoadoresEpitafio lost her way. Best for her, for her men and for the nameless who have come from afar, but not for the six soldiers gambling in the back of what looks like an armored van, nor for El Topo and El Tampón, traveling in the cab of the fake security van, lost in a story that one of them is telling.

VI

'But the son was much worse,' El Tampón says after a second or two.

'Which son?' El Topo asks, letting one hand slip from the steering wheel as he yawns.

'You're bored, aren't you …? I'm sending you to sleep.'

'What the fuck are you talking about?'

'If you want me to shut up, I'll shut up,' El Tampón says, opening the ice box and fishing out a beer.

'I do want you to tell the story …' El Topo insists, reaching for the ice box, 'It's just that I'm tired.'

'Yeah, well I don't feel like telling it any more,' El Tampón says, uncapping the beer. 'This is why you don't know shit.'

'Spoken like a true genius.'

'Why don't you fuck off!'

'Mister Encyclopaedia,' El Topo teases, then, by way of apology, he reaches across and clinks his bottle with El Tampón's. 'Go on, tell me the rest.'

'The son was crazier than the father … Seriously … the stuff he did was much worse,' El Tampón says, picking up the thread of his tales as he balances his beer on the dashboard. 'The son was completely off his head.'

'Which son are you talking about?' El Topo says, then, nodding to the bottle El Tampón has just set down, he adds, 'Don't leave it there, it'll fall off.'

'How can you not know? … Everyone in Lago Seco knows … Everyone living on the fucking *meseta* knows,' El Tampón says, picking up his beer. 'I'm talking about the son that's still alive.'

'He's got a shitload of sons,' El Topo quips, rolling down the window and tossing the bottle he has eagerly downed into the darkness.

'But there's only one who bears his surname … The only surviving Alcántara.'

'You mean the real son … the one who used to hang out with my old man?' El Topo laughs. 'The one I used to see when I was a kid?'

'You bastard … you knew all along,' El Tampón explodes, and, tossing his bottle out the window, snarls, 'Go fuck with someone else.'

'I'm just joking … Don't go throwing a fit,' El Topo says, peering at the distant road sign El Tampón is reading, then, thinking, We're nearly there, he adds, 'I know *which* son, but I don't know what he did … so finish the story, because you won't get a chance after we get there.'

'Now you want to hear the story … You're suddenly all ears because we're nearly there,' El Tampón grumbles, leaning forward and, jerking his chin towards the twinkling lights in the deep darkness, he says, 'Well, you'll just have to wait.'

'Fine, be like that … but I'll remember this the next time you want me to tell you something.'

'When did you ever tell me anything?' El Tampón asks, reaching for the ice chest again.

'You're not going to drink another beer, are you?' El Topo yells, nudging El Tampón and slamming the ice box shut. 'You can't show up there swigging a beer.'

'I've got time enough to finish it,' El Tampón says, opening the box again, then, nodding to the lights pulsing in the distance, adds, 'or maybe you don't realize how far we've got left to go.'

'Now who's fucking with who?'

'Maybe you'll be able to tell when we're a hundred meters away,' El Tampón mocks, but immediately feels a pang of regret and returns to the question he asked a moment earlier: 'When have you ever told me anything?'

'Really? … Who was it told you that the son was deformed?' El Topo says, urging the former municipal garbage truck faster. 'And you wouldn't know about the stuff he did with my old man if I hadn't told you.'

'You're right,' El Tampón acknowledges, flicking the cap off the beer and, feeling the same pang of remorse, he decides not to pick a fight.

'You've no fucking idea what an evil bastard he was … He was the one who hired my father to go out into the scrubland that afternoon … to shoot that crazy fucker … to put an end to his rage and his father's dogs.'

'Who would have thought that faggot would betray your old man … though I suppose he'd already betrayed his own fucking father, so it wasn't much of a surprise.'

'Faggot … the guy wishes he was a faggot!'

'Not every asshole gets to be a faggot!' El Tampón completes the punchline, leaning forward, and, although he'd prefer to carry on joking, he nods to the flickering lights like flames: they are coming to Tres Hermanos.

'I said you wouldn't have time ... You'd better toss that thing,' El Topo says, glancing at the beer bottle El Tampón is holding, then, slowing the truck, he adds, 'Before we get there, swear that you'll tell me the rest of the story later.'

'Do you think they know we're coming? ... Do you think he called them?' El Tampón says, tossing the beer bottle and, gazing at the three huge drums belching flames into the black darkness, he adds: 'The dumb-ass forgets everything ... Sepelio better have fucking called them.'

'Come on, don't be a bastard ... Promise you'll tell me the rest of the story later,' El Topo insists, leaning on the horn of the ex-garbage truck.

'I promise I'll tell you as soon as we leave,' El Tampón says, looking at the blazing drums behind the main gate of Tres Hermanos. 'They've obviously got a lot of work on ... Let's see whether they'll take the ones we'll be bringing later.'

'If they don't, I don't know what the hell we'll do,' El Topo says as he parks the fake security van. 'Unless Sepelio was lying, poor Estela's bringing a fucking shedload.'

'There you go again ... What's with this "poor Estela"?' El Tampón asks, staring at El Topo. 'What the fuck do you care about that old bitch?'

'There they are ...' El Topo mutters, nodding to the two old men in the distance.

'I spotted them a while ago,' El Tampón says, trying to determine the mood of the brothers walking towards them. 'I'll bet you anything that dipshit Sepelio forgot to call them.'

'We're about to find out,' El Topo says and, a moment later, he adds, 'It's your turn to get out ... I did it last time.'

'Bastard ... You always claim you did it last time,' El Tampón says, climbing out of the former municipal garbage truck and walking toward the railings that protect Tres Hermanos.

Reaching across the dashboard, past the dolls dressed in soccer jerseys, the figurine of Christ in a soldier's uniform that they use as a bottle-opener, the tiny Christmas tree and the Smurf dressed as Saint Juan Diego, El Topo grabs the pack of cigarettes and the box of matches, watching as El Tampón reaches the gates, leans his arms against them and waits for the two old men still making their way across their vast empire.

A cigarette dangling from his lips, El Topo tries to strike a match, but as he does so, he realizes he is much more nervous than even he expected, and, closing his eyes, he tries not to think about El Tampón or the two old men slowly approaching. Gliding over the depths of his mind, El Topo repeats to himself: Better to think about something else, and this is how he comes to call up an image of Estela, the woman now driving along mountain roads, who, to avoid thinking about Epitafio, about Father Nicho or about her life, snorts two lines of coke and is thinking about the two sons of the jungle.

The two boys who, a moment earlier, on the main square of the town known to them as Tonée and to those on the far side of the great wall as Oluée, finished laying two blankets on the flagstones on which they are now setting out the things lost in the clearing known as El Ojo de Hierba by the nameless ones that they betrayed.

Exhausted, the elder of the two boys has collapsed on a flowerbed, while the younger boy, excited at the prospect of finally making it to the other side of the fence that divides the desolate lands, is shouting at the top of his lungs, selling off the possessions and belongings left in the clearing known as El Tiradero by the soulless who crossed the border days ago to these creatures who crossed it a few scant hours since.

Closing his eyes and using his hands as a pillow, the elder of the two boys prays to heaven that his younger brother will not sell off everything too quickly, since he has not yet worked out how he will explain that he doesn't want to take him to the other side today: but, Better not to worry about that, the elder boy thinks, changing the image in his mind and, calling up the face of Epitafio, he decides that it was a good idea to work with this man who, right now, is stepping out of his house because he wants to go to the toilet and it is on the far side of the dirt yard.

This yard that Epitafio is crossing as he thinks about Estela, the woman who a moment ago stopped her truck in the high sierra, so she could talk to him and tell him about Father Nicho's betrayal. The same woman El Topo is still thinking about when he suddenly opens his eyes and sees El Tampón standing at the gates, waiting for the old men who founded Tres Hermanos.

Never leaving each other's side, the two surviving triplets of Los Tres Hermanos — a former quarry, now a breaker's yard, that locals call El Infierno — finally reach the railings that circumscribe their world and safeguard their existence, oblivious to the purpose outside their gates of these men who appear from time to time.

'We shouldn't bother to open up for them,' says the white-haired triplet, though he knows that his brother is thinking the same thing: Let them stay out there until they're sick and tired and they leave … Maybe this time they'll finally get the message. The smoke from the great drums dances around the triplets, who stand rooted to the spot, the fire-glow sets the shadows quivering, while a pack of skeletal dogs fight over a bitch in heat.

'I'm not going to open the gates … Let them talk to us from their side,' says the triplet who, years ago, decided to dye his hair, and his words are precisely those that his brother would have uttered. 'Maybe they'll realize that they can't just turn up here whenever they want to,' says the white-haired triplet, standing a few meters from the railings and, gesturing with both hands, he bids those who have come from Lago Seco to extinguish the headlights of the fake security van.

Obediently, El Topo turns off the headlights of the apparently armored vehicle and the shadows of the men standing by the railings become multiple and shifting in the rhythmic flicker of the flames: 'Why have you come here at this hour? … Why come without calling beforehand?' As the first brother speaks and the second backs him up: 'Don't you know we've got rules here?' One of the dogs wins the carnal battle, the bitch in heat whines, while the vanquished dogs snap at the victor.

'Told you that idiot would forget to call,' El Tampón says, turning his attention from the pack of hounds to the former municipal garbage truck: 'I knew he'd forget!' But El Topo cannot hear these words and his mind warps them into something different: it is because he thinks, because he believes that El Tampón needs him to get out of the truck and back him up, that he opens the door and impulsively jumps down. Instantly he hears the blaring horn of a vehicle that all but knocks him down as the tires skid to a halt.

The shriek of rubber on asphalt elicits a laugh from the brothers who manage El Infierno and startles the hounds. The dogs — who all carry the same defective gene: each has one blue eye and one brown — scatter, hiding behind the drums and the skeletal frames of cars, while the dog whose penis is still stuck in the bitch scrabbles frantically, dragging the bitch behind him, her muzzle scraping the dirt of El Infierno.

'Get back in the cab, you fucking idiot!' El Tampón bellows, turning back and taking several steps towards El Topo. 'Why the hell did you get out? Didn't you hear me tell you don't get out?' Hearing their commander shouting, the six soldiers caged in the back of the truck panic and, glancing at each other, wonder: What the bloody hell is happening out there? For their part, the two elderly men in charge of Tres Hermanos laugh like drains as their anger melts away as El Tampón walks back to the gates: 'Good evening!'

'What the devil are you doing here?'

'...'

'Well, answer, boy, or didn't you hear my brother's question?'

'He was supposed to talk to you ... Sepelio ... but I think maybe ...'

'Always the same story,' says the white-haired triplet, shooting his brother a look.

'He told me he was going to call you ... that either he or Father

Nicho would talk to you,' El Tampón says, leaning against the railings.

'No one called us,' says the brother who dyes not only his hair but his beard and his moustache.

'Why don't they ever come up with another excuse?'

'They were supposed … They were supposed to ask you to let us through to the sierra … that they would take care of the cargo later.'

'Nobody phoned here, nobody,' repeats the white-haired triplet, leaning against the gates.

'Not Sepelio, not the priest,' agrees the other, taking his brother's hand in his own and whispering, 'Calm down, you'll do yourself a mischief.'

'…'

'You really have shit for brains if you think you can use our right of way.'

'Get back in your truck and get gone!'

'We can't … I'm sorry but I can't do that,' El Tampón says, then adds, 'They were also going to say that they'll pay more than last time … I swear, Sepelio was going to tell you.'

'Why should we believe you? … Sepelio has never even mentioned you,' Encanecido says, leaning against the railing next to his brother.

'Nor has Father Nicho,' Teñido adds. 'Why should we take your word that you're working with them?'

'We can phone them if you like,' El Tampón suggests, all the while thinking: Shit … I just hope they answer.

'No sense you calling them now … it's too la—'

'Hello ... Sepelio?'

'What the hell are you thinking calling me?'

'Just listen for a minute.'

'How can I get it through your thick skull?' Sepelio says. 'Don't call me when I'm with Epitafio. I've told you a thousand times. I'm the one who makes the calls, not you.'

'I'm at El Infierno,' El Tampón splutters. 'I just got here, but nobody's called them.'

'*Puta madre!* ... El Infierno.'

'Exactly ... and we've begged and pleaded, but they're saying that we can't go through!'

'Those old bastards and their manias.'

'That we can't pass through and that they won't accept the cargo later.'

'Let me talk to them,' Sepelio says, then quickly adds, 'and don't call me again ... The only reason I answered is that Epitafio is on the toilet ... I decide when we talk.'

'Agreed, right, I'll pass you over,' El Tampón says, taking the phone from his ear and handing it through the railings.

'Hello?'

'Sepelio?' says the white-haired triplet.

'Indeed.'

'What the hell is going on?' Encanecido asks, huddling next to the phone that has been handed to Teñido.

'I'm sorry ... I should have called you earlier,' Sepelio says. 'We need ... I need you to let them ... to let these morons ... use your road ... and to accept a cargo on their way back.'

'Well ... only because it's for you and Father Nicho,' Encanecido concedes.

'Is it true you're bringing back a shipment?' Teñido asks, leaning close to the phone.

'That's right ... from the sierra,' Sepelio says. 'And we'll be paying you a lot more than usual.'

'We'll see when it happens,' Encanecido interrupts.

'I swear ... It's the least we owe you.'

'Should I hand you back to the moron here?' Encanecido asks, looking El Tampón up and down.

'Just tell him not to call me again ... Tell him if I want to talk to ...'

Sepelio's words dissolve on his tongue as he hears the line go dead at the other end. Fucking retards ... always want you to call and when you do they're too busy to talk to you, he thinks, then pockets his phone and looks up into the darkness at the night that has entombed this place where he is standing.

Having allowed his eyes to wander the firmament for a moment, Sepelio's gaze slips down to the tallest treetops, along the leafy branches, then down to the place where trunks split into branches, and in the background, the aerial on the roof of Epitafio's house. He studies the cables, the tiled roof, the badly painted walls, the windows and the door.

Getting off the swing on which he has been sitting, Sepelio broods: He said he was only going to be a minute and we've been waiting here for fucking ever. Moving quickly across the unkempt grass of Epitafio's lawn, Sepelio reaches the path leading to the toilet where HewhosolovesEstela is still holed up, then, turning around, he orders Mausoleo: 'Go back and get in the trailer ... Maybe that will hurry him along!' and at the same time he is thinking, Motherfucker ... everything is always done his way.

Surprised that Sepelio is addressing him, Mausoleo digs his heels into the ground to stop the swing that, with great effort, he managed to sit himself on and jumps to his feet. Why has he started talking to me now? the giant wonders, crossing Epitafio's garden, and, as he does so, he realizes that it is something else that is troubling him: Why has he been talking to these people on the telephone while I'm sitting next to him?

Why does he not care that I was right beside him? ... Did he want me to overhear? Mausoleo worries, a few meters from the Minos, but, rather than come up with an answer, he stops in his tracks and turns to face his doubts: He probably thinks I don't understand what's going on ... Maybe he thinks it doesn't matter that I overheard? Clenching his fists and chewing on his rage, the giant turns back towards the garden, but there is no longer anyone there: Sepelio is about to reach the toilet in which Epitafio has locked himself.

VII

Trapped in their cages, six dogs and a pair of parrots start as Sepelio rushes to the door of the outhouse on this patch of land that is home to Epitafio, the wife Father Nicho imposed on him and the son she gave birth to at El Paraíso, and roars: 'What the hell are you still doing in there …? You said, "I'm just going for a quick piss then we'll get back on the road!"'

'We'll go when I say we go … Stop busting my balls,' Epitafio says and, like lightning flashes from the heavens, his words blast from this shack that only recently was a simple pit latrine. 'Who the fuck do you think you are to be telling me to hurry up?' HewhosolovesEstela says, and Sepelio's face flushes with rage and the parrots anxiously ruffle their feathers.

'Who do I think I am? … You bastard … Who do I think I am?' Sepelio mutters and is about to explode when Epitafio roars: 'You're nobody and you've got nothing to say! You're nobody. Nobody!' Epitafio repeats, paying no attention to his words, since his whole body, his whole mind, is focused on the telephone he is holding: Estela called him a little while ago, but he was not able to answer.

He had been in the house, explaining to Osaria — the woman whom Father Nicho abused so often — that he had just stopped by to drop off a few crates, when his phone vibrated. Epitafio had felt a whirlwind of anger whip through him: he knew that the call could only be Estela. At least you made it past La Cañada, he thought, patting his pocket, his eyes still fixed on Osaria, hating her a little more than usual.

Though the phone did not vibrate again, the simple fact of having to remain calm left Epitafio's nerves on edge and, quickly finishing what he was doing, he put Osaria's son to bed, said goodbye to this woman he has never learned to love and went out into the garden, where Sepelio and Mausoleo were waiting: 'I'm just going to the toilet, then we'll set off.' In the toilet Epitafio took out the telephone he is now holding in his hands and confirmed what he already knew: the call earlier had been from Estela, who had stopped on her way down the mountain.

Now you're really going to be pissed off, had been Epitafio's first thought when he had seen Estela's number on the screen of the little phone in his hand: You're going to think that I don't want to call you, that that will just make you angrier, HewhosolovesEstela muttered soundlessly and decided that now was the time for him to call her. But just then he had heard footsteps approaching the outhouse and Sepelio's voice asking: 'Why haven't we set off? … You said, "I'm just going for a quick piss then we'll get back on the road!"'

'Who the fuck do you think you are to be telling me to hurry up?' Epitafio had shouted furiously, his fingers fumbling over the keypad. 'Who do you think you are, Sepelio … you dumb son of a bitch?' HewhosolovesEstela had insisted, leaning closer to the door of the toilet that only recently had been a pit latrine and slipping his phone back into his pocket. But before he can turn the door handle and storm out to confront Sepelio, Epitafio stops, remembering that he needs to talk to Estela, so instead of opening the door, he orders: 'Go back to the trailer right now! ... Stop annoying me ... We'll leave when I say so!'

'*When I say so!*' echoes one of the caged parrots, and Sepelio, who has turned on his heel and is walking towards the trailer, thinking: Fucking bastard ... I won't have to answer to you for much longer, then turns his anger on the bird and roars: 'Who the fuck asked you?' 'What do you mean who the fuck asked me? ... You asked me!' Epitafio bellows as he takes out his phone again and sits on the toilet, only to embroil Sepelio in the misunderstanding.

'I wasn't talking to you!' Sepelio says by way of explanation, only to be interrupted by Epitafio roaring: 'Get back in the Minos and stop busting my fucking balls ... dumb fucking shit!' '*Fucking shit!*' echoes the parrot and Sepelio stalks over and glares into the wooden cage, his pride wounded not so much by the parrot's words, but by the loud belly laugh from Epitafio in the toilet, who has heard everything.

I'm not going to be insulted by a parrot. Sepelio slides open the cage door, thrusts both hands inside and, without thinking, he says menacingly: 'Who do you think you are, talking to me like that?' 'Who the fuck do you think I am, talking to you like that?' Epitafio shouts, laughing heartily at what is happening outside, but then Estela's face floats back into his mind and he picks up the thread of his thought: 'I'll be out in a minute, and you'd better be in that bloody trailer!' HewhosolovesEstela warns, closing his eyes.

'You and Mausoleo better both be ready!' HewhosolovesEstela says again, conjuring on the dark screen of his closed eyelids the image of the woman he so loves: 'And you'd better answer me!' But Sepelio does not hear Epitafio's threat: he is already crossing the garden, the parrot fluttering wildly in his hands. Meanwhile, inside the house, Osaria — the woman to whom, like so many others, Father Nicho became a father — is turning on the television that it might provide a constant noise.

As though she does not want to listen to anything else today, Osaria turns the volume up as far as she can and the jostling, over-lapping voices fill the darkness, joining the chorus of whispers from Epitafio, Sepelio and Mausoleo, each in their several places. For their part, the nameless *who have long since exhausted their tears and spurred by the thought that there-is-nothing-left-to-lose have begun to recount their pasts* fall silent for a moment and do not speak again until they realize that the voices they hear now are coming from a television.

> *'It makes me furious that you're just waiting to leave' ... This is what my father said to me ... 'You should stay here in your own country ... with those close to you, the living and the dead ... There is nothing waiting for you out there ... See how many people come back humiliated ... How many never return and never get there' ... But I did not listen to him ... and now here I am.*

Protected from the others by the noise of the television, the three men who arrived here half an hour ago plunge deeper and deeper into what each is doing: Epitafio is exercising his thumbs and, hoping that Estela will not be furious, is wondering how to greet her; Sepelio is placing the parrot on the swing where he sat earlier as it screeches '*Hijo de puta!*', and Mausoleo is sitting in the cab of the Minos feeling sorry for himself: lifting his head, he looks out into the garden and sees Sepelio as he picks up a rock: What the hell is he doing? 'Fucking parrot,' Sepelio yells, swinging the rock higher and brutally bringing it down, crushing the parrot like an origami bird: 'Who the fuck do you think you're talking to?

'No parrot is going to insult me,' Sepelio roars, raising the bloody rock and, clubbing the bloody mass of bones and feathers, adds: 'Pretty soon now, no one will get to insult me!' Sepelio's words drift across the space to reach the giant's ears, but they do not reach the ears of Epitafio, still locked in the toilet, scrabbling to dial Estela's number.

Epitafio's heart stops and his whole being sinks into the chasm of silence which immediately opens up next to his left ear: I just hope you answer me … that you're not angry. The words passing through the mind of HewhosolovesEstela as he listens to the ill-omened buzz of the engaged tone lose all meaning when a voice at the other end of the line announces: *The number you have dialed is currently switched off or is out of signal range.*

Disappointed, Epitafio gets to his feet and is about to hurl his phone onto the floor, but at the last moment changes his mind: but the telephone slips from his fingers and falls into the cistern, whose lid has been broken since the day the toilet was installed. 'Shit! Shit! Shit!' HewhosolovesEstela roars, searching for something on which to unleash his impotent rage, and finding a target in the noise from the television Osaria is watching.

'Stupid bitch … You know how much I hate that thing, but you can't even wait until I've left,' Epitafio shouts, throwing open the door to the outhouse. 'And it's your fault that I couldn't answer my phone before!' Unaware that the rage now propelling him towards the house is the result of many years and not the setback life has just visited on him, Epitafio races along the path towards the garden from where Sepelio is watching him, still holding the bloody remnants of the parrot: Where the hell is the moron going now?

Mausoleo is paying no attention to watching Epitafio. Sitting in the cab of the Minos, he is sobbing over the dead bird, not knowing why he is crying: Bastard fucking Sepelio! The giant fiercely wipes his eyes and, with great effort, manages to compose himself and, looking up, his gaze drifts out the window: he cannot understand why the contempt he suddenly feels has not already spattered Epitafio or Sepelio, the man who has just taken the path back towards the outhouse.

Opening the cage, Sepelio place the carcass of the bird inside and returns to the garden, even as, in his mind, two phrases flutter, collide and intertwine: A bird in the hand is worth a bushel of learning. Now back in the garden, Sepelio watches as Epitafio goes back into his house and calls to him: 'Are we going or what? How much more time are we going to waste hanging around here?'

What the hell is he doing going back in there? Sepelio thinks; then, walking towards the threshold Epitafio has just crossed, he opens and closes his hands. When he reaches the door, however, Sepelio stops: it is not that he does not want another showdown with HewhosolovesEstela, but that he does not want to have to see Osaria, the woman with whom he shared his life before the orphanage in El Paraíso, the woman he had been unable to protect from Father Nicho and from Epitafio.

Osaria, this woman who gives a start when she notices Epitafio in the darkness of her room, and, startled, says: 'I didn't realize you were still here. Weren't you supposed to leave a while ago?' she asks, getting to her feet as surprise gives way to fear: this husband imposed on her by Father Nicho is furiously coming towards her.

Forcing himself to adopt the mechanical gait he uses when motivated by the anger of the past, Epitafio pushes past Osaria, crosses the room lit by the glow of the television, rips out the cable powering the flickering images, the words, the clapping and the laughter, turns one hundred and eighty degrees and, striding over to his wife, who has gone from fear to sheer terror, breaks her nose with a headbutt.

'Bastard!' Sepelio shouts from the doorway and, although the future and his black fury urge his left foot forward, habit and the past keep his right foot rooted to the spot. 'What the fuck are you doing sticking your nose in?' Epitafio says, turning and moving towards Sepelio, whose left foot, memories and plans for vengeance keep him stock-still, even as his right foot and his desires try to force him to retreat if only a single step: 'I thought I told you to get in the trailer?'

Gazing through the windscreen at Sepelio dancing in the doorway, and seeing Epitafio suddenly appear, Mausoleo attempts to envelop these men with the contempt he feels brimming over, but once again he fails. The giant tries to curse the things these men have done to him only to find his efforts are in vain as he feels his body fill with a strange combination of laughter and tears: What the hell is happening?

Without a thought or a worry for the man watching them from the truck, Epitafio and Sepelio continue their bawling: 'I'm going to count to three and you better pretty soon won't be in seriously if you seriously one of these days different!' Osaria, for her part, gets up from the armchair and shrieks her pain for all the world to hear: a muffled howl that cleaves the space, a howl that Epitafio and Sepelio do not hear, but one that sends a shudder through Mausoleo and the nameless who have crossed the border and who have not yet silenced *their quivering tongues or their dislocated throats.*

> *I lived in my uncle's house … My parents had left … My brothers lived there with me … My cousins and my aunts had left for Oklahoma … I left my hillside and my coffee plants … to take to the roads … I did not say anything to anyone … not even to my wife … I was scared … I didn't know … but now I understand … this is fear.*

Suddenly noticing the murmuring voices, like a drone of insects, of those caged in the back of the Minos, Mausoleo manages to regain control of his body and, withdrawing his attention from the two men still arguing, tries to look at himself in the mirror. It is only now, as he studies his reflection, that the giant finally finds an outlet for the contempt that fills him to overflowing: I am going to get them out of there … I don't care what they do to me afterward.

Still shouting and hurling abuse, Epitafio and Sepelio do not notice the man climb out of the cab and go around the back of the metal container in which the godless hang, their hands bound, who, hearing the creak of the giant as he levers open the heavy doors, once again feel *their voices fettered and their souls crushed.*

The grating of the heavy bolts as Mausoleo lifts them cleaves time and space, but does not reach the ears of Osaria, still weeping in her living room, nor the ears of the two men still arguing in the doorway of the house: 'It's always more thanno seriously I don't want she's not to blamejust go back to the fucking trucknot leaving her think you are telling me what to do?'

Tired of yelling, Epitafio takes the single step separating him from Sepelio and shoves him with such force that he almost knocks him down. Miraculously managing to remain standing, Sepelio feels the urge to lash out, but, determined not to endanger his plans, he manages to control his temper, just as Epitafio realizes what Sepelio has just said: 'Why are you suddenly worried about Osaria? ... When did you start to care about her?'

Unclenching his fists, thinks: You've got a plan, don't go jeopardizing it in a fit of anger ... Think about what you stand to gain if it comes off ... about the pain this fucker will feel, takes a deep breath and tries to calm himself, even as he feels something inside his chest crack: it is the egg from which a bird will soon take flight, then, feeling the ground beneath his feet crumble and slip, he says: 'What the fuck are you talking about? ... I just want us to get the hell out of here!'

'Well then get back to the trailer ... Wait there until I'm done here,' Epitafio orders, then stepping back inside his house, he mutters: 'Why do I have to say everything a hundred times?' Taking a second deep breath, Sepelio fights back his fury and, glimpsing the figure of Osaria sprawled in the shadowy house, he silently vows: I'll make sure this never happens to you again! Then he turns, looks at the truck and, feeling the bird inside his chest emerge from its shell and open its eyes, Sepelio stalks off: he has decided where to vent the rage that only a moment ago he was forced to choke down.

Inside the house, the pain that Osaria has managed to contain as she slumps into the armchair with her head thrown back becomes a scream when, out of the corner of her eye, she sees the looming figure of Epitafio. But before HewhosolovesEstela can say anything, and before Osaria can get to her feet, a silhouette appears out of the gloom and mutters something unintelligible.

'What are you doing out of bed?' Epitafio asks, picking up the little boy and, surprised by the weight, prompts: 'Did the television wake you?' Try as he might, the child cannot say a word. Epitafio hugs him as the shadowy world that envelops him every time he is in this house relaxes and, surrendering to the hug, he takes the child back to his bedroom, whispering words he knows without knowing why: the same words his mother whispered to him every night.

Still holding the child — he weighs a little less every day and his skin bears the marks of Father Nicho's branding iron — Epitafio sees that the window is open and the dark world that envelops him tightens around him again: 'Why do I always have to tell everyone the same things over and over? Stupid bitch … Couldn't you at least remember to close this window?' HewhosolovesEstela mutters as he closes it and pulls the curtain. The last thing he sees before the curtain blocks out the world is Sepelio walking toward the trailer.

Circling the container, Sepelio comes to the rear doors and what he sees there, in the gap that separates his impotence from his rage, leaves him dumbstruck: Mausoleo has managed to open the doors. 'What the fuck are you doing?' Sepelio says and the words numb the soul of the giant who did not hear him approach and does not know how to answer, when, now standing two meters away, Sepelio repeats: 'What were you planning to do with them? ... What are you doing in there?'

Beyond the giant's hulking frame, Sepelio's words rip through the container like a hurricane: 'What the fuck are you thinking, opening this? ... What were you going to do with them?' Each drop of this acid rain is a needle stabbing the ribs, his arms, the bellies, the legs and the faces of the godless who *once again swallow their tongues.*

Sepelio feels a wave of despair as the bird within his chest seems about to come to a standstill, and, just before the giant can emerge from the silence in which he is immured, Sepelio says: 'So you wanted to have a little fun yourself?' Bowing his head and focusing on the space between two crates, Mausoleo once more struggles to speak, but although his lips part and his tongue attempts to give form to the air spewing from his throat, no sound emerges: 'Don't just stand there ... Come over here and help me up!'

Meanwhile, in the house, Epitafio tucks into bed the child he long ago learned to love unconditionally, then he returns to the living room where Osaria is still sobbing, and there, in this prison where his dreams have long since been caged, he asks: 'Why does my son weigh so little? How can you treat a child like this when he is your own flesh and blood?' he says to the trembling Osaria and, catching her unawares, headbutts her full in the face.

Before Osaria has crumpled to the floor, Epitafio has hurled himself on her and, sitting astride her belly, gives free reign to his fury. But then, suddenly, in her bruised and battered features, Epitafio sees the face of Estela and stops: It's your fault I couldn't take her call earlier! It's your fault I couldn't hear her voice and she could not hear mine up in the mountains, HewhosolovesEstela seethes, and, imagining Estela as she drives the Ford Lobo along the mountain road, the self-same road taken by the eight men who crossed El Infierno, he redoubles his blows.

'I couldn't answer her call and she's going to think that what she has to tell me doesn't matter ... that I don't give a shit about her!' Epitafio roars, spitting at Osaria and, lashing out again, finds everything that he is feeling, everything he has been feeling for some time, is now pouring from his mouth and every word is true: 'Because of you she's going to think that I don't care ... that I don't love her ... because of you she's always thought that I don't love her when she is the only person I love ... Hear that? Estela is the only one I love!'

With both hands gripping Osaria's throat and his knees pressed into her breasts, Epitafio stops, looks down at his hands, stares at the wife forced on him by Father Nicho, his eyes filled with disgust, and then rummages through his pockets, searching for the telephone he dropped in the toilet. I'll use a different phone ... I'll keep calling her until she picks up, until she says what she has to say! HewhosolovesEstela decides, glancing around for the house phone.

You won't even answer the call if you find out I've been in this house today, Epitafio thinks and sets down the telephone he has just found. I need his phone ... I need Sepelio to lend me his phone, HewhosolovesEstela says, hurrying towards the doorway from where, across the unkempt garden, he can just make out the colossal shadow of the container truck as Sepelio clambers inside.

'Pass me that bar,' Sepelio says, nodding to the heavy bolt used to secure the doors, but the giant cannot make his feet obey him. 'That bar over there!' Sepelio repeats, pointing to a metal rod. Convinced that Mausoleo does not know which bar he means, Sepelio explains: 'That one there, next to the doors!' He does not know that what has left the giant petrified is the shame that he will not do what he promised: 'Fucking hell … What's the matter with you? Pass me the bar!'

Embracing humiliation, just as, earlier, in the building that once was a slaughterhouse, he embraced cowardice and disgrace, Mausoleo accepts that he will recue no one and, in accepting the mark of contempt that covered his face a moment earlier, he manages to lift his feet from the floor. Leaning towards the door of the container, the giant picks up the bolt and, walking over, hands it to Sepelio, who says: 'You and I are going to have a little fun … If we have to hang around here, we might as well get our own back.'

Slipping past the stack of crates left by Señor Hoyo, Sepelio reaches the far side of the container, where one half of one half of the timeless creatures hang from the ropes binding their hands. He toys with the iron bar and says: 'Why is everyone so quiet?' Then he pounds the sides of the container, not suspecting that the thunderous din of metal will embolden Mausoleo, just as the laughter of the men clutching their weapons did earlier, in the building that towers over El Teronaque. 'Why don't you say something? Why won't any of you answer me?'

'Don't you realize who's talking to you?' Mausoleo roars and, moving toward the shapeless forms, he shoves them hard, setting them swinging, as he did earlier in the garden that Epitafio is about to cross.

The giant's eyes, like two glass beads, are suddenly filled with self-assurance and excitement as he listens to the *men and women whose fears can no longer be expressed in words* but only in *brief whimpers, deep cries and lamentations like howls of pain.*

Hearing the echo of screams and cries from the doorway of his house — he did not go immediately, but went to leave a gift for his son and say goodbye — Epitafio guesses what is happening in the container and, walking as far as the untended lawn, wonders: Why is it that no one ever does what I tell them to? 'Why can't they do what they are supposed to?' he says aloud and feels the dark enveloping world tighten around him.

'You're supposed to be waiting in the cab!' HewhosolovesEstela bellows, but his voice does not reach the container where Sepelio has just brought down the heavy metal bar on a crate on which is stencilled the word: FRAGILE! 'Fragile,' Sepelio reads and, laughing, he approaches the soulless creatures who have come from other lands and he, too, begins to shove and swing them: 'Maybe you want me to force you to talk?

'Or maybe you'd prefer Mausoleo to break the silence?' Sepelio says. 'For the champion here to force you to talk?' Laughing and shoving the body he has been rocking toward the giant as it struggles and sobs, Sepelio announces: 'Choose your punching bag, show me how hard you can hit!'

Mausoleo hesitates for a moment and locks eyes with Sepelio, who growls: 'Hit them or I'll hit you with the bar!' as he turns back to the crates, pick ups the bolt and swings it against the sides of the container. The booming sound thunders through the shadowy night and rolls across the garden Epitafio is crossing in the opposite direction.

'What the hell are they up to?' HewhosolovesEstela wonders aloud, while silently repeating to himself the words he has been practicing since he left his house: I need you to lend me your phone. 'I need Sepelio to give me his phone,' he says, as his footsteps quicken and a thread of ideas urges him on: I'm going to call you right now … My life is finally going to begin.

I will never set foot in this house again … I don't care what Father Nicho says … I am finished with all that, Epitafio promises as he approaches the container. I'll never be separated from you again … Never again be afraid of the woman I love, HewhosolovesEstela vows, smiling into the light that will come and banish the darkness that has enveloped him, and glancing at the trailer that is now only three or four meters away … 'What the fuck is all that banging? … What the hell are you doing in there?'

Despite their power, and the fact that Epitafio is just outside the doors, his words do not penetrate the container in which Mausoleo is pummeling the nameless, while Sepelio viciously rocks the soulless, sneering: 'What's wrong, don't you like being rocked? … You'd think one of you might say thank you.'

Leaning against the back wall of the container and speaking softly as he watches Mausoleo mercilessly beat the swinging bodies, Sepelio says: 'Have you seen how happy canaries are in their cage? They rock and swing, they even sing … Maybe that's why you don't talk … Maybe you'd prefer to sing … What if we all sing together?'

Sepelio's words crumble as the figure of Epitafio suddenly looms in the door of the container. 'What the hell is going on here? … Who told you you could get in the trailer?' HewhosolovesEstela says, all the while thinking to himself: I'll tell you all these things and you'll see, you won't be angry any more … I've decided to listen to you … I want us to be together!

'What are you two doing in here? You're supposed to be ready and waiting in the cab,' Epitafio says stepping into the container and startling Mausoleo and Sepelio, who assumed their boss would bawl them out for beating the shadowless, not simply for being in the container. 'Get out right now and get these doors closed,' HewhosolovesEstela orders, jumping down again from the Minos, then, turning back to Sepelio and Mausoleo and shouting: 'Put on the bolt and the padlocks.

'We're leaving right now!' Epitafio says after a moment, as he thinks: His phone … That *hijo de puta* has to give me his phone. 'We've already wasted too much time. We need to get moving if we're going to sell them!' HewhosolovesEstela explains, then, glaring at Sepelio, he orders: 'You, give me your phone. I need to call Estela right now.

'What's with that look …? I'm telling you to give me your phone,' Epitafio says again, thinking: You're going to be happier than you've ever been! While Mausoleo is padlocking the container doors, Sepelio feels the black bird inside his chest cower, but, bringing his hand to his pocket, refuses to allow it to fold its wings: before handing Epitafio the mobile, he keys in a number he remembers for Estela: one he knows she has not used in a very long time.

'It's ringing,' Sepelio says, proffering the device to this man who is still his boss, as Epitafio snaps: 'Now get in the cab … I'll be there in a minute.' Seeing Mausoleo and Sepelio obey him, HewhosolovesEstela brings the phone to his ear and, for the first time in many years, he feels his soul dilate and smiles at the image of Estela: this woman who even now is speeding the Ford Lobo through the sierra and speeding her mind with another two lines of coke.

To his disappointment, Epitafio once again hears: *The number you have dialed is currently switched off or is out of signal range.* Shaking his head and feeling the joy drain from him, HewhosolovesEstela waits for the beep and leaves a voicemail: 'I don't care what you wanted to tell me this morning ... It doesn't matter, because I've decided ... I'm done with all this ... I want the two of us to be together ... All I want is to be with you!' Then, not allowing himself to be discouraged by this setback, he adds: 'Call me on Sepelio's phone ... Mine just died,' and he hangs up and heads toward the cab where Sepelio and Mausoleo are waiting.

Before he climbs the steps, before he even opens the door, Epitafio surveys the garden, this house and these swings that he will never have to see again, and as he does so he pictures Estela's smile: he cannot know that the phone on which he has just left a message is not Estela's. Controlling his emotions as best he can, HewhosolovesEstela climbs into the cab: 'We've wasted enough time ... We need to get a move on ... We still have to sell these bastards.'

As the headlights he has just switched on illuminate the space that until now has been his exile, Epitafio revs the engine of the trailer truck, shifts into first gear, turns the steering wheel left and drives away from this place, drives away from his past: the only thing he will miss about this place is the child now fast asleep in bed next to the cap Epitafio left on his pillow.

Picking up speed, Epitafio widens the gap between himself and this place where he has lived and the gap between the present and the past. The sudden burst of speed causes the Minos to judder and jolt, lulling the bodiless creatures and bringing a curious sense of peace to the timeless ones still strung up by their bound hands: the tongueless ones, who, seventeen hours ago, were led into the clearing known as El Ojo de Hierba by the sons of the jungle.

The same two boys who, having bought fried chicken on the plaza in Tonée, are at this moment selling off the contents of the sacks they filled in the clearing at El Tiradero. Objects now being bought by those who have just crossed the wall that bisects the wastelands.

VIII

'How much for the sneakers?'

'Twenty.'

'But they're falling apart.'

'Twenty,' repeats the elder of the two boys, gnawing on a chicken wing.

'The soles have come unstuck,' protests the young man who some hours ago dared to cross the wall that looms in the distance.

'I'll let you have them for fifteen,' says the elder boy, tossing the wing he has been eating on the ground.

'Thirteen,' the young man offers, watching the bone skitter across the flagstones.

'Put them back and stop fucking around,' says the elder boy, pointing at the ground and, seeing the pigeons peck at the wing he has just discarded, he adds: 'But you're not going to get anywhere with the ones you're wearing.'

'OK, then … fourteen, and you tell me how to get where I'm going,' says the young man who has been walking now for several days. 'How to get through the jungle.'

'Fifteen, and we'll talk about the rest later.'

'What do you mean, later?'

'Later is later.'

'I'll take them,' says the young man who still bears a name and, gesturing to the younger boy, says: 'That kid there said I should talk to you, but he didn't say anything about later.'

'That kid there is a *pendejo*,' says the elder boy, nodding toward his lieutenant, who is haggling over the price of a pair of trousers with a father and his child.

'He said eight thousand for the trip.'

'Like I told you, later … and not here!'

'Later where?'

'It's fifty for the trainers and a meeting with us in two hours in the courtyard,' announces the elder brother, nodding toward the church at the far side of the square.

'In the church?' says Hewhostillbearsaname, surprised.

'Exactly,' says the elder boy, pocketing the money and turning away.

'What about my change?'

'I'll give it to you in the churchyard later if I feel like it,' says the elder, walking back to the flowerbed next to which they have laid out their wares.

Slumping onto the flowerbed, the boy who assumes the role of leader watches abstractedly — so many things on the square that vie for his attention — as the younger of the sons of the jungle takes money from the father for the pair of trousers he has just bought his little girl: How am I going to tell him … to explain that we're not going to cross to the other side … that he won't be coming with me this time?

Looking away from the boy who is obliged to obey him, who, having taken money has also turned and is now walking toward the flowerbed, the elder boy allows his gaze to wander over the square: I'm sure he thinks that this time he's definitely coming with me, he thinks, admiring the balustrades of the kiosk, the streetlights eaten away by rust, a flowering jacaranda, the trunks of several flame trees, the comings and goings of those who call this place Tonée, and those who know it as Oluée, and the fitful roaming of a starving dog.

But before his younger brother can reach him and distract the boy from the bustle on the square, a cart emerges selling ice cream, the father who bought the trousers hurries off, and a pregnant woman approaches their stall, the night on her face darker than it is on the square. Her sudden appearance interrupts the younger of the two boys; meanwhile, the elder takes a deep breath: What story can I come up with so that he does not throw another tantrum?

I could tell him: I miscalculated the time, thinks the elder boy. Getting to his feet and turning to face the woman with whom his younger brother is bargaining, he feels his stomach suddenly spasm: he has seen this darkened face before. Shaking his head, the elder of the two boys clutches his belly, takes another breath, recovers his composure and thinks to himself: I'm being stupid … Where could I possibly have seen her? At that moment, several dogs begin to bark somewhere on the square, and their growls and snarls are followed by the sound of one of them whimpering.

There's no reason for me to know her … She probably looks like someone else, whispers the elder boy, who, having glanced at the dogs, now returns to his post, conducts a rapid inventory of the remaining objects, then stretches himself, yawning, and allows his eyes to roam the square: in the distance he can see the looming wall he has crossed so many times: It doesn't matter what I tell him … he's bound to throw a fit!

I should never have promised I would let him come to the other side today, thinks the elder boy. Then, looking out of the corner of his eye at his younger brother talking to the woman, he clutches his stomach again: Although, maybe if we hurry … maybe if we can sell the rest of this, I can keep my promise. That's what I'll do … We have to work fast, thinks the boy who acts as leader, and, addressing the men and women newly arrived from other lands who are crisscrossing the square, he shouts: Half price … all remaining stock left is half price!

Surprised, the younger boy and the woman with the tenebrous face, who has only just noticed the presence of the elder boy, turn to look at him for a moment. What the hell is going on now? thinks the younger of the two boys, while the pregnant woman is thinking: That evil bastard … Can it really be the same boy? But their thoughts are interrupted by the sound of bells that have begun to toll in the distance.

Turning away, visibly distressed, the woman with the darkened face rushes off and disappears among the men and women who have crossed the border, who, as soon as they heard the elder boy's cry, crowded around the stall. As he stows the money given him by the pregnant woman and dismisses her from his mind, the younger boy reasons: He wants to work fast to make sure we've got enough time.

He wants to work fast so he can take me to the other side, the younger of the two boys thinks and, just as the church bells fall silent, the dogs begin to howl again, a flock of pigeons who have been hiding between the legs of those who have come from other lands takes to the wing, and the other merchants begin to sell off what remains of their stock.

Beneath the soundless sky of Tonée, tinted orange by the street-lights of the town square, pigeons wheel, tracing a wide circle of shadows. After a brief moment gazing up in awe at the circling birds, those selling and those buying hasten to conclude their transactions: so much so that by the time the pigeons come to earth again, the bustling is over. Those present know that the time to leave is approaching, and with it the time to find out how to leave.

As he puts away the money for the last shirt that he sold, the boy who serves as assistant turns to the boy who serves as leader and watches him sell a flashlight they found the other day in El Tiradero. From somewhere on the square comes the barking and growling of the dogs, and this time it is the younger boy who looks around to see if he can see them, but all he can see are the merchants hurrying to pack away their stalls.

For his part, having sold the flashlight and put the money in a safe place, the elder of the two boys watches a pigeon hurriedly limping after a female, and not knowing why he is doing it, or knowing that the younger boy is watching him again, he clicks his tongue, looks up, sees the other hawkers packing up and thinks of the woman with the darkened face: Could it have been her? … Could it really have been her?

In the meantime, the pregnant woman, now two blocks from the square, stops for an instant and, in that instant, without a second thought, she abandons all the plans that she had made. She pictures the face of the elder of the two boys, chokes back what little courage is left within her body, mentally draws up a new plan and, to the wailing of a pair of sirens, persuades herself that this is what she always intended.

Still mentally redrawing her plans, the pregnant woman starts walking again and, bumping into an old man who has just stepped on to the pavement, apologizes and disappears into the tide of people streaming away from the square. And this old man, who is still staring after the woman who bumped into him as he sees the two patrol cars arriving, will be the last to buy something on the square.

Two minutes earlier, the old man who is now pressed against the wall of a pharmacy watching the two patrol cars pass, bought the threadbare shirt now thrown over his shoulder from the younger of the two boys. And it was also two minutes ago, after taking the money for the shirt now disappearing through the crowd on the shoulder of the old man, that the younger boy began to feel the same disappointment he has felt so many times before: Why am I getting my hopes up? … He's bound to make some excuse again and say we don't have time.

Today will be just like every other day … I won't get to go to the other side, thinks the younger boy and, shaking his head, he stares at the empty square before him, where there remain a handful of dogs, several hundred pigeons, one or two lost migrants and increasing numbers of police officers. Returning his attention to the boy who serves as leader, who is gathering up the sacks and blankets, the boy who serves as his lieutenant walks over to him and says: 'Go on, then … say it! We don't have time to go today!'

'I swear, I really wanted to take you today,' the leader says, looking into the eyes of the boy who must obey him: this time, however, the elder boy cannot hold the younger's stare and looks down. Then, turning his head, the elder of the boys scans the square again and sees that there are only policemen left on the cobbled plaza.

Clicking his tongue, the leader swallows his embarrassment and, since all he wants now is to be on his way, swears: 'I promise I'll take you next time ... We'll stay the night, and you'll see, we'll go across together.' Then, before the younger boy can utter a word, he nods to two policemen, picks up his bundle and sets off down the street: officers are still streaming into the square.

You really think I believe you? says the young boy, setting off after him, while the elder boy ignores him and watches as the police manifest their presence. This is the first time that they have been the last to leave the square, where heavy metal shutters are now coming down in a roar of engines as vans pull away.

'Next time, I swear ... We'll stay overnight and go across together ... Besides, we have to take your medal over there,' the elder boy says. 'We told Epitafio we'd see him on Wednesday ... so we'll have plenty of time to stay longer.' As he crosses a second junction, the elder boy catches sight of the clock on the Tonée government building and says: 'See, I wasn't lying ... Look how late it is ... We can't rest here for very long.'

'I don't care what you say ... I don't believe a word,' the younger of the boys grumbles, stopping on the same street corner. 'Besides, how are you going to explain to them that we're coming back the day after tomorrow ... and that we're planning to spend the night?' 'I don't have to fucking explain myself to anyone ... You're really starting to piss me off now ... Just drop the subject,' the older boy sneers, glaring over his shoulder, his attitude suddenly changed.

Then, looking up at the church towers, the elder boy speaks in his usual tone. 'We'd be better off worrying about what we have to do now … I told people to meet us in the courtyard in two hours … and there are a shitload of them … How many asked you?' 'I talked to a fuckload,' the younger boy says to the boy who serves as leader, following him into the narrow alleyway where they usually rest.

'What do you mean by a fuckload?' the elder boys asks, slumping onto the ground and thinking to himself: Why am I bothering to ask? … How would he even know what a fuckload means? Then, unaware of how or why the thought has popped back into his mind, the boy who serves as leader adds: 'You didn't say anything to that bitch, did you … the pregnant one?' 'I knew you recognized her too … She took one look at you and took off running!' says the boy who serves as lieutenant, then suddenly loses his train of thought: a shadow has stepped into the narrow alley where they are resting.

'What the hell are you talking about? … How would I know her?' The elder boys sounds indignant, but he, too, loses the thread. Moving quickly, the figure that appeared in the alley where they hide the threadbare blankets from their stall is bearing down on their bolt-hole, causing the boys' tongues to shrivel and their bodies to stiffen.

Staring at the shifting shadow, both boys draw their knives and tense their every muscle, then exchange a look that is both question and answer. Just as the elder boy is about to leap out, brandishing the blade, the shadow stops and says: 'This fell out of one of the pockets … I thought you might need it …' And they do need it.

Recognising the voice that has just spoken, the younger boy lights up the face with the flashlight in his other hand, then gets to his feet, pushes his brother out of the way, stretches his hand out and, grabbing the identity card proffered by this man who does not know that he has narrowly escaped being murdered, turns his face to the elder boy and says: 'He bought something from us on the square.'

'It was in one of the pockets … I found it in these,' the man who almost lost his life here says, shaking the pair of trousers he bought from the two boys.

'You scared the shit out of us,' the younger boys says, studying the little card he is holding.

'I came back to the square as soon as I found it, but you were gone …' explains the father who has left his young daughter standing on the corner.

'Going round scaring people is not a good idea.'

'I didn't mean to scare you,' says Hewhostillboastsasoul. 'I spotted the two of you walking and I followed you here.'

'Following people isn't a good idea either,' the younger boys says, raking the shadows with the beam of his flashlight. 'Where did you leave the girl?'

'She's waiting for me on the corner,' the man says and, babbling, adds, 'I just thought you might need it … Forget I was ever here and I'll see you in the churchyard in two hours.'

'And it's not a good idea to split you … You shouldn't leave your daughter alone even for a second,' the elder boy advises, interrupting Hewhostillboastsasoul, 'in a second, anything could happen.'

'I'm really sorry … I hope you'll forgive me,' Hewhostillboastsasoul says, turning and running back to the street corner.

'I hope she's still there!' the younger boy laughs and turns to the elder, who is still studying the little identity card. 'What do you think?'

'Ugly little bitch,' the elder boy says, sitting back on the ground.

'How do you know it's a girl?' the younger boy asks, sliding down onto the ground and, shuffling towards his brother, glances at the card.

'For fuck's sake … She's the moron who was with the old man,' the elder boy says, leaning his head back against the wall.

'What old man?'

'The old guy who said he could tell our fortunes,' the elder boy says, closing his eyes. 'I'm tired.'

'Are you sure?' the younger boy allows his body to relax.

'How can you not remember that stupid bitch?'

'I remember the old guy.'

'He was a bastard,' the elder says, dropping the identity card and closing his eyes again. 'I'm going to sleep.'

'A poor fool.'

'…'

'But I didn't see the ball,' the younger boy says as exhaustion overcomes him, making the words unintelligible.

'What the … who … what ball?' the elder mutters, his head nodding.

'The old guy …' the younger murmurs, his neck sagging.

'The old … woman … that bitch!'

Just before the two of them nod off, the elder of the two boys opens his eyes for a second and, amid the shadows between the beam of the flashlight the younger boy left on, he sees, or thinks he sees, the face of the woman from the square, the woman who filled his belly with fear.

'Fucking witch … didn't give me … You didn't say,' the elder boy tries to say, struggling to keep his eyelids open. 'You did … you did tell her … the churchyard.'

Though the older boy manages to keep his eyes open a second longer, he cannot get a word out of his brother, who is already dreaming, jumbling the events of the day and the phantoms of the night: in the depths of a ravine that opens in a crimson desert, over the waves of a raging purple river, the old man they were talking about is dancing and telling fortunes.

The old man who is imprisoned in the back of the blood-red pickup trailing the pale-blue truck as both follow the Ford Lobo through the mountain passes of the sierra, and is now talking to the oldest woman among the soulless who have come from other lands.

> Give me your other hand … The right hand is no good …
> It doesn't matter that it's burnt … It only seems burnt to
> your eyes … Fate cannot be burned … Promises cannot be
> burned … I swear to you they cannot be incinerated or lost.

In the midst of his speech, the oldest of those who have come from other lands, like all the others, loses his balance and falls to the floor: the slope that the blood-red and pale-blue trucks and Estela's Ford Lobo are now descending is the steepest in the sierra, a sheer drop that the men and women living in the rare shacks hereabouts call *La Caída* — The Fall.

Recovering his balance and once again surrounded by a circle of listeners, the oldest of all the nameless takes the left hand of the godless creature in front of him, who now leans her shoulder against the chest of other men as the truck continues to judder down La Caída. La Caída, the vertiginous slope the driver and co-driver of the fake security van can now see in the distance.

'Look, there, in the distance, La Caída,' El Tampón says, leaning forwards. 'I don't suppose you can see it, but take my word for it I can see it … So put your foot down, that's where we're going to ambush Estela.'

Estela, the woman who is still weaving through the byways of her past even as she weaves through the sierra, leading the convoy in which the oldest of all the nameless caresses a charred palm, before bending to lick the glassy skin.

> To me, the burn is nothing but smoke … and like smoke …
> melts away to reveal what it hides … Melt away and let this
> taste show me what is to come … That's it … That's right
> … I can see what lies ahead … You will return whence you
> have come … You will be happy once more!

In the back of the blood-red pickup, these words, like those of a shaman, fall to the ground as the old man stumbles and falls again, echoing between the bodies of those who have lost their balance and rolling around unheard: the driver has just slammed on the brakes, having seen Estela's Ford Lobo come to a sudden halt; Estela, who a moment earlier heard her phone beep and played the message Epitafio left for her some time ago.

IX

As she listens again to the voicemail that Epitafio left her before setting off from El Teronaque: 'Fucking mountains ... just my fucking luck ... *puta madre!*', Estela brakes sharply, throws open the door of the trailer truck and gets down, feeling more nervous than ever: she must be able to get a signal in this part of the fucking sierra.

If I got his message, he will probably have got mine, ShewhoadoresEpitafio thinks as she strides off, emerging from the past in which she was wandering, lost, and deciding not to carry on driving: We're not leaving here until I've answered you.

I don't want you thinking I don't want to call, Estela thinks, hurrying through the thick clouds of dust produced when the convoy screeched to a halt: she does not know, cannot imagine, that the message she has just heard was recorded by Epitafio hours ago.

'Don't get out ...! We'll carry on to La Carpa as soon as I'm done here!' ShewhoadoresEpitafio shouts from the dust storm that, in the headlights of the battered trucks, looks almost like a living creature. 'And don't turn off your engines!' Estela calls, forcing her legs to move faster as she silently repeats: It has to be possible to get a signal around here somewhere.

But the drivers had already cut the engines of the two battered pickup trucks by the time their boss shouted to them, and so the convoy is shrouded by a dense, deep silence. 'Why did you turn off the engines? Didn't you hear what I said?' Estela roars as she scrabbles away, but the men she is leading can no longer hear her: she is now so far away they can barely make her out in the shadowy darkness.

I guess it's my turn to call you … You've already given up … I knew it … I knew you wouldn't stick it out! ShewhoadoresEpitafio with a smile and a flicker of exasperation hurries along the path in the light from the phone she is holding: You've got your tail between your legs! Then, turning back into the darkness, Estela yells, more mechanical than serious: 'Even from this distance I can hear that I can't hear those engines!

'Start them up again or I'll show you what's what,' Shewho- adoresEpitafio orders and, acknowledging to herself that she no longer cares whether her men are listening, she turns back towards the sea of shadows that swathes everything: I'm going to call you just to hear you say: I shouldn't have hung up on you … To hear you beg me: Don't be angry.

And then I'll tell you what's going on … Tell you what that fuck- ing priest has been up to, Estela thinks as her feet carry her to the place where La Caída plummets, and away from the location of the men who act upon her orders and, where, in the back of the pale-blue pickup, *the women whose souls know only suffering* once more give voice to their fears, under the guise of wishes.

> *'Perhaps they won't come back,' a woman would say each time*
> *they raped us … 'This surely was the last … I think they will not*
> *come again … Let them leave us lying here … We cannot hear*
> *them … We will leave here alone … searching for someone to*

help us ... Perhaps we are close to some road ...
Who knows, perhaps help is at hand.'

Meanwhile, in the blood-red pickup, the nameless are still gathered in a circle around Merolico and still listening to the promises of the old man, who is currently addressing a man whose palm is crisscrossed by a sea of scars.

You will soon forget this time ... forget the days that were
evil days ... Happiness will bury the sadness of these years ...
Well-being will bury the ill-being that is coming to a close ...
You will find a good job ... You will find the woman you have
longed to meet ... Your dreams will be fulfilled ... and you
will fulfill your promises.

How can you not call me back when you'd hung up on me so rudely? Estela is thinking as she moves deeper and deeper into the ocean of shadows that the sierra winds once again set quivering: How could you not call when I'd told you I have something important to tell you? ... How could you? ... How can I? ... Why am I thinking like this? ... Why do I still think that I've won, just because you called?

What does it matter whether I won or you won? ... Fucking hell ... all that matters is what matters ... That Father-fucking-Nicho has shafted us! Estela thinks, shaking her head and hurrying towards the lip of La Caída: There we were, you and me, worried that he might think we were betraying him! Where Estela is standing, the wind from the mountaintops and the wind rising from La Caída meet and mingle in a shriek of squalls.

'There we were, you and me, still thinking we had to do things secretly so he didn't catch on … so he didn't realize that one day we were going to abandon him,' Estela thinks, talking to herself now in a low voice, because the roaring winds dancing before her eyes have set her head spinning and deafened her: 'So you see, you should have listened to me from the very beginning!

'You should have made up your mind long ago … *Puta mierda*… How many times did I beg you to have done with him … to come with me and disappear without a word!' ShewhoadoresEpitafio shouts, standing two feet from the brink of La Caída, then, shouting at the top of her lungs, she adds: 'But you wouldn't do it, and now he's betrayed you!' The winds from mountain and plain continue melding their twin furies, they are blustering faster just as the fake armored truck deep in the ravine of La Caída is moving faster, and their twin roars give birth to a new howl.

'That bastard has played us!' Estela says, standing on the edge of La Caída, and, looking down at her phone, she discovers she has finally got a signal. Frantically, ShewhoadoresEpitafio dials the number she knows by heart: I'd love to see your face fall when you hear what he did to me … when you hear what happened in La Cañada and realize that he has probably laid a trap for you, too!

But the only face to fall is that of Estela as she hears the same voice Epitafio heard some hours ago: *The number you have dialed is currently switched off or is out of signal range.* After a couple more vain attempts, driven by the same fury Epitafio experienced when he reviled the world in the courtyard of El Teronaque, on the toilet at his house and in the cab of the Minos, Estela screams: 'Fuck! ... I need to warn you right now!'

But her scream is drowned out by the whistling winds and, as she lets herself fall on to the stone slabs that cover the ground, ShewhoadoresEpitafio lets her past fall and crush her: the last trace that the present inflicts on her is the stench of a corpse rotting somewhere nearby. But all too quickly even this stench does not matter: Estela is lying next to Epitafio on the first day she woke up in that bed.

What we had to do to keep it from him! Estela remembers and this is all that she remembers: waking with a start, having to hide, and later creep out through the window. *Hijo de puta!* All the time I had to creep out! ShewhoadoresEpitafio thinks and, closing her eyes and smiling, she pictures herself as a girl in the orphanage of El Paraíso. Then she recalls Epitafio as a boy and her smile fades: I have to tell you what's going on with me ... If I'd told you earlier, it might not even be happening ... We might already have ditched that bastard Father Nicho!

Why didn't I say anything? ... Why have I waited so long? ... 'I can't leave here without telling you what's going on,' Estela says again, and though she does not open her eyes, she grips the phone in her hand more tightly: Why am I afraid to say what I have to say? Why am I so afraid of what you have to say to me ... of what you will do to me ... of what others might do to us ... and just as afraid that you might do nothing ... that no one will do anything? ShewhoadoresEpitafio thinks, allowing her cocaine-addled mind to wander: What if there's nothing going on? ... What if he is not thinking of betraying us ... if we're not in danger?

'What if I'm imagining all this ... if it's just an excuse for not talking to you? ... What if I believe it simply because I'm more afraid of telling you the truth ... afraid that even then you won't want to give up everything?' Estela says, as on her closed eyelids an image forms of Epitafio, who even now is driving the Minos ever faster, picturing the woman he so loves listening to the message he believes he left on her voicemail before setting off from his house: a new life together ... a life that would be theirs alone.

Meanwhile, in La Caída, the winds are buffeting harder, shaking the antennae of Estela's hearing aids as she reluctantly opens her eyes. All this fucking noise! ShewhoadoresEpitafio complains bitterly, and angrily brings her hands to her ears and rips out the two tiny implants. Plunged into a sudden, self-imposed silence, Estela closes her eyes again, and once again diverges from the time and place in which she finds herself: What if there's nothing going on, nothing but my own fears?

Why can't I talk to you about what we're feeling? ... Why the hell am I so scared that even then you won't give it all up? ShewhoadoresEpitafio says over and over in the solid, compacted stillness that enfolds her: all of a sudden there is no world, no time, only the doubts in which Estela cloaks herself; there is no other place, no other moment but those in which she has shut herself and from which she will not emerge until the universe has exploded; then, suddenly, flashes of fire and gunpowder set the darkness blazing.

For Estela, in this moment, the mountains and the men do not exist, nor the soulless creatures, nor La Caída, where she finds herself and up whose steep slope the van that only seems to be an armored truck is moving. The fake security van in which sit the captain and the lieutenant who govern the Madre Buena plateau; these two men who, a moment earlier, picked up the thread of the conversation they abandoned at the gates of El Infierno.

'Where did we leave off?'

'The part about what he did to his son … His son and his son's son.'

'That's right … the grandson of El Gringo,' El Tampón says, nodding. 'Crazy fucking pervert … to do something like that to your own son.'

'What? What did he do for fuck's sake? … Stop beating around the bush.'

'I'm afraid you won't believe it …' El Tampón's head is still, 'although, thinking about it, he didn't actually do it to his son … at least not exactly.'

'What the fuck are you saying?'

'I'm saying the boy was dead … He was dead when he did what he did,' El Tampón says, opening the ice box.

'Pass me one.'

'So he did it to his corpse … but he must have thought about it when the boy was still alive,' El Tampón explains, 'so I suppose he did do it to his son.'

'Where's my beer?'

'This is the last one,' El Tampón says, slamming the lid of the box and returning to the subject, continues: 'People say the idea first occurred to him when the boy was sick … some people are twisted.'

'Just tell me what he did.'

'And they say that he talked about it with a guy who had stuffed and mounted his pets,' El Tampon goes on, rolling down his window. 'Used threats to make him do the work ... forced him to measure his son while he was still sick in bed.'

'Are you serious?'

'He arranged for a clock tower to be built and set in the gardens facing the house ... He had everything ready for the moment when the boy finally died.'

'Did you see that light?' El Topo interrupts, pointing to the upper slopes of La Caída.

'What light?' El Tampón says, leaning forward and staring up. 'I don't see a light ... You're just trying to shut me up ... You don't want me to tell you the rest of the story.'

'Of course I do ... I just thought ... It was probably nothing,' El Topo hesitates and accelerates faster. 'Forget it ... What was this clock you were talking about?'

'By the time his son died, it was finished ... They set it in the garden, the clock tower where he later put the child ... They didn't even allow his mother to sit vigil for him ... They dissected him while his body was still warm and carried him up to the top of the tower.'

'This is bullshit!'

'I'm telling you the truth ... The fucking lunatic put his stuffed and mounted child inside this clock, which tolled only once a day at the hour of his death,' El Tampón says, then trails off, leans forwards and says: 'I saw it ... I just saw something up there.'

'I told you so!' El Tampón snaps, stopping the former municipal garbage truck and, forgetting the story El Topo has been telling, says: 'Better if we continue on foot.'

Illuminating the ground with the beam from his flashlight, El Tampón throws open the rear doors of the former municipal garbage truck and the six soldiers nervously jump down. But before they can start to complain, the man who just opened the doors raises a hand and, turning the beam towards the space before them, barks: 'I don't want any of you opening your mouths ... We don't know when there might be someone nearby!'

'And you, point that flashlight down!' El Topo snaps angrily, and, punching El Tampón in the arm, adds: 'You're the one who's going to get us killed! Let me be very clear ... there are to be no lights shining in that direction,' El Topo jerks his chin towards the headlights of the Ford Lobo and the battered pickups in the distance, so far away they are scarcely bigger than six quivering sparks. Then, looking down, El Topo sets off walking, shielding himself from the wind buffeting the landscape and unsettling the men clutching their weapons and the nameless creatures in the pickups high up in the sierra, but not ShewhoadoresEpitafio, who is still lost in her own mind.

'We're going to take this path, but we won't be using flashlights ... OK? ... I don't want anyone turning on a light,' El Topo says, looking over his shoulder, and urges the soldiers. 'You heard him ... no talking ... no stopping ... and no flashlights,' El Tampón says, glancing up at the sky: the Milky Way is so dense it could be mistaken for the shadow of a cloud.

'No slacking ... I don't want anyone falling behind!' El Topo says, striding ahead and, looking over his shoulder again, sees beyond the six soldiers the first sliver of the moon. 'Get your asses in gear, the moon is rising and those fuckers might see us,' El Topo barks as El Tampón turns his head and, seeing the silvery gleam, backs him up: 'First one to fall behind will feel my boot up his ass!'

Meanwhile, inside the cabs of the pickup trucks, the drivers are also staring at the bright circle rising over the mountain peaks. But though she is sitting facing La Caída, Estela does not notice the bright herald burning in the far-flung reaches of the sky: in this moment, the only horizon that exists for her is the one conjured by her memory, the horizon she is gazing at from the rooftop of El Paraíso as she leans against Epitafio: she is still on her inner journey.

'We said no stopping!' El Topo snarls after a while and, turning to his men, is about to hustle them along when El Tampón interrupts: 'We don't know how long they're going to be there.' 'And if they drive off, you're the ones who'll pay!' El Topo adds, cheering his men and watching as the rising moon floods the plain with light. This same moon that, to Epitafio, Mausoleo and Sepelio as they drive along, is barely a faint glow and, far off in Tonée, where the boys of the jungle are in the churchyard, haggling, cannot be seen for the approaching storm.

Thirty or forty meters farther on, as the eight men who come from Lago Seco scale a rocky outcrop, an unexpected sound brings them to a shuddering halt: somewhere in La Caída, one of the walls patiently fashioned by millennia cracks, causing the thunderous rockslide. The echoing rumble of the rocks, now dislodging other stones, also reaches the convoy, alarming the men clutching their weapons, the soulless ones whose bodies have recently recovered the will to live and the nameless one who are still listening to Merolico.

> *'They've finally left us in peace …' the woman said over and over … 'They won't come for us again … Perhaps we have made it …,' the old woman said again and again … then she said: 'Free, though some of us were raped … Free to take to the road again … to move forward.'*

Love and passion lie ahead for you … A tall, blonde man is waiting … Tall and strong, his hair fair as gold … Your lifeline extends for many, many years … A long life awaits you … rich and filled with happiness … Your palm cannot lie to me … You will come through this safe and sound.

For her part, despite the intensity with which the echo of the rockslide rolls through the mountains, Estela does not hear the discordant concert or feel the tremor that accompanies it: the wall she has built between herself and the planet is impregnable, ever since she removed her hearing aids she is holding in her hand. Right now, ShewhoadoresEpitafio can hear only the voice of the man scrabbling to his feet on the roof of the orphanage and challenging her: Let's see who can get to the rocks first.

The rocks where Estela and Epitafio so often hid, that vast fossil hand within whose bone-white palm she struggled to contain her panting breath the first time she opened her body to him: How the hell am I going to tell you that that bastard knows about us? …

How, now that I am carrying the one you do not want to see born? ShewhoadoresEpitafio wonders, oblivious to the new earthquake just beginning: How can I, when I've heard you say a thousand times that the world doesn't need more babies?

The eight men who left the Madre Buena plateau and who, now, having crept a hundred meters closer to the convoy Estela led to this place, come to a halt as El Topo calls: 'Stop, right now!' Then, when the roar of the second tremor has faded to the faint rumble of rocks disturbing the void, El Topo approaches the lone tree he can find and, beckoning El Tampón, commands the six soldiers: 'Don't move from that spot … We're going on ahead for a bit.'

'We need to cross here,' El Tampón suggests as he reaches the branch on which El Topo is sitting and, pointing to the space, adds: 'Duck through those clefts there … Appear from nowhere, all guns blazing.' 'I agree,' El Topo nods, scanning the vast space that opens up before his eyes, which have long since adjusted to the darkness: 'Unless … unless they've already spotted us and are planning an ambush.'

'You think they're lying in wait for us?' El Tampón says, surveying the ocean of rocks lit by the blue metallic glow of the moon: 'You really think that's possible?' he prompts when he gets no response, and it is at this point that he, too, founders in his fears, the same fears that held El Topo's tongue a moment earlier, but not those that have silenced Estela for some time now. Estela, this woman who, still buried in her memories, is stepping into the basement of El Paraíso and once again burning Epitafio's skin with Father Nicho's branding iron: I hope you will forgive me … that you will tell me what you did that day. Nothing you can say now will make me love you less.

Above the spot where Estela is sitting, a muster of storks crosses the sky in a noisy display of bill-clattering, and are disappointed not to have caught the attention of ShewhoadoresEpitafio. And so, seeking others to impress, the flock comes to the place where those who came from Lago Seco are stationed, where their clatter attracts the attention of the eight men; looking up, El Topo breaks his silence and says: 'We might think that they haven't seen us, but we're not going to go through the clefts in the rocks … just in case they did see us … because if they did see us they'll be waiting.

'We'll have to skirt the cleft and go up that way,' El Topo adds a moment later, only to for El Tampón to interrupt: 'Come from behind and take them by surprise … They won't know what's hit them.' 'Exactly, attack them from behind,' El Topo agrees and, as he hops down from the branch on which he was sitting and comes back to earth, he gazes at the storks as they disappear forever into the distance.

When El Topo and El Tampón have explained their plan to the six soldiers under their command, the eight men who left the Madre Buena plateau set off at a run between the rocks frozen by the moonlight. I hope those fuckers don't hear, plead the six soldiers as their hearts beat faster in their chests and their palms are desiccated by fear, while El Topo continues to consider the plan devised back at the tree and El Tampón, in the back of his mind, begins to have misgivings about the plan.

Why do we always have to do things his way? El Tampón thinks as he runs after El Topo, who is also having doubts: Maybe I should have divided these bastards into units. The same bastards who are still silently pleading: I hope they don't hear anything. The six soldiers cannot imagine that, in the convoy where their paths converge, sleep has vanquished, one by one, the men loyal to Estela. The woman who only a moment ago left the basement in which she found herself.

In Epitafio's room, Estela tends to the blisters that will become a triangle of dots on this man she adores and hears again the words he said to her that day: You could never do anything that would make me stop loving you … nothing that happens can ever break us apart. Why have I still not told you? Estela wonders, feeling her heart beat faster in her chest. What does it matter how I say it? Nothing can separate us … You said it to me, and you meant it … and maybe everything will work out … Maybe this will convince you to finally give it up, ShewhoadoresEpitafio thinks and, turning, leaves the bedroom and, quickening her pace, heads towards the stairwell of El Paraíso.

Quickening their pace is also what is preoccupying the eight men who left Madre Buena plateau: 'We need to jump across the clefts,' El Topo explains, pointing into the distance, 'then take that path and see where it leads' … But before his words have trailed off, El Tampón interrupts him again: 'I'm not sure it's a good idea to go the long way round … Maybe it would be better just to go as far as the river, like we planned.'

'Shut you mouth and stop making everyone nervous … Have you seen the state of these guys?' El Topo hisses angrily and, turning towards El Tampón, adds: 'You and I agreed on a plan, this is not the time to have doubts … You'd better to hurry it up or we'll leave you behind.' Swallowing his rage, El Tampón forces his legs to move faster as he thinks: I don't like the way you get to do all the talking … that you never listen to what I have to say.

As the eight hotheads leave behind the rocks, leaping across the fissures, they come to a region where the earth is alive — brushwood grows like veins between the stones, cacti swell like blisters or rise like spectral presences. 'If everyone is ready,' El Topo says, 'the river should be just down there!'

Increasingly wary, the eight men hired by Sepelio and Father Nicho skirt a thicket of acacia bushes and arrive at the river, which is barely a hundred meters from the convoy that has followed Estela to La Caída, and climb down into the dry riverbed. Just then, as the boots of those who have come from Lago Seco wake clouds of the sleeping dust, the wind from the sierra begins to whip up again. El Tampón and El Topo advance, shielding their eyes with their forearms.

For their part, neither the nameless, nor the men loyal to Estela, nor those who left El Paraíso a moment earlier, notice that the wind is once again raging. Leaving behind her past, Estela is now lost in her future: You'll finally have the courage to give all this up … We'll go to La Carpa … We'll live far away from these things, these people.

All I have to do is call you and tell you that I'm pregnant, Estela thinks, standing on the threshold of the house that they will one day build, where she will live with Epitafio: but before she can leave behind this future and call the man she so loves, she finds herself beguiled by hope, which grabs her arm, just as El Topo is grabbing El Tampón's arm at that same moment, and draws her deeper into herself and leaves her wandering through the rooms of this make-believe house.

Shaking his arm brusquely to free his elbow from the grip of El Tampón, who a moment ago said, 'Stop, hold on a minute!' El Topo stops in his tracks: 'What the fuck are you doing? Just as we're … huh … huh … nearly there' … 'It might be best … huh … huh … if we split up … If some of them go with you … huh … and the rest follow me … We need a pincer movement,' El Tampón pants, turning to face the soldiers.

As he, too, struggles to catch his breath, El Topo stares at El Tampón and says menacingly: 'Who do you think you are, giving orders? … huh … I decide how this is played out … huh … Yeah, obviously we're going to do that, but that's not all … just over there, where those things are sticking out of the ground, we'll split up into two units.' 'Where what things are sticking out of the ground?' El Tampón interjects, looking at the convoy which is now barely sixty meters away. 'What the fuck are you talking about?' But he, in turn, is cut short by El Topo, who has already walked off, ordering the men to follow him.

Before El Tampón can protest, the soldiers are gone, he can see only their backs, caught up in a frantic race. A frantic race like the one Estela pictures in her future: Epitafio and their children are running around the courtyard next to their house in La Carpa. Whoever comes first gets to name the new puppy, Epitafio announces in Estela's reverie, just as El Topo announces: 'We need to leave the riverbed and zigzag through these things.'

Pushing past the brushwood, the cacti and the acacias in his path, El Tampón catches up with El Topo: 'Who d'you think huh … huh … d'you think you are … huh … huh … telling me what … huh … huh … what to do? huh … huh … Who said … huh … huh … who said you were the boss?' Smiling into the darkness, now

thirty meters from the convoy, El Topo turns and says: 'OK then …
huh … huh … if that's how you want it … huh … huh … What do
we do now?'

Resting his hands on his thighs and panting, El Tampón explains:
'We split up here … huh … and then we split up again … huh … You
take those three and you split up again … huh … over there by those
huge cacti … I'll take these three and we'll split up, too.'

But before the group splits up and sets off again at a run, El
Tampón whispers to El Topo: 'Throw a pebble at me when you're
ready!' Then, just as the two groups go their separate ways, heading
towards the convoy that brought Estela to this place, the sierra once
again unleashes all its power: the wind howls, stirring up a whirlwind
of dust and gravel.

Shielding themselves against the hail of sand and stones, the soldiers from Lago Seco hunch their bodies, as their leaders wave their
arms in a last, silent order: Face down on the ground, we crawl the rest
of the way! But, having crawled only a few meters, and though they
have nearly reached the convoy, the eight men are forced to stop by
the gravel lashing at their faces, their ambush will have to wait until
the dust storm has passed.

This same dust storm is beating against the bodywork pickup
trucks and Estela's Ford Lobo, but the raging fury of the sierra goes
unheard by the men inside, who fell asleep some time ago, and by
the nameless still singing their hopes or listening to the false hopes
invented by Merolico. The dust storm that whips around Estela
and almost brings her out of her trance: if it fails, it is because
she does not want to leave the future until she has turned it into

memory: Don't open your eyes yet ... Don't go back to the mountains, ShewhoadoresEpitafio tells herself, clinging to the image of her children.

But although Estela does not want to abandon her future, there are events beyond her control: if the stinging of the storm were not enough, the raging wind and hail of stones steals into her dreams and, before she can stop it, raises another storm inside the house she is imagining. A storm that sweeps Epitafio and her children and then, buffeting her, forces her eyes open: she is finally back in La Caída.

X

When the dust storm finally abates, the men from Madre Buena plateau open their eyes, set off at a crawl and come to the place where they are to subdivide again. They have just reached the convoy that followed Estela to this place, where the moon shines like a spotlight underwater.

'You go that way,' El Tampón whispers, looking at the two soldiers to his left, just as El Topo, on the far side of the trucks, orders: 'You head that way and don't stop until you get to the front of the convoy.' Transformed by the moon into pale shadows, the eight men who left Madre Buena plateau creep to their assigned positions and prepare to launch their ambush.

A pebble … I need a pebble! El Topo thinks, and, grabbing the first stone that comes to hand, he hesitates: Do I get up or do I try to throw it lying down? What the fuck is taking him so long? El Tampón thinks, and, raising his head, attempts to see the convoy three meters away. The convoy abandoned some time ago by the woman who is now staring out at La Caída, still unsure exactly where she is.

A moment before Estela finally comes back to earth and to the present moment, El Topo scrabbles to his feet, arches his back, swings his left arm and throws the signal he and El Tampón agreed some time earlier. The gunshots, at first so sparse that someone could count them, quickly become a hail of bullets, a thunderstorm that splits the night and, with its flares and flashes, captures the attention of ShewhoadoresEpitafio.

'*Puta mierda!*' Estela screams, as she sees the silent flashes glittering in the distance, and frantically tries to replace the prostheses she earlier ripped from her ears: 'What the hell is going on? ... How the fuck?'

'Rat-tat-tat-tat!' El Tampón is screaming as the wrath of his semi-automatic and those of his soldiers smites the men still sleeping and slaughters the nameless. 'Rat-tat-tat-tat!' he screams over and over as his bullets pierce skin, flesh and entrails, just as what Estela is witnessing from a distance pierces her very soul: How can I? ... I knew it ... You set this whole thing up, didn't you, Nicho?

'Fucking bastard,' ShewhoadoresEpitafio spits, and her body begins to shudder uncontrollably: Where were they hiding? ... Jesus! Shit ... how can I not have anticipated this? As Estela struggles to reinsert her hearing aids, they slip from her trembling fingers just as El Topo vainly shouts at the top of his lungs: 'That's enough!'

Lying on the flat stones, Estela gropes for the tiny prosthetic devices, while in the distance El Topo roars again: 'That's enough! ... Did you hear me? I said that's enough.' But El Tampón is still shrieking 'Rat-tat-tat-tat!' while his bullets and those of his men continue to riddle the Ford Lobo and the two battered pickup trucks.

'I'm ordering you to cease fire!' El Topo bellows, his anger mounting, but even now he cannot stop the hail of bullets obliterating men and weapons: the only living creature unscathed by the bullets was saved as the bodies of the wounded fell on him and buried him. 'I said cease fire ...! Are you dumb fucks listening?' El Topo vainly shouts again, just as Estela is vainly searching for her lost prostheses and vainly thinking: Forget about the hearing aids, get the hell out of this place!

Get up and get away from here before they realize! ShewhoadoresEpitafio is thinking, but now, crushed by the weight of the present, she ignores her thoughts: I can't just run away ... I need to know who these men are. Raising her head and tearing her gaze from the rocks, Estela once again surveys the disaster zone and holds fast: I need to tell Epitafio who did this to us ... who these fucking bastards are!

'Bastards,' ShewhoadoresEpitafio repeats, champing at the word as she watches the men from Lago Seco, whose leader is still shouting: 'Stop firing or they'll be no use to us afterwards!' El Topo yells as the last salvo from his men illuminates the cloud of smoke and dust like lightning in a pitch-black sky.

As the vascular system feeding the cloud of smoke is finally extinguished and the roaring winds of the sierra are heard once more, Estela decides that she needs to get closer to find out who was responsible for the ambush; and, abandoning her prostheses, she crawls toward the catastrophe where El Tampón is standing, smiling, and El Topo is ranting: 'Look what you've done ... bunch of fucking *pendejos*! How are we supposed to pay the two old men? ... Where's the cargo we were going to give them back at El Infierno?' El Topo waves away the billows of smoke that the wind has begun to disperse.

Then, when the wind has swept away the smoke, the moon's radiance illuminates the scene: the same radiance that, in Tonée, marks the departure of the sons of the jungle and of the men and women who, from henceforth, will follow them, the same glow that lights the path of Epitafio, the man whom Estela is thinking about as she warily approaches the disaster zone.

I need to know who they are ... to make sure, then I can leave, Estela silently says to herself, fearfully moving forward and staring at the shadowy figures moving around the wreck of her Ford Lobo and the two battered pickup trucks. Just a little closer and I'll be able to see them, ShewhoadoresEpitafio thinks, crawling a few meters more; then, as she recognizes one of the men who left Lago Seco, she feels that her chest will explode: fucking bastard!

Son of a bitch! Estela silently curses, feeling her stomach clench as she wriggles along the ground. El Topo, you fucking traitor, ShewhoadoresEpitafio mutters, creeping faster, and the twinge in her belly becomes a spasm as she thinks: If you're caught up in this shit, then Sepelio is in it up to his neck ... that bastard Sepelio ... How could you do this to me? ... How could you do this to Epitafio?

Epitafio ... you're in danger, too ... They won't have set a trap just for me ... I have to call you as soon as possible, Estela thinks, and though every fiber of her being warns her not to, she gets to her feet and flees the scene. 'Epitafio ... Jesus fuck ... Epitafio,' Estela intones the words, over and over like a psalm, forcing her legs and her tongue to work faster, and, calling to mind the deep voice of the man she adores, she remembers her missing hearing aids: only then does she realize that she cannot hear anything.

And since she cannot hear anything, ShewhoadoresEpitafio does not hear the sound or the echo of El Topo's voice barking orders to his men: 'Check and see the engines are still working.' And since she cannot hear anything, she does not hear El Tampón's words: 'There's no one in the Ford Lobo … Estela's body isn't here … All of you, go look for her right now … We can't let her get away!

'We can't let her escape!' El Tampón insists, drawing level with El Topo and, seeing his face distorted with blind fury, adds: 'How could this happen? … Why isn't Estela's body there?' But before El Topo manages to reply, they hear the voices of the soldiers: 'Estela's not in the pickup trucks … She's not here!'

Because Estela is still running, and would carry on running for a long time yet were it not that she has just tripped and fallen on the edge of La Caída. Having been thrown almost three meters, ShewhoadoresEpitafio crashes between two rocks, which, though they leave her injured, manage to hide her and save her from death, though not from the unconsciousness into which she is now sinking, taking with her her fears and the fate of Epitafio, the man who is shifting gears as he says to Mausoleo and Sepelio: 'Make sure you're ready, we'll be stopping soon,' as he thinks of the creatures he is transporting in the container, and the sons of the jungle.

The sons of the jungle, followed by the men and women who crossed the border a few hours since, have just left Tonée behind and are moving into the jungle, thinking about Epitafio, who right now is snorting two lines of coke, as the woman he so loves did earlier, and thinking about Estela, the woman who, now that all ties with consciousness have been broken, does not know that a moment ago a search party set out to find her, nor that the search was quickly cut short.

'Everyone back here!' yells El Topo, brooding and telling himself that he no longer wants what he wants, he gazes up into the sky at the slow, heavy flight of the storks that have returned to La Caída: 'I'm telling you to get your butts back here … Are you listening or what? … We can't waste all night fucking around … We've got to get back to El Infierno!' First to arrive back are El Tampón and the youngest of the soldiers, who, before they have even come to a halt, hear: 'You and me are going to fetch the truck!

'Are you listening or not?' El Topo says, staring at El Tampón, then, turning and giving the youngest of his men a vicious slap, explains to him and to the other soldiers who have now arrived back: 'The two of us are going to get the truck … In the meantime, you lot are going to load the corpses into whichever of these trucks is least fucked … If it won't start up, we'll have to tow it … so work out how we're going to hitch them together!

'And you two,' El Topo growls at two soldiers who are about to pay dearly for not being amongst those he has just been addressing: 'Head over that way and look for Estela. You're not going anywhere, so it's in your best interest to find her … The bitch has to be around here somewhere.' El Topo turns on his heel and, heading back to the place where he left the fake armored truck, he calls back: 'If we don't get back to El Infierno, they'll know something has happened.

'We have to say that it went off without a hitch … We have to tell Sepelio that she's dead … that her body was part of the cargo we gave to the old men,' El Topo says, hastening his pace and, unwittingly, hastening the events that follow: they will reach the fake security van, they will drive back to the scene, they will hitch one of the old pickups to the former municipal garbage truck and leave La Caída forever.

The silence between the two men leading the squadron who left

Madre Buena plateau, as the phony armored truck inches down the slopes of La Caída and away from the place where the two soldiers are still searching for Estela, will not be broken until El Infierno appears in the distance. It will not be broken until the moment when, taking a hand off the steering wheel, El Topo points and says: 'Look, we can see the flames again.'

'You're blind as a bat … I spotted them ages ago,' El Tampón says, and as he does so he realizes that he now wants to say all the things he has been brooding over during the drive: 'We should have stayed up there … No one would ever have known … Why did you side with those bastards? … I should have stayed back there.'

'And miss out on La Carpa?'

'To find that fucking bitch … What has La Carpa got to do with it?'

'What has it got to do with …? What does …? You really don't know shit,' El Topo roars, flooring the accelerator of the fake security van. 'If Sepelio finds out that we've lost Estela, we won't get to go to La Carpa … and if we show up late here, and the triplets talk to him later, he'll work it out.'

'I still think I should have stayed behind.'

'This way, he'll think it all went as we planned … That's why you couldn't stay … because he's bound to call you sooner or later.'

'And I'm supposed to tell him that she's dead … is that what you want?'

'Exactly.'

'How come you're not the one who has to lie to him?'

'You won't be lying to him … It's just a matter of time … They're bound to find her eventually.'

'What if I turn it off?' El Tampón says, staring at the telephone in his hands. 'I turn it off and we wait until they've found her.'

'You really don't get it, do you? … Didn't you hear me? He can talk to the old men,' El Topo gestures towards El Infierno. 'Just listen to me … When he calls, just say it all went off like clockwork.'

'And what if they realize she's not there?' El Tampón asks, pointing to El Infierno, where it is just possible to make out the shadows of the two remaining triplets.

'How are they going to find out if they don't know what's supposed to be in the cargo?' El Topo says, watching the shadowy figures grow. 'Besides, even if they knew, they couldn't exactly go looking for her body, it's like a slaughterhouse back there … You couldn't recognize your own mother.'

'A while ago they were complete bastards, and now look at them … They're straining at the leash … See the way they're eyeing the pickup?'

'Should I stop here or drive right in?'

'Better to drive inside.'

'I feel like mowing them down.'

'Park over there next to those barrels.'

Before El Topo has completely stopped the truck, El Tampón turns, flicks up the lock on the door, wrenches the handle and jumps down into El Infierno. When they see him, the two triplets who still live here — the third left one morning without a word and went to live high in the sierra — start walking towards him, arms waving, through the thick smoke belched by the barrels.

Guided by the headlights of the fake security truck, El Tampón, too, steps into the billowing smoke, and, stopping next to the crackling fires whose flames set the skin of Encanecido and Teñido ablaze, says: 'We've brought you this lot.' A dog's head appears between the barrels, only to quickly run off, scurrying past as the two old men chorus: 'You said you were bringing three trucks, you've only brought one.'

The dog is only a distant memory by the time El Tampón says: 'They all came in one truck … They didn't bring the second truck Sepelio mentioned.' A brief, thunderous flash from the largest of the barrels causes El Tampón to glance to his left, then he returns his gaze to the two old men. 'Well, let's see what we've got then,' Encanecido says and the three men set off in the same direction.

They accelerate their pace, unaware that in doing so they are also accelerating the speed of the events that follow: they will negotiate a price for the bodies and the scrap metal, unload the mangled corpses of Estela's men and of the nameless, and, amid the carnage, discover a body that is unscathed and miraculously alive. They will haggle over a price for Merolico, then El Tampón and the two men who founded El Infierno return to the spot where they met and discuss whether or not the men who left Lago Seco will stay and rest a while at Tres Hermanos.

Without any respite to the speed at which these events are taking place, El Tampón and El Topo will discuss whether they should sleep in the truck or in the workshop of the two remaining triplets, they sleep for a few hours, they and their men, in the steelworks at Tres

Hermanos. Meanwhile, Teñido and Encanecido help the migrant they have recently acquired, they help him to understand what has happened and explain how he managed to come out alive.

Later, while the old men who founded El Infierno are showing Merolico every nook and cranny of their kingdom and explaining what he will have to do from now on, El Topo and El Tampón wake up, argue about whether it is better to head on to La Carpa or go back to La Caída, and, deciding to keep driving towards La Carpa, they leave El Infierno, and with it, they quietly leave behind the story of Estela, Epitafio and the two boys in the jungle, the two boys who are marching through the forest, not talking to each other, nor to those who follow them, filled with hope.

Light and Fire will Return

|

The hindquarters of the vehicle that has just dumped another two bodies fold into the depths of night and its flickering taillights disappear in the distance. Only then do the two old men who founded El Infierno turn and, grabbing Merolico's arms, begin to walk back toward their kingdom.

'They are always supposed to call us first,' Encanecido explains to the old man, who does not understand how he can still be alive.

'Supposed to call, to say how many they're bringing, how much they're paying,' Teñido adds, staring at Merolico for a moment, then, releasing his grip on his arm, says: 'Help me close this gate.'

'That's how they were able to come and go, no problem,' Encanecido explains, watching as his triplet and Merolico close the wrought-iron gates.

'Because they called this morning … They always call in the morning,' Teñido finishes the sentence, shooting home the bolt that locks the two gates. 'Only them as calls are allowed in here.'

'What about the padlock?' Merolico asks, clutching at Teñido as he turns away, then turning to look at the two men, says: 'What if they come back?'

'I'm the one always puts on the padlock,' growls Encanecido, shoving aside his triplet and the oldest of the men and women who came from the wastelands, and the only man who, in the sierra, came unscathed through dust and fire.

'I already said I don't think they'll come back,' Teñido says, dragging Merolico along. 'Least not for several days.'

'And even if they do, you've no need to fear,' Encanecido says, snapping the padlock shut and also turning to face Merolico. 'Those bastards won't hurt you any more ...'

'Don't you get it? We bought you ... You belong to us now and they can't say shit!'

'This here's your new home!' Encanecido says, his sweeping arm taking in the space where fires crackle and smoke dances between broken-down cars.

'You've reached a place where you can finally be safe,' Teñido nods, 'El Infierno.' At this, twin tongues of flame flare from the barrels as though to emphasize his words.

'But back to our business ... Forget about them, let's talk about this ...' Encanecido says, gesturing to the place where the mangled corpses slaughtered in the sierra now lie in piles.

'Let's see if you understand ...'

'If you've understood what you'll be doing here.'

The flames rising from the barrels set the night's shadows scuttering and mark out a path for the men as they trudge through El Infierno without another word. Silently, the two remaining triplets are relishing the fact that they have suddenly acquired a helper, someone to do what their brother used to do. For his part, Merolico is embracing his fate and determined not to fail the two men who saved him just a few hours ago.

Prowling around the old men, who, as they walk, cleave the stone-gray clouds of smoke, come the dogs who live here: when their masters walk abroad in their kingdom, the beasts are always at their heels. High up, where the rising smoke melds into the darkness, a flock of storks is migrating to another world.

A few meters from the place towards which they are headed, where the pile of broken bodies is bleeding out and the warm, snaking, ashy smoke from the furnaces becomes thick, sweltering and unbreathable, the two old men who founded El Infierno and who are growing older every day cover their faces with their hands and, beneath their cupped palms, set their tongues wagging again.

'I hope that you don't fail,' Encanecido says, turning to Merolico, and adds, 'and that you're not too bothered by the stench.'

'I can tell you won't fail us,' Teñido says as he, too, turns to face the oldest of the men and women who crossed the border only to meet the hail of bullets in the sierra: 'You'll get used to the smells, you'll see.'

'I don't know whether I could get used to it,' Merolico blurts suddenly, stopping to spew the acrid liquid that has been churning in his gut, welling in his throat until it found the miniscule church of the fortune-teller's mouth.

'Everyone gets used to it,' Encanecido declares, tugging Merolico's arm and laughing at the way he arches his body.

'One of these days you won't even smell it,' Teñido agrees, tugging at the oldest of the soulless, then, gesturing to the flames rising like huge sunflowers from one furnace, adds: 'You'll start here with this fire.'

'You'll see, you might even get to like it,' Encanecido says with a sudden laugh and, stopping next to the barrel his brother just mentioned, turns towards the limbs severed in the hail of bullets. 'We threw up ourselves the first time.'

'We'd never smelled burning flesh before either,' Teñido says, chuckling, then, turning to the mangled bodies, quickens his step.

'Someone brought in a car that had been shot up, and we found the body of a woman inside,' Encanecido explains, following his triplet brother and dragging Merolico in his wake. 'They wanted the car back, so we charged them for cleaning it and disposing of the body.'

'Later, they came back with another bullet-riddled car and this time there were lots of bodies inside,' Teñido finishes his brother's sentence as he stops next to a heap of corpses. 'That day we turned this business around … We turned it into a real breaker's yard.'

'We diversified, you might say … These days we don't just break cars, we break bones,' Encanecido said, laughing even louder. 'In business, you have to adapt. If you don't, someone else will and then you're fucked.'

'That's true … We're not turning our backs on the past,' Teñido says gravely and his laugh trails away. 'We couldn't give up the old business altogether … but these days meat is as valuable as scrap iron.'

'If they leave the vehicle with us, they get the bodies burned for free,' Encanecido explains, bending over the pile of bloody, emaciated limbs; then he picks up an arm and, waving it in the air, says, 'If they want to take the junker away, we charge them for each body.'

'But we explained all that already,' Teñido says, as he, too, picks up a severed arm and pretends to lunge at the body of the oldest of all the bodiless creatures.

'I lied to them,' Merolico babbles, but before he reaches the end of his sentence, the surviving triplets interrupt him with another burst of laughter.

'Ha Ha Ha! ... Too much chatting and not enough working,' Encanecido growls between booming belly laughs.

'Best you get to work and stop wasting time,' Teñido says, tossing the arm he has been waving back on to the pile. 'You finished hacking up this lot a while ago and you still haven't tossed one on to the fire.'

'So get a move on, there's a lot to burn, we'll be watching you ... and don ...'

'And don't go stopping, even if other people show up.'

'If anyone shows up, we'll open the gates,' Encanecido explains. 'You don't move from here until you've finished your work.'

'When you're finished, come see us,' Teñido agrees, turning and pointing to the shack where he and his brother live, then adds, 'Not when you've finished burning the bodies ... When you've finished cleaning the pickup.'

'We'll be there waiting,' Encanecido in turn gestures to the shack and then heads in that direction.

'And remember ... we can see you from there,' Teñido says and trudges off in his brother's footsteps.

||

The echo of the door Encanecido has just slammed rolls around the vast breaker's yard, but does not penetrate the ears of the oldest of those who left their lands days ago. He raises the machete Teñido has just set down and, as he does so, memories rise of the voices of the men and women who crossed the border with him: How could I do that to them?

All around Merolico, the dogs prowl and growl and flames crackle in the drums, but these sounds do not reach his ears. Why did I lie to them all? wonders the oldest of the shadowless and, as he does so, he raises the machete he is holding to his eyes. What good did it do me? Merolico mutters over and over as the edge of the blade cuts through his sightline, then he tosses the knife on to the jumbled pile of corpses.

The sound of the machete as it strikes a shaft of bone that rises from the bodies like the mast of a sunken ship sets the dogs' yapping louder, but this sound, too, does not pierce the ears or the mind of the oldest of the voiceless, who is now staring at the palms of his hands in the nervous, flickering glow of the flames. In the end, it won't save me … It's written here in the lines of my hand, Merolico thinks and, without knowing why, he starts to laugh.

What the hell am I laughing at? Merolico is wondering as he laughs, but the thought is interrupted by Encanecido's voice like a whipcrack, booming across El Infierno, lashing the oldest of all the voiceless and startling the baying pack of dogs: 'Get to work, you fucker! … We're watching you!' Shaking his head, Merolico shakes off the thoughts and the laughter the way a dog shakes itself dry: he must not fail these men.

I can't afford for these bastards not to like me, Merolico mutters silently to himself and as he does so, finally trudges towards the pile of corpses and severed limbs. Just as he is about to raise his machete, Teñido's voice rumbles in the distance, and more than urging him on, the words that reach him further numb the oldest of the godless: 'Get your ass in gear! We want to see that work done!' At Teñido's roar, the barking of the hounds rises to a howl, and the howls take Merolico back to the years when he was a soldier.

'We're not going to wait around all night … We're not going to put up with you if you can't do your job!' yell the brothers, but Merolico is no longer listening: he is not simply reliving the years he spent as a soldier, but those after he joined the paras, the years he spent wiping out whole populations, eviscerating pregnant women, hacking children and old people: Even then I knew that light and fire would return.

I can see it written on my palms as clear as day … The past is always waiting up ahead, Merolico thinks, and as he does so, finds himself laughing again and it is the sound of his own laughter that rips the oldest of the nameless from his trance and drags him back to El Infierno, where the two brothers, watching from their window, are suddenly puzzled: something has changed in this man who now picks up the machete from the ground and, raising it high, begins to slash and roar, scattering the baying dogs skulking around the corpses.

Merolico's roar serves only to further madden the dogs, whose yowls rise to shrill yelps and, hearing this cacophony, the man who tried to give back to the world what he stole from fate to fashion a future for himself, pauses once more and pictures himself back in the jungles of the desolate lands. But before those squandered years return to overwhelm him, he is startled by a booming laugh he does not yet know is his own.

When Merolico finally realizes that it is his own laugh that has dragged him from the depths of the forest, he suddenly notices that the brothers are shouting at him and that the restless dogs are crowding him again. Taking a step forward, the oldest of the soulless who forsook the wastelands plants his feet on the pile of corpses, raises the machete over his head and furiously lets it fall.

One after another, with quick and expert slashes, Merolico hacks away arms, legs and skulls from the corpses as the dogs are whipped into a frenzy and, watching from a distance, the brothers are shocked to see how well he is doing, this man who no longer seems bothered by the stench or the smoke or the flames rising from the barrels; the barrels spread all over El Infierno like the tattoos spread all over the skin of this man who now rips off his shirt and carries on hewing at the corpses.

When, finally, he has finished cutting up the bodies, Merolico tosses the machete aside and, ignoring the hand truck left for him by the brothers, picks up a pile of arms with both hands and stacks them on his shoulder. Eyes half-closed, mouths wide open, the two old men who founded El Infierno gape at the oldest among all of the voiceless: they do not understand what is going on in their kingdom;

they cannot understand the behavior of this man whom they bought just a few short hours ago.

This man who even now is moving towards the barrel they told him to use, and, as he moves, he is thinking about the bundle of arms hanging from his shoulder and about the men and women whose arms they were: How could I have lied to them? Merolico wonders and feels a spasm shudder though his belly: At least the light and fire will return, he thinks stubbornly, as he pictures himself back in the jungles of the desolate lands, watching himself as he torches a village whose inhabitants are locked inside their houses.

Increasingly confused and alarmed, Encanecido and Teñido watch as Merolico strides towards the barrel, and notice that he is talking to the arms that he is carrying on his shoulder: the brothers cannot know, cannot imagine that not only is he talking to the lifeless hunks of flesh he has just hacked to pieces, the oldest of the shadowless is addressing his own destiny: the past is always waiting up ahead.

Stopping as he reaches the huge brazier, Merolico takes one of the arms from his shoulder, examines the hand and, prising open the fingers clenched into a fist, studies the palm. Then he laughs without knowing he is laughing and, having licked the palm with his tongue, tosses it into the fire, where it emits a mute, silent cry that echoes around this world as it falls into the flames. 'What the fuck is he doing?' wonder the two old men, and they hurry towards the door of their shack. 'He's lost his mind!'

After he has tossed the arms he was carrying into the flames, Merolico picks up the can of gasoline the brothers left next to the barrel and, dousing the blaze, watches the flames erupt with savage power, just as in the jungles of the desolate lands mighty flames once razed cities, towns and villages.

It is all here within me ... My past, my present, my future, laughs the oldest of the godless, his laugh growing louder as he raises the can of gasoline above his head and, as he does so, sees the two old men who founded El Infierno rushing towards him, screaming: 'You fucking lunatic!'

'What the hell are you doing?' Encanecido roars and Teñido shouts: 'What the fuck is wrong with you?' But the old man they are addressing does not hear their words: dousing himself in the gasoline that streams down his body, he turns, moves towards the fire, and plunges both hands into the flames. 'You crazy bastard! ... Stop that right now!' the brothers yell as they pass the pile of corpses where the starveling hounds are finally sating their hunger.

Still laughing, Merolico steps closer to the barrel and, using his hands as torches, sets himself ablaze: jaws clenched, flaring like a firebrand, the oldest of the voiceless then leaps headlong into the flames, deaf to the voices of the old men who founded El Infierno still babbling as they reach the barrel: 'What the fuck are you doing? ... Don't you know how much you cost us?'

The Book of the Sons of the Jungle

|

Flanking the procession of those who only recently crossed the great border, tramping beneath the thin, constant drizzle of rain that has begun to muddy the paths through the jungle, the two boys who were born here and who live nearby move at a brisk pace, without approaching or speaking to each other: traveling with them is the pregnant woman on whose face the night is darker than it is on the wet stones.

'How many times do I have to tell you? We're not supposed to bring back pregnant women,' said the elder boy as they passed the outskirts of Tonée, though what he really wanted to say was very different: I've got a bad feeling about that woman ... I've seen her somewhere before. 'What the fuck are you talking about? ... When did anyone ever say that?' says the younger boy, turning towards him, and although he wanted to say something more, he was cut short by the boy who serves as leader: 'Shut up and get to the back of these fuckers!

'Today it's your turn to make sure no one gets lost,' the elder boy said, and so began the long silence in which they are now immured. Moving away from the boy who serves as lieutenant, he ordered the group following them: 'Stick together and no talking!', before setting off through the towering *cuajilotes* and the smaller flame trees that separate Tonée from the great forest, through which they have now been walking for an hour and a half: an hour and a half during which he has not stopped thinking about how and where he met this woman he finds so troubling.

For his part, the boy who serves as lieutenant has spent the hour and a half prodding those who have just arrived from other lands, who are constantly seeking some excuse to stop for a while and catch their breath: the first was Hewhostillbearsaname, who stopped next to a towering *amate* on the pretext of changing his shoes for sneakers; next it was an elderly woman who held them up, stopping to babble a prayer next to a *chujume*, whose branches seemed to form a crucifix: ShewhostillcallsonGod had barely begun her supplication when the younger boy caught up with her and shoved her back on to the path.

Further on, it was Hewhostillboastsasoul who wandered off the path, taking his daughter's hand and using her as an excuse: 'She needed to pee ... She couldn't hold it,' he said, but the younger boy angrily bawled him out: 'We said no one fall behind ... Piss yourselves if you have to!' Later, it was a small boy who suddenly stopped and started gasping for breath: he wanted to search his rucksack for the little inhaler that would open up his bronchial tubes, but instead collapsed on the grass: the younger boy, furious, strode over to Hewhostillhasabody and smashed the inhaler with his flashlight.

Now it is the pregnant woman about whom the older boy has been thinking, who clutches her swollen belly, slows her pace, leans against one of the huge sapote trees and, clawing at the bark, tenses every muscle in her shadowed face and lets out a muffled howl. '*Puta mierda!* ... How many times do I got to tell you!' says the younger boy, trembling with rage and, grabbing Shewhostillhashershadow by the arm, he wrenches her from the tree and rants: 'Move it ... I'm not letting you cause us problems!'

'I'm not going to spend my time prodding you ... The next one to stop is going to pay dearly!' warns the boy who serves as lieutenant, already bored of the task he has just been assigned, and thinking — much to his own surprise: Poor thing ... She's probably going to end up giving birth here in the jungle. Then, shining his flashlight on those who crossed the border only today, grips the wrist of Shewhostilhashershadow, feels a stabbing in his chest and broods about what he wanted to say an hour and a half ago to the boy who serves as leader: All you had to say was: She's not coming ... We didn't have to bring her if you didn't want to ... You should have said something back in the churchyard instead of making up shit later about how we never take pregnant women!

Releasing his grip on Shewhostillhashershadow now that she is steady on her feet again, the younger boy repeats his threat: 'First one of you to stop will be left behind, I swear ... and anyone who's left here will never get out of here.' The power of his words harries these men and women who still cling to hope, then he cuts a path through the mist and, fighting his way through the stubborn drizzle, reaches the boy who serves as leader, who turns to him, thinking: That dumbass is bound to show up soon.

Couldn't hack bringing up the rear any more, the older boy thinks silently, then, turning and using the beam of his flashlight to find the face he has seen so often, he roars: 'Shut the fuck up! Stop shouting!' The power of the leader's voice startles a troop of howler monkeys; they rise up on their branches and hurl their cries like stones at the ground; terrified, those who recently arrived from other lands suddenly stop and cower, turning their faces to the sky.

When the howls of the monkeys have faded to an echo, the men and women still clinging to their dreams find their ears suddenly attuned to the ordinary sounds of the jungle: the crack of a branch that can no longer bears its own weight, a ripe fruit falling, the thunderclap that announces that the drizzle will soon become a downpour. Then their hearing returns to normal and can no longer distinguish the drone of the jungle from the rustle made by their own bodies.

Why the hell have you stopped? … Move it, the lot of you! the sons of the jungle are about to roar, but just at that moment the sweet, supple drone gives way to a sound they have never heard, one that not only renders them speechless, but startles them and puts them on their guard. 'What the fuck is that?' older and younger say as one, and, feeling their flesh creep, they walk towards each other: 'Where is it coming from? What can be making that noise?' they repeat as they walk, shining their flashlight beams at one other and meeting in the middle of the huddle of those who have come from other lands.

'What the fuck is it?' mutter the sons of the jungle and, raking the sweltering darkness of the forest with their flashlights, prepare to move on, but the shriek turns into a raucous howl and their unease turns to dread. There comes a sound of running footsteps and both boys turn their flashlights: from the tangle of ferns and orchids lit by the beams comes a shadow that almost knocks them over, leaps on to a branch and scrambles into the treetops.

The drone of the jungle is suddenly drowned out by the terrified chattering of those who have crossed the border, and if they do not turn and flee it is only because their fear of getting lost is even greater than that instilled by the screeching they can still hear, by the shadow they have just glimpsed. The two boys turn their flashlight beams on each other and, seeing each other's startled faces, wonder what the hell is going on, then glare at the men and women following them: they need to shut the fuck up right now.

'Shut up, all of you!' orders the boy who serves as lieutenant, and, turning his attention to the elder boy, brings his free hand up to his ear, turns towards the jungle and waits to hear what his leader has to say. The older boy turns to those who have recently arrived from other lands and, dragging the younger by the arm, barks: 'Get on the ground, keep quiet and wait until we get back!' He clenches his jaw and sets off towards the ferns that vomited up this shadow and, pointing his flashlight beam towards the distant howling, says: 'You and me are going to see what's going on.'

The shrieking that draws the boys on, as dried blood draws insects, swells as they set off and find themselves crossing an area thick with branches, dense foliage and tall grasses. As they move, the boys, who know this jungle as someone knows the garden where he grew up, unsheathe their machetes and slash a path through the undergrowth, feeling their hearts beat faster: 'You should go first ... I'll cover your back,' says the boy who serves as leader and the younger boy walks on: 'Shit ... I always have to go first.'

Their machetes in one hand and their flashlights in the other, the two boys plunge deeper into the jungle, heading toward the source of the wailing and away from those who still believe they are fortunate, and who for the first time now turn to each other: 'What if they don't come back?' asks Shewhostillhashershadow. 'Why would they leave us?' says Hewhostillboastsasoul. 'What if that noise was a …?' begins Hewhostillbearsaname, only to be silenced by a peal of thunder.

The echo of the thunder and the sound of the lightning as it splits a jacaranda tree silences the wailing for a moment and sets the boys' hearts racing faster still, and they wander a short distance off track. 'It wasn't coming from this direct … I'm sure it was coming from over there,' the younger boy nods, turning and pointing the beam of his flashlight to the left. 'You're right, it came from that side,' says the elder boy as the space is once more filled with the keening lament that both alarms and excites them.

Retracing their steps, the two boys skirt a thicket of philodendrons, slash their way through a wall of orchids, and jump over a clump of shrubs and aloes, advancing toward the sound. Trembling with anxiety and impatience, the two boys wade across a ford thickly carpeted with moss and, stepping out of the stream, their hearts about to explode, they finally come to the place they have been searching for. 'It's coming from behind that fig tree,' says the younger boy, pointing the beam of his flashlight.

'We'll take opposite sides,' orders the elder boy with a pang of jealousy, illuminating the thick trunk of the Banyan fig from whose sides strangled vines and great broken branches hang like moth-eaten curtains. Then, raising his machete into the air and gesturing with his hands, the boy who serves as leader says: 'We have to pounce at the same time.' When they are within a few steps of the source of the wailing, the younger boy, still crouching in the tall damp grass, turns to the older, marking a rhythm with his weapon that signals the countdown before they leap.

The scene illuminated by the light of their flashlights as they drop down on the other side of the banyan brings a surge of relief and also disappointment; their teeth chatter as they let out a laugh that not only relieves the tension in their gut, but rids them of their terrors and fears: dangling from the ravening roots of a strangler fig is a howler monkey, its legs have been severed, its arms dangle limply and there is a gaping wound in its belly.

Despite the intensity and the proximity of the flashlights, they do not startle the monkey, whose face is expressionless: there is not a trace left in its features, in its eyes, that this is a living creature. All that remains is the howl, a lament that does not even seem to come from its throat: it hisses from the gaping wound that has slit the creature's stomach like air from the neck of a balloon. And the sound is more a herald of death than a promise of life.

'I told you ... I said it couldn't be human,' says the elder boy when he has stopped laughing and, approaching the monkey, he adds: 'Son of a bitch ... You scared the shit out of me.' 'When did you say that?' asks the younger boy, also taking a step forward and, shining his flashlight on the one who serves as leader, adds: 'Neither of us said anything.' But the elder boy is no longer listening to he who serves as lieutenant: 'I don't like being scared ... piece of fucking shit.'

'Why did you say that you said that when you didn't say anything?' the younger boy perseveres, but his brother ignores him and, raising his machete towards the darkness, says again, 'I don't like being scared!

And I won't stand for being fooled … Certainly not by a fucking monkey!' roars the boy who serves as leader, raising his weapon higher still and, to the astonishment of the younger boy, bringing it down on the animal: as the creature is split like a ripe fruit, a piece of the howler monkey falls on to the grass, and the wailing dies away.

'Let's get back, we've wasted too much time,' says the older boy, wiping the blade of his machete against the trunk of the banyan. Then, as he lights the path by which they came and listens to the rustle of the jungle, he once again takes possession of this space. Still in the grip of his astonishment as he stares down at the severed hand of the howler monkey, the younger boy cannot manage to voice an objection — much as he would like to — and so tramps along in the footsteps of his leader.

Wading across the ford again, and jumping over the fallen trunk of the Guanacaste tree, the two boys hurriedly follow the path they cut through the jungle. Meanwhile, the men and women who crossed so many borders convinced that they might change their fate, have once again begun to talk amongst themselves: 'I told you they weren't going to abandon us here,' says ShewhostillcallsonGod. 'What if that's not them?' says Hewhostillhasabody. 'Why wouldn't they …?' says Hewhohasnotyetsunghisfears, but his words are cut short by a roar.

'I told you to shut up! Fucking hell!' shouts the older boy when he hears the murmuring voices and, quickening his pace, he turns the flashlight on his brother. 'We need to hurry before they get fucked up …' 'Not in my eyes!' the younger boy interrupts. 'Shine that bloody flashlight in my eyes again and you'll see what happens,' he says, sucking in air and spitting on the ground.

'Nobody fucking threatens me!' snaps the elder boy, stopping in his tracks and, smiling, he turns around and the younger boy laughs and shines the beam of his flashlight full in the face of his leader: 'So, tell me, what are you going to do?' 'You spiteful little son of a bitch!' says the older boy, laughing harder and hitting the boy who is supposed to obey him: the metallic sound as it strikes home stirs both boys with a memory of their childhood games.

'You want to fight?'

'What I want is to beat you again.'

'Like you've ever beaten me!'

'Bastard … You're the one who's never beaten me!'

'Whoever wins today gets to keep it.'

'Gets to keep what?'

'Whichever of us wins keep this,' the older boy says, slipping a hand into his shirt and taking out the medal hanging around his neck.

'Seriously?'

'Whoever wins gets to keep it!' The older boy drops the medal and it bounces against his sternum, then he brandishes his flashlight like a sword.

'You're serious — if I win I get to keep it?' says the younger boy again, but before he can raise his guard, he is attacked.

'And the champion slays him while he's still off guard!' crows the older boy, planting the glowing beam that serves as his sword into the belly of the boy who does not serve as leader.

'Not fair … we hadn't even started!'

'And the champion gets to keep the medal of all time!'

'You cheated … You cheated like you always do,' the younger boy says, storming off, then he turns and heads towards the place where those who recently arrived from other lands are sitting on the ground.

'And the loser whines because he lost again!' says the older boy as he walks towards the group.

'Go fuck yourself!'

'I've got a better idea … Learn to lose like a man instead of throwing a tantrum.'

'…'

'Are you pissed off?'

'…'

'What are you angry about now?' asks the older boy as he reaches the huddled mass of those who still believe they might change their destiny, as they stare at him, dumbfounded and relieved.

'I don't want to start a fight here,' says the younger boy, training his flashlight on the men and women who, recognizing them, struggle to their feet.

'I don't want to fight either,' says the older boy, walking through the swarm of men and women staring at them without making a sound.

'Let's not talk about it right now,' says the younger boy, flanking the group on the other side. 'You all better keep up … No one's going to look out for anyone who lags behind.'

'Look, let's say I didn't win the medal … Best of three, what do you say?' the older boy offers, turning towards the men and women now following behind. 'You heard him … No one's going to be bringing up the rear.'

'Anyone who falls behind stays here!' growls the younger of the sons of the jungle, walking faster, and then turning back to the older boy, says: 'It's raining harder than it was earlier.' 'And it's likely to carry on for a long time,' says the boy who serves as leader, turning his face towards the sky and staring at the leaden, lowering clouds. From time to time a lightning bolt illuminates the heavens and a guttural clap of thunder sends a shudder through those who have come from far-off lands.

Looking down from the clouds to the earth, the older boy spots the flickering flames rising from the jacaranda tree struck by the earlier thunderbolt, which is still blazing despite the incessant drizzle. When, finally, they reach the jacaranda, the older boy turns to the junior who follows his orders and, breaking the silence that has hung over their long march, he says: 'How could you think we were going to keep it?'

'How could I think what?' the younger boy says, though as he speaks he hears the words: 'I told you we were going to sell it on the other side of the border.' Then he watches as the leader once more slips a hand into his threadbare T-shirt and holds up the medal that, many years ago, was awarded to Mausoleo. Mausoleo, who is still sitting between Epitafio and Sepelio in the cab of the Minos.

Minos, the container truck that is about to meet with an accident that will put an end to its flight, a headlong race brought about by the events that preceded it: having left behind the house in which Osaria still lies unconscious, Epitafio, Sepelio and Mausoleo raced along the road leading from the great forest to the scrubland, arguing about whether they would arrive too late in Los Pasos, the village they reached just in time to climb down from the cab and sell the nameless women to Sepulcro, the man who had come to buy them.

More happy to have made it on time, than with the profit from the sale, Epitafio, Sepelio and Mausoleo sealed the container, bought half a kilo of beef from a roadside barbecue and, as they wolfed their tacos, they set off through the scrubland, goading each other, though each was really lost in his own thoughts: Mausoleo was wondering what happened between the two men now separated by his body; Sepelio was angry with himself that he had not taken the time to call the men from Lago Seco; while Epitafio could not understand why Estela had still not called him back.

More apprehensive than nervous, Epitafio, Sepelio and Mausoleo left behind the scrubland — each slipping a little deeper into himself, even as the tone of their taunts, whenever they emerged from themselves and spoke, grew more vicious — and reached the village on the edge of the vast, uninhabited Llano de Silencio — the Plain of Silence. They stopped again at Siete Cruces, where, having negotiated the sale of the soulless men to Doña Cárcava, they climbed back into the cab of the Minos and quickly headed towards the one road that crossed the Llano de Silencio.

The vast, desolate plain that Mausoleo, Sepelio and Hewhoisdeafofmind have been driving through at breakneck speed for half an hour now, arguing with each other fitfully, yet constantly preoccupied with their own thoughts. It is here, a moment from now, that they will be forced to stop, much as they do not want to, and it is here, in circumstances beyond their control, that this frantic sequence of events will be brought to an end. The mayhem that will end here, in the middle of the Llano de Silencio, when the Minos meets with an accident.

||

'How much do you want to bet he'll make a run for it?' Epitafio asks, resurfacing from his inner depths, and his words rouse Sepelio and Mausoleo from their own thoughts. 'Who wants to bet that this fucker will move first?' he says again, flicking on the truck's high-beams and lighting up the distant silhouette of a stray calf in the middle of the road.

'I bet he stays where he is,' Sepelio says, shaking his head and, dismissing all thoughts of the men from Lago Seco for a moment, he leans forward and claps, still gripping the telephone in his left hand: 'I bet you the dumb animal won't move — but you're not allowed to sound the horn!' Mausoleo also leans forward, watching excitedly as the Minos barrels towards the calf that is rooted to the spot with fear.

Before Epitafio or Sepelio can decide on the stakes for their bet, in fact before Hewhoisdeafofmind can make up his mind whether to honk the horn, the Minos reaches the spot where the calf clenches its jaws, turns its face towards the darkness, closes its eyes and tenses every muscle in its body. The clang of metal hitting flesh rolls around the Llano de Silencio, punching holes in the night, jolts the cab of the Minos and the three men who, before they realize what is happening, hear the snap of bone and tendon: none of them realizes that a prime rib has punctured the engine propelling them.

The sickening crack of the mangled body rips through the thick rolling darkness of this vast plain unlit by the moon or the army of stars flaunting their colors — blue, green, red, copper, yellow — it stirs the beasts in the sheltering shadows, sets to lowing the cow that has just lost her calf, and, for a brief moment, silences the nameless imprisoned in the Minos, who continue to sing their fears.

> *What can they be doing to him? … This is what we wondered*
> *every time they came for someone else … Why are they taking us*
> *out, one by one? … Slowing down … The one with the largest*
> *pistol came from behind … laughing, insulting, threatening*
> *… 'Bunch of lowborn bastards' … Then we set off again … the*
> *lowborn trembled.*

'I told you it wouldn't move,' Sepelio says when the crack of bone beneath the mortally wounded engine fades: 'I told you, so you have to pay up … Those dumb fucking animals never move … They just tense their bodies!' 'How do you expect me to pay you when we didn't even settle on the stakes?' Epitafio says, cackling and, bending over to the dashboard, has a quick snort and grabs the pack of cigarettes: 'If you want someone to pay up, you have to tell them what the stakes are … assuming there's anyone left to accept the bet!'

'What do you mean anyone? … What the fuck are you tlak-nig about hwat od uyo mean nayeno?' Sepelio rages, but, having snorted a line himself, his tongue twisting the words just as the beams of the headlights begin to twist as Epitafio's hands wrench the steering wheel: something in the engine implodes and the arms of Hewhoisdeafofmind flail like snapped cords: 'Shit! … What the hell? … Fuck, fuck, FUCK!'

Having steeled himself as the truck slewed across the tarmac, left the highway and threatened to barrel-roll, before miraculously managing to steer the Minos back on to the road to a chorus of screams from Sepelio, Mausoleo and himself, Epitafio feels as though his heart — the heart he finally opened to a new life back in Osaria's house — is about to burst in his chest, and, choking back the slivers of a scream, he takes a deep breath and slams on the brakes: outside, the screech of tires still echoes across the plain of silence.

Still feeling shaken, Epitafio blinks his eyes, takes a drag on the cigarette his trembling hand managed not to drop, pats his head, looking for the cap he left behind in Osaria's house, then turns to the two men who are also struggling to choke back their screams. Seeing terror written on the faces of Sepelio and Mausoleo, Hewhoisdeafofmind bursts out laughing: 'Chickenshit faggots …! You should be ashamed … The look on your faces …! All that for nothing!'

Outside, silence lays claim to this wasteland that reeks of burning rubber, while inside the cab Epitafio is still laughing at Sepelio and Mausoleo, who are silently opening two more beers and snorting two more lines; in the container of the Minos, the godless who crossed the borders so long ago gradually stop their wild swaying, regain control of their fears and begin to speak of them again.

> Fucking hell … What happened? … Is it over? … How the fuck? … What was that? … It was nothing … It's nothing now … Just carry on … That's right … carry on talking …
> *I am making this journey … Back there I had a family … I*

didn't want to leave ... They evicted me from my home ... They
slaughtered my family ... I have nothing back there now ... That
is why I'm making this journey.

'Shame on you ... If you could see yourselves ... How can you be such cowardly faggots? ... I can't even look at you!' Epitafio says, stubbing out his cigarette and uncapping another beer and, realizing that his hands have stopped trembling, he thinks: Nearly went belly up there ... Very nearly didn't get to start my new life ... Another inch and our story would have ended before it even began. Then, Hewhoisdeafofmind takes a long breath and says: 'At least I don't have to look at the two of you any more ... Get out and assess the damage.

'And don't come back until you've fixed it!' Epitafio growls, staring at the back of the giant who is following Sepelio's unsteady progress. 'And make it fast. I don't want be stuck here forever,' Hewhoisdeafofmind warns as Sepelio and Mausoleo disappear into the cloud of steam belching from the engine; then, picturing the woman he loves, he silently rephrases what he has just said, I don't want to be stuck in this life ... I'm done with all this ... As soon as I finish this run, it's all over ... There'll be no more days like this.

Inside the scalding, stifling cloud of steam still rising from the truck and spread into the darkness that envelops the vast Llano de Silencio — a white cloud that seems almost golden in the beams of the six headlamps — Sepelio and Mausoleo look at each other, then, sweating profusely, they hunker down on the ground, lie on their backs and inch themselves under the engine, and there they see the bloody shards of the mutilated calf.

'Do you know anything about this stuff?' Sepelio asks, and before Mausoleo has a chance to reply, he wipes the desiccating sweat from his eyes, thinking: I should use this opportunity to call those clowns. Sepelio says: 'Because I don't know shit about engines.' In the distance, the invulnerable silence that slows and intensifies the hours on this plain, is pierced by the roar of an approaching vehicle.

'Don't worry, I'll have it sorted in a minute ... You'll see, it'll be fixed in a second,' Mausoleo says in a low voice, silently vowing to himself: I'll fix it and the two of you will be grateful ... You'll both owe me ... and I won't have to confront anyone ... I won't even have to fight one of you to make both of you happy ... Maybe this is my lucky day. Far off, the roar of the vehicle grows louder as it gets closer, and since, across the vast expanse of the Llano de Silencio, no sound contends with it, it hurtles towards the spot where the Minos has stalled.

But Sepelio and Mausoleo cannot hear the sounds belched by the vehicle about to pass over the roar of their own engine; Epitafio, on the other hand, hears the sounds and, steeling himself, he scans the flatlands and peers into the wing mirrors to find the culprit responsible for spreading fear in his cab once more. Where the hell are they? wonders Hewhoisdeafofmind as he fumbles again for the cap he left on the bed of the son he has always loved, and says aloud: 'You and I can start our lives together getting my son back!'

You and I can start our new life together kidnapping my boy! Epitafio repeats silently to himself, and, as he does so, he feels an excitement he has never felt before. It is at this moment, through the windscreen of the Minos, that he sees the headlights of the engine that has been making the noise he heard, and watching the vehicle about to pass him any moment now, he says: 'So that's what was making the noise,' even as he silently thinks: You and I can … or maybe not … because first you have to answer my call … to begin our new life together, you have to talk to me!

By the time the vehicle finally passes the hulking Minos, trailing the rattle of its ramshackle engine, the shriek of frayed shock absorbers and the muffled creak of springs worn down by time, Epitafio can no longer hear it: his attention is focused on his thoughts, on this other plain of silence where he is wandering between doubts and fears and dreams: Why haven't you called me back? … Why haven't you talked to me when I've already told you it doesn't matter what you had to say to me? … That I've decided … I'm done with all this … I want us to be together, you and me … I just want to be with you!

For their part, the creatures who have come from other lands, the bodiless still hanging by their hands, also hear the rattle, the shriek and the creaking that have now begun to fade: yet, for the first time these shadowless creatures do not know what they are hearing and so they continue with their song:

> *I was living happily when they came to my village one day …*
> *They killed almost everyone and left … They left a chainsaw on*
> *my bed … Then the police came and I told them what happened*
> *… They asked for the chainsaw, but we couldn't find it … so*
> *they accused me … They said I was the one who had murdered*
> *everyone … so I was forced to run away.*

Unlike earlier, Sepelio and Mausoleo also hear the vehicle passing and fading into the distance as they lie next to each other under the malfunctioning engine splattered with calf's blood, suffocating in a swelter that combines the heat radiating from the mechanical heart of the Minos, and that which is already beating down on the Llano de Silencio, though morning has barely broken.

'That's the first I heard pass round here.'

'What the hell are you talking about?'

'It's the first car that has passed since we started crossing the plain,' Mausoleo says, adjusting the engine above his head.

'Stop thinking about that and focus on your job,' Sepelio orders. 'Fix this heap of shit.'

'I'll have it fixed in a minute,' Mausoleo says, plunging both arms into the tangle of metal threatening to scorch him. 'The problem is this bone, here.'

'How could a bone have caused this?'

'The fucker snapped the timing belt,' the giant says, looking at the shard of bone he has just pulled from the mass of iron and setting it down. 'Then it buried itself in the crankcase.'

'So, can you fix it?'

'I told you, I'll have it sorted soon,' Mausoleo promises, picking the pieces of the broken drive belt from between the crankshaft and the pistons. 'How come the engine doesn't have a casing? … It's a piece of shit.'

'Well, quit with the talking and fix it,' Sepelio says, glaring at Mausoleo. 'Got it?'

'…'

'That's good ... keep your trap shut.'

'If you want, I can do this on my own ... You don't have to stay here,' Mausoleo says. 'You don't have to stay here suffocating with me.'

'That's ... even better. Now you're starting to catch on,' Sepelio says and, rolling over on to his front, he starts to drag himself out on to the road. 'Maybe this is your lucky day,' he says, all the while thinking, I'll call them now ... I can use this time to phone those dumb fucks.

'Of course it's my lucky day,' the giant says without knowing why, and immediately regretting it, he begins to babble, words, he babbles, 'Don't mind mehow am I supposed to knowjust leave me here justgo before you melt andleave me to it justleave me your belt I'll can use it to fixit I'll get her runningeven if only as far as the next townwe can buy a new one there.'

'So you think this is your lucky day,' Sepelio says with a faint smile, taking off his belt as he hunkers in front of the truck. 'So tell me, why do you think it's your lucky day?'

'...'

'I'm asking you to tell me why you think you're lucky ... Do you have a fucking clue what's happening?' Sepelio says, handing the giant the belt he has just taken off.

'...'

'Don't be a fucking coward, say something!' Sepelio roars, and glaring again at Mausoleo, he shouts, 'Tell me right now what you think is going on.'

'I will be you in a while ... by the end of the day I will be who you have been,' Mausoleo says, his voice feeble and faltering, then, reaching out his left hand, he grabs the belt that Sepelio is proffering.

'You're going to be me later … Are you sure?'

'I'm sure … Whatever happens I'll be who you've been until now … who you've been to Epitafio,' the giant's voice drops even lower. 'Whether it's with him or with you, I'll end up in your position … I'll take your place.'

'Jesus, who would have thought? … Just look at the dumb fuck … Not so dumb, though, are you?' Sepelio says and his smile broadens into a laugh, then, leaning on the bumper of the truck, he threatens: 'If you know that much, you know what you've got to do … So don't fuck up … Don't pick the wrong side … and don't fucking say a word to him.'

'I won't fuck up, you'll see … I know what I've got to do … I'll make sure you're happy with me,' Mausoleo says, bringing a new enthusiasm to his words as he prises the buckle from the belt, thinking: Good … you were right to say something to him … There was nothing else you could do … You had to offer him something, too.

'I'm serious, you better not fuck up … and you better not be playing me … playing that other fucker's game,' Sepelio growls, moving away and, wiping his hands, he creeps round the side of the trailer without standing up completely.

I can't let him see me … He needs to think I'm still under there, Sepelio thinks as he walks, half-crouched, along the side of the truck, not stopping until he reaches the container, where he straightens his body, but not his legs. Then, taking out his mobile phone, hiking up his trousers, which, without a belt, are about to fall, Sepelio stares out into the darkness and thinks: I should get the hell out of here now … hide in the shadows so I can talk to those clowns … Otherwise he might overhear ... and I don't want him to know what's going on yet.

Without stopping to think, clinging to the idea that has just occurred to him, as he does to every idea: pathologically, obsessively, brutally, Sepelio starts to run into the Llano de Silencio, and when he feels that he is totally alone, that he is far enough away from the Minos, he stops, turns his body into the shadows that envelop the earth and looks back at the cloud of steam still hanging in the air: there is not a breath of wind.

Hiking up his trousers again, Sepelio stares at the illuminated cab of the truck, and the figure of Epitafio, who suddenly senses that someone is watching him, thinks: I don't want you suspecting anything ... I don't want you to have the slightest intuition ... I need to know that when I strike, it will hit home ... that everything will go according to plan ... the way I've always thought it would ... I want to see you doubled over ... I want to see you crumple when you see her body riddled with bullets.

Still keeping an eye on the figure of Epitafio — who shifts nervously in his seat and, though he is still wandering through another different plain of silence, pleading with Estela: Why haven't you talked to me? ... Not a single fucking word! is still peering through the windows of the truck for the eyes he can feel upon him — Sepelio thinks: I want everything to work out the way I always planned it ... I want you to see her utterly disfigured ... I want to end your life only after I have destroyed you ... You owe me that ... You've owed me that and more for a long time now.

A plane glides over the Llano de Silencio and, since there are no other sounds here, the roar of the turbines startles Sepelio, who shakes his head, smiles at the figure of Epitafio, then tears his eyes away and looks up at the plane and, with a rictus grin, punches in the number of the men from Lago Seco. They better have gotten her ... They better have done what I told them to do, Sepelio thinks as he listens to the ringing tone that only serves to irritate him: You better not have fucked up ... You better have done exactly what I said ... I want that photo ... I want a picture of Estela's corpse on my phone. Estela, who still lies unconscious back in La Caída as the two soldiers left behind in the sierras search for her on the orders of El Topo and El Tampón.

El Topo and El Tampón, who, seeing the screen of the phone on the dashboard flashing, burst out laughing and congratulate themselves that they have just spoken to Father Nicho, and, seeing the phone slide off the dashboard and fly out the window of the van, they laugh harder, convinced that they will not have to deal with Sepelio, the angry man now listening to the same voice that tells everyone: *The number you have dialed is currently switched off or is out of signal range.*

Believing that they did not hear the phone ring, Sepelio dials the number again: but the chasm that opens up in his left ear leaves him anguished and desperate. Furiously, he hangs up, shaking his head, then slaps his forehead, kicks out at the darkness, only to once more dial the number of the men from Lago Seco, who can no longer hear the telephone chirruping in the grass somewhere on the sprawling plain that separates El Infierno from the site where, years ago, Estela built La Carpa, the compound that El Topo and El Tampón now plan to appropriate: La Carpa, the place where hundreds of migrants work as slaves.

Meanwhile, freed of the pressure of the eyes he felt upon him, Epitafio allows his own eyes to roam, leans back in his seat and studies the cloud of steam that has still not dissipated, picturing Estela's face in the misty curves that hover in the air. Spellbound, Hewhoisdeafofmind once more sinks into his private plain of silence: *Maybe you haven't called because you don't want what I want … If you haven't called me back, maybe it's because you don't want anything … Maybe that is what you wanted to tell me … that you're tired of wasting your time on me?*

'What if that was the important thing you needed to say? … To tell me to fuck off … to say: "I don't love you … You disgust me … How could I carry on loving you?"' Epitafio mutters in his plain of silence and, as he does so, his eyes suddenly open and his hands suddenly lash out at the steering wheel, pounding out his rage on the horn in a blare of trumpets that booms around the plain.

The clamor sets every creature on the Llano de Silencio on the alert; it alarms Mausoleo, who is just about to finish repairing the damaged engine; it startles Sepelio, who furiously grumbles: 'What the fuck is Epitafio up to now?' even as he resigns himself to the fact: *Those bastards aren't going to pick up*; it shakes the shadowless souls still strung up in the container, their feet still shackled to weights they can no longer feel.

I left because everyone else had already fled … The old people and the kids … the women and the men … there was nothing left … not even people's voices … nothing … absolutely nothing … Why are they hammering …? Why have they started up again … They'll come for someone else … Who will they pick this time?

After a moment's hesitation — while Epitafio is still flailing in his fears, while Mausoleo finishes repairing the Minos, while the luckless listen to each other's song — Sepelio opens his eyes, decides he had better call Father Nicho and, his thumbs flying, he punches the tiny keypad and dials the old man's number.

'Hello?'

'Sepelio?'

'I've been trying to get through to those two clowns, but they're not picking up ... I've called the fuckers a couple of times, but they haven't answered ... Did you hear what I said? Those bastards aren't taking my calls!'

'Calm down, Sepelio ... get a grip on yourself.'

'How do you expect me to calm down? ... They've let us down ... I'm sure they didn't manage to capture Estela!' Sepelio protests, trembling with rage. 'I don't know what the fuck to do now.'

'Listen to me ... this is what you have to do ... listen ... First off, you need to calm down,' Father Nicho bellows into the phone. 'They called me a while ago.'

'A while ago ... they called ... the two ... when exactly?'

'What does it matter? ... All that matters is that I've spoken to them ... They said they tried to call you, but you didn't pick up!' the priest says. 'What matters is that they said they've done the job ... that everything went like clockwork.'

'How could I take the call when I had Epitafio breathing down my neck? I've only just managed to get away,' Sepelio explains, his tone calmer. 'So they said everything went to plan?'

'That's what they told me ... they said they killed her.'

'And they didn't say whether they'd done as I asked ... whether they'd carried out my plan?'

'Who cares? All that matters is that Estela is gone,' the priest says, then, caressing each word with his tongue, he adds, 'What matters is that you're free now.'

'What matters is what matters,' Sepelio interrupts the priest, who listens in astonishment. 'Why shouldn't it be important? ... It's important to me ... very important ... I want to know exactly how they did it ... I want to know if they followed my plans!'

'...'

'Whether they did all the things I have thought about so often ... whether they skipped even part of my plan ... whether they trashed my ideas ... whether those *pendejos* even looked for her corpse ... or found it, but didn't take a photo ... the photo that I insisted ...'

'Shut up for one fucking second,' Father Nicho roared, interrupting Sepelio. 'I have the photo right here ... They sent me the fucking photo ... If you hang up now, I'll send it to you ... I don't want to ...'

'Send it now, I'm hanging up.'

Without another word, Father Nicho rings off and searches for the picture sent to him some hours back — he doesn't understand why Sepelio wants him to send the photograph — he finds it, attaches it to a brief message that reads: 'What's important is that now you can take down Epitafio'; sends the message to Sepelio and then tosses on to his desk this phone he has no desire to use again for a long time.

When he receives the message sent by Father Nicho, Sepelio opens the attachment, stares at the image before his eyes, grits his teeth, kicks out again at the darkness, sucks in a lungful of air and grumbles: 'Fuck ... I told them I wanted a photo of her on her own ... In this picture, you can't tell if it's her or not ... This is no good to me ... He might not believe that the body in the picture is Estela.'

Then again, why wouldn't he believe me? Sepelio wonders after a moment, and feels his face relax: You've no reason to disbelieve ... After all, you've no idea what's been happening ... You're not expecting something like this to happen ... You'll believe me because you can't believe it ... You'll see her in the photograph, despite it being blurred. Jubilant now that he has convinced himself, Sepelio hitches up his trousers and stares at the Minos, thinking: Today I'll finally get to see you crushed. He puts away the phone and says to himself: But I'll do it the way I've always planned ... First I'm going to drive you insane.

A few meters from the Minos, Sepelio tears his eyes from Epitafio, who passed from shadow to figure to effigy to face as he approached the truck, then he turns his head to the right and another dark, spectral shadow makes him shudder and sets his heart hammering. Once more a panicked babble spills from his mouth: 'Fucking bastard, you just scared the shit out of me!' He cannot know that the urgency of his words will govern the events that follow.

Laid one above the other, as though someone were laying out a row of slides relating the stories of Epitafio, Estela and the sons of the jungle above another that tells the stories of Sepelio, Mausoleo, Father Nicho and Merolico, the events that now follow will blur the boundaries and put all of them to flight: Sepelio and Mausoleo will climb back into the cab of the Minos, the truck will pull away, eating up the ribbon of road that crosses the Llano de Silencio, and with every meter that flashes past, with every second they share, they will become more nervous, more tense, more agitated and, in the end, will set off for other territories, each once again immersed in his innermost thoughts.

Then, after a while, having bought and fitted a new drive belt for the Minos, and another six-pack of beer, Hewhoisdeafofmind, Mausoleo and Sepelio will reach Bermajío, each lost amid his deepest fears, each gnawing at his bitterest words: They can't realize that I'm playing them both, Mausoleo will think for the thousandth time, while Sepelio will clench his jaw and, twisting his face into a rictus, will doubt himself for the hundredth time: What if he doesn't believe it's Estela … that she is among the charred, mangled bodies? … I need to be sure he'll believe me … that everything will go the way I've planned … I want to see him ruined … The bastard owes me that … I want to see him founder before I kill the *hijo de puta*!

Meanwhile Epitafio, briefly forgetting that he is no longer alone, will growl a litany of complaints that will make Sepelio and Mausoleo laugh against their will: 'Why would you tell me to fuck off when I've just told you I love you?' And a thousand times Hewhoisdeafofmind will grumble: 'Shit … Where is this fucking village …? Why aren't we there yet?' … though in his mind all he wants is to go to the place where he believes he would find Estela. The same woman who, up in La Caída, suddenly opens her eyes and, petrified, emerges from her oblivion: What the fuck happened?

III

What am I doing lying here? Estela wonders as her eyelids flicker open and she raises her head from the stones and makes an inventory of her injuries: she feels a shooting pain in the femur and tibia of one leg, a smarting from two irregular lacerations in her collarbone and neck, six broken ribs are stabbing at her flesh, and her guts are in spasms as though gripped by a hand.

When did I fall on to the rocks? ... How long have I been lying here? Estela wonders, and, heedless of the pain in her back and her hips, she presses her palms against the ground and slowly sits up, bends her knees and struggles to her feet amid the shadows of night. She has lost several things: she no longer has her gun, her flashlight or her telephone, nor, more importantly, the prostheses she needs in order to hear.

Turning her head, spitting a thick gob of saliva and leaning against the rocks to stop herself from tumbling into the abyss where the shadows are thicker, Theblindwomanofthedesert recognizes where she is: to her right the sheer drop of La Caída plummets, before her and behind are rocks that threaten to fall at any moment, to her right is the steep slope of the hill where she was standing when she fell, and where the two soldiers left here by El Topo and El Tampón are still searching for her.

The same two soldiers who, having vainly scoured this ledge that towers over La Caída stop for a moment, look at each other and give a helpless shrug. 'How are we going to tell them that we couldn't find her?' says the first soldier, but his words meet with no response except the throaty whistle of the wind still whipping through the sierra. 'Seriously though, what are we supposed to tell them?' the first soldier says, holding up the telephone in his hands.

'We don't need to tell them anything yet,' the second soldier says, walking along the edge of the chasm and then suddenly turning his head as he hears barking in the distance. 'We need to keep searching … We have to find her, otherwise we'd be better off not calling … not having any contact with them,' the second soldier says, training the beam of his flashlight into the depths of the shadows: the barking they can hear is coming from the slope were La Caída plunges towards the plain.

'The slope … we haven't searched that slope,' the second soldier says, still peering into the depths of night as he begins to walk. 'She could be hiding there … I bet that's where we'll find her!' 'She could just as easily have climbed higher up,' the first soldier says. 'Hang on a minute, she might have gone the other way, into the hills opposite La Caída.' 'She could have, but I mentioned the slope first,' the second soldier says and, turning, walks back to the first and takes out a coin: 'Heads, I go with you up into the hills … tails, you come with me down the slope!'

Catching the coin in mid-air, the second soldier claps it between his hands, and, as the clapping sound is whisked away on the wind, he opens them to reveal the coin glimmering in the light of the rising moon. 'Tails it is … Let's head down the hill!' Without another word, the two soldiers sling their rifles over their shoulders, turn their flashlights towards the spot where La Caída begins its descent, and set off walking, unhurried and with little hope, to the spot where Estela has just struggled to her feet and where her memory has just quivered into life, stirring up images of fire and dust.

'You bastards … treacherous fucking pigs … It's your fault I'm here,' Estela curses, recalling the faces of El Topo and El Tampón framed against the cloud of smoke lit by gunfire and, leaning against one of the rocks that broke her fall, she adds: 'And if that wasn't bad enough, I bet they know … They're bound to have realized … bastards … but I won't give them the satisfaction … I'm not going to let them take me!'

I have to get out of here … get anywhere, Estela thinks, surveying the place in which she finds herself, and, without a second thought, she chooses the gaping chasm that yawns to her right. She takes her hands from the rock against which she was leaning, but her left leg is not strong enough to support her and she crumples to the ground again. The burning ache in her femur and tibia has become a deep, stabbing pain, but, squeezing her eyes shut and clenching her teeth, Theblindwomanofthedesert growls: 'I'm not going to let this leg stop me … I'm not going to let a couple of broken bones be the end of me … I'm going to get up and get out of here!'

Biting back the pain throbbing through her limbs and pounding in her head, Estela remembers something that Epitafio once said, something she mentally repeats as she remembers: Pain is all in the mind, not in the body! Pain is all in the mind, not in the body! Theblindwomanofthedesert thinks again, opening her eyes and looking at the stars high in the dark sky, flaunting their colors — blue, green, red, copper, yellow. 'Pain is all in the mind, not in the body!' she mutters, and in doing so she manages to struggle to her feet, to think about descending the steep slope, to begin the long walk. First one foot, then the other, Estela thinks as she grits her teeth harder, stretches her arms wide to keep her balance, and deep down in La Caída where shadows reign she notices two tiny, flickering lights at a spot where dogs are barking, though she does not hear them; however she does see the two soldiers who are coming to the top of the slope. 'First right … okay, good … then left,' Theblindwomanofthedesert murmurs, lifting her feet and shuffling away from the place where she fell.

But after only a few meters, Estela stops, rests her hands on her hips, takes a couple of deep breaths and feels an agonising spasm in her chest: the broken ribs are grating against the pleura protecting her lungs. Take shallower breaths, Theblindwomanofthedesert thinks and, careful not to fill her lungs, she sets off again, still gazing, spellbound, at the lights like twin stars that have fallen from the dark heavens: If I can just get as far as that house … I might be able to hide there … There has to be someone there.

There has to be someone still awake … They haven't turned off the lights … There's bound to be someone, and that someone is going to help me … They'd better help me or I'll have to make them, Estela thinks, shuffling across the stones as fast as she can. They might have a gun there … maybe even a car, she thinks, convincing herself that the pain has now left her body, and, quickening her pace, she crosses the patch of ground where, any moment now, the two soldiers who left Madre Buena plateau will appear. Convinced that nothing now can stop her, Theblindwomanofthedesert begins to run down the slope that grows steeper and darker, and soon she is leaping along: I don't feel the ache in my leg any more ... my hips don't hurt.

The pain in my head and my ribs has gone, Estela persuades herself as she takes longer leaps down the slope of La Caída and, urged on by a strength that quickly convinces her that nothing now can stop her, not taking her eyes off the twin lights glittering at the bottom of the chasm, she plunges into the shadows, sucks in the lungful of air and once again feels her broken ribs jabbing at her lungs. 'Don't overdo it ...' Theblindwomanofthedesert whispers, and she no longer knows whether she is talking to the stabbing pain inside her, the gathering shadows that are growing more dense or the fear that has suddenly taken possession of her body: just ahead, the gradient becomes vertiginous and the track she is following is impassable.

Slowing the rhythm at which she inhales and exhales as she massages her aching side, she persuades herself that she has to calm down and hesitates as to whether she should retrace her steps or sit down and shuffle on her buttocks down this increasingly dark, steep and treacherous slope. The moonlight cannot reach the depths of the ravine. Estela turns her head, her neck aching despite her conviction that she is feeling no pain and, on the high plateau where she was some moments ago, she sees the nervous dance of the beams from the flashlights of the soldiers searching for her.

'Fucking bastards ... I knew they'd find me eventually ... but they're not going to catch me!' Estela mutters and, without a moment's hesitation, she lets herself fall to the ground, raises her heels, throws her head and shoulders back and, using her hands to push against some loose stones, she thrusts herself into the void, into the cold, impenetrable gloom. The clatter of the stones that fall with her, a sound Estela cannot hear or even imagine as she falls into nothingness and darkness, is carried on the wind up the steep slope and, reaching the top, it startles the two soldiers.

'Did you hear that?' says the second soldier, taking a few steps forward, peering into the abyss, where he trains the beam of the flashlight in his left hand. 'It's that fucking bitch — what else could it be?' roars the first soldier as he, too, peers over the edge, and as his flashlight picks out the distant figure of a woman letting herself slide down the sheer slope, he feels his heart pound in his chest: 'We have to go down and get her ... We have to reach her before she gets to the bottom!

'If she reaches the bottom, she's bound to get away,' the first soldier says, taking a few steps, then coming to a sudden halt as he reaches the chasm: 'How are we going to get to her? ... How are we going to get down?' The first soldier's words are interrupted as the second of the soldiers who left Madre Buena plateau pushes him towards La Caída and strides after him: 'Shut up and get a fucking move on or we'll lose her ... We can't let her get away!

'Even the flashlights will be no use to us down there ... If she reaches the bottom, we'll never find her ... If she actually makes it,' the second soldier says, setting off down the slope, but this time it is his companion who interrupts: 'You go that way ... I'll head back and take the road ... I'll go down the other side, that way we're bound to catch her,' he calls, as he stops his descent with the help of the two rocks that earlier saved Estela.

'No one's taking the fucking road!'

'But that way she can't escape.'

'No fucking way!' the second soldier grunts, looking over his shoulder as he urges his legs to run faster: 'Now start running, or she will get away!'

'Follow me, or everyone will know you're a fucking coward,' the second soldier yells, turning back and training his flashlight on the woman who is now trying to slow her descent.

'Fuck, fuck, fuck …' the first soldier grumbles and, taking his hands from the two rocks, sets off at a run down the slope.

'I'll tell everyone that you let her get away … Get a move on or I'll tell them you were so scared you allowed her to escape.'

'Shut up and keep the light on her … I'm right behind you,' yells the first soldier as he, too, begins to lose his balance: with every meter the slope grows a little steeper, meanwhile the woman they are pursuing has just succeeded in breaking her fall.

'She's stopped … The bitch has stopped and she's started running again!' the second soldier yells, trying to plant his feet between the flat stones: they have just reached the point where the wind-swept surface of La Caída makes it impossible to continue on foot.

'Shut up, keep the flashlight on her and shift yourself, because she's already reached the bottom,' the first soldier says as he crashes into the second, who has to dig his heels into the cracks between the stones to stop himself from tumbling into the abyss. 'Why the fuck did you stop?'

'Why the fuck didn't you stop? … We nearly took a nosedive,' the second soldier rages and, turning around, adds: 'Can't you see it's impossible for us to continue on foot?'

'So what the hell do we do now?' the first soldier says, staring at the sheer drop, scanning for the woman now at the bottom of the ravine and spotting the two lights that he has not noticed until now. 'She's heading for that house ... We have to catch up with her before she gets there ... We have to get down any way we can.'

'Shit ... I hadn't noticed the house,' the second soldier says, and, dropping to the ground, he propels himself with his hands the way Estela did: 'Come on ... get moving ... we don't have time.'

'Don't take you eyes off her ... and don't move your flashlight!' the first soldier commands as he, too, begins to slide down the slope, trying to keep Estela in the circle of light from the flashlight he is gripping in his left hand, and as he drops he hears the distant barking start up again.

'That's ... those fucking dogs,' the second soldier shouts excitedly. 'Maybe they've stopped her ... There's no way they'll let her get near the house.'

Neither the first nor the second soldier realizes that they are about to reach the point where Estela broke her fall and scrabbled to her feet again, that the woman they are chasing cannot hear the barking they can hear. Just as they cannot imagine that this woman who is racing toward the house, whose outline they can finally make out, is also running toward the jungle: the powerful beams now illuminating her have led her back to the clearing known as El Tiradero: 'Epitafio ... Epitafio ... I have to call you ... I have to tell you what has happened!

'You're in just as much danger ... I'll call you from this house

... warn you that we've been betrayed!' Theblindwomanofthedesert mutters, forcing her legs to run faster and, as she chokes back her pain and a fury made sharper by her love, she begins to sense the spectral presence of the dogs amid the shadows of La Caída that the moonlight cannot reach: 'There has to be a telephone here ... I need to tell you that I saw El Topo clear as day ... that El Tampón ... What the hell? ... What's that moving in the darkness?'

Running as fast as she is able, while behind her the soldiers urge each other on — 'Move faster, she's going to get to the house ... Move it, she'll find a place to hide' — Estela watches as the spectral forms are transformed into six dogs, and she is about to stop, but the instinct pushing her onwards is much stronger than the fear that the dogs inspire: What do I care? ... I have to call Epitafio ... If there are dogs here, there must be people ... and if there are people, there will be some way to phone you ... They'll lend me a phone or I'll force them to.

I'm going to call you, to save you ... to let you know that fucking priest is behind this ... that I saw El Tampón and El Topo ... that Sepelio must have planned the whole thing ... Fuck you, Sepelio ... How could you do this to Epitafio? Estela's thoughts are racing as fast as her legs, as fast as the six dogs now careering towards her. The baying hounds and the woman whose broken ribs have once again begun to ache are just about to clash, meanwhile the soldiers who came from Lago Seco are still frantically urging their legs and their tongues to move faster: 'They'll stop her ... the dogs are going to attack her!'

But when Estela and the dogs finally meet, Theblindwomanofthedesert bends down, pretends to pick up a couple of stones and, feeling a sharp pain below her armpit forcing the air from her lungs, lets out a scream that rises to a guttural howl. She does not even have to throw the stones she did not pick up: when they hear her howl and realize she is wounded, the six hounds — who all share the same defective gene: each has one blue and one brown eye — stop in their tracks, tuck back their ears and their tails and, now friendly and intrigued, approach the woman who begins to stroke them.

'Take me to your house ... take me inside,' Estela implores, her voice weak and faint, and begins to run again, though her leg has begun to ache again. 'Show me the way,' she begs, looking at the dogs that escaped El Infierno. Then, looking at the windows of the shack and thinking she has seen a door opening, she says: 'Take me there ... I need to call him ... I have to say: "I told you he was up to something ... I didn't suspect Sepelio ... I don't know how he could do this to us ... after all the time we've lived together!"'

Surrounded by the dogs, now howling in turn, leaping and turning in circles, begging to be petted, Estela comes to a cactus hedge, goes through a narrow gate into a small yard where her presence sets a few listless hens aflutter and a rooster crows in defense of what is his. The black-and-red cockerel stretches its neck, pointing its head towards the darkness and crows again, a sound that goes unheard by Theblindwomanofthedesert, but rolls across the plain and encounters the two soldiers, who have stopped running, turned off their flashlights and are now standing idle and anxious.

'What the fuck do we do now? ... How are we supposed to catch her? ... We can't just walk in there!' the second soldier says, kicking at the shadows, then turns back to the first soldier who has set off toward the house, saying: 'Why the hell not …? Let's go in there and finish this … We won't leave a single dog alive!' 'Stop, wait up … and don't talk such shit … use your brain for once in your life … What if she knows them? … What if she's setting a trap?' the second soldier says, stopping the first and looking toward the shack, where two more lights have just been turned on.

As the lights flicker on, the cockerel falls silent, the six dogs cease their barking, leaving Estela standing nervously in the middle of the yard, from where she sees the door swing open and a silhouette framed in the doorway and hears, or believes that she hears: Pain is all in the mind, not in the body. Theblindwomanofthedesert does not hear the greeting offered by the shadow, who quickly reveals himself to be an old man: the creature now hurrying towards her is the triplet who abandoned El Infierno.

'I need you … to lend me … need you …' Theblindwomanof-thedesert stammers as the triplet who came to the mountains arrives at her side. 'What's going on? … What the hell has happened to you? Who did this to you?' the old man says, while Estela tries to get her lips to form words: 'Tell me that … you have … there is … a.' But her words disintegrate beneath the weight of the effort that has brought her to this place.

Once more, in the silence of her mind, Theblindwomanofthedesert hears: Pain is all in the mind, not in the body. 'A telephone … I need … lend me …' Estela once more tries to say, but seeing the triplet's mouth repeat: 'What happened …? Who did this …?' her efforts turn to ashes in her mouth as her resolve drains from her body: I need … tele … Theblindwomanofthedesert does not realize that she is only thinking these words as she passes out and the triplet catches her as she falls.

Dragging the woman who appeared in his yard a moment earlier, the triplet who left Tres Hermanos heads back toward the house, escorted by his six dogs, where he once again transforms into a silhouette: the silhouette the two soldiers are gazing at as the shadows of the house envelop the triplet and Estela. The soldiers are still wondering: How do we … when she's got someone with her? … We should never have come here … What if they're lying in wait? … What if this is a trap?

The two soldiers left behind at La Caída by El Topo and El Tampón spend some time trying to decide what to do, how to assail this house whose lights are still twinkling in the darkness. This house in which the old man will spend a long time trying to resuscitate the woman who is now lying on his living-room floor, struggling to return to the present, to break free of her past that beckons her only to abandon her on the worst of all the days she spent living in El Paraíso: the day when Father Nicho said to her and to the man she so loves: 'Epitafio will marry Osaria … They will go to live up in the mountains … I need them to be somewhere else.'

The day when, for the last time, Estela and Epitafio went to hide among the rocks and where, for the last time in many years, they gave themselves to each other. The day on which they swore their undying love, while Estela, resting her head on Epitafio's chest, took a pen and traced lines between the dots she herself had burned into her lover's skin with Father Nicho's branding iron: suddenly, as in a children's book, Estela saw beneath her hesitant, faltering lines, a wind rose appear, transforming Epitafio into a map before her eyes; on that day he became a map of her entire existence.

'How can I …? Without my map …?' Theblindwomanofthedesert murmurs over and over as she lies on the floor of the house, while the old man who lives there continues to try to bring her round, to understand the words of this woman who is being hunted by the men still planning their assault. 'I can't ho … how … without you … my side,' Estela tells the triplet, who does not know that the delirious woman is not addressing him, but the image of Epitafio. The same man who floors the accelerator of his trailer truck and, seeing the distance they have yet to cover, announces: 'There's the fucking village!' while silently thinking to himself: Why haven't you been in touch? … Why are you ignoring me?

Why are you casting me aside when I've finally made my decision … when I'm finally ready to face up to that bastard priest … to face anyone and anything! Epitafio mutters soundlessly as he opens another beer, fires up his mind with three more bumps of cocaine, and says in a hoarse voice: 'We've finally reached the village … I hope you're ready, because we're going to have to get out.' And as he accelerates the Minos, he hastens the events that will ensue: they will arrive at the outskirts of the village, they will stop the truck, step out of the cab, climb into the back of the container, unhook one of the nameless ones, negotiate a sale, climb back into the cab and they will head off again in the trailer.

Later, as the landscape and the darkness begin to merge in the windows of the Minos, the three men in the cab will once again be plunged into their greatest fears, in a rush of cocaine and beer, going over and over the doubts that have been plaguing them for hours: If you keep playing his game, sooner or later Epitafio is going to realize, Mausoleo will think, glancing at Sepelio, who, in turn, is thinking: I need to convince this fucker that Estela is one of the bullet-ridden corpses … that it's her mangled body in the photograph.

Meanwhile, Hewhoisdeafofmind will continue to torture himself: I could call you back … no … that's the one thing I can't do … I've already told you that I love you … I can't call you again … I've told you how I feel … to say it again would be humiliating. And from time to time he will continue to blurt out something causing the two men next to him to laugh: 'Shit … not even a word and I've told you I love you!' And it is the scornful laugh of Mausoleo and of Sepelio (who, when he hears Epitafio mutter, thinks: That's it … you just keep driving yourself up the wall!) that will force Epitafio to regain his composure: Try to think about something else.

And each time he does so, each time he thinks about something else, Epitafio will see the faces of the boys from the jungle: the same two boys who, to herd the men and women from other desolate lands toward the caves where they must wait until daybreak, have been forced to abandon the front line for the past forty-five minutes and walk behind these creatures who still have a God, a name, a soul and a shadow.

IV

'Get a move on, the caves are just up ahead,' shouts the elder of the two boys, using the beam of his flashlight to whip the backs of the men and women who crossed the border only recently and who, stooped and bowed by exhaustion, by the incessant, lashing rain, by the sounds that in the dying hours of night burnished the gathering dawn, filling the space of threats, shamble forward ever slower and more scattered. 'He said get a move on!' roars the younger boy, using his beam of the flashlight in his left hand to herd the men and women still trailing their hopes like shadows: 'Round up, we're nearly there … Once we get there we can rest up for a while … Shift it! We're nearly there!' says the boy who serves as lieutenant here, the beam of his flashlight pointing through the rising mist that hangs in the air toward the caves that the people of the forest call El Purgatorio.

'I really thought we wouldn't all make it today,' says the older boy, quickening his pace as he illuminates the four immense subterranean caves through which the jungle channels the water that rushes down from the sierra, then, turning briefly to glance at the boy who acts as lieutenant, who is urging himself faster, and those of the men and women who still have a name, a body, a tongue and a shadow, the older boy adds, 'I can't believe we made it here with all of them.'

'It was hard work today … So much rain so much mud … so many dumb fucks brought here by you … so many old people so

303

many young ... not to mention that pregnant bitch ... It's amazing they all made it ... We're not likely to lose any of them now ... The path from here to the clearing is easy going,' says the boy who serves as leader, coming to a halt a few meters from where the subterranean caves open their flinty throats to the night: the four caves known as El Purgatorio, that people here call Cuatro Bocas — the Four Mouths.

'Stop! We're going to rest up here for a while,' barks the younger of the boys, yawning and turning his flashlight on the men and women recently arrived from other lands, stopping them in their tracks: 'No one is to wander off ... Stay close by ... go no further than the caves.' Yawning again, the boy who serves as deputy sinks a little into the mud and, training his flashlight on the face of his leader, protests: 'Why are you blaming me for this? You brought them here just as much as I did!'

'I told you not to shine that thing in my eyes,' growls the older boy, batting aside the flashlight and, yawning himself, he turns his own flashlight on the men and women who have dragged their hopes through the jungle: 'You know full well why I said that ... Don't play the fool ... just look at the ones you selected, then look at the one I brought!' Turning again, the younger boy trains the flashlight on the creatures who have meekly stopped: like diminutive searchlights, the flashlights bring from the shadows the bustle of those who once more feel their hopes swell.

Hewhostillboastsasoul is now sitting on a branch and on his knee is the little girl he carried all this way, who whispers a few words in his ear and hugs him, nestling against his shoulder. ShewhostillcallsonGod is wandering toward one of the caves with Hewhostillhasabody, who is taking out the inhaler he uses from time to time and which he will use inside the cave they have just entered. Behind them, a small group comprising two unnamed old men and a middle-aged woman are walking decisively toward one of the other caverns.

As they pass, the group of those unnamed step over Hewhostillbearsaname, who is framed against the giant movie screen that is the jungle, lying on a rock next to which stands another rock against which a woman who has not been named is leaning: the two huge rocks are sheltered by a flame tree that, in the movie projected by the flashlight of the two yawning boys, looks as though it is bleeding out. Farther off, between the roots of a copperwood tree, Hewhohasnotyetsunghisfears has laid out the plastic sheet he carried with him and, settling himself on it, he watches Shewhostillhashershadow who is wandering aimlessly, muttering to herself in a low voice.

Silent, bewildered and increasingly exhausted, the two boys watch the movie their flashlights project on to the shadows, then, slumping to the ground and, without even realizing, they contemplate the dance of the rain, which has now become a downpour: from time to time there is a crackle as lightning flashes hurled upon the world by the great black clouds light up the shadows that their flashlight beams cannot reach: a squirrel scampering along a branch, a bird in flight whose vivid plumage does not fear the raindrops, a ring-tailed snake frantically slithering across the mud.

Each time the lightning flashes fade, the rumble of thunder lingers and when the echo of the thunderclap falls silent, the sons of the jungle, whose eyelids long to rest if only for a moment, lose themselves in the murmur of the jungle: the croak of frogs in the river that spews from the vast caverns, the screen of hundreds of bats inside the caves, in the distance a panther of these latitudes roars while a stubborn bird pecks at the soft trunk of a towering avocado tree. And so, as they unravel the sounds that weave together the thrum of the jungle they can hear, the boys' eyelids surrender and the nervous tongues of the men and women who recently breached the wall that divides the ravaged lands begin to awaken.

I just need to get there I've got people waiting for me ... My two sons and my husband ... Four years they've been here ... I haven't seen them in all that time ... so they're bound to throw a party for me.

I come from there, but there's nothing there any more ... That's why I'm leaving ... as all my friends left ... I'll have a job here ... I'll have a life here ... I'll meet up with my friends again ... They're waiting for me.

I am leaving so I can forget ... forget what I had ... forget what I don't have ... what I don't have any more ... I've come here so I don't have to live in fear ... because I won't be afraid here.

I want to go so that I can come back and keep my promises ... I promised my daughter a laptop ... my son a Cubs jacket ... I promised my wife I'd bring back money ... That's why I've come here ... so I can go back weighed down with promises.

So I can give birth there, so he won't have to make the journey ... I want him to be born there, so he never has to make this journey ... That's why I'm going ... to finish this pregnancy.

'She says she can't carry on ... The woman over there keeps saying she can't carry on,' says the boy who serves as lieutenant, his eyelids suddenly flickering open, thereby exploding the silence in which he and his leader had been plunged until now. 'That even if she wanted to she couldn't ... she couldn't take another step,' the younger boy says, clapping his hands and training the beam of his flashlight on Shewhostillhashershadow. 'It will do her good to get some rest ... Maybe she'll stop fucking with things she can't change.'

'What the hell are you talking about?' the older boy asks, opening his eyes and slapping his cheeks before turning toward the men and women following them. 'What did you say? ... What the fuck are you talking about?

'I had to pretty much drag her here,' the younger boy says, once more shining his flashlight on Shewhostillhashershadow.

'That idiot ... You should have left her behind,' the older boy says, looking at the woman illuminated by his lieutenant's circle of light; and, feeling a stabbing pain in his chest, he adds, 'How many times have I got to tell you? ... We don't bring pregnant women.'

'You don't care that she's pregnant ... Something happened between you and her,' mutters the younger boy, barely noticing as he lets his flashlight fall on the ground.

'What the hell are you talking about?' the elder asks, picking up the other's flashlight and training it on Shewhostillhashershadow. 'You know the rules … There's only one fucking rule … No old people, no amputees, no pregnant women.'

'I could tell back there that you'd seen each other before,' the younger boy says, closing his eyes and leaning back. 'I even told you then that I knew.'

'One simple rule!' the boy who serves as leader says, ignoring the fact that the younger is now lying down and peering at the pregnant woman, who has been wandering around and is now heading towards one of the caves.

'I knew that she recognized you, too … She took one look at you and ran off.'

'Don't talk shit,' the elder boy says, his tone more perfunctory than before and, as he turns towards the younger boy he feels another stab in his ribs. 'Why don't you get some sleep? … I'll come by and wake you later.'

'Back there in the alley … maybe in the churchyard … it was … it's true … did tell you …' mutters the younger boy, allowing his body and his mind to mingle memories with the noises of the jungle and the voice of the boy who between them serves as leader.

'I'll come back and wake you, then when you're awake I can get some sleep, so we'll both have had some rest,' the older boy says, the words pour out mechanically and, as he waits for the other to nod off, he tries to ignore the impulse that has risen from his chest to his brain and there become a thought.

'While I'm asleep … I said back in the jungle … back in the

churchyard … then you sleep,' the younger boy murmurs, memories not twining with the dream he is having and the words that seem increasingly distant.

'Sleep, get some rest. I'll be back later to wake you. Right now I'm going to go and check on them, make sure they're not up to something,' the leader says, still looking at the younger boy and, embracing the idea that blossomed in his mind a moment earlier, he jumps to his feet.

'Please don't hurt her,' the younger boy pleads, opening his eyes, feeling again the curious stabbing in his chest as he sees the older boy race off.

'What?' the older boy spins around, more angry than nervous. 'What the hell are you saying?'

'You know … I'm saying …' the boy whose role is to obey closes his eyes again, feeling the needle withdraw from his chest and once more confounding wakefulness and dream, '… to her … nothing … I'm …'

'Why do you suddenly care about her? You weren't even there the day when …' The leader begins, but trails off in mid-sentence, realizing that the younger boy is now asleep.

'…'

'That's right … you just get some shut-eye,' the elder boy says, and, turning on his heel again, walks away from his lieutenant.

Illuminating the space with his flashlight and the flashlight that the younger of the two boys has been using until now, the older boy slips past ShewhostillcallsonGod and Hewhostillhasabody and comes to the entrance of the huge subterranean cavern Shewhostillhashershadow has just entered. The rain is falling harder on the place where he is standing, on the body of the older boy and on the idea urging him on while the lightning flashes grow more frequent: the deluge has become a thunderstorm.

Ignoring the storm and allowing himself to be led on by the idea that has brought him to this place and now grips him, the boy who serves as leader thinks: I saw her at the entrance to this cave ... I'm sure of it ... She must be inside. Then, walking on, he illuminates the interior of the cave, burying his rage and his fear: If you recognized me, you shouldn't have come ... You should never have come to the churchyard.

Racing inside the rocky gullet that spews forth the river that cleanses the essence of the forest — El Purgatorio is the liver and the kidneys that purge the jungle — the older boy grips both flashlights in one hand, unsheathes the machete hanging from his belt, feels the idea that a moment earlier governed his existence become a plan and, pushing aside two other men who have not been named here, cajoles them: 'Where did the pregnant woman go?'

'Did you not hear me or did you not understand?' the boy who serves as leader here insists, training the beam of the flashlights on the men, who seem to fuse with the rocks, as though they were drawn on the rocks there several eons ago. Then the elder boy raises the machete and, his eyes boring into the fearful eyes of Hewhostillhashisvoice and Hewhocanstillusehistongue, snarls: 'Where is she ... the pregnant woman ... Where is she, the fucking pregnant bitch?'

'I saw ... I saw her ... I saw her sitting ... sitting there ... then I saw her go deep inside,' Hewhocanstillusehistongue says, gesturing to the point where the earth's gullet divides into two tunnels. 'That way?' The older boy asks, shining the twin flashlights towards the tunnel that snakes towards the right. 'If you want I can come ... I can show you ... If you want I can show you the way,' Hewhostillhashisvoice says, raising his head.

'*Hijo de puta* ... Don't even set ... What do I care?' growls the boy who serves as leader, staring hard at Hewhostillhashisvoice, then, leaning his face so close the man can smell him, he adds: 'Just tell me which tunnel ... which path she took ... and don't think it will earn you any favors ... That's all I need, you thinking I owe you something ... There's nothing to be gained here.' Bowing his head again and forcing his feet to walk, Hewhostillhashisvoice leads the elder boy to the place where the cave divides and, stretching out his hand, he points: 'She should be down that way.'

'If I don't find the bitch down there, you're the one who is going to pay,' the elder of the sons of the jungle warns. 'I'll come back and you're going to pay,' he says and stalks off towards the vast cave, then steps into the stream and plunges off into the bowels of the forest dark, using the twin flashlight beams to illuminate the shimmering epochs of the earth and his blade to startle the bats, who flutter off, wheeling in the air.

Once embarked upon the path, the boy who serves as leader sees the woman he is seeking and who a moment ago, just as the most distant of her ancestors did a thousand years ago, looks up and knows that her time has come. Crouching on the rocks, Shewhostillhashershadow brings both hands to her belly, smiles at the elder of the sons of the jungle and returns the water she has just poured into her mouth to the river that sweeps along the odours of all things living and all things dead: this place smells of the very essence of the earth.

Exploiting the impulse that has led him to her, the elder boy furiously brings the machete down and with a single stroke cuts the throat of the woman, so robbing her of her shadow. 'You didn't have to come … If you recognized me, why the fuck did you come? … You should never have gone to the churchyard!' the elder boy roars, slashing the shadowless creature over and over with his blade. 'Or you should have said something to me … You were the one who should have remembered … You shouldn't have seemed so unsure … so uncertain … You should have acknowledged me!' the boy howls and falls into the stream as a strange, garbled moan escapes his lips.

Crouching in the stream, the water lapping at his thighs, the older boy looks to the ruined body, glances at his machete, contemplates the reflection of the bats returning to their roosts as the moan becomes a long, hoarse whimper and then a plaintive howl that ebbs and flows. Setting down the flashlights on the rocky bank, the boy who serves as leader plunges his weapon and his hands into the water and, watching the water sweep away the blood still dripping from his body, he sobs for a long time.

When, finally, he gets to his feet again, the elder of the two boys picks up the flashlights, slips the machete back into his belt and, wiping the tears from his face, he clenches his jaw: 'But you didn't recognize me.' He smiles briefly and sets off back to the entrance of the cave and, as he does so, without quite knowing why, he recalls the face of the man to whom he and the younger boy sold the nameless only a day ago: No, you're not thinking about that man … Don't be an idiot, the elder boy thinks, smiling, and realizes he is thinking about the woman he saw in the clearing known as Claro de Hierba.

Then, when he finally emerges from the cave, the boy who serves as leader finds that he is still smiling and that the dappled night has given way to gray-blue dawn. 'Come on …! Get up … We're on the move again!' he orders the men and women who so recently crossed the border, and, heading back to the place where the younger boy still lies, sleeping, he searches his memory for an image of the woman he saw in El Tiradero: this time, however, he realizes that he is thinking about Epitafio, the man who is still behind the wheel of his truck and who is growing more worried with each passing moment.

That same truck that, some time ago, left behind the vast plain known as the Llano del Silencio, the uninhabited plain that unites the south and the center of the land that is the birthplace of Epitafio, the sons of the jungle and Estela. Estela who, back in La Caída, sprawled on the floor of a shack belonging to the triplet who took off one day for the mountains, briefly regains consciousness and, lost in an ocean of pain and fear, babbles: 'Him too … going to leave me … kill him … no coordinates … must phone him … betrayed us … with no map … without him I don't want … without my Epitafio.'

Epitafio, the man who still does not understand why Estela has not called him and who, as he slows the truck and twists the steering wheel, leaves the motorway and, shifting gears, takes the road that crosses the high plateau called Sombras de Agua — Shadows of Water. The high plateau that forms the center of his homeland and which leads to the north, a place Hewhoisdeafofmind will never reach.

V

Gazing into the distance, yet oblivious to the dawn breaking over the volcanoes that rise from the center of the plateau known as Sombras de Agua, since for him the outside world and indeed the cab of his truck do not exist, Hewhoisdeafofmind reaches out, flicks down the sun visor that protects his eyes and, without realizing, launches into another tirade: 'Fucking hell ... Why haven't I heard anything when I said I love you!'

Startled, the two men sitting next to him in the cab of the Minos — the same two men who, in Epitafio's mind, ceased to exist some time ago when the truck pulled up next to a derelict building and they sold the girl with the oversized head to the man with particular tastes — turn to look at him, but say nothing. Each is still carrying on a conversation in his mind: It couldn't have worked out better for me ... I haven't even started and the lunatic is already half-crazed, Sepelio is thinking, while Mausoleo reasons: I stepped aside just in time ... I've managed to play them both.

Who would have thought you were so fragile ... so strange? Mausoleo thinks, looking at Epitafio, whose chin and neck and chest are bathed by the sweltering sun rising in the distance. Who would have thought that some woman could get you so worried? the giant broods to himself, since he cannot imagine a woman unsettling a man: Mausoleo cannot imagine, will never be able to imagine that; to this man who came from nothing into the world and who, adrift in this nothingness, has tried to live in the world, a woman is the only home on earth.

You were such a bastard a while ago! ... Deciding everybody's fate ... Now you're begging for her to call you! Mausoleo thinks and, looking away from Epitafio to gaze through the windscreen of the Minos as silhouettes are formed by the sun rays on Sombras de Agua, he adds: A fucking bastard, now you're begging for her to call ... for some woman to love you!

Just some random woman, Mausoleo thinks as he watches the swooping ballet of a thousand blackbirds in the sky: just as he is incapable of imagining that this woman is a home to Epitafio, so, too, he cannot imagine that Estela — who, high in the sierra, has lapsed back into unconsciousness under the startled gaze of the triplet who struggles to his feet since his dogs have sensed other presences — aside from being Epitafio's only home, is his whole world.

Epitafio who, at this moment, having seen the flock of blackbirds quiver and whirl in the sky like a cloud of smoke, drives faster and edges dangerously close to a trailer filled with pigs. 'I wanted to be away from here by now ... This road always has too much traffic,' then, turning the steering wheel and shifting up a gear, he floors the accelerator and overtakes the truck blocking his path, while Sepelio and Mausoleo turn to stare at him: for some time now Epitafio's only utterances have been ravings.

'I was hoping we'd be long past the plateau by now ... fucking traffic,' Hewhoisdeafofmind grunts, weaving back into his own lane, shifting gears again and startling his fellow travelers. But before

THE BOOK OF THE SONS OF THE JUNGLE

Sepelio can react and distill his rage into words — I need to leave Epitafio to his terrors, don't let him step back from the brink of the abyss that is consuming him — Hewhoisdeafofmind slaps his head: 'How can you not love me? ... Why now when I've finally made up my mind?

'Why haven't you said anything when I've said I want only you ... or maybe you don't want the same thing?' Epitafio cries, taking both hands off the wheel and slapping himself in the head again, fueling the exultation of Sepelio, who is staring through the windscreen at the sun as it pales on the wheatfields and silhouettes the tractors, the rocks, the houses, smiling at the morning and at his good fortune: There I was thinking you wouldn't believe me ... that you'd believe me only because you couldn't believe it ... Who would have thought you'd do the work for me ... that you would further my plans ...?

Who would have thought that you'd believe me because you want to believe ... because you cannot bring yourself to believe anything else ... that you would have more faith than me in my plans! Sepelio thinks, stroking the mobile phone he is holding and smiling excitedly at the trees and the grain silos in the distance. But Sepelio's glee is burst by a sudden scream: 'What the fuck are you doing?

'Jesus fuck ... what are you doing?' Mausoleo roars again, cowering in his seat, squeezing his eyes shut and throwing his head back: brought abruptly back to earth by the screams — even as Sepelio withdraws into his shell — Epitafio savagely jerks the wheel of the Minos and returns to his own lane, narrowly avoiding the oncoming truck blaring its horn. He's going to get us killed ... The dumb *pendejo* is going to kill us! Mausoleo thinks, while Sepelio silently gloats:

That's it ... he's finally lost it ... This is my moment! and Epitafio pleads: Fucking hell ... what's going on with me? but the words from his mouth are: 'Fucking Estela ... what's going on with you?'

Meanwhile, inside the container of the Minos, the nameless not yet sold who are hanging by their hands wait for their bodies to stop swinging and, when they have finally regained their balance, go back to talking among themselves.

This is the third time I've come ... The second time was worse than this ... We were kidnapped, piled into a truck and taken to a house ... They took our phones away and phoned relatives to demand a ransom ... They broke the women's legs. They used a club to break the men's backs ... so they couldn't run away ... so they didn't have to guard them ... They left everyone just sprawled on the floor ... to be used when they needed us to talk.

This was my first time ... I'd never ... I never really wanted to make this journey ... I was all on my own back home ... I held out better than most ... I watched everyone leave ... I stayed behind until there was no one left ... nothing but my house ... my village ... nothing but the deserted fields ... nothing but silence and a soundless wind ... until even the flies fell silent.

I can't even begin to count ... I don't know how many times I've come ... The last was a long time ago ... nine years or so ... and I made it ... I even had a house here ... a job and a house ... but

immigration officers raided the fields and rounded up everyone
… Back again, the little dream was over … Now here I am …
back again … What can I do except try … keep on trying?

Epitafio switches off the headlights of the truck; they are no longer necessary since the power deep within the earth that sets the volcanoes blazing now bathes the plateau known as Sombras de Agua in light. He pushes the engine to the maximum, and once more says: 'Fucking Estela, what's going on with you?' although what he intended was to tongue-lash Mausoleo: *¡pinche puto!* … what's wrong with you? … get a grip. Don't be such a faggot coward! Then he laughs to himself, overtakes a couple of cars and comes to a tanker truck.

Having passed the tanker, Epitafio reaches out an arm, snorts two lines to shake himself into life, grabs the pack of cigarettes, pops a bottle of beer and completes the thought that has been nagging at him: Fuck's sake, Estela … what's going on with you? … Why don't you want to love me? … Why not now forever! Meanwhile, Mausoleo is brooding: Bastard … Who are you to decide my fate? … You're more likely to fuck it up completely … You're going to get us killed because you're hung up on some woman!, while Sepelio, turning back toward the window and watching two mustangs racing in the distance, is thinking: Now I know you're going to believe me!

Now I know you're going to believe me, not because you don't suspect anything … but because you already suspect something … You've started to suspect something is wrong and I didn't even have to say a word! Sepelio thinks again, diverting his attention from the distant mustangs to the interior of the cab where his excitement is piqued as he watches as Epitafio, coughing smoke from his lungs and trying to allay his panic, gestures to a road sign by an area of common land that reads EJIDO SADA 27 and says: 'We're going to stop there … just before that *ejido*.

'Make sure you're ready, we're going to stop here … just next to that area of common land we'll be sell … You promised me that what we had was real … that it would never end … that wherever you went you would carry me within you … Why haven't you called me?' Epitafio adds, without realizing that midway through the sentence he has allowed his fears to overcome him again and without realizing that his fears have turned Sepelio's elation into pleasure: You'll believe me because you already believe it … I didn't even have to plant the idea in your head … You don't know it yet, but you have made a trap for yourself … You have created the very pain I wanted to inflict on you!

'Why won't you talk to me when I've told you that you will always be my home … that I will always be your refuge? … Up there among the rocks and in my room and in the fucking truck I told you over and over … that you were born in me and I was born in you … What's going on with you that you won't even talk to me?' Epitafio roars, alarming Mausoleo and transforming Sepelio's pleasure into something pure and translucent: You'll believe me because you already think it has happened … though you don't yet know that's what you think … You manufactured these terrors yourself … Now you're just waiting for something to have happened to her … You'll believe me because all you can think is that she hasn't called you because she cannot call you!

'I don't believe you don't love me … It's impossible … It's not

possible that you haven't called because you don't want to call me ...
Something must have happened to you!' Hewhoisdeafofmind protests,
and, while Sepelio continues to gloat over himself and his plan, this
time Mausoleo's shock, which until now was no more than a reflex,
takes the form of a warning and then, finally, a decision: glancing at
Epitafio, Mausoleo thinks: I was right not to stake everything on him
... to play them off against each other ... This idiot is not the good guy
... He's not the tough bastard I thought he was ... This fucker can't
even decide his own fate.

And all over some woman ... all this over a woman! Mausoleo
carries on, and will continue to carry on even when all this is over,
incapable of understanding that Estela is not merely a woman. Estela,
who, a moment earlier, awoke high up in the sierra and was petrified
to see the window glow with the light of day and to find that the man
who took her into his shack has vanished. Mausoleo looks away from
Epitafio, he will never understand that, more than simply a woman,
Theblindwomanofthedesert is a history: the only history in which
Epitafio ever imagined his life might one day be written.

On the other hand, this bastard is a lot calmer now ... more com-
posed, self-controlled ... and much more excited, Mausoleo thinks,
observing Sepelio: the giant will never understand that Estela — who
now struggles to her feet as best she can and, as best she can, sets
about looking for the man who helped her, because she needs a telephone and a gun — is the sole, the unique foundation to Epitafio's
entire universe: the only constant in a life that began in uncertainty
and here, in uncertainty, is about to end.

While Hewhoisdeafofmind begins to rant again: 'Something

must have happened to you … Otherwise why haven't you called me … Shit … Someone must have done something to you!', Sepelio smiles at the giant, closes his right eye and gives a little nod, then turns back to the window: You'll believe it, because you want to believe that something has happened to her … because you want to believe that someone has hurt your Estela … You'll see her in the photograph because you're convinced that something like that has happened, Sepelio thinks, savoring the moment. You will see her in the photo because you can already see her in your mind, Sepelio thinks in his heart of hearts and his moment brings with it a surge of bile: finally all the years of bitterness are over, finally the moment has come for revenge, a revenge he has been plotting for so long and is now playing out as it did so often in his mind: with Epitafio falling to pieces: Everything will go exactly as I wanted … I'll finally put an end to all the time I've spent dealing with your shit … to all these years!

Sepelio's interior monologue is suddenly interrupted by a new outburst from Epitafio: 'Why would something have happened? … Nothing can happen to you … You don't want to call me … That's what's happened!' Sepelio's smile broadens to a laugh, even as he realizes that he must hurry, that he needs to exploit Epitafio's doubts, he turns away from the window and, in a tone that is firm yet deliberate, says: 'What if she hasn't called because something has happened to her?'

'What?'

'What if she wants to call but she can't?' Sepelio says, suddenly feeling as though his cage is closing on him.

'What the hell are you talking about?' Epitafio asks, reducing the speed of the truck, but not the speed of his thoughts, 'What the fuck did you say? Why would you—?'

'What if Estela wants to call you, but can't?' Sepelio interrupts Epitafio, feeling his heart pound in his chest as the cage in which he was prisoner begins to open again.

'Why couldn't she talk to me? … Why wouldn't Estela be able to call?' Hewhoisdeafofmind says, allowing the Minos to slow further, even as his mind races faster. 'You'd do better to get yourself ready, we're almost there … Stop spouting shit … The *ejido* is right over—'

'Maybe something happened to her … Maybe that's why she hasn't called,' Sepelio interrupts again and the walls of his prison crumble to dust. 'Don't tell me it hasn't occurred to you.'

'Why would anything have happened?' Hewhoisdeafofmind says, pulling over to the side as the shudder threatening his spine finally shakes him. 'Maybe something has happened … Maybe someone has done something to her.'

'That's what I was just thinking … Something's happened to Estela,' Sepelio says, shaking off the dust and the rubble from his prison cell and, feeling his anger swell to blind fury, he adds: 'Someone has done something to Estela!'

'Who would want to hurt her?' Epitafio says, turning off the ignition as the shudder racing down his spine fills his head with the faces of a thousand men. 'Who would dare pick a fight with Estela?'

'It could be anyone … at the checkpoint or up in the mountains,' Sepelio suggests, smiling to himself and feeling his fury transformed into sheer hatred. 'Maybe even someone at the orphanage …'

'Why did you mention the orphanage?' Hewhoisdeafofmind snarls angrily, but in his mind the thousand faces melt away leaving only that of Father Nicho.

'Maybe it was Father Nicho,' Sepelio suggests, as his private smile turns to a inward laugh.

'Bastard fucking priest … that son of a bitch Nicho.'

'How many times did she tell you … I must have heard her tell you a hundred times … You shouldn't trust that old man … he's plotting something,' Sepelio says as his laughter rises to a cackle.

'That damn priest … I've been an idiot … why didn't I listen …? You're right, she did tell me,' Hewhoisdeafofmind wails, beating his head with his fists as the face of the priest is transformed into that of Estela.

'That treacherous bastard.'

'That's what you were trying to tell me,' Epitafio howls, forgetting for a moment where he is and once more addressing those who are absent. 'That's what you wanted to tell me back in the jungle … Why didn't I listen to you when we were in the truck?'

'Father fucking Nicho … How could you do this to them … How could you betray them?' Sepelio says again, choking back his jubilation and, feeling his rage transform into hope, he asks: 'Why don't I call him?'

'"When I wake up, remind me I have something to tell you" … That's what you said back in the clearing … but I wasn't listening to you and now it's too late,' Hewhoisdeafofmind howls, speaking to the memory of Estela, and, feeling his world collapse around him, he adds:

'It's my fault … if anything has happened to you it will be my fault.'

'So should I call him or what?' Sepelio says, waving his phone — and the silent laugh inside him dies away as he sees Mausoleo cower in his seat.

'If they've done anything to you, it's my fault, it's my fault … I let you down and I promised I would never let you down,' Epitafio howls, as a reel of memories spools past, showing him every day he spent with Estela, the woman who, even now, is in the mountains still looking for the triplet who brought her into his home.

'I'm going to phone the bastard … I'm going to talk to that traitor!'

'I failed you and I shouldn't have failed you … I let you down and I told you that I would always be your map … I promised you!' Epitafio says, picturing Estela in the rocks behind the orphanage, on the roof of the ancient building, in the basement that reeked of burning flesh, on the bed in his room, in the cab of his battered old truck, in the bedrooms of a thousand and one hotels, in La Carpa, where she governed for many years: in every single place where, thanks to her, he felt he was a man and not simply a scab.

'I'm calling … I'm phoning Father Nicho,' Sepelio says, pretending to dial the number of the old man who founded the orphanage known as El Paraíso. 'It's ringing … I'm going to give that bastard a piece of my mind.'

'How could I allow something to happen to you? … I let you down and I let myself down … how could I have failed myself so badly?' Epitafio roars, pounding his head with his fists again, watching as they crumble, the memories of the moments he spent with Estela crumble, those moments when he was truly a man, accepting that his world has fallen apart and feeling himself crushed by the weight of nothingness.

'He's not answering ... The fucking bastard isn't answering,' Sepelio says, taking the phone from his ear, then, glancing at the giant who has so shriveled in his seat he has become a dwarf, and, seizing the moment, the moment when he feels he will finally be reborn, he stares at the back of Epitafio's head: 'He's sent a message ... the bastard has sent a photo.'

'How could he do this to us? ... Why didn't I listen to you while there was still time ... How could he betr ...?' Hewhoisdeafofmind trails off in mid-sentence, because he has heard what Sepelio has said, and, turning his face, he feels the weight of nothingness crush the present moment.

'That son of a bitch ... Epitafio ... Fuck ... The bastard ... You need to see this!' shouts Sepelio, who is sitting next to a dwarf attempting to disappear altogether, then, offering the phone to Hewhoisdeafofmind, he says, 'You really need to see this ... The bastard ... He's killed her.'

'Who ... What ... What the fuck?' Epitafio says, oblivious now to what he is saying, since he already knows who and what, 'Who ... What ... Why?' he babbles, stretching out his hand, grabbing the phone and feeling the nothingness that ravaged his memories now come for his desires.

'Father Nicho ... Father Nicho has murdered her ... She's riddled with bullets,' Sepelio says, pointing to the phone he has just handed to Epitafio, and, seeing the man who humiliated him for so long crumple, he feels the black bird in his chest that opened its wings so recently, finally take flight: 'You should have listened to her ... You should have listened!'

'Shot … Estela … murderer there … father dead … I listened …' Hewhoisdeafofmind whispers, squeezing the telephone he is holding in his hands, as he realizes that it is not simply his past and his future that are being obliterated, but his present, and he tosses the phone on to the dashboard, opens the door of the truck and clambers out.

'They've taken your Estela!' Sepelio shouts, leaning over the dwarf who was once a giant and vainly trying to reach the open door: yet the something that manages to reach the open door, leaving behind the bottomless well of emptiness and solitude in which it lived, is the black bird from his chest: 'You should have listened to her … She told you a hundred times … She told you over and over … You should have listened.'

Clambering over the body of the dwarf, Sepelio reaches the open doorway and watches as Epitafio wanders aimlessly along the road: 'Even I listened to her … because you wouldn't,' he calls and laughs once more, and as he does so he feels the emptiness that the bird inside his chest left a moment earlier filled by a creature of hope and the stillness that comes only with revenge. 'Why didn't you listen to Estela? … I would have listened to Ausencia!' he shouts, expecting Epitafio to turn, if only briefly, before he Hewhoisdeafofmind does what Sepelio knows he will do.

'I would have listened to her … I would never have ignored Ausencia … never!' Sepelio insists, relishing this vengeance he has spent so long planning as he watches Epitafio stagger and weave: Hewhoisdeafofmind is about to mimic Cementeria, he is about to make the plan Sepelio devised so long ago a reality: 'That's something I never did ... I never disregarded Ausencia ... I always listened to her ... I'm listening to you now ... Why didn't you listen? ... Why didn't you listen to Estela?' Sepelio says it over and over, convinced that Epitafio will turn around or look over his shoulder. But, having decided he will never again listen to anything or anyone, Hewhoisdeafofmind continues to walk away, now disconnected from his mind and disconnected from the earth.

Without a second thought Hewhoisdeafofmind waits for the moment that happened some time ago and when the truck his mind has chosen is about to overtake his, he takes two steps, almost two leaps forward: the thud of metal against flesh makes Sepelio shudder and flattens Epitafio, whose last act is to beg forgiveness of Estela: Estela, the lone person in this world who could have made him different to this world.

Estela, who, back in La Caída, gives up searching the shack and decides to look out the window, only to see that the man who helped her earlier, whose face she can scarcely remember between dreams, is outside.

VI

Staring at the window she has just peered through, Estela pushes away the chair she has been using as a support, takes a couple of panicked breaths and once more feels the ribs broken against the rocks bite into her flesh: He must have gone outside … I'm sure there was a man here … that he dragged me inside … I can't have imagined it, she thinks, while reminding herself to take short, shallow breaths.

If he left the house he is in danger … If there was an old man and he went out, they might attack him, Estela reasons silently as she takes two faltering steps and looks through the window at the morning light: the sun's rays have reached the depths of La Caída and the world is alive with those creatures stirred by the heat, who lie on rocks, sating their hunger or basking in the sun.

But maybe there was no man, Estela thinks, leaning against the table that bisects this shack that belongs to the triplet who left El Infierno after quarreling with his brothers. At this point she realizes that she can go no further without dragging her left leg and the numbing pain that has spread to her shoulders and her neck: There must have been a man … What the hell am I thinking? … He was the one who brought me in here … Now I have to warn him … to save him from danger.

No … I don't care that he is in danger … If he went outside, then that is what he chose to do … He should have waited for me

… He should have asked me! Estela thinks, shuffling closer to the window whose glass flames in the morning light: I don't care what happens to him … but I need him to lend me his phone before they hurt him … He must have a mobile phone … I saw a phone charger when I was looking for the landline … I saw it just a minute ago, Theblindwomanofthedesert thinks, turning her head.

Scanning the room and realizing that there is no phone in the house and nothing that she can use as a weapon, Estela sees the charger plugged into the wall: a cable trails along the floor, lying there like an earthworm in a puddle. 'The man must have his phone with him … I need him to lend it to me,' Theblindwomanofthedesert mutters, turning back to the window, and moving two steps closer to the pane of glass where three cracks glitter in the sunlight.

I need to call Epitafio … to warn him … to let him know he's in danger, Estela thinks and, gritting her teeth, releases her grip on the table and quickens her faltering steps, mentally repeating the words Epitafio once said: Pain is all in the mind, not in the body, while screaming at the top of her lungs: Nearly there … just a few more steps … a little further and I'll be able to see him … to ask him.

But just before she reaches the window Theblindwomanofthedesert collapses and, for a moment, Epitafio and the words she needs to say to him and the words he said to her so long ago are pushed from her mind. Lying broken on the floor, all that is Estela is now reduced to a struggle with her body and a desperate urgency to save the man who went out into La Caída some time ago: I hope he's safe … that they haven't hurt him … at least not until he lends me his fucking phone, so I can talk to Epitafio.

As Theblindwomanofthedesert resurfaces in the mind of Estela, so too does her strength; raising both arms, she clamps her fingers onto the edge of the window sill and, using every ounce of energy, hauls herself to her feet: but a second before she can look out at La Caída, the dogs begin to bark, and though she cannot hear them, she somehow senses this and her body slackens and falls: 'Fuck ... fuck ... that must be them ... They're going to slaughter him,' Estela yelps as her words and her breaths come faster.

The stabbing pain from her ribs is more brutal this time and the lungs of Theblindwomanofthedesert spasm: little by little, the light streaming through the window and bathing the triplet's house begins to fade to black and the warmth Estela could feel becomes an icy coldness. From her mouth comes a panicked rush of words which lose all meaning and then they too trail away: 'Kill me and kill him ... the old man ... no more me here nothing ... fuck they ... can't call him ... could ... save him.'

A second before slipping into oblivion, in the echoing emptiness of her mind, Estela repeats the last words she will ever utter: 'Save him.' And it is these words that accompany Theblindwomanofthedesert to the place where she suddenly finds herself, trailing with her the memory of Hewhoisdeafofmind, who embraces her for a moment and then disappears, stripping all meaning from the dream in which Estela is floating: a dream in which she is saying to Epitafio: Without you the earth has no center ... without you everywhere is anywhere ... nothing but distance ... nothing but nothingness.

When Estela emerges from her blackout, the sun — which even now is stifling those still trudging through the jungle that divides the ravaged lands, and beating down on Sepelio's truck in Sombras de Agua, where he and Mausoleo are selling another of the soulless — shimmers on the floor where she lies curled into a fetal position and floods this house that delimits the madness of Theblindwomanofthedesert. This woman in whose mouth words of wakefulness and coma are commingled: Pure nothing ... to borrow his phone ... Without you there are no compass points ... not here he must be outside.

'He must still be outside ... He must still be alive ... Otherwise they would have come in here ... He's outside and when I call he will come,' Estela says to herself, believing she has completely regained consciousness, and, forgetting her dream, she grits her teeth again, reaches up and, clutching the windowsill, she hauls herself up with a strength she has never felt before: 'He has to come and help me ... He'll hear me and he'll come ... He'll lend me his phone,' Theblindwomanofthedesert mutters as she finally draws herself to her feet: 'I just have to call him ... to ask him to come back!'

Opening the window and sticking her head out, Estela looks at a world robbed of its shadows, she is surprised by the calm that reigns over La Caída and excited when she finally sees the triplet who long ago left El Infierno and came up to the mountains: the old man is standing next to a tin barrel. 'Please ... señor!' Theblindwomanofthedesert shouts, looking at the fire that the man is stoking and seeing from the rising smoke how high the sun is in the sky. Then Estela feels a sharp pain in her chest, tells herself that it is too late and, summoning up Epitafio's face, she begins to slip back into the dream from which she has barely emerged.

But before she becomes lost in this world that is calling to her again, Theblindwomanofthedesert manages to regain her self-control, to reduce her terror to agitation, to remember what she has to do, and to scream: 'Please … señor … help me … Please … I need … your phone … I have … to call him!' Less surprised by the screams of the woman stumbling towards him than by the fact that she has already managed to get to her feet again and is able to scream, the triplet who left for the mountains hurries back: 'Keep calm … Please, don't strain yourself … I'm coming … We can talk.'

For her part, Estela is surprised by the silence that issues from the mouth of the triplet, who is now racing back towards the house, and by the soundless barking of the dogs under the window, then she remembers that she lost her prostheses among the rocks up in the sierra and her deafness turns agitation to sheer terror and her worries to grief: How can I call him now … How the hell can I talk to him? Theblindwomanofthedesert wonders and the silence of the planet suddenly becomes the silence of the nothingness in which she found herself moments earlier.

'I need to phone Epitafio … Please … you have to help me … I need to talk to him urgently,' Estela pleads even as she racks her brain: But how am I going to talk to him … How, if I can't hear anything? Meanwhile the triplet approaching the house forces his legs to run faster and shouts: 'Don't worry … Please, just stay calm … Please, sit down again,' as he silently wonders whether he truly heard or merely imagined that the woman used the name Epitafio.

'Epitafio … is that what you said?' the man calls, unable to imagine that the man he now dredges up from his memory can be the center of Estela's world, the meaning that prevents nothingness from taking hold, the certainty that glimmers in her eyes, the desire that makes it possible for her to embrace her hopes. 'Epitafio? Did you say Epitafio?' the triplet calls again and his words collide with those Theblindwomanofthedesert inside the house is still shouting: 'Epitafio … Epitafio!'

Epitafio, the man who a moment earlier — a moment that could be a minute or an epoch — was betrayed by Sepelio. Sepelio, the man who has just brought the truck to a halt, and, after ordering Mausoleo to get out of the Minos, climbed down and headed towards the rear of the container. The container that the giant opened a second ago and which he and Sepelio are now climbing into, singing *'Eeny, meeny, miny, moe … catch a tiger by the toe … and the last man standing … is the one hanging here!'*

'Take him down and get him outside … We need to sell him and get moving … We have to keep heading north … We shouldn't be driving around here at this hour … It's not safe to be on the motorway in daylight,' Sepelio shouts, signaling the last of the godless, and, watching Mausoleo, he smiles and thinks: He was right, you really are huge … and you'll be very useful to us … and it's true that we're better off traveling by night … during the day anything could happen to us … because he was right about almost everything … Epitafio … Epitafio.

'Epitafio … Epitafio!' Estela wails as the triplet stands in front of her: 'Calm down, woman … I'll help you … Please calm down, you're not as strong as you think … You've lost a lot of blood. Calm down, you've taken a serious blow to the head … Come on, calm down and

I'll help you ... He helped me many times ... He even helped me to get away,' says the triplet, but the silence streaming from his mouth makes Theblindwomanofthedesert even more agitated.

'Your phone ... I need you to lend me ... no ... no ... I need you to talk to him ... I can't hear anything ... I need you to call Epitafio,' Estela shouts to the man standing in front of her and, sensing that the desert, the void, the nothingness now brood over her life, she tries to read at least some of the words on his lips: '   call him want ...   don't   really understand   two men guns ...   following you   what   do to you!'

'Exactly ... those bastards ... They were coming after me to kill me ... They were trying to hurt me ... They're going to try and hurt Epitafio, too ... The people who work for Sepelio and the priest,' Theblindwomanofthedesert explains, looking up and, picturing vultures circling overhead, she mumbles: 'Shit ... it might be too late,' then she stares into the eyes of the triplet, who is now smiling proudly and, though he knows that she cannot hear, he excitedly exclaims: 'Those two   no problem ...   killed ...   hack to pieces ... bodies   burning barrel.'

If he's killed them and burned the bodies, that means a lot of time has passed, much more than I thought ... It's too late to warn Epitafio ... too late for me to save him, Estela realizes and the hope in her eyes gutters out and the desert descends on the world: The three vultures I feared have landed. 'Call him right now ... Call Epitafio,' Theblindwomanofthedesert cries, and, though she no longer really knows where she is, she tries to read the old man's words: ' calm!   in danger really   help you ...   not listening   call him if you can …   phone now.'

'Yes, yes … you have to talk to him … You have to phone Epitafio … Tell him we've been betrayed … that he's in danger … that's what you have to tell him,' Estela pleads, even as she silently resigns herself to the fact that it is futile, that it is too late, and, realizing for the first time that, without this man she has loved for so long, there are no longer two worlds, that without Epitafio the world of her dreams is the world of her waking: '   the number?   Tell me …
talk to him   number to dial   you want to …   ? '
says the triplet, who owes so much to Epitafio, and this time, as his lips move, Estela surrenders and allows herself to fall, accepting her defeat and her misfortune, she turns the knife in her own wound since she believes it is deserved, and rather than give the number to this man, she spits in the face of the world of Sepelio, while, in heart, soul certainty, meaning and hope crumble to dust as her body musters all its strength and stands up.

Leaning against the window again, Estela stares out at the court-yard where the barrel is still blazing and, having seen what she was looking for, she clambers on to the window ledge and allows herself to tumble outside. Struggling to her feet again, without knowing how or why, Theblindwomanofthedesert shoos away the dogs trying to lick her wounds and is about to start walking when she feels a claw-like hand grip her and, turning, she sees the triplet who one day left El Infierno.

'   is dead …   some man   Epitafio …
run over …   threw himself … oncoming truck   told me he
laughed   I'll tell him   and laughed   happening

laughing …   to understand …   the other one
about Cementeria!' the man shouts, but Estela has already
turned and is walking away. Around her the six dogs silently yap
and, up ahead, the flames crackle soundlessly: for the first time
Theblindwomanofthedesert does not miss the hearing aids she lost
up in the mountains: for her, the only sound in the world was the
voice of Epitafio.

Looking up for a moment, Estela sees the summit of La Caída,
glances at the dazzling, distant sun, spots a flock of storks, stares at
the steep slope she came down some hours ago, catches a glimpse of
the road that brought her to the place where she now finds herself.
Then she watches as they crumble, the place where she finds herself,
the road that brought her here, the flock of storks, the dazzling sun
that shimmers on the summit of La Caída: for Estela, the only sight
in this world was the sight of Epitafio: without it, her world is already
in ruins.

Crouching next to the blazing barrel, Estela picks up the machete
the triplet used to dismember the bodies now burning in the drum,
looks at her reflection for the last time, and, as the triplet now running
towards her screams something that neither she nor we will ever hear,
she decides that she cannot kill herself because of the thing she is carrying in her belly and so puts out her eyes: why would she need them
when she will never again see Epitafio, when her world is a perfect
circular void, pure distance, pure nothingness?

'   !' the triplet shouts
again as he reaches Estela: it will be many years before he will understand, this man whom life is soon to make a godfather, why this

woman now struggling to her feet again has just done what she did, this woman who, feeling a hand grasp her, cries out: 'Pain is all in the mind, not in the body!' This woman who, in the midst of her desert and using her new blindness, summons up the first image of the world that Epitafio made visible, not quite knowing why it is this rather than another image that her memory offers: it is an image of the sons of the jungle.

The same two boys who, at this moment, are urging on the men and women who recently arrived from other lands for they have almost reached the clearing that some know as the Eye of Grass and others simply call The Shooting Range.

VII

'We're almost there ... get a move on, we'll be there any minute now!' shouts the elder of the two boys, pointing into the distance and considering the colors the sun has imposed upon the world: the procession of men and women who will soon lose their names are framed by every possible shade of green, the brash, smoldering reds of a poisonous creeper, the muted purple of the bromeliads that infest the kapok trees, the black and blood-red mud and the symphony of browns made by tree trunks, roots and vines.

Meanwhile, as the younger of the two boys watches light play on the damage wreaked by the storm — the rays of the great star glancing off pools of rainwater, the damp leaves of the shrubs, the wet rocks and the mud which look as though the jungle has been sprinkled with slivers of metal — he echoes the words of his leader: 'You heard him! Get moving ... We're nearly there ... Just a little farther and we'll be there!'

'That's the clearing up ahead ... just past that line of sapote trees,' the elder of the boys says, forcing his legs faster until he is almost running as he listens to the cacophony of jungle voices that daylight imposes upon the world: the calls of crows and mockingbirds, the chatter of magpies and the croak of ravens. He looks over his shoulder at the boy who serves as his lieutenant: 'It's amazing that we got here on time ... I didn't think we'd make it back on time.'

'Almost on time … You mean almost on time,' the boy whose role is to obey contradicts him, racing towards the clearing called El Ojo de Hierba as he, too, listens to the shifting sounds of the jungle in the light of day: from all around, though invisible to the eye, comes the cackle of turkey buzzard, the snort of a wild boar, the bell of a deer, the drone of bees and the sound of furtive laborers: the thwack of axe against wood and, further off, the clang of a machete against a rock concealed by grass.

'What do you mean almost on time … surely we're …?'

'We're a little late,' the younger boy interrupts the elder, bringing a hand up to shield his eyes from the scorching, blood-red sun. 'If you want me to believe what you say, don't tell lies!'

'What the fuck are you talking about?' asks the elder boy, also shielding his eyes from the sun as it blazes through the huge flowers of a flame tree that mimic its blaze. 'Why are you angry with me?'

'We wouldn't be late if we hadn't stopped at the caves,' the younger boys says, and he quickens his pace and, looking over his shoulder, yells at the those who are following: 'Don't get left behind … This is the last stretch!'

'We're not so late that it's going to cause trouble,' the elder boy says, lowering his hand since the sun is now hidden behind a philo-dendron, 'Besides, they couldn't carry on any more … If we hadn't stopped, we'd have lost some along—'

'We stopped because you wanted to stop,' the younger boy once more interrupts the boy who serves as leader. 'Because you wanted to do what you did to her.'

'Why are you going on about her?' the older boy yells, turning his head. 'What the fuck do you care?'

'I couldn't give a shit about that bitch,' he whose duty is to obey calls, now twenty meters from the wall of roots, trunks and vines that separates the jungle from the clearing called El Tiradero, 'I'm just angry that you didn't tell me.'

'Didn't tell you what, exactly?' says the leader, also quickening his pace.

'That it was her,' the younger boys says, leaping over a fallen tree trunk.

'I can't believe that that's what's made you so angry.'

'The fact that you didn't tell me that it was her, and that you didn't even let me help.'

'I knew there was something else … So I didn't let you help me!' the older boy says, using one arm to sweep aside the liana and stepping into the clearing.

'…'

'You've never done the things I've had to do back there,' the boy who serves as leader says, surveying the empty space blazing in the sunlight, then, turning around, he threatens those who all too soon will lose all hope: 'Right, all of you together … stay in a group … no one wander off.'

'I've never done … I've never gone … I've never got to carry the money … I've never got to do anything,' the boy who serves as lieutenant says, turning to those who have come from other lands: 'You heard him … keep close together!'

'Exactly … Why would you need to do it? … I'm already doing

it,' the elder boy says, coming to a halt. 'You see, we are here on time … They haven't even arrived yet.'

'It's strange that they're not here yet.'

'Yeah, it is strange,' the elder boy agrees, then, pointing to some holes in the grass, he says: 'What are those?'

'That's weird too,' the younger boy says, looking at the curious holes and, following the boy who serves as leader who is already heading there, adds, 'But don't change the subject … tell me who she was.'

'Who she was?' the elder boy echoes mechanically, paying no heed to his own words or the question posed by the boy who serves as lieutenant, so fascinated is he by the strange excavations.

'Exactly … Who the fuck was she?' he whose duty is to obey insists, forgetting the hole in the grass for a moment. 'I want to know who she was … Why are you making such a big deal about it?'

'*Puta madre!*' the older boy says, peering into one of the holes.

'*Pinche mierda!*' the younger boy says, as he, too, recognizes the body lying there. 'What the fuck happened?'

'All of you, shut up right now!' roars the boy who serves as leader, turning to the men and women who crossed the borders and, backing away, he glances around: 'Who could have done this … Who did …?'

'On the ground … all of you, get down on the ground right now!' the younger boy orders, not realizing he is contradicting his leader, and he throws himself down. 'I told you they never show up late.'

When the elder boy realizes that he is the only one still standing, he too drops to the ground and, crawling through the grass and squelching through the mud left by the rainstorm towards the one who serves as lieutenant. 'What the fuck do we do now …? Who could have done this to that idiot?' the older boy asks, staring at the ground and listening to the whisperings among the men and women who have come from other lands.

'Who gives a shit?' the younger boys says, but before he even finishes his sentence, he digs his elbows into the mud and crawls towards another hole. 'There's another body here,' he says, and the murmur of the beings that crossed the borders raises several decibels just as, in the distance, they hear the approaching *swarm of fleas or flies or gadflies come to prey on things and on men.*

'Shut the fuck up … Shut up or I'll do it for you,' the elder boy growls, turning his head and, hearing the growing drone of the swarm he cannot see but can sense, he turns to the younger boy, who is crawling off again, and barks, 'Come back here and forget about those fucking holes!' Meanwhile, for the first time, those who will never be allowed to leave the ravaged lands begin to weave their song, and for the first time their tongues begin to tell their terrors.

'What the hell is happening?' says Hewhostillboastsasoul.

'Who are those dead people?' asks Hewhostillbearsaname.

'What is going to happen to us now?' says ShewhostillcallsonGod.

'That noise … Where is that noise coming from?' says Hewhostillhashisvoice.

'We made it this far!' screams Hewhostillhasabody.

'It is all going to end here … You'll see what …!' roars Hewhocanstillusehistongue.

'Shut up … I'm serious … If you don't shut up, you'll see what happens,' the boy who serves as leader interrupts Hewhowillnot-usehistonguemuchlonger. Then, raising his head above the grass, the older boy looks around for his lieutenant and, hearing it grow louder still, this swarm of horseflies, blowflies and locusts, he feels a twinge in his bladder and suddenly relaxes his sphincters.

'And you! Get over here, right now!' the older boy shouts, only to be silenced midway through the sentence by the younger boy calling: 'Another one … There's another body in this hole! They're all riddled with bullets!' the younger boy shouts a moment later, and just as he who serves as leader is yelling: 'Get over here, forget about them … Get back here, now!' the drone of the horseflies, blowflies and locusts deafens everyone in earshot, even as the song of those who will soon forsake their creator, their history and their name, is transfigured to become a lament.

By the time that he who serves as lieutenant finally reaches the place where his leader is lying, face buried in his hands, nose pressed into the grass, crushed by the sound of the horseflies, the blowflies and the locusts that rises to the apocalyptic rumble of the plague that it is, the sons of the jungle silently realise that the music they can now hear is being blasted from a dozen speakers.

The thunder of the approaching music crushes the ears of the sons of the jungle, but not their dignity or their spirit: realizing that they have no other choice, he who serves as leader and he who serves as lieutenant exchange a brief glance and, smiling at each other, jump to their feet. Forming a perimeter all around them, the men clutching their weapons are now loyal to a different man, and from his perch on the roof of the battered pickup truck, he issues new orders with a wave of his arm.

Taking each other by the hand, the two boys glance at each other once more, thrust out their chests and close their eyes, and a hail of shots and shrapnel knocks them to the ground where their mangled bodies form one single hole in the grass, and their blood nourishes the mud lit by a rising sun that sets off a thousand sparks: this is how, it is as though here, in the clearing known as El Tiradero, the earth is suffused by threads of gold.

Stepping around the two boys bleeding out on the ground, the men who now lay down their arms and follow the orders of the man on the roof of his hulking truck at the top of the hill, who, with a slight wave of his hand, set them marching, while the men pushing the heavy wheelbarrows carrying the heavy speakers that deafen and terrify the men and women who are still lying on the ground, gradually tighten the gruesome circle.

Jumping over the bodies of the boys of the jungle, who have just left the clearing called El Ojo de Hierba as they have just left the story of Epitafio, the story of Estela, and this, which is their own story: the story of the last holocaust of its kind, those loyal to this man who is now clambering down from his huge truck reach the place where the godless are lying, haul them to their feet and train the still smoking muzzles of their rifles on them: it often takes place by night; this time it takes place by day.